For my Mum a True Se<!-- cut -->

SECOND HAND JANE

By
Michelle Vernal
Copyright © 2014 by Michelle Vernal
All Rights Reserved
No part of this work may be reproduced in any fashion without the express, written consent of the copyright holder. *Second Hand Jane* is a work of fiction. All characters and events portrayed herein are fictitious and are not based on any real persons living or dead.

Acknowledgements
Paul I couldn't do it if you and the boys didn't believe in me.

MICHELLE VERNAL LOVES a happy ending. She lives with her husband and their two boys in the beautiful and resilient city of Christchurch, New Zealand. She's partial to a glass of wine, loves a cheese scone, and has recently taken up yoga—a sight to behold indeed. Michelle's written six novels to date along with the popular Guesthouse on the Green series. All her books are written with humour and warmth and she hopes you enjoy reading them. If you enjoy Second Hand Jane then taking the time to say so by leaving a review would be wonderful. A book review is the best present you can give an author. If you'd like to hear about Michelle's new releases, you can sign up to receive her VIP Newsletter:

www.michellevernalbooks.com

To say thank you, you'll receive the first ten chapters of her novel, Sweet Home Summer FREE!

Prologue

TO: NIALL FITZPATRICK
From: Jessica Baré
Subject: First Draft Amy's Story

This story starts with a children's book published in 1969, a fairy tale bought by a mother in Northern Ireland on behalf of her youngest child to give to his sister for Christmas 1973. It's no fairy story, though, nor is it just the sad relaying of brutal facts that ended in Lisburn in 1983. It might have finished there, though, if not for her family and had that little book not found its way to me. I don't mean to sound proprietary because neither the book nor the story I am going to tell you belongs to me. This is Amy's story and in order to tell it to you, I have to begin where it all began.

My full name is Jessica Jane Baré or Second-hand Jane as my friends have started to call me. Why? Well, it's because I love the pre-loved—just like that old cliché, someone else's junk is my treasure. My real passion, though, is for old children's books—it's something about the smell of them, I think. It conjures up the innocence of a bygone era of children called Dick and Ann and tea at five o'clock, trapped forever within their much-thumbed pages. I covet the Ladybird Series 606D books in particular—the classic fairy tales every child grows up with: Rapunzel, Cinderella, The Elves and the Shoemaker, and most pertinent of all, Snow White and the Seven Dwarfs. It wasn't the bold black typeface, however, that had me poring over the books as a child and hoarding them as an adult but Eric Winters' fabulously detailed illustrations. They brought those stories to life and were the source of a childhood fascination with witches, fairies, princes, and princesses. The delicate colours of the foxgloves planted by the thatched cottage's flag stone path, the grand white Bavarian styled castles in which as a little girl I had no doubt I would one day grow up to live in, were a world away from the suburban pocket of New Zealand I inhabited. When a young imagination is fuelled, though, the impossible becomes possible. Good versed evil within those pages and always won. If only we could hold onto that analogy forever.

I often wonder, when I open my books to find another boy or girl's mark inside, whether that faceless child felt the magic, too. Who were they, these little people who had scribbled their names inside books long since forgotten by adulthood?

Snow White and the Seven Dwarfs arrived with neither pomp nor ceremony but rather by mail thanks to an online auction I was determined to win. Inside the tatty cover, in precise, big print was the dedication:

To Amy with love from Owen Christmas 1973

Beneath this, scrawled in orange pencil pressed deep into the cardboard, she had forever made her mark:

Amy Aherne
Glenariff Farm
Ballymcguinness
6 years old

As I looked at the scribbled inscription, I began to wonder. Who was she, this six-year-old girl from the seventies? Was she a dreamer like me, who was now learning the hard way that princes don't just pop up every day and that there are an awful lot of frogs out there? Or perhaps she was a realist who didn't believe in a man supplying her with a ready-made happy ever after? Might we have been friends if we had met? Where was she now? What had she grown up to do with her life?

I felt a compulsion that was almost a physical tug. It was one that I have never felt before—this overwhelming need to know. I would find her and tell the story that lay within the name inscribed in the storybook.

What I found, though, was not at all what I expected.

Chapter One

"OI, NICE SLIPPERS, love!" A broad Dublin twang shouted down from the heavens.

A lack of privacy was the downside of apartment living, Jess thought as her gaze shot upwards to scan the myriad windows overlooking the courtyard. She was rewarded by the sight of a lad with a crew cut who looked far too young to be the proud owner of such a bulbous drinker's nose. His purpose, judging by the plume of smoke he had just exhaled through his nostrils, for hanging out the window on a Saturday morning was not to spy on other residents but to have a sly smoke.

Having been there and done that, Jess shrugged. Each to their own was her motto because she, better than most, knew what it felt like to always have someone else sticking their ten cents' worth in. As her mother's face floated before her, she gave Puff the Magic Dragon a little curtsey and got an excited wolf whistle in return before opening the door to her block and disappearing inside.

It was true, she mused as she waited for the lift, that along with a sagging bottom and boobs, age—almost as though it were compensation—brought confidence. There was a time when she would have blushed a shade of beetroot upon being whistled at like that. That was back in the days when men were still allowed to down tools on building sites in order to harass the young women hurrying past. Funny, too, how when you were a nubile, barely post-teen strutting your stuff around Auckland's CBD, you took those whistles for granted—almost as your due—and then when you reached a certain age, you became pathetically grateful for them.

Jess knew that before the morning was out she'd be texting her best pals with the exciting news that she had received a wolf whistle *and...wait for it...* she was wearing her elephant suit, as her friends liked to refer to her Penney's tracksuit ensemble.

Her apartment was housed on the second floor of the Sandbank Wing of the Riverside complex. Although she often joked that by the state of the Liffey when the tide were out, perhaps the *Smelly Mud Flat Apartments* or *Abandoned Shopping Trolleys Apartments* might have been more apt names. Being on the second floor was something that made her feel happier when she spied the diehard smokers like ole randy, big nose boy—her reasoning being that if there was a fire, at least she had the option of jumping.

This cheery trail of thought was interrupted as the lift door opened and disgorged Gemma from across the hall. She looked to be a woman on a mission, judging by the water bottle in hand and the amount of skin-tight black spandex on display.

"Morning, Jess!" chirruped the svelte redhead with the bouncy ponytail and perky everything else. "Glad to see you're up and at it." She gave Jess's track pants and slippers the once-over. "Well, kind of anyway."

"We can't all be gym bunnies like you, Gem. Besides, you'll do yourself an injury on that cross-trainer one of these days. Just you mark my words." Pushing past her, she stepped inside the lift. "Besides, my old bones have a good ten years on yours."

Gemma laughed. "Listen to you—you sound like my Gran and she at least does aqua-aerobics twice a week! You really should come with me, you know." She winked conspiratorially. "There's lots of hotties there."

"Yeah, yeah. I'll think about it," Jess muttered, hitting number two. She had no intention of breaking the golden rule by which she lived her life. No man would ever see her in spandex nor would she get hot and sweaty in front of the opposite sex unless there was something fun in it for her!

"You've been saying that since Easter and we're into September already, so why don't you put your money where..." Gemma's voice trailed off as the doors slid shut in her face.

Gemma was right, she supposed. She did sound like a granny, even though she had only just turned thirty-four, which in this day and age of forty being the new thirty meant that technically she was twenty-four. Cheering up at that thought, Jess let herself into her apartment.

THE TIRED HARDBACK cover peered up at her as she tossed the paper the book had been wrapped in onto the floor—she'd pick it up later. Being a slob on a Saturday was every single girl's prerogative. She stroked the cover reverently; this was it!—the copy she needed to complete her collection. The rest of the Ladybird books were piled into the worn, leather suitcase she'd swooped on after spotting it at one of her favourite local second-hand haunts.

The collection the case contained wasn't overly valuable, given that most of them had someone else's name scribbled inside. What was it with kids needing to put their mark on everything? It was this graffiti that devalued the little they were worth. For Jess, though, their value wasn't monetary; it was magical. She could pore over her tattered copy of *Cinderella* for an age, mesmerised by Cinder's beautiful ball gowns. There was just something so enchanting about the whole idea of living a life of rags to riches.

Oh, she knew that these days such stories weren't considered PC but in her opinion, things in that department had gone too far. Take, for instance, the day her local library had banned Enid Blyton's Noddy books. Sacrilege! To say she had been heartbroken at the ridiculousness of it was an understatement. How on earth was a child supposed to make the connection between the Golliwogs and black people? And it had certainly never crossed her mind that Noddy's relationship with Big Ears was based on anything other than platonic friendship.

She understood now, though, that this was because kids don't view the world the way adults do. With kids, there are no hidden agendas. But then it's not the children who pay for the books, is it?

Jess dismounted her high horse at the remembered injustice of it all as the phone began to jangle.

"Hey, it's me. What are you doing?—Harry, put that down!?" Brianna shrieked and Jess, holding the phone away from her ear, grinned at the mental picture her friend's tone invoked.

"The book arrived."

"*Snow White*—the one you bought off eBid?"

"That's the one."

Brianna could see the romance in collecting old books, unlike their mutual friend Nora who, upon spying the vintage suitcase and its contents for the first time, had exclaimed, "What on earth do you want with that old pile of mouldy shite? Honestly, Jess, you'll be coming home with second-hand smalls next." A second-hand Jane Nora was not.

"Yes, and oh Brie, it's just gorgeous." She began flicking through the little book's pages, gazing at the pictures as she did so. "You want to see the wee cottage in the woods; it's..."

"Like something out of a fairy story," Brianna finished for her with a laugh that was cut short. Jess could make out some sort of scuffling noise which was swiftly followed by, "Harry Price, you give that to Mammy right now! If Daddy catches you playing with his new razor, there will be murder." She gave a heartfelt sigh that sounded like a long, slow hiss down the phone line. "Whatever you do, Jess, don't ever have children."

"Ha! It would be the Immaculate Conception if I did and did I hear you right? Did you say Harry was playing with a razor?" She was mildly alarmed—Brianna had a laidback parenting style but that was a bit much, even by her standards.

"It's electric and he's pretending to shave like Daddy."

"Phew, that's alright then. Oh and Brie, if perchance I do meet Prince Charming before the menopause and have babies, then I hope they're as gorgeous as your Harry. Put him on for me, will you?"

"Huh! Not so gorgeous at five o'clock this morning when he decided to pay us a visit. Honestly, the concept of a weekend being for sleeping in is completely foreign to him—wait a minute... Harry, love, it's your Aunty Jess wanting to say hello."

A few moments later, heavy breathing signalled Harry had taken over possession of the phone.

"Hello, sweetie pie, how are you today? Are you being a good boy for your Mummy?"

The heavy breathing stopped. "Yes but she's not being a very good Mammy."

Jess choked back a laugh. "Why's that then, Harry?"

"I *need* to use Daddy's razor or I will get prickles."

Brianna's voice trilled in the background, "You won't get prickles, Harry, because you are not in the throes of puberty just yet even though some days I could swear I am living with a hormonal teenager in the body of a five-year-old. Now give the phone back to Mammy and say cheerio to Aunty Jess."

There was a thunk as he dropped the phone in protest and then the line went dead. Jess smiled to herself and shook her head. It really was lucky for Harry that he was such a cutie. Hanging up her end, she waited for it to ring again. She didn't have to wait long.

"Sorry about that. His Highness is being a right sod this morning. We've both got cabin fever, so I'd better keep it short before he gets himself into some real mischief. Now I know it's a bit of a crap day and you'd never know it was supposed to be the tail end of an Indian summer, but we do live in Ireland after all and if I don't get out and about with Harry, I will go mad!"

"I take it Pete's at work then?" Jess interjected. Despite having the look of a builder about him, Brianna's nearest and dearest actually worked in IT, doing that cryptic kind of stuff that IT people do. She had once asked him to explain to her in layman's terms exactly what it was he did do for a living. To which Pete had replied in painstaking detail and in slow, drawn-out syllables as though talking to a simpleton. The thing was, he might as well have been because her eyes had glazed over halfway through his explanation and she was still none the wiser when he'd finished. It was something or other to do with contracting his computer skills out to a major retail outlet, for which he got very highly paid. Well paid enough for Brianna not to have to work and for them to live in a lovely home with all the latest mod cons.

"Yeah, he's finishing off an urgent job and won't be home until late. So how do you fancy a trip to Bray? We could do the Greystones walk, followed by a glass of wine in the pub. A lemonade and bag of crisps will keep Harry quiet and then we could all hop on the Dart back to mine for a BBQ dinner. Nothing flash—sausages in bread with salad—but I've managed to entice Nora, so long as they're the low-fat chicken sausies, mind."

Brianna lived in a pretty red brick, two-storey house in the bustling seaside hub of Bray, a mere thirty minutes outside of Dublin. With the hills of North County Wicklow surrounding it, there was no better place for a Saturday afternoon ramble. Jess glanced out the window at the grey old day. Exercise hadn't been on her agenda but a spot of fresh sea air, some good company followed by an ice cold glass of sav—well, it would do her the world of good, she decided. Besides, if it meant she didn't have to cook a dinner for one, she was all for a BBQ!

"You can't beat a good old banger, even if they are low-fat, so count me in. Meet you at the station around two?"

"Perfect! We can head off from there. I'll let Nora know and we'll see you then."

Jess hung up the phone and twiddled her toes inside the soft fleece lining of her slippers. She'd have to take them off in a minute but not just yet—they were so comfy.

The slippers were a Valentine's Day gift from her mother last February. For as long as she could remember—or at least since Jess had been of a marriageable age—she had been buying her a little something on Valentine's Day. She said it was her way of making her daughter feel loved and once upon a time, the gifts had been saucy knickers. Inappropriate items for one's mother to be buying her daughter, perhaps, but when your mother worked on the lingerie counter of Auckland's iconic Smith & Caughey department store, she got to buy them at cost. Hence, Jess was sure she boasted a more exotic underwear drawer than most red-light workers!

More years ago now than Jess cared to remember, she had really pushed the boat out and given her a pair of lace-topped stay-up stockings. She'd volunteered a demo on how to put them on, too, but Jess declined the offer as sexy stockings were not really the kind of thing she wanted to see her Mum in. Yes, indeedy, the sight of that would have been enough to make her hoist her pantyhose as high as she could get them for the rest of her days!

These little gifts were given on the annual day of romance in the hope that Jess would use her feminine wiles to maximum capacity in order to seduce a doctor or solicitor or some such other professional.

Marian Baré, you see, suffered from delusions of grandeur. She herself was married to a carpet layer and there was absolutely nothing wrong with that, in Jess's opinion. Her dad was a hard worker who had always provided for his girls, as he liked to call his wife, Jess, and her younger sister Kelly.

As the years had passed, however, and she had unwrapped yet another lacy thong, her mother had abruptly changed tack.

"Jessica, your father and I would be just as happy if you married a tradesman, you know. They make good providers *and* they're practical. That's so important, sweetheart; I mean, a man needs to know how to unblock a toilet or change a light bulb. Look at how your father's always looked after us."

Marian's voice softened as she thought about her obliging hubby Frank but then she'd gotten back to the matter at hand. "Speaking of whom, your father was saying the other day that the firm's just taken on a new apprentice. He's only a year or two younger than you, which is nothing when you think of Catherine Zeta and Michael, so perhaps Dad could arrange for you..."

"No way! I am not desperate, Mum, and I haven't forgotten that awful Jeremy you got him to set me up with last time! And since when were you on a first name basis with members of the Hollywood A-list?"

"Don't be clever, Jessica; it doesn't suit you. Your problem, my girl, is that you're too fussy for your own good because there was absolutely nothing wrong with poor Jeremy that a dab of antiseptic cream on his spots wouldn't have sorted out."

"Yeah, and a bottle of mouthwash, a deodorant, anti-dandruff shampoo, and soap for that matter. Personal hygiene issues aside, Mum, in case you haven't noticed, we do not live in the 1950s anymore. I don't need a man to be happy. I have a career of my own, from which I gain plenty of personal satisfaction, thank you very much." Actually, now that she thought back on it, she had sounded a tad *"And I am off to get a crew cut and stop shaving under my arms."* No wonder her mother had begun to narrow her eyes whenever her girlfriends popped around after that little statement.

At the time, though, she had merely reiterated, "Yes, sweetheart, and we are very proud of you. That's why we put you through university but a job won't keep you warm at night, will it? Why can't you have both? Lots of women work and maintain a relationship. I mean, I've hardly sat on my backside all these years, now have I?"

God. She was so frustrating and probably the main reason Jess thanked her lucky stars for her UK ancestry, which meant she could live and work on the other side of the world from her! She flatly refused to refer to her daughter's chosen line of work as a journalist as a career. It was always referred to as a job—a means to an end until something better came along: aka, a man. Jess gritted her teeth in anticipation, knowing what was coming next and she was proved right.

"Jessica, all your father and I want for you is to find *someone* to settle down with like your sister has. That's not too much to ask for, surely?"

It irked Jess the way she always included her father in the equation. It wasn't him who put the pressure on her to get a ring on her finger at every opportunity. And, at the very mention of Kelly, she rolled her eyes. Married she may be but did it count if it were to a Martian? Okay, so he wasn't green but he was odd and he wasn't very attractive and she had no idea how her sister actually managed to have sex with him but she obviously did—and quite often, too, judging by their numerous offspring. Who, if she were being honest, were complete and utter little shites. Although as their aunt, she obviously loved her pretentious eight-year-old niece Mia, know-it-all six-year-old Bella, bossy four-year-old Ethan, and of course she couldn't forget her three-year-old tearaway nephew, Elliot, who still wasn't properly toilet trained. Nor could she forget the incident whereby he'd wet himself all over her favourite velvet Balenciaga skirt the last time she had been home. She had picked up the vintage skirt for an absolute steal on one of her op-shop forays and it would now forever bear the mark of her nephew. Kelly had tried to appease her by saying that he only peed on people he felt comfortable around. She'd tried to convince her sister that really, she should be pleased because despite his having not seen his aunt since he was six months old, he obviously had a soft spot for her. Jess was too busy wiping at the wet spot he'd left on her lap to care.

Suffice to say she loved them all but she loved them even more from afar. Which was why she had left behind her gigs writing a weekly column about Auckland's movers and shakers—she refused to call it a gossip column—along with the regular trickle of commissioned work that had started to come her way as she carved a name for herself to inadvertently flee to the Emerald Isle in the first place.

Now that she thought about it, her mother never said much when she made reference to her brother-in-law hailing from the red planet. Jess reckoned this was because deep down she secretly agreed with her but the fact Brian was something or other high up in the world of banking was all the compensation she needed.

There was no doubt about it; Marian Baré was a snob, she reflected fondly. Though where it stemmed from, Jess had no idea because it really wasn't in keeping with her South Auckland upbringing or her parents' current suburban address of Hillsborough in Auckland. It may well have straddled the more fashionable Mt Eden, as Marian liked to point out whenever she got a chance, but their three-bedroomed brick and tile still firmly had its foundations dug into Hillsborough.

Then there was the thing with their surname. Whenever anybody pronounced it as the rather blunt "Bare," Jess was instantly reminded of that old TV show *Keeping up Appearances*. The one where Hyacinth Bucket always insisted her name was actually Bouquet. *It's not Bear, thank you very much; there is an accented 'e' on the end. Beret, dahling; it's Beret.*

"Your sister's making noises about having a fifth baby, you know," she announced during one of their last cosy mother-and-daughter transatlantic chats.

"More fool her; then she'll be run ragged." This wasn't true. Kelly was not averse to getting their Mum, the world's most devoted grandmother, to help out and she would be in her element with another baby. She was a proper earthmother, which to Jess's mind simply meant not wearing makeup, not getting one's hair done, and talking about nothing else other than your boobs and your baby's bowel motions, both of which her sister majored in.

"All I am saying is that your eggs are a-cooking, Jessica Jane, and once they're fried—no matter what these medical experts say—there is no turning back the clock. Surely there must be some eligible men in Dublin. Isn't it choc-a-block with famous musicians and actors? We don't want any more of your wounded birds, mind."

What was it with her mother and all things avian? Jess had sighed. "All I will say with regards to my eggs, Mother, is that I am quite partial to the odd fried egg despite their being high in cholesterol and that four, possibly five grandchildren, in an overpopulated world is enough for anybody. Stop being so bloody greedy! As for your reference to Irish men, think about the Corrs—three beautiful girls to one unattractive male. And for your information, so far as wounded birds go, I do not always date men with problems."

"Yes, you do. What about that Peter—the one who didn't know whether he liked Arthur or Martha?"

She cringed. Typical, making her relieve that painful memory. It had been said more than once that she had a tendency to gravitate toward the problematic members of the male species and there was the teensiest grain of truth in that, she supposed, given her dodgy track record. Peter had issues over his sexuality and she'd been convinced she would be the one to help him make his mind up one way or another but apparently not—he'd dumped her for his mate Matthew. Then there had been Simon, whose parents had divorced when he was a child and their ensuing bitter custody battle had left him damaged goods. Paul had followed shortly after. His former fiancée had cheated on him and he was mistrustful of the female species to the point of obsession. A stalker was born.

She'd thought she was on to a winner with Andrew the lawyer and last man she had dated, though. Christ, for a girl who didn't attend church, she was following a bit of a biblical theme here. Marian had gone into a rapturous state when she'd mentioned what he did for a living to her but well-paid job or not, he'd managed, after only three dates, to put her off the opposite sex for a good long while. For starters, he began their every conversation with, "Well, if you want to know what I think." She didn't but he wasn't very good at reading body language, i.e., rolling her eyes. However, the real clincher had come when he asked as they got amorous on her couch one evening whether she had any objection to being dominated in the bedroom. The penny dropped as to what the handcuffs she had seen on his back seat were actually for—not for restraining his criminal clients on the way to court after all.

Marian had derailed her train of thought.

"If like you say, Jessica, and the odds are really not in your favour, then you should come home. I'll say no more on the subject."

If only she would say no more, Jess had thought. Frustratingly, she refused to entertain the idea that perhaps her daughter was happy in her life and that maybe, just maybe, she didn't want to hear the pitter-patter of little feet in her future and that maybe, just maybe, she was managing quite nicely without a man.

Jess shook the spectre of Marian Baré away and, kicking off her slippers, she went in search of a pair of trainers.

Chapter Two

JESS DIDN'T OWN A CAR. There really wasn't much need for one when she could walk nearly everywhere in the city. Besides, Dublin's roads were congested enough without her adding to the problem. Not to mention the fact her budget didn't stretch to paying for a permanent car parking space in Riverside's underground garaging. She'd soon learnt on arriving in the city that she could get to wherever she needed to be faster on foot than she could in a car or on public transport, especially come rush hour, and it kept her relatively fit at the same time. As for all the carbon monoxide fumes she breathed in every time she marched down the Quays—well, the Chinese had it right with those masks they wore but she herself was far too vain to do a Michael Jackson.

Slamming the main doors of Riverside Apartments shut behind her, she stared for a moment at the steady flow of cars. Some had people half hanging out the windows, waving flags. Obviously victorious after the morning's football match, she thought before setting off at a steady pace along pavements that had seen better days. Her new trainers were almost neon in their whiteness and she hoped they wouldn't give her blisters as she passed under the shadow of the domineering Four Courts building. The bodies of those who partook of the hard stuff and slept rough in the building's grand entrance way had all shuffled off for the day. All except for one chap who was still huddled under his grey greatcoat. Jess paused; it was so sad to see—with all that grey, he blended into his surrounds. Most passers-by wouldn't even notice him. Rummaging in her bag, she found what she was after and stuffed a tenner into the bag that lay open next to him. She hoped he'd use it to buy breakfast and not his next fix.

A Saturday afternoon stroll down the Quays was usually a much more relaxed affair than an early morning weekday one when the traffic was at its worst. Once, she'd almost been knocked down by a car mounting the pavement in an effort to get out of the way of an ambulance. The emergency vehicle had been trying to manoeuvre through the middle of the two-lane traffic on a road that had originally been designed for a horse and cart. After she'd gotten over her fright, she'd fervently hoped that she was never in a position where she needed help in a hurry.

Reaching the Ha'Penny Bridge in good time, Jess rocked from foot to foot as she waited her turn to cross over to the Southside. Even from that distance, she could see that the bridge was thronging with its usual horde of both tourists and what her mother would call ne'er-do-wells. *He* was there in his usual spot, too, she thought, wrinkling her nose as she spied the chap with the gingery dreadlocks sitting on his piece of cardboard. His back was pressed up against the iron railings and he was decked out in what some might call an alternative and others might call the wastrel uniform of army fatigues and Doc Marten boots.

In the past, she'd always done her bit for him—flicking a couple of euros into the tin cup he'd hold out whilst worrying about the likelihood of his getting piles sitting so close to the ground like that. That was until the day she'd spotted him fine dining in the latest hip little French bistro to open up in Dublin with a lady friend. So much for on the bones of his arse—he was creaming it! Jess shot him a disgusted look as she marched past, carrying on to her destination of Tara Street Station.

THE TRAIN DIDN'T KEEP her waiting long and she settled back to enjoy the short ride. This was her favourite route on the Dart and not just for the scenery but for the celebrity spotting, too. She was busy trying to spot signs of life down in U2's The Edge's pink house. It resplendently perched on the rocks overlooking the sea but she was distracted by the couple sitting across from her. Neither looked to be the full packet of biscuits, Jess concluded, giving the woman's frumpy floral, nylon housecoat the once-over. Her legs were splayed in that slightly apart stance of the chubbily well-blessed and her greasy, grey hair was short and to the point. Hubby looked like he would be called Errol and he was in a brown suit. There was no need for him to stand up for Jess to know it would be an ill-fitting one. He had an impressive comb-over going on, too, which was presently flapping up and down as his wife gave him a couple of slaps about the ear-hole before calling him a "Fecking Eejit."

Jess sighed happily; she did so love Dublin public transport theatre. It was great fodder for her column—a Kiwi girl's take on life in Ireland's capital. Take, for instance, the occasions when she caught the bus. The harried housewives travelling on it seemed to incorporate the word "fecking" into every sentence, pausing momentarily in their cussing to cross themselves as they passed by St Patrick's Cathedral.

Now, though, the husband beater turned toward her and muttered something about, "Fecking useless eejits." This was Jess's cue to smile in polite agreement with her before averting her gaze back out the window. Dublin public transport theatre was all well and good so long as she wasn't on the receiving end of it.

The waves below the tracks were crashing onto the rocks but even on a grey day, the view from the train's smeared window was a stunning one as it hugged the rugged coastline. As they neared Enya's castle, which wasn't really a castle but an impressively purposely-built pile of rocks, Jess risked a glance over to her right. She always hoped to spot the singer wandering ethereally around the grounds in a billowing white dress. She refused to believe that she was more likely to be decked out in jeans and a sweatshirt, pulling weeds or hanging out her washing like every other mere mortal. There was no sign of Enya today and catching the husband beater's eye, Jess swiftly returned her gaze to the sea and shuddered. God, she hoped she didn't wind up like her. Still, at least the woman had a husband whereas she was well on her way to spinsterdom. She'd really have to help herself and get out and about more.

Nora was forever offering to escort her along to various speed-dating events or 90s Dance Revival nights at her local pub but it was all a bit of an effort these days—putting on her glad rags, only to be jostled back and forth in a crowed pub. Or, if the lights were dim enough, being chatted up by cubs in search of a bit of cougar action. It was enough to make a girl feel cheap!

Not Nora, though. No, Nora was blatantly proactive in her search for a mate. Her pretty soft blonde, blue-eyed features, breathy Monroe voice, and petite build all combined to give men the false impression that here was a woman who was in dire need of their protection. However, having clawed her way up the professional ladder into a high-flying career in cinema management, Nora was in actual fact what you could call a strong woman. Or, to put it more plainly, she had a tendency to frighten men off with her "say it like she saw it" manner because they never saw it coming.

Brianna and Jess had referred to their friend fondly as the Praying Mantis—an insect who bites the head off its mate after sex—ever since the night they'd first borne witness to Nora in all her glory.

The three women had been propping the bar up in some pub buried deep in the cobbled zone of Temple Bar when a chap had bravely stepped forth from the crowd and offered to buy Nora a drink. She'd acquiesced like the Queen accepting a bouquet of flowers from a commoner by going on to order the most expensive drink on the menu. She'd then delved deep into her handbag and just when the girls thought she would never come up for air, she'd resurfaced, waving a business card as if she had won the lotto. It wasn't just any business card, mind; oh no, it belonged to her dental hygienist.

"She'll sort your halitosis out lickety-split, love," she'd told the poor sod, placing it in his shirt pocket before accepting the drink he proffered and cheerily raising her glass.

Brianna, by contrast, reminded Jess of Bambi. She was pretty and sweet of nature yet tall and gangly and her bobbed chocolate hair and big round brown eyes suited her perfectly. Her olive skin colouring was most definitely that of her ancestors—the Celts. Brianna was also the first of the trio to say "I do" to anything other than the offer of a drink and for the past seven years, she had been happily married to Pete, who was both big and burly and loved the bones off her.

Five years ago, Harry had arrived in the world and while his mother professed that he drove her potty, he was a child Jess actually did really like. He was by no means saintly—as Brianna often attested—but he had such of sense of fun, not to mention a penchant for makeup. He was a veritable magpie where cosmetics were concerned and when his two spinster aunties, Jess and Nora, weren't spoiling the little boy rotten, they were keeping a tight hold of their makeup bags. "He'll grow out of it, Brie," Jess had assured her the last time he had been caught red-handed literally with her new Bobbi Brown lippy. "Honestly, my nephew used to do some unspeakable things."

"What does he do now then?" Brianna had asked hopefully.

"Oh, more unspeakable things. My sister says that if you try to analyse what your children do, you'd send yourself mad. She reckons life with kids is just one continual phase after another."

When she wasn't playing happy families, however, Brianna still occasionally liked to live vicariously through her single friends but if the truth be known it was she, the old married woman of the trio, who got the most action on a regular basis. So, in point of fact, it was Jess and Nora who lived vicariously through Brianna's sex life. She was also a fiend for committees and belonged to everything from the PTA at Harry's school to Save the Manatee, the latter being a mermaid-like sea-creature she encountered and went on to bond with on her Florida honeymoon.

Jess had never figured out exactly where she fitted into their friendship equation, not just because she was the polar opposite of Nora and Brianna in her taste for all things vintage. Her idea of a great day's shopping was not trawling the High Street for the latest fashions with them but rather rummaging through an Oxfam store or hitting a car boot sale. She definitely had her own sense of style, too, with her love of vintage designer clothes, and had gone through many phases in the fashion stakes. At Uni, she had fallen in love with the 1950s floral frock, eventually moving on to the Boho look of the early 1970s. She was currently enthralled by all things 80s, although she drew the line at horrendously oversized shoulder pads. Looks wise, she was out on a limb, too, with her green eyes and unruly crop of auburn curls that simply refused to do what they were told, no matter how many times she singed them between the hair-straighteners.

She was neither quiet nor what you could call outspoken and the three girls often had a laugh that they were like Bananarama, the female trio from the 80s, before launching into an off-key version of "Venus." Jess, however, was the only one who actually looked the part with the side bow in her hair and pinafore smock dress. What she did know, though, was that leaving London and arriving in Dublin back in 2001 was the best choice she ever made. The Celtic Tiger had been roaring and Dublin was rocking when she met the girls and the three of them had just clicked. This was surprising given their inauspicious start:

Jess had booked in for a haircut with Miss Brianna—as the salon's receptionist had referred to her—the morning of her job interview at the Marriott, the Marriott being an established Dublin guesthouse near St Stephens Green where she'd wound up working for slave wages during her first year in Dublin while she tried to establish a name for herself as a freelance journalist.

Brianna, who never was a very good hairdresser and for whom half of Dublin's female population breathed a sigh of relief when they heard she'd hung up her scissors in favour of being a stay-at-home mammy, had managed to brutalise her fringe—and that's when Nora had walked into the salon for a lunchtime shampoo and blow-wave.

Flopping down in the seat next to Jess's, Nora called out a hello to Brianna, who was hopping nervously from foot to foot. She was gripping a mirror, waiting to show her already unhappy client the concave she'd attempted and which she had now decided was not such a good idea on hair that was as thick and curly as this girl's was. Nora took in Brianna's latest victim's mortified expression as she frantically tried to stretch her shorn bangs down over her eyebrows and shook her head in commiseration.

"My God, she's done a job on you. You're not going to be able to do much with that, now are you?"

Distracted, Jess turned her attention to the blonde woman seated next to her, surprised that one so petite and dainty had such a big gob and feeling a stab of envy—a proper fringe! "Fringe envy"—now that was a new one, she'd thought. Still, the woman had only stated the obvious and so she'd blinked back the tears that were threatening and confided, "I know. I look terrible and I have a job interview this afternoon."

"I'm really sorry but you did say you wanted quite a bit taken off and well, your hair is curly and it all just bounced up a lot higher than I'd expected," Brianna interjected with her bottom lip wobbling ominously.

Jess almost felt sorry for the pretty stylist with the big doe-like eyes.

"Too late for that, Brianna. They'll think your woman here's escaped from the funny farm looking like that and, where on earth did you buy that dress? My Gran had one just like it," the blondie butted in again.

Jess ignored the comment about her dress as she studied her fringe in the mirror. Blondie was right, she concluded; it did give her face a rather simplistic quality. She couldn't help but omit a little laugh at how ludicrous she looked and then that little laugh had turned into a rip-roaring snort, which proved to be contagious and soon all three women were falling about laughing.

Thus, a decade later, the Celtic Tiger may have rolled over and died a long and painful death but the three women still just clicked and Jess had long since grown her fringe out.

Despite her butchered locks, though, she had gone on to get the job at the Marriott and her big break had come the day she'd organised a conference room for Nigel, the head reporter from the *Dublin Express*.

Nigel was going to be interviewing Shane Moriarty from the latest boy band to dance their way onto the Irish charts in it. Shane, who was milking his new-found fame and fortune, had demanded all sorts of both legal and illegal treats be placed in the room if the reporter wanted him to dish the dirt. Jess, along with her contact (a fat man with crew cut and gold chains around his non-existent neck who loitered outside the Mary Street McDonald's behind the Jervis Centre—she was by no means a regular customer, just a good observer and lover of the Big Mac), had managed to acquiesce to his every demand. This was to Nigel's surprise and relief because it meant he got a coup in his candid interview with pop star Shane, who was extremely relaxed by the time he arrived revealing that, yes, he did have an illegitimate love-child being raised in the wilds of Connemara.

To show his appreciation for getting his scoop, Nigel agreed to return the favour by sliding the sample piece Jess had written of her take on life in Dublin under Niall Fitzpatrick's—his editor—nose. Considering how the Irish had for years been heading for pastures greener, Niall had been tickled by the idea of the tables turning and by condensing an Antipodean's impressions of boom-time Ireland into a weekly column. This was ideal because she was still free to write the novel she planned to get around to writing one day but now she had her bread-and-butter job.

"My column is called 'Jessica Baré does Dublin,' Mum," she'd breathed excitedly down the transatlantic connection the day Niall had sent through her contract.

"It sounds like those old porno movies—you remember? *Debbie Does Dallas*. But well done, dear, and be sure they accent the *e*," her mother had congratulated her down the phone.

Jess decided not to ask how she happened to know the title of old pornos and why on earth she would think her daughter would be familiar with them.

It had started out as very much a Carrie Bradshaw/Sex and the City styled column and had evolved from there. Just like her fictitious New York counterpart, her column had been a hit, too, but even more surprisingly, despite the boom times being a distant memory, it still was a hit. She could only assume that her loyal following of downtrodden Dubliners liked to read about the happenings in her hapless life as surely it could only serve to make them feel better about their own! Thinking about her hapless life brought her back to the here and now as the train continued to judder along. Maybe she would tag along with Nora next time she suggested hitting the hotspots of Dublin. Mind you, the last time she'd shaken her groove thung until the wee hours, it had taken her days to recover—so much for being twenty-four, she thought with a rueful sigh.

THE TRAIN SAILED INTO Bray Station at five minutes past two o'clock and she spied the girls waiting on the platform. Harry's hand was held firmly by Brianna, the buggy parked beside her with a backpack sitting in it. All three waved out when they saw her disembark.

Nora, Jess noticed as she leaned in for a quick hug, looked as if she meant business in her obviously expensive all-weather parka, cargo pants, and hiking boots whereas Brianna was a bit more casual in her sweatshirt, old jeans, and sneakers.

"Oh goody, you're wearing the elephant suit!" Brianna grinned, kissing her friend hello on the cheek and causing Harry to erupt into giggles and make trumpeting noises.

Nora frowned and shook her head. "I'll never know why when you finally did go and buy yourself something new, you chose that."

Jess pulled off Harry's woolly hat, causing him to squeal and, handing it back, she told him to pipe down before stating, "Because me and the elephant suit are a match made in heaven. It is the most comfy outfit I have ever owned. Besides, I'll have you know I got wolf whistled at this morning while"—she did a twirl—"wearing this, my Penney special, *and* I had those pink fluffy slippers Mum sent me on, too."

"You never did?" Brianna's eyes widened.

"I did."

"You go, girl!"

"Were you walking past St Vincent's then?" Nora sniggered, referring to the Fairview-based psychiatric hospital.

Jess hit her playfully on the arm. "Don't be so awful, action woman! Come on—you look like you're about to climb Everest, so we better get a move on before we get crushed in the melee." She was referring to the handful of passengers getting on and off the train and the other two laughed.

The foursome wound their way down to the promenade, which would take them to the start of the cliff walk. The tide was out, Jess noticed, looking at the crab hole-pocked sand as she listened to her friends chatter on about their weeks that had been. Harry trudged alongside her, looking mutinous and muttering about wanting his lemonade and crisps now. It was a good job Brianna had had the foresight to bring the buggy, Jess thought. He might like to think of himself as a big boy of five these days but his little legs still got tired and there was no way he would manage the two hour's walk ahead of them. The big girls would struggle enough without having to take it in turns to piggyback him as well!

AN HOUR LATER, THE trio paused to draw breath and survey the scene splayed out before them. Craggy green and brown cliffs stretched down to a churning sea, its recalcitrant colour meshing with the sky. Occasionally, a marauding gull would provide a splash of white against the vista. The sense of nature's power was overwhelming up here, Jess thought, inhaling deeply and trying to harness a bit of it.

"Even on a day like this, it's gorgeous, isn't it? We could be the only people in the entire world." Brianna sighed happily before plopping Harry into his buggy. "You've done so well walking all this way, sweetheart. I think you deserve a bit of a nibble. What do you think?"

Harry's hand was already outstretched in anticipation of sustenance and as Brianna handed him his lunch box, a couple sailed round the corner on mountain bikes, nearly mowing them all down.

"Oi, watch it!" she called out, receiving no more than an apologetic wave as the cyclists disappeared down the hillside.

Jess laughed. "Well, almost the only people left in the world, aye Brie? And you're right; it is gorgeous. It reminds me of home." She felt a strong pang.

Brianna patted her on the shoulder. "Did you know that your accent always get broader when you feel homesick? It must be hard sometimes being so far away from your family."

"Yeah, it is sometimes but then Mum phones me and I get over it pretty quickly."

"What's the male-to-female ratio like in New Zealand?" Nora butted in, producing a fancy looking silver foil wrapped bar from the depths of her rucksack.

"I don't know but I bet my Mum could tell you. She knows the stats for most countries—I'll ask her next time she phones." She frowned, watching her friend hoe into the unappetising-looking snack. "Nora, you're not doing the Boston Marathon. What's with the bar?"

"Protein bar." Crumbs spewed forth. "Low in fat and packed full of protein."

Brianna held out a bag of chocolate chip cookies and Jess helped herself to one.

Nora suddenly looked coy. "I've got another date with Ewan next Thursday and I want to fit into that little black dress of mine—you know, the one with the halter neck you two helped me pick?"

The two friends nodded and exchanged a glance; it was a gorgeous dress. If Nora was pulling out all the stops on a second date for this Ewan, then they needed to find out more.

"So I'm Dukaning myself." Nora finished the bar and looked longingly at the bag of chocolate chippies.

"You're what?" Jess and Brianna chorused.

"It's this four-stage French diet that's all the go at the moment. You start off by eating nothing but protein and then slowly reintroduce vegies and other stuff. Kate Middleton's done it. I'm on day three, so girls, it might be advisable to let me bring up the rear because you don't want to be downwind of me at the moment. All that protein can be a little bit constipating."

Her face was so serious that Jess had to laugh before adding, "Say no more! And if your friend Kate's done it, then it must be the biz." Her reply was very much tongue-in-cheek. "Personally, I think all those diets are a waste of time because losing weight is all down to exercise and portion size."

"Says the girl who hasn't seen the inside of a gym since the 1990s and who can put away two whole Big Mac burgers *and* a large fries in one sitting."

"Once! I did that the one time! And you know I had the hangover from hell. I needed stodge fast and loads of it."

"So what's he like then, this Ewan? He must have something about him if you're seeing him again." Brianna butted in, successfully heading off any further dietary discussion.

"Well, put it this way, girls: I knew right from the off I was looking at a pretty good candidate to father my babies—yep, a top quality sperm donor."

The other two women nearly choked on their chocolate chips and Nora smirked. If there was a reality TV show called *The Shock Factor,* she'd have a starring role on it.

"You can be so crass, Nora Brennan, but speaking of sperm, you just reminded me—Mum told me my sister is thinking of having another baby."

"What would that be then?"

"Number five. I think she's mad, though she and Brian have a pretty good babysitter to help ease the stress of it all."

"Who's that then?"

"My Mum."

"Oh right, good old Mum. Well, if Mr Good Quality Sperm doesn't work out, I could always ask your sister to be a surrogate."

"Ooh, now that really *is* gross."

"All the celebrities are at it."

"Not with my sister they aren't," Jess muttered darkly.

"Anyway, back to my possible donor. How are you placed next Thursday night? Because he has a friend..."

"I will not go down the blind date route, Nora."

"At least it might get you a root!" This was a phrase Nora had picked up on her year-long Australian overseas adventure a decade or so ago.

"Give it a rest, you two! Little ears are burning." Brianna set off at a brisk pace, sending Harry's cheesy-corn snacks flying. "Come on, shift it; there's a glass of wine waiting for us in Greystones."

Nora and Jess did as they were told.

BY THE TIME THEY REACHED the little harbour town of Greystones, the weather had closed in and a steady drizzle was descending. The Beach House Pub was a welcome sight looming over the little horseshoe-shaped bay and they hurried inside to where a welcoming fire was roaring.

Once they were settled with their drinks in front of them, Nora picked up the threads of their earlier conversation. "Ewan said his friend is a big fan of your column and he's really keen to meet you." She frowned. "He said he loves your eclectic style, whatever that means."

"You're making him sound like the male version of Kathy Bates in *Misery*—'I'm your biggest fan,'" Jess mimicked, trying to smooth down curls she just knew had frizzed in the damp air.

"I love the series you're doing at the moment on all the different culinary schools in Dublin. This week's one on Croatian food was really funny—I giggled out loud trying to picture you flipping pancakes. What were they called again?" Brianna loyally read her friend's column every week and always gave her biased feedback.

"Yeah, it was a sight and I had to scrape more than one off the floor. Cooking is not my forte, Brie, that's for sure but Marija, our teacher, felt sorry for me and let me eat hers. Mmm, they were scrummy—Palacinke Sa Sirom or pancakes with cottage cheese." Jess was enjoying her once weekly forays into foreign cuisine, as was her waistline. The walk today would have done her some good, she thought, determined not to think about how many calories her glass of wine contained.

"When are you going to do one on good old Irish tucker? Because you can't beat my Gran's stew with a hunk of soda bread to mop it all up with—yum! It's the best." Brianna's eyes glazed over at the very thought of a bowl of it.

"I've only got a couple more weeks to run with the cooking school theme and no offence to Granny Dierdre, but I'm booked in on a Cajun course and then I'm looking at a Portuguese class. After that, I need to come up with something completely different. Niall's giving me the hard word—he wants something that will really hold the reader's attention, so put your thinking caps on, girls."

"Well, if you go on this blind date Nora's jacked up, you could write about that. I for one would be most interested in finding out how you get on and I think you should go, by the way." Brianna opened Harry's bag of Prawn Cocktail flavoured crisps and handed them to him. "Because if you don't go, you'll never know, will you?"

"Know what?" Jess frowned.

"Whether or not he's the one, of course!"

"Humph. Or he could be this Ewan of Nora's ugly, desperate mate."

"Ewan assured me there is absolutely nothing wrong with him. They went to school together and he's done really well for himself, dealing in property, apparently." Nora leaned toward her. "Come on, Jess. Brianna's right: if you don't come along, you will never know and you might be letting the opportunity of a lifetime slip you by. What's the worst thing that could happen?"

"He could be a serial killer."

"Well, now that would make for riveting reading," Nora replied and Brianna sniggered.

"It's not funny."

"Look, I'll lay it on the line for you." Nora leaned forward earnestly. "I am actually rather keen on Ewan and he asked me on behalf of this old school chum of his—whom, like I said loves your column and your weirdo style—to set up a double date for this Thursday. Please, *please* don't make me let them down."

Jess knew when she was beaten. "Well, I have to go when you put it like that, don't I? But I'm warning you, Nora, I will make you suffer if he turns out to be a freak of nature." She took a slug of wine. "And you have to come shopping with me this week, Brie. I have a feeling I won't get away with wearing my trusty old 1960s rose print cocktail dress."

"You most certainly will not!" Nora exclaimed.

"I didn't think so. Looks like I shall have to splurge if I am going to find a dress worthy of being seen out with the halter neck."

"Ooh, goodie! I love shopping." Brianna grinned. "Especially when it's someone else's credit card getting a hammering."

Nora smiled too and raised her glass. "Thanks, sweetie; you're the best. To the One—you never know."

"To the One," they chorused.

Harry joined in clinking his lemonade against their wine glasses so enthusiastically that he managed to slop half of it over the wooden table top. "Whoopsie."

"Never mind, love; it was an accident." Brianna produced a roll of paper towels from her bag.

"My God girl, have you got the kitchen sink in there as well?" Nora asked in disbelief.

"I was in the Girl Guides—I'm always prepared," she replied, mopping up the sticky drink. "So come on then, tell us a bit about this Ewan. What does he do? And more importantly, what does he look like?"

"He's an actor and he's not bad-looking at all."

"Oh? Anyone we would have heard of?" Jess asked. Nora had dated actors before—bit part players she'd come across at the various premiers she got to attend in her role as cinema manager for the Movie Max chain. Jess had always found them to be a bit self-absorbed for her liking.

"His name's Ewan Reid."

There was a split second's silence as Jess and Brianna digested the name that had just been dropped in a big way. Then both girls screeched, "EWAN REID! As in *The Suburban Man* star Ewan Reid!"

All heads swivelled their way to see what all the excitement was about. "Shush, you two! Honestly, you're worse than a pair of star-struck tweenies. Yes, Ewan Reid, star of smash hit film *The Suburban Man*." Then Nora broke into uncontrollable giggles and wrapping her arms around herself, gave away her own excitement. "And he's absolutely fecking GORGEOUS!"

"What's he like in real life, how did you meet him, and more to the point, how come it's taken you so bloody long to tell us? We're supposed to be your best friends, for goodness' sake!" Jess shrieked, now on her second wine, having downed what was left of the first one in one large gulp at the shock of it all.

"I'm sorry. I really, really wanted to tell you but I didn't want to jinx it. I felt like if I said the words, 'I have a date with Ewan Reid' out loud, I'd wake up and find I had dreamt the whole thing. To be honest, girls, I could hardly believe it myself when he asked me out. I mean, he's a movie star and I'm, well, I'm..."

"You're Nora Brennan, gorgeous, successful career woman," Brianna put in loyally. "So come on then, tell us—how did you meet him? Was it in a book shop? I saw him interviewed on Graham Norton a few weeks back and he said that he's an avid reader."

"No, you eejit, that was in the movie *Notting Hill* and anyway, he's far better-looking than Hugh Grant, and I am hardly Julia Roberts." Nora laughed. "We met at the after party for the Irish premiere of *The Suburban Man*. Honestly, girls, he is lovely and so normal—not at all like some of those other affected actor arses I've been out with in the past. Apparently he asked his agent, Maria, to find out who I was and introduce us. We got talking and basically didn't stop talking all night. He even ignored that skinny cow, the one who looks a bit like Victoria Beckham, from *Big Brother* when she came over and tried to stick her set of tennis balls under his nose!"

"He didn't!" Brianna's eyes were like saucers. "Ooh, she wouldn't have liked that."

"She didn't." Nora looked pleased with herself as she glanced down at her own pair of natural 34C cups. "I've always said a boob job won't get you anywhere in this world."

"Maybe but it would be nice if mine didn't have such an up-close and personal relationship with my belly button these days—bloody breastfeeding," Brianna lamented.

"So what did you talk about then?" Jess wanted details, details, details; it was the writer in her.

"Well, it turns out he's a bit of an adrenaline junkie, like me."

"Nora!" she couldn't help but exclaim. "The only remotely adventurous thing I have ever seen you do is a spot of rock climbing at Clondalkin Leisure Centre when we went there for Harry's birthday last year. That hardly even counts as abseiling, let alone as an adrenaline rush."

Nora's expression grew petulant. "The instructor said I was a natural and for your information, I've always wanted to go white-water rafting."

"Come on you two, we can talk about Nora's penchant for thrill-seeking at home. I need to get Harry back for his tea and there's a packet of chicken sausages with your names on it sitting in my fridge." Brianna got to her feet and began helping Harry back into his coat.

At the mention of food, Jess and Nora suddenly realised they were ravenous and followed suit with Nora talking non-stop about the delectable Mr Reid and what she would like to do to him all the way back to Brianna's.

"THANKS FOR A LOVELY afternoon and for the sausages," Nora called, picking her way down the darkened garden path later that evening. She cursed as she narrowly missed tripping over Jerome the Garden Gnome the girls had bought Brianna and Pete as a housewarming gift on her way to the front gate. "If I have a headache in the morning, it will be all down to you, Brianna Price!" she tossed back over her shoulder.

"Don't worry. I am sure all that protein you're eating will soak up the alcohol! And I don't recall having to twist your arm to open that second bottle of vino. Be sure and ring me, won't you, after your big date?"

"Of course I will."

"Don't do anything I wouldn't do! And for goodness' sake, buy yourself some De-Gas pills!"

There was a snorting sound followed by something unmentionable from the footpath and Brianna giggled.

"Easy for you to laugh when you're not the one having to sit next to her on the train for the next thirty minutes," Jess muttered. "I couldn't believe the one she dropped in the Dart on the way back from Greystones. The poor chap opposite us looked like he was going to pass out and then she had to go out and make out it was down to me! Typical Nora—she always looks like butter wouldn't melt in her mouth." She finished shaking her head before making the arrangements for Tuesday morning. They'd meet up at St Stephen's Green for a spot of serious shopping after Brianna had dropped Harry at the little Catholic school he'd started back in January.

IT WAS LATER THAT NIGHT as Jess sat curled up on her couch that she realised Brianna had indeed given her an idea for her column. She would be going on a double date with a Hollywood Movie Star, so why not write about what it was like to hang out with a celebrity in Dublin? Pleased the pressure to come up with something pronto was off, she began idly channel surfing and it was then that she spotted *Snow White and the Seven Dwarfs* lying on the coffee table where she'd left it. Picking the little book up, she opened the cover and gazed thoughtfully at the names scribbled inside it. She was getting that tingly sensation she always got when the seeds of a potentially brilliant idea for her column began to germinate.

Chapter Three

"DOES MY BUM LOOK BIG in this?" Jess wondered how many conversations she had started over the years with that sentence whilst trying on clothes with Brianna or Nora—too many to be counted on one hand, that was for sure! It was ten thirty on a Tuesday morning and the two women were holed up in the changing room of the third exclusive boutique clothing shop they'd happened upon in the labyrinth of streets surrounding the city's main shopping hub of Grafton Street.

She had come to the conclusion that the less a shop had in it, the more hideously expensive the little it did have dangling from its rails was likely to be and the more skinny and hoity-toity the shop assistant was likely to be. Another reason she preferred charity shops—the people who worked in them were genuine, kind-hearted souls who quite often volunteered their time, not like Shop Girl No. Three.

When Jess had audibly gasped at the price tag hanging off the dress she was currently wearing, the underweight little madam had told her, "Well, *it is* Italian." She'd left the *what did you expect, you South Pacific commoner?* to hang in the air unsaid between them.

"No, not at all." Brianna answered her friend's question in a pitch just high enough to bring her back to the present and to let her know that she was telling a little white lie. She smiled to herself, thinking that if it had been Nora who was with her, she'd have said something along the lines of, "Good God, yes! Get it off before you split the arse out of it!"

As she wriggled her way out of the fitted green dress that had looked absolutely perfect on the hanger, she couldn't help but sigh—it was bloody hard work, all this getting dressed and undressed business. She wished she hadn't opted to wear her old Levi's because it would have been much easier had she donned a sack suitable for whipping on and off.

"Was the garment to madam's liking?" The angular redhead standing behind the counter studying her blood red talons sniffed when she emerged from the cubicle, clutching the dress.

She tapped her own un-manicured nails on the counter until the woman finally looked up with her bored expression firmly in place.

"Nah, it wasn't," Jess drawled in her best put-on Aussie accent, "'Cos it made madam's arse look humongous." She tossed the dress down on the counter and stalked out the door.

Brianna hurried after her, sniggering. "Did you see her face?" She linked her arm through Jess's.

"Snooty so-and-so. I reckon that plumy English accent was a put-on. I am ninety-nine percent sure I could detect Liverpool undertones creeping in! Anyway, it was probably a good thing the dress didn't look right, otherwise I'd have had to of taken out a second mortgage to pay for it."

"Mmm, you're right; it was on the pricey side. Why don't we try good old Debenhams instead?" Brianna suggested as they turned the corner back onto Grafton Street.

"Okay. I usually have far more luck at the Goodwill Thrift Shop on Capel Street, though, but if you recommend Debenhams, then Debenhams it is. Although I don't know why I'm going to all this bother of trying to find a new dress anyway because I bet you this friend of Ewan Reid's will probably be the Beast to his Beauty."

"So what if he is? At least you'll get to go out on a Friday night looking gorgeous—I can't remember the last time I got dolled up for a night out."

Jess was about to make a mental note to offer her babysitting services when she was distracted by the strains of a Coldplay tune. "I love that song," she said, elbowing her way through the semi-circle of people gathered round the busker who'd set himself up outside Marks and Spencer's. He had a mouth organ and a guitar and was doing a surprisingly good rendition of "Clocks" despite the lack of a piano. The girls clapped along with the rest of his audience when the song came to an end and flicked him a couple of coins before making their way down to Debenhams' Henry Street shop.

It was on the second floor of the department store that Jess spotted "the Dress." It was like a beacon in a sea of nondescript change of season fashions as it beckoned to her from the Jacques Vert designer collection. Racing across the shop floor, she whipped the brick red cowl neck off the rack and holding it out in front of her, admired the way the thousands of tiny beads stitched onto it shimmered under the bright lights. The dress had a 1920s feel to it—very Mary from *Downton Abbey*, she decided, calling out to Brianna to come and have a look. "What do you think of this one then?"

"Wow, it's gorgeous, so it is, and it's definitely your colour. Go and try it on."

Two minutes later, Jess stepped out of the changing rooms and did a pirouette for her friend.

"Oh yes, that's definitely the one! It looks amazing! You remind me of your woman out of *Downton Abbey*. You know, the one who was supposed to marry the chap in the wheelchair—go on, do a curtsey!"

"Lavinia?"

"Yes, that's her; she's got the same colouring as you."

Jess was pleased with the verdict, even if she would rather have been likened to the elegant and austere Mary because from what she could recall of the television series, Lavinia had not gotten her happy ever after. Still, she wasn't superstitious and the dress—even if it was brand new—had felt right the moment she'd slipped it over her head. It helped that it was on sale, too! When she'd taken a step back to look at her reflection in the dressing room mirror, she'd realised that it was definitely a Cinderella dress. So who knew? Maybe this friend of Ewan's would turn out to be a bit of a Prince Charming after all. Stranger things had happened and she was due a bit of luck on the man front.

"Best of all, it's under a hundred euro! So shall we head to the café for a spot of lunch—my treat?"

"Great—I'm starving."

"SHOPPING IS SURPRISINGLY hard work, isn't it?" Brianna said, not really expecting an answer as she flopped down into her chair.

Jess nodded, laying out their well-earned sandwiches and coffee. "It is when you are looking for something in particular. That's what I like about op-shopping—I just happen across really cool stuff. Do you know what I was thinking earlier when I was busy getting dressed and undressed?"

"What?"

"That I wish to God someone would open a shop with fitting rooms that are dimly lit. I hate those horrible fluorescent lights that show every lump and bump. It's not good for one's psyche."

"What lumps and bumps?" Brianna was indignant. "You wait until you have a baby—then you'll know all about lumps and bumps, my girl! You want to see the muffins Harry's left me with?" She reached around the back of her jeans and squeezed two imaginary pockets of fat. "It doesn't matter what size I get down to; the only way I'll get rid of these blueberry babies is by lipo." Picking up her rather delicious-looking gourmet sandwich, she took a greedy chomp out of it.

Jess looked glumly down at her own meagre low-fat bean sprout veggie sarnie and silently cursed all dressing room mirrors.

"Don't you have that Cajun cooking class tonight?" Brianna mumbled through her full mouth.

"I do. I'm looking forward to it. Apparently we will be making jambalaya, which sounds vaguely familiar and very exotic." She frowned. "It also sounds calorific, which is why I am on the bean sprout sanger. Next week, I'm doing a cod fish casserole, which doesn't have quite the same ring to it. It's a Portuguese class and I know nothing about Portuguese cuisine apart from the fact they eat a lot of fish."

"Well, I can't help you there. We're having Gran's bangers and mash for dinner because I've got a PTA meeting tonight—good old plain, hearty tucker; you can't beat it. My Gran says all men need a good serving of potatoes on their plate each night in order to fill them up."

"So that's what you do to keep your Pete happy, is it? Serve him up loads of spuds. Anyway, it's alright for you and Granny Dierdre to advocate bangers and mash because you're both built like whippets. It sucks—I so much as sniff mash spud and it goes to my waistline, whereas you eat what you like and never put a pound on."

"It's running around after Harry. Have a baby, Jess, and you'll never have to worry about your figure again except for the post-birth muffin overhang, of course, and the sagging boobs and stretched stomach skin," she lamented.

Jess subconsciously crossed her legs under the table. She was fairly sure Brianna wouldn't be getting a job as a Weight Watchers advocate in the near future if that was the best dietary advice she could dole out.

"Have you had any more thoughts on your column? What you're going to write about once you have finished the cooking school series and had enough of stuffing yourself silly on jumbaywotsit and Portuguese cat fish casserole?"

"*Cod* fish, not cat, and I have had a couple of ideas, as it happens. I thought I could write about the celebrity lifestyle in Dublin now that one of my best friends is dating a Hollywood Hottie. Actually, it was you who gave me the inspiration."

Brianna looked pleased. "When I told you to write about the blind date you were doubling on?"

"Yeah, except we didn't know then that the other half of the double date was a major celebrity, did we?"

"I know and I still can't get my head around the fact Nora kept it quiet and that our best friend is actually dating Ewan Reid." She pulled a face. "It's not fair you get to meet him first."

"Yes, but we don't know at what cost yet, do we? I may have to suffer through an evening with a Gollom clone."

"Or—ha-ha," Brianna snorted, "he could be one of those weird Trekkie guys in a giant nylon baby-gro." She giggled, giving Jess a Vulcan two-fingered salute.

Jess gave her a two-fingered salute of a different kind back. "Yeah, thanks, that's not helping. Anyway, I don't want to talk about it anymore. I had another idea as well I wanted to run past you. It's to do with a name in a book."

"You've lost me. What name in what book?"

"Well, remember the *Snow White and the Seven Dwarfs* book I bought for my collection not long ago?"

"Yes. That reminds me—Harry's right into all those traditional fairy stories at the moment. I made the mistake of reading him *Hansel and Gretel* the other night and managed to give myself nightmares. I'd hate to think what my poor son made of it. Though, to be honest, I don't know what disturbed me more about the story: the abandoning of children in the forest, the wicked witch putting Hansel in a cage in order to fatten him up, or the fact that Harry didn't seem at all fazed by it! I'd forgotten how horrible some of those old tales actually are."

"Yeah, you'd have to wonder what was going through the mind of the Brothers Grimm when they penned that one. They wrote *Little Red Riding Hood*, too. Please don't read that to Harry just yet. I had a phobia about wolves for years thanks to that little minx."

"Don't worry—we're sticking with good old *Hop on Pop*, Dr Seuss for the foreseeable future. But, come on then, spill—what's this idea of yours?"

"Okay, you know how one of the things I find intriguing about second-hand things is the thought of the life they have lived before they come to me?"

Brianna nodded. "That and the thrill of a good bargain."

"Yeah, well there is that too. But books, especially children's ones, are really special."

"Because of the illustrations, right?"

"Definitely that yes but it is more than just the pictures. Children love to mark their territory and every book in my collection has its original owner's name scrawled inside the cover."

"I don't get it—you told me once that decreases the book's value."

"It does but I don't collect them for their monetary value. It's hard to explain it properly but there's just something about the idea of another child having loved that book the same way I loved it and I often wonder who they were or are now. Does that sound weird?"

Brianna grinned. "If I was Nora, I would say it definitely sounds weird but since it's me you are talking to, I think I get it. You'd like to know the story behind the name in the book, is that it?"

"That's it exactly! Who was that child? Did he or she pore over the stories and the pictures like I did? Were they daydreamers too? Who did they grow up to be?"

"Jaysus, you are such a romantic, Jessica Baré. Where are you going with this?"

"I am going to find her."

"You've lost me again—who exactly are you off to find? And please don't say yourself because you're far too young for a mid-life crisis."

Jess laughed. "Don't worry; I'm not going to do an *Eat, Pray, Love* and frolic round Bali. I am going to find out what became of Amy Aherne from Ballymcguinness. She was six years old when her brother Owen gave her *Snow White and the Seven Dwarfs* for Christmas in 1973. So I am going to write about my journey to find the forty-six-year old Amy. I will do the detective work to find out who she is now, what she went on to do with her life and what that book meant to her. What do you think?"

"Wow, it's a bit out there but at the same time I think it's a brilliant idea!" Brianna was wide-eyed, imagining Amy Aherne, wherever she might be now. "Gosh, she could have grown up to be anything; how fascinating to find out. She could be an airhostess or an actress or a writer like you." Brianna's eyes became saucer-like. "Oh my God, what would you do if you found out she was a prostitute?" Before Jess could reply, another thought occurred to her. "What if she doesn't want you to write about her?"

"Whoa, slow down. Who's the writer—me or you? If she doesn't want me to write about her, I guess I will just have to come up with another brilliant idea. So what have you got on for the week then?"

"I've a PTA meeting Thursday night; it's full-on at the moment because we're organising the school fair in October—tonight's topic is the cake stall. I expect you to contribute, you know."

"But I can't bake."

"I meant buy something from the stall, you eejit. We can't all hang out with the rich and famous, you know. Some of us have responsibilities." She grinned. "Pete and I might try to get out for a meal down at the pub on Friday night, if Mammy's free, and Saturday afternoon I am meeting up with a group of mams to discuss saving our local playgroup."

"Harry doesn't go to playgroup anymore, though."

"I know but I have fond memories of when he did."

Jessica laughed. "You call me a romantic! Well, you're the queen of the community-minded. Bray would grind to a halt without you." She frowned, glancing at her watch. "It's two fifteen already, Brie. What time do you have to leave to pick Harry up?"

"CRAP! I'd forgotten about Harry. Come on, I've got to get a move on!"

"YOU LOOK FABULOUS. I love that dress. The colour is great on you—very Lavinia from *Downton Abbey*."

"You look lovely, too—very Naomi Watts in *King Kong*." Nora had gone for old-time glamour, too, and it suited her.

"Thanks. It's silly, isn't it? But I think I'm more nervous going on this second date than I was on the first."

"You should be nervous because I'll murder you if this friend of his turns out to be a big hairy gorilla."

"At least you'll get a column out of it."

There was no time for further discussion as Nora's intercom buzzed, signalling Ewan and his mystery mate had arrived.

The two women looked at each other and giggled with Nora announcing, "God, I feel like I'm sixteen and off to my school ball!"

They tottered down the stairs of Nora's Georgian two-storey manor house. Its bricks were laid firmly in the heart of fashionable Rathmines, where she paid a premium rent to live in the house's converted second-storey apartment. On the quiet street outside, Ewan Reid—looking as swarthy and gorgeous as he did on the big screen—was lounging alongside a tall, blonde handsome stranger; their backdrop was that of a sleek grey convertible.

Thank God the roof was on, was Jess's first thought, or her artfully tousled auburn curls would have been an artfully tousled bloody fright by the time they got to wherever it was they were going. Not to mention it would be bloody freezing. Her second thought as the stranger stepped forward, introducing himself as Nick before homing in to drop a kiss on her cheek, was that he was not bad, not bad at all. Nora might just get to live after all.

JUAN'S WAS BUZZING, Jess noticed, glancing round the popular Spanish restaurant's bar. It was standing room only and by the harassed look of the maître de, they would probably have to wait ages for a table. She was proved wrong and was only halfway through her Singapore Sling—she'd thought it sounded suitably sophisticated for the company she was keeping, even if sangria would have been more in keeping with the restaurant's theme—when Manuel from *Faulty Towers* appeared in front of her.

She had to bite back a laugh when he introduced himself in a dodgy Spanish accent as Miguel, their waiter for the evening. It was her first taste of a proper celebrity lifestyle, as in his next breath he began bowing and scraping to the great Ewan Reid before whisking them away from the minions who kept coming up to ask for his autograph.

Actually, she mused as Miguel held her seat out for her at their table that overlooked lively Harcourt Street below, the whole being famous thing—while having obvious perks like fabulous seats in fabulous restaurants—was also kind of annoying. No sooner did Ewan attempt to start up a conversation than some stranger would butt in, asking for an autograph. People seemed to think that because his face was familiar it gave them the right to be pushy—especially the women. Still, underneath Nora's fluffy blonde exterior and white silk sheath dress lurked a woman with the strength of King Kong, so if things were to get serious between her and Ewan, his female fans would have to watch out.

No, fame certainly wasn't something she hankered after, she thought as Miguel made a show of flapping the crisp white linen napkin before draping it across her lap. At least with writing she got to retain a certain amount of anonymity because while people often looked twice at her, they didn't usually twig that they recognised her from the passport-sized photo featured alongside her column. Though Nora would beg to differ; she maintained that the reason people looked twice at Jess was more to do with what she deemed her friend's bizarre choice of clothing.

Once the others were seated, she turned her attention from the window back to Nick, who was telling her he did something or other in property and that he had known Ewan since school. The convertible had been his, so whatever it was he did with property he obviously did well, she concluded, feeling slightly ashamed of how easily impressed she was.

Now though, as he smiled across at her, she couldn't help but notice that as well as driving a fancy car, his eyes were impossibly blue against the tan of his skin and blonde, stylishly cropped hair. Very Pierce Brosnan in his younger days but with blonde hair cut into a much better style. Oh my gosh, she thought, grinning inanely back at him and admiring the pearliness of his perfect teeth—my mother would absolutely love you!—and wondering at the same time whether he'd mind whether she whipped her cell-phone out and took a photo as proof that she was on a date with a man who so far appeared to have no underlying issues and was obviously successful.

At that moment, she received a sharp kick to the ankle and biting her lip, managed to stop herself from crying out. Bloody Nora, she swore silently but nevertheless took her friend's hint and wiped the sappy look off her face.

"So tell me about you, Jessica." Nick leaned forward, toying with his empty wine glass as they waited for Miguel to come back with the bottle of red they'd all agreed on. "Although, I have to say that having laughed out loud at your column many times, I can't help but feel like I already know you."

Jess preened ever so slightly; he had just scored some major brownie points because she loved it when a man took the time to ask about her instead of banging on about his achievements all night. "Ah, well, don't believe all that you read."

"I'll vouch for that." Ewan joined in the conversation. "My agent showed me an article in some woman's magazine the other week that strongly implied I might be the one to heal Demi's broken heart. All I bloody did was shake her hand when I was introduced to her at Cannes. The woman terrifies me. I was still in short pants when she did *Ghost*, for Chrissakes!"

They all laughed and after Ewan had sampled and approved the wine, much to Miguel's obvious relief, an animated conversation about the media ensued.

Jess had just finished relaying her tale of how her column came to fruition thanks to Shane Moriarty from Bad Boyz milking his new-found fame when Miguel magically popped up again. This time, he had his pad and paper in hand, ready to take their order. Nora opened the menu and Jess leaned in to read it as Nick announced that the paella was absolutely fantastic. The menu was snapped shut and it was agreed that they would all share in a plate of Spain's national dish.

"Teez a good choice, Meester Reid," Miguel gushed before giving a little bow and scurrying off toward the kitchen to click his fingers and tell the chef to snap to it.

That was another thing Jessica was noticing about the power of celebrity: it was as though Ewan were the only person seated at the table the way Miguel addressed everything to him. The rest of their little group was all but invisible.

As Nora and Ewan embarked on a conversation about paragliding, Nick refilled Jess's wine glass. "So what made you leave New Zealand? It's a stunning country."

"Have you been?" She was surprised; most Irish only got as far as Australia, arriving at Sydney Airport with their passports and dream that life from hereon in was going to be like one big scene from *Home and Away*. Not many jumped the ditch to New Zealand. Mind you, Nick didn't look like the kind of man who'd watch *Home and Away* or *Neighbours*.

"To Auckland on business, yes, but I managed to get up to the Bay of Islands for a few days R&R before I had to fly home. The fishing was fantastic and I'd liked to have stayed longer and seen more—you know, catch the big one that got away." He grinned and shrugged. "I'll definitely get back there in the near future, though."

Jess had no doubt that when he said something, he meant it but his words had seemed to hold an unspoken invitation and she felt herself grow hot. Knocking back her wine to cool down, she told herself off for always reading something into what was probably nothing. She'd only known him for an hour, for goodness' sake! Placing her glass back down on the table, she hoped he didn't think her a lush and then realising he was waiting for some sort of reply, the best she could come up with at short notice was, "Yes, it is beautiful." Risking a glance over at him, their eyes locked and the jolt of excitement that ricocheted through her literally made her catch her breath. It was either that or the wine had gone down the wrong way. Either way, the moment was ruined as she began coughing and spluttering, sending a spray of red wine across the table. Nora, thinking she was choking, leaped out of her seat and began walloping her on the back, which only made her cough harder.

It was then that Miguel appeared and excitedly told Nora to stand aside as he announced loudly and proudly, "I will perform ze Hymen Manoeuvre."

Thanks be to God he didn't get a chance to perform anything on her! Jess thought, because after a sip of the glass of water Nick was holding to her lips, the coughing subsided. By the time the steaming pan of rice and seafood appeared to take centre stage at their table, she had managed to regain her composure—well, almost.

By the time the third bottle of wine was opened, she, too, could see the funny side of Miguel and his "hymen" manoeuvre and she found herself relaxing and enjoying Nick and Ewan's company, though she did wish Nora would stop going on like she was the stunt woman out of the *Matrix*.

From there on in, the evening passed in a jovial wine-addled blur and before they knew it, they were the last patrons in the restaurant. It was time to go but not before they'd given Miguel a generous tip. As they led the way down the stairs and out the doors to the car park, Nick made one last joke about Miguel's Spanish accent and as she laughed the darkness in front of her was suddenly split by blinding flashes of light. She felt her mouth form a startled "Oh!" as Nick took her by the elbow and herded her over to the car.

"Who's the mystery blonde, Ewan! Does Tessa know you've called it quits?" Several different voices called and by way of reply Ewan growled, "Fecking paparazzi!" as he and Nora ducked inside the little car just as Nick began revving the engine. They exited the car park in a blaze of burning rubber.

"It's okay, Nick, man; slow down—nobody's following us," Ewan urged a moment later. "I'm sorry about that, ladies. The fecking pap get everywhere." He had turned around in his seat but he only had eyes for Nora as he added, "And Tessa and I broke up amicably aeons ago."

He was referring to his stunning *Suburban Man* co-star Tessa Adamson. Jess felt Nora relax next to her as she reached over and stroked his arm. Her eyes, in the darkened interior, were still glittering from the adrenaline rush of what had just happened and Jess had to concur that it had been rather exciting. She could see how the novelty would soon wear off if it happened every time you went anywhere, though. Imagine being photographed doing something as mundane as going to the corner shop for your morning paper or just collecting your post? A mental picture of herself in the elephant suit with pink slippers gracing the cover of *The Women's Friend* sprang to mind and she shuddered, pushing it aside.

Nick proved to be the perfect gentleman when they pulled up outside Riverside Apartments five minutes later. He got out of the car and, opening her door, helped her out before walking her to the main doors. While she fished around in her purse for her keys, he told her that he had really enjoyed the evening. "I'd like to do it again sometime." He looked at her expectantly.

"So would I." She blushed, all too aware that Nora would be sitting in the car with her face pressed up to the window, phone at the ready to text Brianna should there be snogging.

"So it's okay if I get your number off Nora and give you a call?"

"Yes, I'd like that."

"Great." Nick leaned in and she felt his lips airbrush hers before he stepped back, waiting for her to head inside. It was all she could do not to drag him in behind her.

Chapter Four

THE PHONE TRILLED BRIGHT and early the next morning—ridiculously early for a Saturday, in Jess's opinion—but nevertheless she forced herself to get out of bed and stumbled through to the living room to answer it.

"Hi, honey, it's Brie—okay if Harry and I pop round shortly? Because there's something I think you need to see."

Jess's brain gave itself a feeble kickstart. Bloody Brianna—what was she doing phoning at such a godforsaken time of the morning? Honestly, just because Harry always ensured she was up at sparrow's fart didn't mean everybody else had to be. "What's so important you're ringing me at the crack of dawn then?"

"It's actually after eight but never mind that. I will show you what it's all about when I get there."

"I thought you had your Save our Playgroup meeting this morning?"

"I did but I cancelled. See you in an hour."

She'd hung up before Jess had a chance to quiz her further and wide awake now, she padded through to the kitchen, puzzling over what it was she wanted to show her. Whatever it was, it had sounded like something worthy of an extra strong caffeine fix, especially if Brianna was missing one of her meetings in order to pop over.

IT WAS SOMETHING WORTHY of a triple shot of vodka but Jess didn't drink in the morning. "Sweet Mary, Mother of Jesus!" After nigh on ten years living in Ireland, she had at last grasped the lingo. She screeched, staring in horror at the open newspaper Brianna was holding up under her nose. All the while, Harry puff-puff-puffed his Thomas train up and down her kitchen tiles.

"You're not allowed to say that!" His five-year-old voice was outraged.

"You're entitled to sweets under the circumstances. Don't mind Harry; he's just begun religious instruction at school. Ignore him. I do." Brianna shot her son a look that would silence the most evangelical of preachers.

Jess's own face loomed back at her from the *Dublin Central* newspaper's weekend colour celebrity supplement.

"It's not that bad, really," Brianna lied. "And your dress is gorgeous. It's a lovely one of Nora, though, don't you think?" she finished rather lamely.

"I don't care what bloody Nora looks like and it *is* that bad. Nobody will give a rat's arse about my dress either because they'll be too busy laughing at my teeth—God! How will I ever show my face in public again?"

There were more shocked noises emanating from the kitchen but Harry wisely kept his thoughts on blasphemy and swearing to himself this time round.

"Ah, nobody will notice except your nearest and dearest like me and Nora. The general public will be far too busy wondering who it is Ewan Reid's dating now to wonder who your woman with the bad teeth is. I mean, look at the heading—'Ewan's Reid's Mystery Blonde.' There's no mention of you or your man—Nick, was it? He looks tasty, by the way."

"He was and there weren't a pair of handcuffs lurking in his back seat nor did he have a nervous disposition due to some trauma or other—not that he'll ever want to see me again, not after this." Jess stabbed at the photo depicting the foursome leaving Juan's the night before. The photographer had caught her with her gob hanging open gormlessly as she laughed in what she had thought was a coquettish way at Nick's little joke. Nora and Ewan, looking glamorously furtive, were bringing up the rear. Ordinarily, she'd have been quite chuffed to have made the celebrity pages but not with the dodgy set of gnashers she was flashing in the photo.

From over her shoulder, a little voice chirruped, "Aunty Jess, you are supposed to brush your teeth in the morning and before you go to bed. Mummy sings the 'Happy Birthday' song and I am not allowed to stop until she's finished."

This time it was Jess who shot him a look. Enough was enough and grabbing her phone, she punched out Nora's number. "Oi, have you seen it? I am holding you responsible, you know."

"Morning, hun," she sang cheerily down the line. "I take it you're talking about the *Dublin Central* pic?"

"Why didn't you tell me my teeth were black from all the red wine?"

"You were rather knocking it back, now that I think about it. Mind you, can't say I blame you. It was a nice little drop, I thought—quite cheeky…"

"Shut up, Nora!"

"Alright, alright. If you must know, I was too busy staring at Ewan to notice your teeth—so sue me. I'm seeing him again tonight, by the way."

"Humph. It's alright for some."

"Listen, I'm sorry, Jess, I am—but hey, nobody will notice and if they do, they will have forgotten all about it by tomorrow, especially if you don't smile at them and jog their memory." There was a little snort down the phone before she added, "Anyway, nobody reads the *Dublin Central*."

"I heard that snort! You better not be laughing at me, Nora Brennan, and for your information, forty percent of Dubliners read that newspaper. I'm officially mortified!" It was the *Express*'s rival paper and she wouldn't have put it past the paper's weasel-like editor, Jimmy Mulroney, to have put the photo in just to spite her. He was known to hold a grudge and she had turned him down flat when he'd tried to poach her from the *Express*. As far as she was concerned, she'd definitely made the right decision and he had just cemented his reputation as a mean git who suffered from short man's disease.

"It's not fair," she whined. "I really liked Nick but I've no chance of hearing from him, not now! Bloody hell, choking on my wine was bad enough but this… this is…"

"Enough to send a gal off for her annual check-up at the dentist's?"

"Shut up Nora!"

"Look, if that's what you're really worried about, rest assured—I saw the kiss Nick planted on you last night. You'll hear from him again. Trust me."

HE RANG ON SUNDAY NIGHT.

"Hey, Jessica, it's Nick Jameson. How are you?"

Her stomach did this funny sort of a flip-flop somersault at the sound of his voice and she sat up straighter on the settee, turning the television down.

"Hi, I'm good, thanks, Nick. How are you?" She hoped her voice didn't betray how wobbly her tummy felt.

As the conversation moved swiftly on to the weather, she steadied her nerves. It was a subject they didn't mull over for long. They did live in Ireland and it was mid-September after all. There was only so much you could say about rain.

Jess was unwilling to mention the photo in the paper just yet, happy to let Nick make small talk about a hailstorm he'd gotten caught in earlier that day.

She'd only left the apartment once over the weekend and that was out of desperation. She'd needed to get a carton of milk and a loaf of bread, so she'd donned a hoodie and dark glasses. Nevertheless, she'd expected to be on the receiving end of cat calls along the lines of, "Hey, Jessica, when are you auditioning for the Pogues!" as she'd scurried down to her local Spar shop. As it was, nobody had looked twice at her, so perhaps she had overreacted after all. Chewing on her nail, she decided it was no good; she'd just have to bite the bullet and put herself out of her misery. It was that or she'd start talking about squally showers and drizzle. She cut him off just as he was saying something about the hailstones being the size of golf balls. "So, um, Nick, did you happen to see the *Dublin Central* yesterday morning?"

"Nope, I'm an *Express* man myself. There's a column in there I never miss on a Saturday."

A smile spread involuntarily across Jess's face and she was glad they weren't on Skype because she knew she'd look like a dippy fool.

"Besides, I don't like all that gossip fodder in the middle of the *Central*: most of it's a load of shite. Some of the crap that gets written about Ewan is unbelievable and who cares where so-and-so has their lunch or where the latest place to be seen is. Why do you ask?"

Jess allowed herself to exhale. Thank goodness he hadn't seen it! Somebody upstairs was looking out for her after all. She'd have to apologise to Harry next time she saw him and from now on, she promised, looking heavenward, she would never blaspheme ever again. "Oh, um, just a bit of a survey my boss asked me to conduct—you know, to see who reads what." It sounded pretty lame and she cringed but thankfully Nick didn't seem to pick up on it as he got to the point of his call.

"Oh, right, well, I'm heading over to London on a late flight tonight for business back on Thursday and I was wondering whether you'd be free that evening? I've been invited to the opening night of Esquires. It's a new cocktail bar on Dame Street."

Jess decided not to reflect on the irony of his inviting her to a cocktail bar opening after his "who cares where the latest place to be seen is?" spiel. Nope, it didn't matter if she had an interview with the Queen of England next Thursday evening. She'd cancel, because for Nick super hottie Jameson, she'd be free. Hoping she didn't sound too eager, she told him that yes she would love to catch up next Thursday and so he arranged to pick her up at nine before ringing off.

Jess sat on that couch for an age, hugging herself, and every time she recalled that ever so soft kiss good night, her tummy did that funny forward roll thing. It had been ages since a man had given her butterflies like the ones she had flittering around at the thought of their next date. What did one wear to cocktail bar opening nights? she mused. Should she dig out her 1970s black wool Anne Klein dress? It was classy and elegant but not what you'd call sexy. Nora would know the look she should go for, she decided, picking up the phone to ring her with her news. It clicked straight on to her answerphone, which Nora's mobile only ever did when she didn't want to be disturbed. Hmm, she thought, eyes narrowing; perhaps she was up to no good with Ewan. Nora was a firm believer in trying before buying so it wouldn't surprise her. She'd make sure she got the lowdown tomorrow. She'd try Brianna instead. The same thing happened—God, was everybody at it? Her new-found piety was short-lived as a naughty smile played at the corners of her mouth. Who knew? If she played her cards right, she might be in the club soon too—no, not literally of course. God no!

Flicking the television off and opening her laptop, she decided she couldn't sit here dreaming about Nick all night and she certainly didn't want to dwell on the fact her two best friends were more than likely having sex. There was nothing else for it—she'd have to do some work.

Leaning away from the screen, with her fingers forming a steeple she was holding to her lips, Jess pondered the best way to handle her humiliation at the hands of the *Dublin Central*. The more she thought about it, the more it became clear that she should make light of it—turn it into a bit of a joke.

Show that it didn't bother her. It was with that thought in mind that her hands began flying over the keys as she tapped out an article bound to make the most pokerfaced of *Express* readers crack a smile—at her expense, of course. She had just begun writing about how close she had come to having the "hymen" manoeuvre performed on her by a Manuel from *Fawlty Towers* lookalike (naming no names, of course) when the phone jangled into life, disturbing her flow. Jess felt a surge of irritation; it was ten o'clock and there was only one person who rang at this time on a Sunday night. Stretching over, she answered it with a lemon-lipped hello.

"Well, if there was ever a tone to frighten potential suitors away, it's that one, my girl."

"Hey Mum." She sighed, having guessed right. "I was just about to do some work."

"Yes, well, work can wait. It's Sunday night over there, isn't it? Frank, you did work out the time difference properly, didn't you?" Marian called out.

Jess held the receiver away from her ear, a mental image of her father seated in his favourite Lazy Boy chair forming. "Yeah, it is but..."

"Well, you shouldn't be working on a Sunday night, for goodness' sake, so put whatever it is you were doing down. It can wait until Monday, surely? We can have a nice little chat instead. So *how* are you, sweetheart?"

Jess frowned, hating the way she stressed the "how," inferring she couldn't possibly be happy. Her complete lack of interest in Jess's work stung too. She would have loved to have told her Mum about the black teeth debacle or her plans for finding Amy but there was no point. She closed her laptop with resignation, knowing full well there would be no fobbing Marian Baré off when she was in this mood. Still, she thought, on the bright side, at least this time she had some news that would definitely please her. "Actually, Mum, since you ask. I'm good. Really good, in fact...I've met someone."

There was a split second's silence broken by a scream and followed by, "Hallelujah! Frank, turn the telly off! She's met someone!"

Jess could picture her dad hitting the mute button, a tiny act of rebellion, on the telly as he flicked his favourite armchair upright. It might have been a Sunday morning at home but there would still be some form of sport on the box and it would take a major world disaster for him to forfeit his fix. It had been the happiest day of his life when he had gotten the Sky Sports channel.

"Oh, that is fabulous, Jessica, just fabulous. But first things first—any issues? Is he normal?"

"*Mum!*"

"I have to ask, darling. You can't blame me worrying, not with your track record."

She couldn't really argue with that one. "He is tall, blonde, and handsome."

"So was Ted Bundy."

"He had dark hair and he's not a serial killer, Mum; he's a successful property developer and he drives a convertible." She added this last bit to prove her point. It worked.

"Frank, he drives a convertible!"

She heard something muffled in the background.

"Your father wants to know what kind of convertible."

It had sounded more like her father had said something along the lines of *bully for him* to Jess, which seemed a far more likely response from the laid-back Frank.

"How should I know? But you can tell Dad that it was shiny and grey, oh and it went quite fast."

"It was shiny and grey, Frank, and it went fast." She paused for a moment. "I hope he wasn't speeding. So come on, then, what's his name?"

"Nick Jameson."

"Jessica Jameson. It has a nice ring to it. Jessica Jameson—Frank, what do you think? Your dad's nodding, sweetheart; he likes it too."

God, with Darby and Joan for parents, was it any wonder she was still single?

"How old is he?"

"Er, I'm not sure. He is an old school friend of Ewan Reid's, so I guess he must be around thirty-eight."

"Ewan Reid? As in Ewan Reid the actor?"

"Yes, Nora's just started dating him."

There was another eruption as Marian shrieked this trivia across the living room to Frank, who gave an unimpressed sounding grunt, and then her voice grew suspicious. "Hmm, thirty-eight, you say, and he keeps the company of celebrities? Has he been married before?"

"I'm not sure."

"She's not sure, Frank—didn't you ask him?"

"It didn't really come up, Mum."

"Well, it should have. Have I taught you nothing over the years? Be sure to ask him next time you see him. If there are children from a past relationship involved, you won't have an easy time of it, my girl, so think on." She drew breath, not ready to give up on her potential son-in-law just yet. "What exactly does he do?"

"I already told you he's a property developer."

"Yes, I got that but what property is it that he develops? I hope he's not one of these rogues we're always reading about here that turf old people out of their homes to make a quick buck."

Jess shook her head. "Of course he's not."

"So what does he develop then?"

"Um, I don't know...expensive property?"

"Oh, for goodness' sake, Jessica, what on earth did you talk to him about all night? Where does he live? Tell me that at least."

Jess cringed. "Ah, not sure," she squeaked, realising she didn't know much about Nick Jameson after all.

"Well, when are you seeing him again? Think very carefully before saying I don't know, my girl."

"Thursday night, actually. He's taking me to the opening of a new cocktail bar."

"Oh, thank goodness for that. Thursday night, Frank—she's going to a cocktail bar with him."

Her suspicious tone returned. "He doesn't have a drink problem, does he?"

"*Mum!*"

Marian ignored her. "What are you going to wear? Please tell me you won't be donning one of your weird and wonderful thrift shop creations."

"I don't know yet and for your information, some of my weird and wonderful creations are actually designer vintage collectables."

"If you say so, dear, but in my opinion that's just gobbledegook for old. Take it from your mother, the voice of experience: you can't go wrong with a little black dress."

"Well, I do have an Anne Klein black wool dress I was thinking of wearing."

"I'm not sure about wool sending the right message and for goodness' sake, don't you go wearing any of those awful big knickers that come in packs of six I found in your drawer that time. Decent knickers with lots of lace, my girl, if you want to land yourself a decent man. I could get some couriered over express if you don't have any."

"*Mum!*"

"*Marian!*" She heard her father protest in the background.

It was no good, though; she was not suitably chastised. "I'm not naïve, Jessica Jane. I know what you girls get up to these days but whatever you do, don't let him hit a home run. Are you listening to me? First base maybe but a home run so early on in the piece is a no-no."

She had made the excuse she was desperate for the loo after that and had gotten off the phone quick smart, determined not to listen to any more of her mother's sex education class.

PEERING INTO THE DARKNESS to where the red digits of her alarm clock glowed, Jess saw that it was gone three a.m. and she was still wide awake. Talking to her Mum always gave her a good dose of insomnia and left her feeling wound tighter than a pair of knickers two sizes too small. She gave a long, drawn-out sigh because she knew she was wasting her time tossing and turning in bed when she could be doing some work. She'd managed to finish the piece she'd been working on earlier and despite the interruption halfway through thanks to her mother, she was pleased with the way it had turned out. It would definitely get her into Niall's good books, she thought, stretching with satisfaction.

Whenever she wrote something, though, she liked to leave it at least twenty-four hours before going back over it. It was amazing the mistakes that jumped out glaringly when she cast a fresh eye over her work. So there was no point working on her brief brush with celebrity life anymore tonight. She could get ahead of her game, though, she thought, tossing the duvet aside and sitting up, by making a start on tracking little Amy Aherne down.

Dragging the duvet into the lounge behind her, she dumped it on the couch and switched her laptop on before padding into the kitchen to make a cuppa.

The problem was, she mused, setting the steaming mug of tea down on the coffee table next to her computer, *Little* Amy—as she had begun thinking of her—wouldn't be so little now. In fact, she'd be a middle-aged woman of forty-six and had probably been married for years. Plonking down on the couch, she flexed her fingers and then let them hover over the keys as she pondered what she should begin to search under. Unless she had decided to become a nun, keep her own surname or hyphenated it, it would be a waste of time searching under Amy Aherne. Still, she had to start somewhere.

As she'd expected, she got no hits—just a whole lot of stuff to do with the Troubles, as the sectarian fighting spanning the late 60s to the mid-1990s in Northern Ireland was referred to. She didn't want a gloomy history lesson, so maybe she would be better off doing a Google search for the brother Owen and seeing where that got her. A moment later, something about W.B. Yeats cropped up, as did a genealogy website with Ahern listed minus the *e* on the end and oh dear, she thought, as her eyes scanned the list and settled on a death notice. She double clicked and closer inspection revealed that this poor soul had lived in Tipperary—opposite ends of the country. Just like the song, Ballymcguinness was a long way from Tipperary, so the odds of this being her Owen Aherne were slim.

Picking up the mug, she blew on it and thought for a moment before taking a sip. She'd try good ole Facebook and see what that threw back at her. Settling back to wait for the onslaught she'd have to trawl through, she could hardly believe her eyes when the search told her there were no Owen or Amy Aherne registered. Unbelievable in this day and age of social networking!

Right, well, Ballymcguinness sounded like a mere dot of a place; surely this search would yield the result she was after. A website welcoming her to Ballymcguinness filled her screen with a grainy black-and-white photo of a small town. It kind of looked like the start of *Coronation Street* with all the roofs of the houses—not very inspirational and not very helpful either. She didn't want to know how many grocery stores or hairdressers the town had. She wanted to know where she could find Amy blinkin Aherne, she thought in frustration.

Flopping back onto the couch, Jess closed her eyes for a second and racked her brains. Sometimes having all this technology at your fingertips was a waste of time. Then, it came to her. Duh-uh! Still, it was the middle of the night; she was entitled to be a little bit thick. This time, she searched the white pages and lo and behold after narrowing her search down, up popped two listings for Aherne. The first was for an M J Aherne, who was registered at a retirement home in the village of Dundrum and the second was for an O M Aherne, Glenariff Farm, Pyke Road, followed by a phone number. She had her man and unbelievably he still lived at his childhood address.

Jess's eyes strayed over to the telephone but then she shook her head. She might be up and about but she was fairly sure Mr Aherne would not appreciate being on the receiving end of her dulcet tones at this hour of the morning nor would his wife appreciate a strange woman telephoning her husband in the middle of the night. Besides, she was beginning to feel sleepy, she thought, yawning as she saved her search. Switching the laptop off, she took herself and her duvet back to bed.

WHEN SHE WOKE IT WAS gone nine a.m. and her head felt heavy after her disturbed night's sleep. She'd gone off quickly enough when she had got back into bed but had still slept lightly as she dreamt about an imaginary Owen Aherne serenading her with "It's a Long Way from Tipperary" while her mother clapped along in the background. Still, she thought, pouring her morning coffee, it was nothing a paracetamol wouldn't fix. As she poured out her cornflakes, her mobile broke into song, causing her to cringe mid-pour. "Barracuda" by Heart was belting out from where her phone lay atop the microwave. Bloody Nora had programmed the song as her ringtone in punishment for their having lost a pub quiz due to her lack of knowledge about all-women hard rock groups throughout the ages.

Granted, Nora had had a few drinks under her belt and they'd all thought it was a great joke at the time but now she had no idea how to change it back. It wasn't a good look when one was enjoying a civilised latte or riding on public transport. Picking it up, she squinted at the inbox.

C tht u rng lst nite was out Ewan hot wot u wnt?

Speak of the devil! It was Nora; her texting shorthand was always so bloody cryptic and she never included any social niceties like a x or luv Nora, Jess grouched, deciphering the curt message out loud: See that you rang last night—was out—Ewan hot—what you want?

Nick phd me we have a date this thurs nite -did you have sex last nite?

A reply that didn't require a code breaker this time bounced back almost immediately.

Told u so!MYOB PS:kncking off erly to jmp ot plne.

Jess stared at the glowing screen; if she didn't know better, she'd have read that last bit as *knocking off early to jump out of a plane*. No, that couldn't be right; it was more likely she was planning on knocking off early to jump Ewan's bones again. She'd phone Nora for the lowdown this evening. She knew from experience it was useless trying to hold a conversation with her when she was at work. With that decided, she raised her spoon to tuck into her cornflakes.

"*OOOOH Barracuda*" pounded out again. It made her drop her spoon. "Piss off, Nora!" she said out loud, aware that talking to herself was a side effect of living alone, but this time the message was from Brianna.

Morning Jess sorry missed your call was having sex - what did you want sweety?

Jess had to smile. Nora and Brie might have hailed from different planets but she loved them both the same, though at this moment in time she probably loved Brianna a teensy bit more. She was nicer, after all.

After a series of frantic texts bounced back and forth about her upcoming date with Nick and thankfully not about Brianna's Sunday night delight, she finally managed to finish her breakfast. Dumping the bowl in the sink, Jess glanced at the phone. She might try to contact Amy's brother before jumping in the shower.

As she punched in the code for Northern Ireland followed by his phone number, she decided it was probably a pointless exercise. It was ten o'clock on a Monday morning, after all. This Owen chap would probably be hard at work, toiling in the fields or whatever it was that farmers did on a Monday morning. As it connected and began to ring, though, she decided to hang on—she could always leave a message on his answerphone as to what she was calling about.

To her surprise, the phone was picked up on the fourth ring. It wasn't a good line but she did manage to detect a gruff male voice as it was answered.

"Hello?"

"Oh, hello, is that Mr Aherne?" she inquired, putting on her best journalistic tone.

"Aye." He sounded wary.

"Er, right, well." So much for consummate professional, she thought. "My name's Jessica Baré and I write a weekly column for the *Dublin Express*."

"Aye." He sounded even more suspicious.

"Well, what I am ringing about, Mr Aherne, is your sister, Amy?"

There was a static-filled silence.

"Are you still there, Mr Aherne?"

"What are you wanting, dragging all that up again?" His voice, despite the gruffness, had the sing-song quality of the North to it.

What was he on about? she wondered. Maybe he and Amy weren't on good terms or perhaps she'd done something illegal? Her nose twitched the way it always did when she sensed she was onto something and whatever it was that had happened, she was sensing there was definitely a story to be told here.

"It's just that I've got her book, you see. It's a children's storybook that you gave her for Christmas back in 1973. She wrote her name inside the cover; that's how I know it was hers." She rushed on and he didn't interrupt her—he probably thought she was mad, so in for a penny, in for a pound, she ploughed on. "It's a bit of a long story but I collect old Ladybird books—Series 606D to be exact. The stories are all the classic children's fairy tales but it's the illustrations I love and well..." She paused momentarily, wondering whether he would interrupt and tell her she was mad but he remained silent. "Nearly all of the books in my collection are pre-loved, with other children's names scribbled inside them. It devalues the book for most collectors but I like it—you know, the thought that another child has loved that book." There was still no response. Jess twirled her hair round her index finger with her free hand. She couldn't blame him—not really, because her brilliant idea was beginning to sound pottier by the minute. She inhaled deeply before telling herself to just cut to the chase before he hung up, writing her off as a crackpot caller. "Anyway, Mr Aherne, to get to the point, as I mentioned before, I recently acquired Amy's old copy of *Snow White and the Seven Dwarfs* from an eBid auction and that's when the idea came to me. Where is she now—the child who used to own that book? And that's it—really, that's what I'd like to write about."

If she expected him to begin filling her in with enthusiasm as to what it was his sister had been doing for the last thirty-odd years, she was out of luck. "The thing is, Mr Aherne..." she said, filling in the crackling static that was, if she were to be honest, getting a tad creepy, "I'd love to get in touch with Amy to see whether she'd be open to my idea." Christ, she thought, he really wasn't making this easy. "Erm, so that's why I have rung you, to ask whether you could give me your sister's contact details? I couldn't find a listing anywhere for her, and I tracked you down easily enough because Amy had scribbled the name of your farm inside the cover of her book too."

At last he broke his silence, clearing his throat before answering her. "Ah, well now, it's the sorta ting she might have been open to for sure but you could find it a bit hard getting in touch with her seeing as our Amy's been dead for the past twenty-nine years."

Chapter Five

HE'D HUNG UP ON HER after dropping that bombshell and Jess sat for an age staring at the phone, which was now dead. Dead, just like little Amy from her storybook was. Whatever she had been expecting Owen Aherne to tell her about his sister, it certainly hadn't been that.

She was too numb right at that moment in time to feel awful but she was angry. Angry with herself for being so naïve and caught up in her own big idea to have never even considered the possibility in the first place. What an earth could have happened to her?

Jess mentally worked out the years. Owen Aherne had said she'd died twenty-nine years ago, so that would make her around sixteen years old when she passed away. God, that was so young. She'd have had her whole life in front of her. Maybe she got hit by a car or perhaps she'd been ill? Whatever it was that had happened, she'd never know now and all her big idea had served in doing was raking up a whole lot of remembered grief for a man she had never met. Thank goodness she hadn't inadvertently contacted the poor girl's parents.

After a few minutes, she put the phone back in its cradle and getting to her feet, decided to go and have that shower. The numbness had definitely worn off now and perhaps drowning herself under a hot shower faucet might make her feel marginally less worse about the tactless, one-sided conversation she had just had. She was halfway down the hall when she heard the phone shrill. Retracing her steps, she picked it up and found herself pressing it to her ear a little tighter as she heard that same broad Northern Irish twang from a few minutes earlier.

"It's Owen Aherne here," he said brusquely. "Listen, I'm sorry I hung up on you, and I hope you don't mind me calling you back like this—caller display—but when I thought about what I said to you, well, you didn't deserve that reaction so I'd like to apologise."

Jess was taken aback; she could tell from his voice that an apology was not something that tripped off this man's tongue easily. "You don't need to explain yourself to me, Mr Aherne. I can't imagine what an awful shock my phoning out the blue like that was and with such a convoluted story, too. Really, it's me who should be apologising to you, and I am sorry, really sorry. I should have done my homework properly before contacting you. It was terribly unprofessional. I just...I got so caught up on the whole idea of finding her that it never crossed my mind that your sister might no longer be with us."

"Call me Owen; it's me Da who is known as Mr Aherne. You weren't to know that she'd passed on but aye, it was a bit of a shock to hear her name like that, with it being thirty years like this October."

He pronounced his "that" like *dat,* Jess noticed as he began to talk.

"She was older than me by two years and turning into a bit of a hallion."

That surprised Jess because for some reason and she didn't really know why; she had assumed he was the older brother. As for a hallion, well, he'd lost her there. "Sorry if I'm being thick but what's a hallion?"

"Aye, sorry, it's the lingo up my way. It means she was a tearaway, a right typical teenage girl, you know? Mouthy like and what came out of it was usually directed at me Ma."

Yes, a familiar scenario, Jess thought, picturing herself at the same age. Actually, as her own mother's face floated before her, she realised not that much had changed.

"Anyway, the day it happened she told Ma she was going to her friend Evie's house, and Evie told her Ma she was going to Amy's; then both girls caught the bus up to Lisburn. Back then, Lisburn was classed as a borough of Belfast but it's a town in its own right now, so it is." He coughed then and Jess couldn't tell whether it was because he was getting choked by the story he was relaying or not, and she found herself clutching the receiver a little tighter.

"She had her eye on a lad who worked up that way, so Evie told us later. She'd met him briefly at a dance and was determined to see him again even though according to Evie, he didn't want to know. That was our Amy all over, though—determined. If she set her mind to something, there was no stopping her."

Jess could recall doing the same thing herself, just at a different time and place. She felt a surge of empathy for the teenage Amy and her unrequited love.

"The fighting was bad back in '83 and there were a lot of tit for tat killings going on, you know? So Amy knew that there was no way in hell she'd have been allowed to go anywhere near Belfast or the like if she'd asked permission." He cleared his throat and Jess looked down at her bare forearms. The downy hairs covering them were standing on end. "But Ballymcguinness is a small place and it was even smaller back then, claustrophobic for teenagers. I know because I wasn't whiter than white myself, if you get my drift, so I got where she was coming from, sneaking off like that."

Yes, Jess thought; that was the mentality of a teenager. They were all ten foot tall and bulletproof.

"Don't get me wrong, though, because she wasn't a bad kid nor was Evie. They had itchy feet, though, and going somewhere they knew they had no business in going—well, it would give them a bit of kudos with their pals. God knows we were naïve living here tucked away from the worst of it all. It was like the Troubles were happening somewhere else, not in our backyard, you know?"

Having grown up in Auckland, a city of just over 1.5 million people, Jess couldn't relate firsthand to the frustration of small town life for a teenage girl but she did know that sometimes living in the city could be just as claustrophobic.

"Evie told us later that she left her bag in the café they'd been hanging out in for most of the day, eyeing up this lad Amy fancied who worked across the road at a mechanics'. They'd sat smoking cigarettes, trying to look sophisticated and drinking manky, bottomless coffee until it was time to get the bus home. Evie had run back down the road to get her bag while Amy waited at the bus stop outside O'Hara's the butchers to make sure they didn't miss it. She knew there would be murder to pay at home if it came out what the two of them had spent the day doing."

Jess inhaled shakily and felt a wave of nausea; she had a feeling she knew what was coming next and she was right.

"It was a Loyalist bombing that went wrong. There was a meeting due to be held in the back of the butcher's shop. Christopher O'Hara, who was an

IRA hard man back in the day, and his cronies were supposed to be gathered there except they weren't and seven innocent people including my sister were killed instead. We were told she died instantly and that she wouldn't have suffered, which was a blessing for her but of no comfort to me Ma, who spent the rest of her life suffering." He paused and drew a ragged breath. "It's a hard thing to accept that you've no body left to bury, just the pieces left behind. Me Da was an armchair Unionist back then who liked to spout off with his pals down at Murtagh's Pub on a Saturday afternoon but after what happened to Amy, he never stepped foot in there again—he lost his spark."

Jess was speechless as she swiped at her eyes with the back of her hand. What did you say to someone who had been through what this poor man and his family had been through? In the end, the only thing she could do was whisper, "What about you—what did you do?"

"Oh, I grew up as you do and went over the water to England to get my law degree and to forget. I wanted nothing to do with Northern Ireland. I practised law in London for fifteen years."

"And now you're back?"

"And now I'm back and I am sorry to burden you with our family history like that." The curtness was back in his voice and she felt his wall go back up.

"You didn't really have a choice, Mr Aherne; it was me who rang you, remember?"

"Aye but this isn't about me and that's partly why I rang you back. Like I said, it's coming up to thirty years since that bomb went off and I'm thinking it needs to be marked somehow. Maybe by remembering the girl our Amy was and could have been instead of focusing solely on an event that was out of her control. I mean, when she wasn't causing me Ma and Da to pull their hair out, she was a normal girl, you know. She liked messing around with makeup, listening to music, and trailing round all moony-eyed after boys. She wasn't political in the slightest but what happened that day meant that's all she is remembered for and I think the story you are talking about putting together is something she would have approved of." He coughed, as though embarrassed by the depth of feeling behind his words. "What I'm saying, I suppose, is that if you are up for a visit to Ballymcguinness sometime, I'd like to tell you a bit more about my sister."

There was absolutely no doubt in Jess's mind that she had to tell Amy's story now. The book lay open where she had printed her name all those years ago on the coffee table in front of her and she traced her finger over the letters. "Is tomorrow too soon for me to come? If you give me your mobile details, I can text through what time I will be arriving."

AS IT TURNED OUT, THE operator for Bus Eireann told her there were only two buses every day to Ballymcguinness: one in the morning and one in the late afternoon. Jess decided to get on the eight a.m. bus and return at five p.m. later that day.

"You'll arrive sometime around twelve o'clock, in time for your lunch, so you will," the operator informed her as she booked a return ticket. "It's around about a four-hour trip each way, with a few wee stops along the way."

She assumed he didn't mean "wee" stops literally. Nothing was ever precise in Ireland either, she thought with a half-smile, thanking him for his help and hanging up. Next she banged out an email outlining to her boss, Niall, the story idea she wanted to put together in the vague hope of some travel expenses coming her way. Fat chance of that, she thought; the *Express*'s coffers were tighter than Olivia Newton John's spandex pants in *Grease*. Oh, well, the fare wasn't going to break the bank, she thought, sighing and shutting her laptop. Besides, she'd write Amy's story for free if it came to it.

After texting the number Owen had left her to give him her guesstimated arrival time in Ballymcguinness, she decided to give Brianna a call and fill her in on the latest instalment where Amy was concerned.

"OH MY GOD, JESS! I didn't expect that—I bet you didn't either. That's unbelievably awful. Whenever I hear things like that, I want to hold Harry and never let him out of my sight—speaking of whom, he was last seen heading toward my room with a look of intent on his face. I've just bought a new nail varnish and he's determined to get a hold of it. Remember what happened last time I was gassing on the phone?"

Jess did indeed remember; she didn't think she would ever forget. Harry had decided to put his mother's fuchsia colourfast lippy on all his teddies. They'd looked like they belonged in a teddy bear brothel, not a little boy's bedroom, by the time he had finished. She held the phone away from her ear while Brianna yelled, "Harry, come here please. Mammy needs you."

"Sorry about that," she said a few moments later. "I've plonked him in front of the telly—his favourite *Sponge Bob* is on so we won't hear a peep out of him. Now, then, your girl Amy—I still can't believe she died like that. I mean, I grew up hearing about what was happening in the North and seeing bits of it on the news while my Mammy and Da tut-tutted over it all but it always seemed like it was happening in another country."

"In someone else's backyard." Jess echoed Owen's earlier words.

"Exactly."

"It's a real tragedy, isn't it? And I bet Amy's story is only one of hundreds but it is a story I get the privilege of telling. I'm catching the bus to Ballymcguinness tomorrow morning to meet with Owen."

"The bus? Jaysus, you're game! Why did you not look at catching the Dublin to Belfast Express? The train only takes a couple of hours at the most. You could have got a bus down from there to this Ballymcguinness. Sure, it would have only been a hop, skip, and a jump away."

"I didn't know express was even a word in the Irish language."

"Ha-ha! Well, I'll get the last laugh when you're clutching your bum as you bounce over every pothole from here to the back of Ballybeyond."

Mental note to self, Jess thought: bring a cushion. Her cell-phone announced an incoming text and she quickly glanced at the new message. It was from Owen, asking why she hadn't booked herself on the Belfast Express. She decided not to mention the text to Brianna, whose tone had grown sombre.

"Seriously, though, tread lightly, Jess; it's bound to be emotional for this Owen chap, talking about his sister in-depth with you like that after all these years."

"I'm not Nora, Brie. I won't bulldoze my way in."

"Sure, I know you won't but hey speaking of Nora, I got the weirdest text from her. You know what they're like to decipher but I think she was on about skydiving. Surely not, though; Nora's terrified of heights."

"Ah yes, but she's also mad about Ewan. Question is—is she mad enough to throw herself out of a plane for him?"

Both girls chorused, "No way!"

ER, YES WAY, SHE THOUGHT, shaking her head in disbelief at seven thirty that night. She was scrolling through photos Nora had just sent through to her email as evidence that she, Nora Brennan, had indeed done a skydive. Jess's eyes widened as she took in the impressive sight of one of her best friends, spread eagled and decked out in some hideous padded suit with goggles on, blonde hair flayed out behind her and mouth forming a perfect terrified *O* as she launched herself into the great blue yonder. Crikey, Jess thought; she really does have it bad for Ewan.

Spying a new message from her boss, she opened it and to her surprise read that Niall was so enthused over her story idea he wanted to run it as a full-page article, independent of her column for which, if the figure he had quoted as payment was correct, she was to be generously reimbursed. Her eyes widened further as she carried on reading. The *Express* would pay her travel costs to Ballymcguinness, too, and any other additional costs she incurred. She felt inordinately pleased that it wasn't just her that recognised Amy's story was one that needed to be told; it was just a bummer that she hadn't booked a first-class seat on the train after all.

BY TEN THE FOLLOWING morning, she was not only wishing she had taken heed of Brianna's warning regarding the bus she was also wishing she had donned a sturdy sports bra instead of the non-underwire one she had worn, opting for comfort. Not only had the bus done a loop inland, passing through all sorts of out-of-the-way towns before finally getting back onto the road that spliced through Drogheda and headed north, but Brianna's warning regarding the potholes had proved prophetic too. She was fairly sure the bus driver whom she had nicknamed Leery Len—his badge declared his real identity to be one Leonard O'Reilly—was deliberately hitting each and every one of them to see just how much bounce her boobs actually had in them.

At this rate, they'll be down to my knees by the time we get to Ballymcguinness, she thought despondently, crossing her arms over her chest before catching Leery Len's gaze in the rearview mirror. Humph, she huffed; the bloody heating was turned up so high in the bus that it wasn't as if she could put her jacket back on over her top to cover up—she'd expire before she even got to Ballymcguinness! She fixed Len with her evil eye instead and received a wink for her troubles.

Turning away in disgust, she gazed out the window. They were officially in Northern Ireland now, although crossing over the border had been a nondescript event since the days of army checkpoints were long gone. Still, she thought as they sailed past rows of Newry's white stucco identikit houses edged up against the grassy verge of the motorway and Irish flags blowing from their brown tiled roofs in the chilly autumn winds, even from here she could sense the undercurrent. It sent a shiver through her.

The bus veered inland, winding its way into the green heart of County Down where they passed through the town of Banbridge and then on through the smaller village of Dundrum. Spying the ruins of a castle perched hillside and keeping watch over the villagers, Jess fell a little bit in love. She'd heard of the father complex but she reckoned she had castle complex. There was just something so romantic about them, she thought, sighing wistfully and imagining the grand banquets that it once would have hosted and the gallant men bravely going off to battle as the bus left the village behind. She hoped Ballymcguinness would prove to be just as much of a chocolate box village as Dundrum.

UM, FIRST IMPRESSIONS—NOT overly fabulous, she thought, peering out the window as the bus topped a hill and headed down toward the little village some twenty minutes and at least one hundred potholes later. The grainy Internet photo she had seen of Ballymcguinness had been a good likeness and, from her vantage point, she could see a narrow, curving street from which a pile of semi-detached houses two streets deep ran off either side.

There was a mishmash of power lines dangling over the rooftops, stretching off toward a hill dotted with pylons that lay over to the right-hand side of the village. At the base of the hill stood an austere grey stone church with a tall and wide spire. The location, of which, had been chosen no doubt to keep the villagers in line. It was one of three smattered around the surrounding countryside, she noticed—three churches and not one single castle in sight.

The bus slowed to a crawl as it headed down the main street of the village, passing by half a dozen off-white pebble dash, two-up two-down houses. Their flowering window boxes added a welcome splash of colour to the overall greyness of the day, Jess thought, spying a grocer's shop followed by a pretty, pastel yellow painted pub, next door to which was a hairdresser's called Maura's Place.

As they passed by another pub with a decidedly more serious drinker's-hole look to it than the first one, Jess decided they were now officially on the wrong side of town. This was reinforced when they drove past another cluster of not-so-well maintained pebble dash houses. The bus came to a juddering halt at the end of this metropolis outside a school that looked at odds with the period of the rest of the village. It was a one-level red brick building with the bland building style of the 1980s and was obviously a much newer addition to the town. Outside, a dozen or so children were running around in the yard, screeching and enjoying the fresh air despite the damp chill pervading it.

"Last stop, Ballymcguinness!" Leery Len called out the obvious as he swung his head round for one last lingering leer.

Pulling her laptop in its shoulder bag down from the overhead rack, Jess ignored him and glanced down the bus to see that there was only one other passenger left on it. An elderly woman, her spindly frame well rugged up against the cold in a tan wool coat she'd probably held onto since the sixties, was struggling down the aisle with her case. As she peered out from under her headscarf at Jess, she saw the woman had a face like a pushed-in jam tin, as her mother would say.

Oh, well, hadn't she always been taught not to judge a book by its cover? She's probably a real sweetie and if it were my Nan, I'd like to think someone would give her a helping hand. She decided she'd ask her whether she wanted help carrying her bag as Len apparently was not the chivalrous type. She didn't get a chance to, though, as with all the manners of an old codger on a motorised scooter who thinks he owns the pavement, the elderly woman shoved past her, sending her flying into the seat opposite. She glared back at Jess, who was open-mouthed at finding herself plonked with her legs swinging over the side of the armrest as though to say *well, it was your own fault for getting in my way* and then her hunched back disappeared from view as she disembarked.

"Rude old cow!" Jess muttered, struggling to get out of the seat.

"What was that—do you want a hand, luv?" Len called down the aisle.

She could well imagine where his hand would inadvertently slip to. "No thank you."

It was with a face on *her* like that of a pushed-in jam tin that she got off the bus, sending up a little prayer that not all the Ballymcguinness locals were tarred with the same brush as the nasty old biddy who was now hobbling off down the street at a surprisingly fast pace. She sent a second prayer up in quick succession as she heard Leery Len mutter something about *get a load of the rump on that prize filly* that he would not be the driver on her return trip to Dublin.

"Er, Jessica?"

She quickly rearranged her features from that of a smacked bum to that of a sensitive writer. The tall man clad in an Aran knit jumper and thick brown corduroy pants that were stuffed into a pair of wellingtons standing over her looked nothing at all how she had pictured the severe sounding Owen Aherne to look. She caught him giving her a quick once-over and was surprised to see his expression change to one of amusement, although she couldn't understand why.

In her opinion, she had toned it down for her day in the country, opting for a tight-fitting white top (okay, the top had been a bad move) tucked into an artfully worn pair of jeans. The leather belt with its wide brass buckle had been a recent find in one of her trusty little boutiques—code for her favourite second-hand shops. As had the scarf, which she had tied in a jaunty knot around her neck in what she liked to think was a cowgirl sort of a fashion. Her brown leather ankle boots, although reminiscent of the 80s, were a practical choice because there wasn't much call for owning a pair of wellies in the city.

"Er, yes, that's me. Hello—you must be Owen. It's nice to meet you." She decided to repay the favour by giving him the once-over before peering up at him. His hair was dark brown, almost black, with a smattering of grey around the temples and his eyes were a light, almost luminous grey. It was a disarming combination—one that took you unawares, she thought, holding her hand out to him. He looked surprised by the gesture and for a split second as he took it, she thought he was going to raise her hand to his mouth and kiss it but instead he shook it like he meant business.

Jessica Baré, here you go again, she told herself sternly; one of these days you are going to have to stop behaving as though you have just stepped out of the pages of a romance novel every time you meet a man. At least he didn't have sweaty palms. That was a good sign, she decided, as he let her hand drop from his firm grasp. She could never trust a man with sweaty palms. It conjured up all sorts of unpleasant connotations. Unaware of her scrutiny, Owen followed the direction in which she had been looking so disgruntled a moment earlier and said somewhat formally, "Welcome to Ballymcguinness. You didn't just encounter Mad Bridie, did you?"

"If you mean that bad mannered elderly lady making her way down the street like the Bionic Woman, then, yes, I did. She pushed me over on the bus."

Owen omitted a low, throaty laugh. "Ah, pay no heed to her; she's mad as a hatter, poor old thing. Besides, that's mild by Bridie's standards. She once chased Teddy O'Shea the postman down the street with her walking stick. Waving it around like a woman possessed, she was, shouting at him for being a Peeping Tom. All the poor sod had done was to push some letters through her door. So there you go; think yourself lucky she only gave you a bit of a push."

She had to raise a smile at the mental picture he had invoked of Bridie and the postman. She was relieved, too, that underneath his bluster, he had a sense of humour.

"So did you have a good trip up?" he asked, heading across the road to where a battered and mud splattered Land Rover was parked.

"Let's just say it was a bit of a bouncy ride," she replied, deciding not to elaborate further as she clambered up into the passenger seat.

"The farm's about a ten-minute ride from here and it will be another bouncy ride, I'm afraid." Owen jammed the gearstick into first and muttered something under his breath about the old bloody beast as the jeep set off with a judder back through the village. The flash of humour she'd seen a few minutes earlier had disappeared.

Damn this bloody bra, she thought, feeling her own short-lived good humour dissipate as quickly as Owen's apparently had as at the juddering of the jeep her boobs began a wobbling all over again.

Considering the place had been devoid of street life five minutes earlier, it suddenly seemed to have come to life, she noticed, as they drove past an old man sitting on the low wall outside the drinker's pub she'd spied on her way in to town. He was wearing the requisite tweed jacket and cap and his nose was a bulbous red. As Owen raised his hand in acknowledgement, the old man raised his walking stick in greeting.

"That's Ned; he was a great mate of me Da's in their day. He's waiting for the pub to open. You can set your watch by him. He's there perched on that wall every day at ten forty-five a.m. come rain or shine even though the pub doesn't open until eleven o'clock."

Outside the hairdresser's, a woman with a plastic cape and a headful of tin foil stood chuffing on a cigarette. She nearly dropped her fag as Owen scowled out at her. "Katie Adams—she's our local busybody and barmaid at the Primrose Arms up there." He nodded in the direction of the pretty yellow pub. "And over there, that's Billy Peterson, the grocer. His wife left him for another woman—took off to Spain with her. I tell you, Katie pulled pints on that one for months on end."

Jess glanced over to where a world-weary looking man who was probably only in his early fifties despite his stooped gait was piling oranges into a crate outside the grocery store.

Two young mums in tight jeans and puffer jackets pushing their prams toward each other had a head-on pushchair collision as Owen drove past, giving them a mock salute.

It was all very *Twilight Zone* like, she thought, sneaking a peek at Owen and as though reading her mind he growled, "That's village life for you. Everybody knows everybody's business. It's a bit like living in a goldfish bowl;

that's what Amy struggled with. You mark my words, I'll be the talk of the town by lunchtime."

"Why?"

"Because I have a strange woman sitting in my passenger seat, that's why."

Oh, she realised, suddenly understanding the stupefied looks on everybody's faces. It obviously was not a common occurrence.

"Oh well, at least your wife knows what I'm doing here. That's all that really matters," she said cheerfully.

"I don't have a wife," he growled.

"Oh, I'm sorry. I just assumed you were married," she stuttered—just like she had assumed his sister was alive when she had contacted him.

"Do you have a husband?'

"No."

"There you go then."

She wasn't sure she knew what he meant by that but she decided not to analyse his comments. Or antagonise him more by asking him to explain. So she settled back in her seat as the village disappeared behind them, giving way to an unmade road with hedgerow on either side. Ah-ha, that explained the mud splatters then, she thought, as the jeep nosedived into a giant brown puddle and her boobs smacked her on the chin.

"The dairy farmers at home would love this," she said, looking out at the lush, flat green fields stretching to the horizon on the other side of the hedgerow. Healthy looking cows chomped happily on the grass and determined to make cheery conversation, Jess ploughed on, "How many cows do you have?"

Owen's scowl deepened. "None, actually. I'm a pig farmer."

Crap! She'd got it wrong again. She was silent for a moment—she'd never actually met a pig farmer before. It wasn't a glamorous sounding profession but then, hey, she liked a nice bit of bacon as much as the next girl. She was saved from having to make any further embarrassing small talk by Owen announcing, "We're here."

He swung the jeep to the right and as it veered round into an entranceway, she hit her shoulder against the door.

"Sorry. I'm not used to carrying a passenger."

The jeep bumped its way down a long gravel driveway, at the bottom of which sat a scene straight from the pages of a Beatrix Potter book.

"Welcome to Glenariff Farm," Owen grunted, wrenching the handbrake up and sending her lurching forward.

Chapter Six

JESS SAT MOMENTARILY speechless as she gazed at the stone, limewashed cottage, complete with Jemima Puddleduck and her offspring swimming contentedly in a pond out the front of it. "It's like something out of a picture book! This is where you live?" It definitely did not fit with the hardened exterior of the man she was sitting next to. She'd envisaged him in a tumbledown shack, eating only wild foods he'd caught or foraged for himself.

In a burst of chattiness, he informed her, "Aye, the farm's been in our family for four generations but I renovated it fully before I moved back in. When I was a lad, my room could have been used for storing meat. I used to sleep with a woolly hat on."

Jess couldn't imagine Owen as anything other than the somewhat moody man he obviously had grown into and try as she might, she could not conjure up an image of the little boy he'd once been with a beanie on his head at bedtime. Following him up the path to the front door, she paused to say hello to Jemima and received a hiss in return. It seemed she was not a duck after all but rather a goose. She nearly trod on Owen's heels in her hurry to get inside. She'd once seen a show on when animals attack featuring a rabid goose and she had no intention of being pecked to death in the wilds of County Down.

Once the door was safely shut behind them, she took a moment to survey her surrounds. The front door led straight into the living room, where the ceiling was held up by low timber beams bowed with the weight of a century or so past. She watched Owen duck his head, obviously an automatic reaction, as he walked through to the open door at the far end of the room. A fireplace full of kindling waiting to be lit, above which a heavy timber mantel housed a clustered group of framed photos, took centre stage in the room. Jess would have liked to have been a nosy rosy but she resisted the urge to wander over for a closer look at the pictures and instead soaked up the ambience of the rest of the room. The overall feeling it gave off was masculine, emphasised by the worn but inviting leather couch and its matching armchair. A Persian rug covered the bare timber boards, giving the room a sense of quality and cosiness. He was obviously a man of understated but good taste.

"You must be parched. I'll put the kettle on."

Jess trailed behind him through to the farmhouse kitchen. Oh wow! she thought, her eyes widening as she entered the light, airy room because there, in pride of place, warming the room, stood a majestic old Aga. It was the oven of her dreams.

Owen caught her admiring gaze and shrugged. "Me Ma had her put in way back when she and Da were first married. She always insisted she couldn't cook on anything else. Have a seat." He gestured awkwardly to the chunky pine table upon which she could see the outline of what she hoped was a dish of food covered by a cloth—she was starving. She reckoned all that bouncing around on the bus must have been the equivalent of at least an hour at the gym.

Setting her laptop down on the table's scrubbed wooden surface, she pulled a chair out and sat down. If she closed her eyes for a moment, she knew she'd conjure up images of all the hearty meals this table had played host to and the stories that would have been swapped back and forth over it. Then, she remembered why she was here. Perhaps not so many stories being swapped jovially. Perhaps Owen and his parents had eaten in silence, all too aware of the empty chair at the table for all those years after Amy died.

"Would you like a tae or coffee?"

Shaking away the reverie, she smiled at his pronunciation of tea. "Coffee, white and one please."

While Owen set about banging mugs and opening the fridge, she cast her gaze around the kitchen. It was homely and inviting. All it needed to complete the scene was a rotund middle-aged woman with apple cheeks in a white pinny as she baked scones for the farm workers' afternoon tea. There was a set of French doors at the end of the room, which flooded the space with natural light, even on a day like this when gloom pervaded the air outside. The doors opened out onto the back garden and she peered out into it. It looked like Owen was green fingered, judging by the sturdy looking cabbages and gosh, was that broccoli? Yes, she was fairly sure that's what the tall spindly green stuff was. It had been a long time since she had seen vegetables in their natural state and not in the bins at her local Tesco. There was a gate tucked away in the hedgerow at the bottom of the garden and Jess hazarded a guess that behind that there would be fields. She was just wondering whether that was where Babe and her mates hung out when Owen set her drink and a plate down in front of her.

"Oh thanks."

"You're welcome." His face turned ruddy as he added, "I made us a spot of lunch before I picked you up because I figured you wouldn't get a chance to grab a bite on your way up."

"I didn't and I'm starving actually—my goodness, I didn't expect you to go to so much trouble. That looks delicious!"

Magician-like, Owen had whisked the cloth off to reveal a delicatessen spread that made Jess's tummy grumble embarrassingly. There was a selection of thinly sliced cooked meats, fat black olives, and sundried tomatoes nestled alongside a decent wedge of cheddar cheese, all to be eaten with rustic slabs of soda bread. This man really was an enigma, she thought; one minute he was gruff, the next the host with the most. She definitely preferred the latter.

"Aye, it was no trouble; tuck in."

She didn't need to be asked twice.

"Did I tell you my editor liked my idea so much that he wants to run Amy's story as a full-page article instead of just in the weekly column I write?"

"No, you didn't say."

Whatever enthusiastic response she had expected, she obviously wasn't going to get it and perhaps she was being insensitive, so she moved on.

"So tell me," she asked between bites, the food making her feel brave, "and I know you said you didn't want to talk about it over the phone, but I can't figure it out. How did a lawyer living in London come to be running his family's farm?"

"Ah." He waved his hand. "It's not that interesting a story, that's all."

She raised an eyebrow and his mouth twitched at the corner. When his brow wasn't furrowed, those uncannily shaded eyes of his softened and they were really rather kind, she decided.

"Why do you want to know?"

Sawing off a chunk of bread, she explained, "It's the writer in me. I can't help being nosy."

"Fair enough, I suppose, but there's not much to tell except that when my marriage broke up, I decided I didn't want to stay on in London. I'd had enough of life in the city. It was time to come back."

"London can be an awfully lonely place." Jess remembered her own aborted attempt to set up camp there before hot-footing it over to the smaller, friendlier city of Dublin.

"Aye, well, it was time for a change. I needed a fresh start. Ma passed away eight years ago and me Da struggled on here but his heart wasn't really in it once she died. He got old all of a sudden and it was too much trying to run the farm himself. So I made a deal with myself: I'd come back and give it a go for a year. See if it was a lifestyle I could stick with."

"You grew up here, though; you'd have known what it was like."

"Aye, true, but I hated the farm when I was younger." He stated this as a matter of fact. "Now, I don't know if it was the farm I hated or the atmosphere in it after our Amy died." He shrugged. "Sometimes you have to leave a place for a while to appreciate what it is you had."

His words sounded prophetic to Jess's ears. "I've been away ten years and I have no intention of going home for anything other than a holiday."

"Fair play to you; it's five years since I came back and I couldn't imagine living anywhere else. It's a much simpler life and I like it."

"Apart from the goldfish bowl syndrome." She raised an eyebrow.

His mouth twitched again. "Aye, apart from that."

"Does your dad still live here too then?" Jess cast her eyes about, as though expecting the senior Aherne to suddenly appear.

"No, he showed me the ropes then handed me the reins. He went into a home near Dundrum a couple of years ago. He's made some good pals there and he knows the farm's being taken care of, so he's right enough."

"Oh, right, so the other listing I saw in the phone book belongs to your dad then. I passed through Dundrum on the bus on my way here. It's very pretty." She carved off a greedy girl's slice of cheese and began arranging it on top of a slice of prosciutto. "Gosh, this is so good," she mumbled, spraying crumbs over the table. "How much land do you have here?"

"Twenty questions," he mumbled, chomping into the sandwich he had put together. He sat there chewing silently and she didn't think he was going to answer her but unlike herself, he obviously didn't speak with his mouth full because once he'd swallowed, he told her, "The farm's thirty acres, which works out at ten acres for every two hundred pigs I run. It's boutique by comparison to the commercial piggeries but we're totally organic and there's a good living in it now that people are demanding a better quality meat."

"I always try to buy free-range." It sounded self-righteous even to her own ears and she guessed it was easy for her on her own to buy top quality meat but she'd seen how Brianna had to budget her shop and it didn't leave room for free-range meats seven nights a week.

"Good for you."

She couldn't decide whether he was being smart or not.

Amy sat between them, a silent third party at the table, as they finished eating. Jess didn't want to bring her up until she knew that Owen was relaxed and comfortable with her, though from what she had seen so far, she didn't think relaxed and comfortable were part of his genetic makeup. He hadn't alluded to the reason behind her visit yet so she decided to leave it for the moment. He was definitely more at ease when he was talking about the farm, so perhaps she should ask him to give her a guided tour of Glenariff and see whether that loosened his tongue.

"Right-ho," was all he said to her request and getting up, he began to clear the table.

"OH, HE'S ADORABLE. You have to call him Wilbur—you know, like in *Charlotte's Web*?"

"Aye, so long as you are not comparing me to John Arable."

Hmm, the comparison had crossed her mind but she'd kept that to herself, impressed that he knew the name of the farmer who'd wanted to off poor Wilbur initially in the famous children's story and she told him so.

"Ah, well now, you couldn't be a pig farmer and not know the story of *Charlotte's Web*. It was one of Amy's favourites."

"It was one of mine too." She felt pleased to have found something she shared in common with Amy and that Owen had been the one to bring her into the conversation.

A moment later, her maternal instinct had thrown off its heavy overcoat, sunning itself as she sat cross-legged in the old barn on a pile of straw, feeding the newly christened Wilbur. The tiny, hairless pink bundle was slurping feebly at the bottle Owen had handed her.

"I feed him every two to three hours."

"What? Even through the night?" Her eyes were wide at his dedication and she felt her tummy do a little flip at the thought of this large and gruff man caring so tenderly for the tiny piglet trembling in her arms.

"I put a drip bottle up at night. His last feed is at nine thirty; then he is on his own until the morning."

That shattered the picture she had invoked of Owen trooping across the darkened fields in the wee hours with his heated bottle of milk, as did the frantic squealing of Wilbur's healthy, hungry brothers and sisters as they vied for space, butting into their patient mother in the stall next to them. Owen had explained to her that Wilbur had to be taken away from his mother and siblings if he was to have any chance of survival. Overhead, a long heat lamp not unlike the old school classroom fluorescent lights warmed the wooden box stuffed with straw in which the tiny piglet slept.

"I try not to name the girls. I did it once when I was a kid, even though me Da told me not to. Broke my heart the day Florence was taken away."

"Florence?" Jess looked up at Owen and saw that twinkle in his eyes again; she wasn't sure whether he was having her on or not. "I didn't think farmers could afford to be sentimental about their animals?"

"Hard not to be but I like to think I give them a good life before I pack them off to meet their maker or Sean O'Flaherty—the local butcher I use."

She flinched involuntarily at the mental image of Sean O'Flaherty with a big white apron and long carving knife that flashed before her eyes. Owen was right, though, she thought. Perhaps it could be said that she watched far too much television but she had once seen an undercover expose on pigs being kept inhumanely by farmers who supplied well-known supermarket chains. Those poor animals hadn't had much chance for wallowing or foraging, not like Owen's fat, happy sows.

"They're amazingly intelligent animals—pigs, you know—more so than any other domestic animal."

She didn't know but then it had turned out there was an awful lot about pigs she hadn't known, like for instance the fact that pigs have very good memories and that the reason they wallow in mud is not because they are dirty—they were, according to Owen, extremely clean animals—but because they can't sweat and the mud cools their body temperature down.

She had become a mine of information on all things swine, listening to Owen as he walked her around the first and closest of his paddocks. She'd watched him curiously out of the corner of her eye as he became positively animated, pointing out the area where the pigs wallowed before showing her the little huts or kennels they used for shelter. Initially, as he had held open the gate at the bottom of the garden for her and she'd wandered out into the paddock, she had felt slight trepidation at the sight of two hundred or so free-ranging pigs. However, once she realised she wasn't going to be charged and trampled to death, she listened to Owen with interest. It was hard not to when he was so amazingly passionate about his animals. He was like a different person when he was amongst his pigs; it was as though he came to life. His enthusiasm for them was catching and she knew instinctively that from hereon in she would never pick up a packet of budget pork sausies in the supermarket again.

Jess glanced down at her flat brown boots. She'd just squelched through a particularly boggy part of the paddock but her feet were still dry and her boots would clean up with a scrub under a hot tap, no bother. She might have got the bra wrong but at least she'd had the sense to wear sensible footwear. It was at that moment she'd nearly gone flying, tripping over those same said sensibly clad feet. It was all Owen's fault, she thought, as he grabbed her elbow and steadied her; he had just pointed out the area in the paddock set aside for the pigs to root in—his words, not hers. As he caught sight of the look of horror on her face, he'd let rip with a loud laugh. It was only the second time she had heard it since he picked her up from the station and she looked at him startled as he informed her, "No, I don't have a herd of rampant lesbian pigs! Rooting is the term we use for the way the girls forage in the soil."

Jess had the grace to look sheepish and once he had stopped laughing, he had led her over to the barn, where she had met and fallen in love with Wilbur.

"Would you like to feed him?"

"Can I?" Her eyes were wide, taking in the pink bundle whose plaintive squeak was nothing like the robust squealing of the piglets she'd seen in the stall next door. It tugged at her heartstrings.

"Here, hold him like this." He placed Wilbur carefully in her arms and she gazed down with adoration as he began to suck feebly at the bottle.

"Is it cow's milk?" she asked.

Owen's mouth did that twitchy thing at the corners again. "No, it's a sow's milk formula."

She didn't see his expression; she was too concerned about Wilbur. "What will happen to him?"

"Ah, well now, runts don't have a great survival rate so I don't know for sure but if I manage to get the little bugger up to a decent size, I will put him back on his mother once her other piglets are weaned. That would catch him up to his brothers and sisters in no time and prevent his mother getting a bout of mastitis."

Jess cringed, remembering the terrible time Brianna had had with the breast infection. She wouldn't wish that on any mum.

"Tickle his tum. They love that," he said as the little piglet finished the bottle.

He was right, she thought, with delight; if Wilbur could coo, he would be cooing. She sat contentedly like that, rubbing his tummy until she saw his eyes beginning to shut. Gently placing him back in his box, she got up and brushed her jeans down. "You will let me know how he gets on, won't you?"

Owen looked bemused for a moment before he nodded and then their eyes met and locked for a split second in an unspoken agreement that it was time to head back to the cottage. They couldn't avoid Amy any longer.

"THAT'S HER," HE SAID, plucking one of the photos Jess had spied on the mantelpiece earlier and holding it out to her. "That was taken a few months before she died."

Jess was settled into the leather armchair and she placed the cup of tea he had made her when they'd come back inside down on the side table before leaning forward to take the frame from him. She didn't know what she expected really, but the young girl who was smiling out at her made her draw a sharp breath.

Amy was quite beautiful. Her hair was dark like her brother's but her skin was much fairer than his. They both shared the same startlingly light grey eyes, though. She looks just like how I always pictured Snow White, Jess thought, wondering at the irony of that as she mentally swapped the seventies orange-and-brown knit dress and the long straight hair, parted down the middle, for a long red dress with puffy sleeves and waves of shiny black curls. This was the girl she had come to meet.

"She looked just like me Ma," Owen said, handing her another picture.

This one was a group shot, showing a much younger Owen. He looked like a typical boy with a shock of sticky-up hair, the kind of lad who would have pinged the girls' bra straps in school. He also looked as if he would rather be anywhere than standing around having his picture taken with his older sister and parents. Mr and Mrs Aherne rested their hands on their children's shoulders, their pride in their offspring evident as the foursome stood together frozen in time out the front of the cottage.

Jess couldn't help but think it was a good thing that none of us knew what lay in store for us and our families. Mrs Aherne was indeed a beauty while her husband had that certain swarthiness about him—Owen had it, too, now Jess realised. His parents made a handsome couple. Amy, Jessica could see instantly, was the spit of her mother, and she would have grown into a stunning young woman given the chance. Owen was a real mix of both his Mum and Dad. He obviously got his dark colouring from his father. Their noses were identical, too; slightly bent to the right and with their heavy eyebrows, it gave them both an almost hooded, brooding look. They even had the same tall and rangy builds but Owen's grey eyes and full mouth were those of his mother and his sister.

"I can see the family resemblance, alright. You were a handsome lot," she murmured, handing him back the two pictures.

He gazed at them himself for a moment before placing them back on the mantel. "Aye, peas in a pod, us Ahernes."

"Amy would have grown up to be a real stunner. She looked so much like your Mum."

"Aye, she did. All me mates had a thing for her. I was the most popular lad at school thanks to her. As for Ma, she was Miss County Down when she met Da."

Jess caught a glimpse of that rare smile as he crouched down to light the fire. "He used to tell me and Amy a tale about how he'd won Ma over with the gift of a pig and a bunch of roses."

Looking at him over the rim of her mug, Jess was unsure where this story was going because it certainly wasn't the romantic tale befitting the woman in the photo that she had been expecting.

The fire suddenly roared into life and Owen took a step away from it, catching her bewildered expression as he did so. "Not exactly Cinderella, is it? But Ma had a soft spot for animals and roses—she planted all the bushes out the front of the cottage—and the wee pig Da gave her was a runt, not unlike your Wilbur out there. Ma called her Marigold and she grew up to be a very fat, spoilt old sow. The way she told the tale was that she took pity on the tiny runt and Michael Aherne the poor pig farmer who needed the love of a good woman. If the truth be told and you do the maths, Da got her up the duff. That was the end of her reign as Miss County Down because she had to become Mrs Michael Aherne and pronto."

Jess laughed. "They were happy, though? I mean before Amy, well, um, before..."

Owen interrupted her. "I know what you mean and aye, they were happy enough. Farming was a hard life back then, though, and they had their share of hard times. I sometimes felt Ma wondered about what might have been, you know, if she hadn't been forced to settled down so young. They both changed after Amy died, though, blaming themselves for a long time. They kept her room like a shrine for years and Ma used to sit on her bed, holding Amy's teddy for hours on end. When she came out, all she would go on and on about was how she should have put her foot down and made us all leave the godforsaken North years ago." His gaze flickered to the mantel. "She'd wanted us to go over to the family she had in Liverpool or even go to the States to start a new life. Da wouldn't hear of it, though; this place was his home and I think she blamed him for not wanting to leave the farm. I can understand it, though. What would he have done? The farm was his life; he didn't know anything else." Owen shrugged. "I've learnt that you can't rewrite the past, no matter how much you might want to and this farm is the only bit left of our past now, so I am glad we never left in that respect."

"You said your Mum kept Amy's room like a shrine? Would I be able to have a look? It would give me a real sense of her."

He shook his head. "No, she got rid of everything in the end—took a couple of bin bags into her room and filled them. She was so angry—part of the whole grieving process, I suppose. It wasn't long after that she got sick. Cancer like."

"That must have been so hard for you and your Dad."

"Aye, it was but she left us emotionally the day Amy died. For his part, though, Da never stopped adoring her. He always called her Bridgette his Beauty Queen and it didn't really matter that she could never bring herself to forgive him for not wanting to leave Glenariff because he could never forgive himself. Amy was the apple of me Da's eye." His eyes moved toward the front door. "He was a great one for the stories. Do you see that old walking stick over there?"

Jess followed his gaze to where an umbrella stand housed a battered-looking black brolly and an old cane walking stick. She nodded.

"Well, it belonged to me Grand-da and it was Da's wee joke that he kept it there because it would come in handy one day for beating all the boys off when they came a-calling for our Amy."

Jess smiled at that, thinking briefly of how her mother would have kept a walking stick by the front door for quite a different purpose. It would have been used to hook any red-blooded males under the age of forty who came-a-calling around the neck, drag them inside and then marry them off to her first born.

"He stopped telling his tall tales after Amy died."

They were both silent for a moment, Owen lost in the flickering flames of the fire.

Something was puzzling Jess, though. Owen had told her that that terrible day in Lisburn Amy had gone up to see a boy who, according to her best friend, wasn't the least bit interested in her. Having seen her photo, Jessica couldn't understand how any young man in his right mind could have been anything but smitten with the gorgeous teenager. She voiced her bewilderment and Owen frowned; it leant a harshness to his face and his voice grew bitter.

"Evie told us that Amy had chatted up the lad at a dance in Banbridge a few weeks earlier. She wasn't shy in coming forward, our Amy. She had that awareness about herself that young girls have, you know?"

Jess nodded. Yes, she could remember thinking she was pretty hot to trot at the Blue Light Discos she had frequented many moons ago.

"Anyway, this lad—he didn't belong in Banbridge and he should never have been at the dance in the first place because he was asking for trouble like. Sure enough, it wasn't long before one of the local lads took umbrage with him talking to one of their girls and the dance ended with a fight. Amy was like you—into her stories. She was a right dreamer and she was always waiting for something exciting to happen and for her, that was it." He picked up the poker and stabbed at the fire. "I suppose she saw the situation as a Romeo and Juliet scenario, you know? That whole forbidden love rot, and she was determined to see this fella again despite him telling her in no uncertain terms to leave him alone after the fight. He'd gotten a battering and he didn't want any more trouble. She wouldn't leave him be, though, even though there was no way in hell that lad would have even looked at her again."

There was a hole in the story Jess just couldn't figure. "What do you mean 'one of their girls'?"

"We're Proddies. It was a Protestant dance and this lad was Catholic. It was more than his life was worth to go near her again but Amy was motivated by fashion, not by politics, and she couldn't understand why what religion you were mattered so much. 'We're all human beings, so why can't we all just get along?' she once asked our Da and he told her it wasn't that straightforward. She just said, 'Why not? It doesn't seem that complicated to me.' Then she shrugged her shoulders and walked away from him."

Chapter Seven

THE BITTERNESS WAS etched into Owen's features. "I never fathomed the point of it all. Where did it get any of us?" He shook his head. "Live and let live, I say, but things were different then and like Da said, it wasn't as straightforward or simple as that—feelings ran too deep for too long for there ever to be an easy answer. Still do, if you scratch beneath the surface. It never seemed to touch us, though, not here. Da down at the pub, rolling out his stories of marches gone by or putting on his orange colours and heading up for the parade was the closest we came to being involved with any of it. I saw them once, though."

"Who?" Jess asked quietly.

"They were UDA men."

Even with her limited knowledge of the different Loyalist fighting factions, she knew this stood for the Ulster Defence Association, Ulster being the northerly province of Ireland.

"I was ten at the time, cutting through the paddocks, taking a shortcut on me way home from school when six of them crashed through the hedgerow, wearing balaclavas and carrying guns. I dropped down and lay flat in the grass, me head this close to a cow pat." He held his hands up to demonstrate the distance. "The last one spotted me and he stared right at me, two slits for eyeholes in the balaclava, before raising his finger to his mouth. He didn't need to tell me to keep quiet; I was too shit-scared to do anything but lay there. I didn't move until it was dark and I never told a soul about it until years later."

It must have been terrifying for a young boy, Jess thought, contemplating what she had just heard and trying to understand what it would have been like to have been raised in the heat of those troubled times. It wasn't the Ireland she knew and loved, though she guessed it was still there—that resentment and anger. All you would have to do to find it would be as Owen had just said—to scratch lightly at the surface where it simmered away, threatening to boil over again. The flags she'd seen flapping on the wind declaring where the occupants of each house's loyalties lay had brought that home to her today.

The Troubles were something for which there was no real solution and so there was no real point in her sitting here now in 2013 questioning why it was they had affected the people who called Glenariff Farm home in such a brutal, firsthand way. She was sure it was something Owen and his parents had asked themselves a thousand times.

"What was she like?" she asked, deciding to move past the images of a violent past, wanting to get to know the girl Amy had been.

"She was me sister. A right royal pain in the ass most of the time." He smiled at that and Jess thought about her own right royal pain in the bum of a little sister. Yes, Kelly bugged the hell out of her growing up—still did, for that matter—but she would never want to be without her.

"She could make us all laugh, though she had a right ole sense of humour when she wasn't being a moody mare. I don't have that much experience of teenage girls but I'm guessing Amy was pretty typical. Her room was covered in posters—you know, your man with the white spiky hair—Billy something or other."

"Idol," Jess supplied helpfully.

"That's him, and your pretty boys Duran Duran—her room was plastered in them."

"When I was sixteen, I loved Nirvana. It broke my heart when Kurt topped himself. Funny how your tastes change, isn't it? Nowadays, if I were to meet him, I would probably tell him to go and give his hair a bloody good wash!"

Owen looked nonplussed at this titbit of information she'd just shared, so Jess decided to get back on track. "What games did Amy like playing when she was younger?"

"Dress-ups—she was mad on dressing up and putting on shows for us all. She'd have us in bits with some of the stuff she'd come out with. She loved ballet, too, though I don't know if she was any good at it. I heard Ma tell Da once that she was like an elephant in tights clomping round the stage." He smiled at the memory before adding, "She liked to read right from when she was a wee dot, so I'm guessing she would have loved that Snow White book of hers. I remembered what happened to it."

"What?"

"We had a village fete and Amy had a stall. I can't remember what she was saving up for but she would have sold it there."

"And now I've got it," Jess said, pulling it from her bag.

Owen reached out and took it from her, opening the cover and staring with a lowered gaze at the inscription his own hand had written all those years ago.

"I remember Ma standing over me, making sure I wrote that out neatly."

"It's a pretty good effort for a little fellow, and I'd like you to have it back."

"Ah, no, it's only a book sure."

"Maybe but it belonged to Amy first. You were the one who gave it to her, so it should be here with you. I think that's what she would have wanted." As she uttered the words, Jess felt something. It was as though the atmosphere in the room had changed. There was a frisson in the air that hadn't been there a moment before. It was like an electrical current of sorts and Jess felt her skin prickle with goose bumps. She glanced at Owen but he was still intent on the book, seemingly oblivious of the subtle change in the room's tone. She shook away the impression that Amy had just joined them. Surely it was no more than her fanciful imagination at work as per usual and as she did so, the ambience settled once more.

The silence that pervaded the room apart from the crackling of the fire wasn't an uncomfortable one and Jess drank her tea, imagining a dark-haired little girl who had once danced in front of that same fire dressed as a fairy or in tights and a leotard practising her ballet.

"She had a cat called Tiptoes," Owen offered up after a bit.

"Ha! I have that book—*Tiptoes the Mischievous Kitten*. It's a Ladybird one, too, but it's older than that one." She indicated her head to the book Owen now held in his hands.

"Well, there you go; maybe our Amy had it, too, and that's where she got the moggy's name from. It was a stray who just decided to move in on us. Ma didn't want anyting to do with it, saying it probably had fleas and that it would give her worms but Amy wouldn't stop feeding it. It'd wait at the gate for her to come home from school, more faithful than any dog. I reckon it pined away after she died, just like Ma did."

Grief had a roll-on effect, Jess realised.

"It wasn't just our family who suffered. There was poor Evie and their gang of pals, too. What kid of sixteen should have to deal with something like that? Those girls should have been allowed to carry on, playing their music and dreaming about boys, not dealing with the shite that happened. Evie told me years later that she couldn't come to terms with the guilt she felt at having escaped the bomb. She reckoned that no matter how many times people said it wasn't her fault, she could never bring herself to believe them."

"Survivor's guilt."

"Aye. That day played out in her head constantly, along with the 'what if' game. You know—what if they'd never gone to that dance in Banbridge? What if she hadn't been so keen to join Amy on that trip to Lisburn? What if she had put her foot down and refused to go with her? What if she'd told our folks about what Amy was planning on doing? It would send you mad going down that road."

"Where is she now?"

"She got married young but it didn't last—my guess is too much baggage."

Jess wondered whether that was the same reason Owen's own marriage had broken up.

"She met an Australian backpacking his way around the country and the last I heard, she immigrated with him to Australia. I hope she got her fresh start."

They sat in silence as Jess mulled over what Owen had just said. He was right, she thought, picturing herself at sweet sixteen. She might have thought she knew it all but underneath the makeup and attitude, she had still been a child trying to come to terms with the fact that she would soon be a grownup. She had been in no way emotionally equipped to deal with the death of a pet goldfish, let alone her best friend. Life was not fair, she mused. Some people got to breeze through it, never encountering anything more than the death of elderly parents—the natural course of life—while others had to cope with horrendous trials like the death of a child, a sister, and a friend.

"Did she enjoy school?" Jess decided to change the subject and was rewarded by Owen's lightened expression.

"Aye, when she was younger, she did. Not so much the high school; she was too busy messing about. She loved to draw. I remember seeing her sitting at the kitchen table, doodling away for hours. Dress designing, she called it. If she wasn't drawing, she had her nose in a book. She was a dreamer, Amy—no good with the practical stuff like maths. Da was always threatening to take her record player off her if she didn't start applying herself."

"My Mum and Dad used to say the same thing, except with me they always threatened to snap my Guns N' Roses record in half. It made no difference, though; I still got lost at fractions." Jess thought for a moment. "Amy obviously liked music but was she musical?"

Owen gave a short laugh. "I don't know if it was the music she liked or if it was that Simon Le Bon fellow and his tight trousers but no, she wasn't musical—not unless you count the god-awful racket she used to make with a recorder. She had lessons once a week. It is my firm belief that whoever invented the recorder deserves to be locked in a room for twenty-four hours with a child practising it. Even when the bloody thing is played well, it still sounds awful."

"My niece is learning the recorder and sometimes when she is practising, my sister puts her on the phone for me to listen to. I agree—it is terrible."

"What did you do to your sister to deserve that then?"

"Oh, I don't know—moved to Ireland and made myself unavailable for regular babysitting services."

She almost didn't hear Owen when he said, "She used to give me and me mates a hard time because we were annoying little sods, always spying on her and her pals. She'd tell us to piss off and leave them alone but sometimes when it was just me and her, we'd talk. Talk properly like. She asked me once what I made of the violence—I mean, like I said, we were kind of isolated from it growing up here but it was there all the same and you were always aware of the undercurrent. There were places you couldn't go and things you wouldn't say too loudly. Amy hated it; she said she couldn't understand why everybody just couldn't get along."

Jess was beginning to form a mental picture of Amy as a creative child with a wilful personality who, if she had had the chance to grow up, might have gone on to do something really fabulous with her life. She had just got caught up in something she couldn't understand and something that had nothing to do with her at all.

"Where is it you come from then? Your accent's not strong enough to be an Australian's so I am guessing that you must hail from New Zealand?" It was Owen's turn to abruptly change the subject.

"Well done! Most Irish assume I am from Aussie. I once had a chap ask me if I'd ever bumped into Kylie at home or if I used to take my holidays in Summer Bay."

Owen laughed and Jess felt inordinately pleased with herself.

"I always fancied New Zealand but it's too far to go unless you go for a decent spell and these days it's not so easy to just up and go, what with the farm."

"No, I guess not and especially not when you've got young Wilbur out there to bring up." Jess caught sight of the old carriage clock ticking away on the mantel. The day had flown! It was four thirty already and she would have to be making tracks if she was going to make it to Ballymcguinness for the bus at five. The return journey back to Dublin was not one she was relishing the thought of.

She gathered her things and followed Owen out to the Land Rover, scurrying past Jemima, who gave her a sly hiss.

Owen turned the key in the ignition and instead of the engine roaring into life as it had done earlier, absolutely nothing happened. He tried again and again and again, finally slamming his hands on the steering wheel and announcing, "Bugger, it'll be the starter motor gone. It's been grumbling for a while."

"Er, should I get a taxi then?" Even as she said it, Jess knew it was a pointless statement. Ballymcguinness was the size of a postage stamp; the village would not stretch to a taxi service.

"Tell you what—I'll ring old Joe over on the farm next door to see if he can give you a lift down to the station."

Jess dug her phone out of her bag and checked the time; it was marching on. "Here, you can use this."

Sadly, old Joe wasn't home, Owen informed her a minute later. Apparently he had left a message on his answerphone to say he had headed down to the bachelor festival at Lisdoonvarna. That gave Jess pause for thought. She had been down to the tourist spa town's festival with Nora a few years earlier in the vague hope of meeting a wealthy land owner. Ye gods, some of the sights that had staggered out of the wild west of County Clare in the search of a wife had just about been enough to make the girls head for the hills themselves. The dance they had attended had seen them both visiting chiropodists on their return to civilisation—Dublin.

"Well, you can't walk into town; it's too far. And by the time I can tee up a ride for you, the bus will be long gone anyway."

"Oh," was all Jess said. What the hell was she supposed to do now?

They had both gotten out of the vehicle that obviously wasn't going anywhere and Owen kicked the door. "Damned thing."

He looked so annoyed that Jessica found herself saying, "Hey, it's okay. It's one of those things; don't worry about it." Actually, she thought, it wasn't okay because she was bloody well marooned.

"I'm sorry about this," he muttered brusquely in that tone that implied apologising was a foreign concept to him. "Come on, it's getting too cold to be standing around out here. I'll phone Mick from the garage and get him to come out with a new motor. There's a bus that swings through just after ten tomorrow morning. I'll have you on that."

"Oh," was all Jess could come up with again as she stayed where she was.

He looked back. "Well, you'll have to stay the night, won't you?"

Jeepers, Jess thought, taking in his surly expression. He was as enamoured at the thought of having her stay over as she was about staying. She didn't think she could face the long evening that stretched ahead alone with him and his moods. She didn't want to have to make conversation with him. What she needed was to be alone with her thoughts to process what she'd learnt about Amy today.

Owen was right, though; the temperature had dropped and the air was filled with that real autumnal chill that had begun setting in every afternoon once four o'clock rolled around. It was a taste of the winter yet to come. She thought of that blazing fire he had going inside the cottage and reluctantly followed him back inside. Spying Jemima a safe distance away under the rose bushes, she poked her tongue out at her before closing the front door firmly behind her, just as the pudgy white goose charged.

This was so not what she had planned. She should be sitting on the bus: boobs-a-bouncing, evil-eyeballing Leery Len as he drove her back to Dublin. Yes, by rights, she should be well on her way home to her own cosy apartment with all the noises of city life wafting in thanks to the building's crap soundproofing. She should be looking ahead to an evening spent slopping around in her elephant suit as she dined on beans on toast with a big handful of grated cheese on top for dinner. After which she'd pour herself a nice milky cuppa and curl up on the settee to think about Amy and begin writing her story while the emotions were raw and fresh.

She didn't suppose there was much point in telling Owen that she couldn't possibly stay overnight because she hadn't a clean pair of knickers with her, either. She had never been a very good Brownie, never quite getting that whole "be prepared" bit. Oh well, there was nothing she could do about it, she thought with a sigh as she followed him through the lounge and out through a door she hadn't ventured past since arriving.

Jess found herself in a hall with a huge skylight in the middle of it. If it weren't for that and the electric light coming in through the lounge with the remnants of daylight thrown in from the three other rooms all running off the hall, she guessed it would be pretty much pitch black.

"That's my room," Owen stated, pointing to the first door that was ajar. She paused to catch a glimpse inside what was a surprisingly big room. It was spacious and painted white with a big overstuffed armchair placed by a picture window that looked out at the gardens to the side of the cottage. An ottoman was placed at the foot of the chair. Though the light was fading, she could make out a book resting open on top of it and Jess wondered what he was reading—*A Guide to Rearing Healthy Pigs* perhaps? A huge double bed dominated the room and it was neatly made up with a masculine chocolate duvet with cream piping around the edges.

The next room was a large bathroom, complete with a gorgeous clawfoot bath and a walk-in shower. The room next door was to be hers.

"It's always made up. I have friends who pop over from London regularly," he told her, opening the door.

Jessica couldn't imagine him having friends who "popped" in but there you go—as she had discovered earlier, Owen Aherne was by no means a straightforward man.

This room, too, was large but had been made to feel warm and welcoming with a double bed made up with a plain white bedspread; there was a folded patchwork quilt at the bottom of it. At the end of the bed sat an old sea chest.

"You'll find towels and an extra blanket in there if you need it," Owen said, pointing to it. "There's an unopened toothbrush in there too."

She hoped he wasn't implying she had bad breath. "The room is lovely, thank you." She wondered whether this was Amy's old room.

"I knocked the wall out between what was mine and Amy's old rooms and turned it into the master bedroom," he said as though having read her mind and then, turning on his heel, he left her to it.

Ah, so this room had once upon a time been his parents', she thought, noticing that it was well and truly evening outside now. Jess pulled the heavy white drapes, too, before tossing her bag down on the bed and switching the little bedside lamp on. She should text the girls and let them know what was happening; otherwise, the pair of them would put two and two together and come up with five. Wresting her phone from her bag, she perched on the end of the bed and tapped out a message explaining what had happened. Sending it off, she sat there for a moment, unwilling to go through to the kitchen and face the long evening that stretched ahead. What on earth would she find to talk about other than Amy between now and nine—which was the earliest she'd be able to sneak off to bed without appearing rude. She sensed Owen, too, was exhausted from trawling his memories and would have liked nothing more than to wave her on her way so he could reflect on the day. Sighing, she got to her feet. She couldn't hide away in here all night; besides which, she was getting peckish. It must be all that fresh country air.

Owen was in the kitchen, making up a baby's bottle. "Would you mind taking this out to feed Wilbur? Mick said he'd be here in the next half hour and that was fifteen minutes ago."

Jess took the bottle from him happily. She was glad of the escape hatch and more than happy to go and see her little baby again.

THE CACOPHONY FROM the stall next door settled down as the sow, and her demanding brood, grew used to her presence. They couldn't see her but they certainly sensed she was there, she thought, crouching down and stroking Wilbur.

"Hello, little man," she whispered, picking him up, sure that the squeal he emitted, although weak, was one of delight. As she settled down to feed him, her mind played over what Owen had told her that day. She was still trying to process the sadness of Amy's story and she didn't want to make that the sole focus of her article. She wanted to paint the picture of a girl who had laughed and made others laugh with her for the short time she was here. The article began to take shape in her mind as Wilbur drained the rest of the bottle and so, settling him back into his box, she stood up. It must be around five thirty, which would mean he would be due another feed around seven thirty. She could handle that one—even the nine thirty feeding—but she was grateful that she wouldn't be pulling an all-nighter thanks to the drip bottle. She really did take her hat off to all new mothers, she thought, making her way back to the cottage.

An outside light was on and she could make out the shape of what looked like a Ute parked next to Owen's Land Rover. The bonnet was up and Owen stood next to it, talking to a little roly-poly man.

That must be Mick, she decided, registering the surprise on his face as he clocked her making her way toward them. Owen waved her over.

"Mick, this is Jessica Baré—she's a writer up from Dublin. She's doing a piece on Amy for her paper. I was supposed to drop her back in the village to get the bus back to Dublin but the old beast died on me."

Mick nodded and the knowing twinkle in his eye as he gave her the once-over reminded her of a beardless Santa Claus. "Pleased to meet you. Aye, she was a bright spark, Amy. Terrible thing. Terrible thing." He shook his head then and turned away to make himself busy under the bonnet.

"Right, well, I'll leave you to it. Owen, is there anything I can get underway in the kitchen for you?" She was fairly sure it would be a simple dinner of chops and mashed spud or some such farming fare.

"You could top and tail the beans, thanks. I've knocked up a smoked chicken pasta bake; it's in the oven. We should be eating in half an hour or so, alright?"

Jess was gobsmacked and Owen looked bemusedly at her for a moment before turning away to help Mick.

He probably got the sauce from a jar, she thought, going back inside and having a quick look around to see whether she could spy the evidence of this. There was an empty cream bottle and a block of parmesan on the bench, as well as half a bunch of fresh herbs. He'd made the sauce from scratch. It was her turn to look bemused as she picked up a knife and began doing as she'd been told to the beans. They were freshly picked and obviously home-grown. Just who was this guy—a distant relative of Gordon Ramsay? He certainly had the same cranky demeanour but thankfully he didn't use bad language and he was definitely better looking.

She'd just finished the beans when she heard an engine revving outside. Owen appeared in the doorway a few minutes later, looking pleased with himself as he headed over to the sink to wash his hands.

"All sorted then?"

"Aye," he grunted, drying his hands off before opening the Aga's door, sending out a waft of something delicious as he did so.

Jess's tummy rumbled. "Shall I set the table?"

"Aye. I'm heading off for a shower. Do you want one?"

Jess must have looked shocked because Owen's face flushed a mottled red and he stammered, "I, uh, meant after me, of course. There's time before dinner's ready."

It was quite fun seeing this normally reserved man flustered, she thought with a grin before answering. "Oh, right, yes, I suppose I probably should." She had spent the best part of her day wandering around a pig farm, after all, even if they were extremely clean animals.

Owen recovered himself and pointed to where she'd find the cutlery, plates, and glasses before disappearing down the hall.

By the time she'd laid the table, he had reappeared, heading straight over to the stovetop to put the beans on. "The bathroom's all yours."

He had changed into a clean pair of jeans and a loose sweater. Without the thick corduroy pants and gumboots on, he looked a different man. He'd lost the farmer look and for the first time she caught a glimpse of the man who had been a successful lawyer in London. His hair was freshly washed and he had that scrubbed look of someone who had done a hard day's work and earned a hot shower at the end of it. I bet he wears Old Spice, she thought, her nose twitching to identify the cheap aftershave that had been a Father's Day staple when she was growing up. Instead, she received a whiff of something citrusy but fresh and rather delish.

"Er, thanks. I won't be long," Jess said, feeling slightly awkward about her silent inventory as she made a hasty retreat through the door. She checked her phone on her way through to the bathroom to find as expected that there were two messages—both from the girls. She read Brianna's first:

Take care sweetie behave yourself and phone me as soon as you get home xox PS: Harry's in big trouble he used my Coco Chanel as toilet freshener

Jess smiled. Poor Harry—he would be in the poo! Grinning at her inadvertent pun, she opened Nora's message next which was as usual indecipherable at first glance:

Wht u doin on pg frm - wnt xtrme mntain bking 2day feckn scry – wld hve bn lkin fwd 2 xtreme actn of anthr knd 2nite but cnt wlk Bloody hell, she's getting worse, Jess thought, re-reading it and slowly beginning to make sense of what she was saying:

What are you doing on a pig farm– I went extreme mountain biking today with Ewan – would have been looking forward to extreme action of another kind tonight but can't walk.

God—movie star or not, this Ewan Reid would be the end of Nora, she thought, grabbing a towel out of the chest. What would be next—abseiling down the Empire State Building? She shook her head at the thought of Nora leaping off tall buildings—before heading off for her shower.

Chapter Eight

OWEN WAS PULLING A bottle of wine from the fridge when Jess came back in, feeling refreshed and pleased with herself for having the nous to turn her knickers inside out. Maybe she could have gone on to the Girl Guides after all.

"Have a seat," he said, placing the bottle on the table. "I've got juice or a soft drink if you'd rather that?"

Jess sat down and leaned forward to read the label on the wine.

"Are you kidding? Oyster Bay is my favourite sav." The grapes were a taste of home. "Pour away," she said, holding out her glass.

"Aye, well, you Kiwis do produce a good drop," Owen replied, doing as he was told.

The meal was even scrummier than it had promised to be. Owen had poured lemon-infused vinaigrette over the beans and tossed a sprinkling of roasted walnuts on the top. There was a crusty loaf of garlic bread on a wooden bread board for them to share and as for the pasta, it was carb heaven. She hoped he wouldn't think her too much of a pig—whoops, better make that glutton, she quickly admonished herself—if she helped herself to seconds.

"Can I get the recipe off you?" she mumbled, her mouth full.

"Aye, it's pretty simple, though."

"Nothing is simple where me and cooking are concerned, believe me."

"It's just fresh penne pasta, shredded smoked chicken, white wine, cream, zest of orange, dill and grated parmesan. You literally throw it all in together and you can't go wrong." He shrugged. "I take it you're not a cook then?"

"No, not really. I am more of an eater. I like to eat far more than I like to cook, probably because I am not very good at it despite having just completed half a dozen different cooking schools."

Owen raised an eyebrow and she told him all about her column, regaling him with her useless attempts at flipping Croatian pancakes and how she'd nearly hit the roof upon taste testing her heavy handed chilli-flavoured attempts at Creole cooking.

"You obviously enjoy cooking, though, if you can knock something up that tastes this good," she said, pointing her fork at him before stabbing another piece of penne.

"Aye, I do. When I practised law, I found it helped me wind down at the end of the day. There's nothing like dicing an onion or chopping garlic to make you forget about a shitty day."

"Chopping onions always makes me cry. What kind of law did you practice then?"

"Commercial law mostly. It wasn't me, although the money and the lifestyle it gave me certainly suited for a bit."

Jess was itching to ask him about his ex-wife but didn't want to spoil what was turning out to be a surprisingly enjoyable evening. She didn't know whether it was the wine or the fact that Owen had resigned himself to being in her company for the entire evening but he had become quite affable and she'd found herself relaxing in his company for the first time since he had picked her up from the bus stop earlier on that day.

"So what about you then? How did a girl from Auckland come to be writing a column in a Dublin newspaper? That sounds far more interesting than commercial law."

She filled him in on what she had done briefly for a crust back home in Auckland and he broke in with, "So you were a gossip columnist then?"

"I was not! I merely passed on information to my readers about people who liked to be seen about town."

Owen smirked.

She ignored him.

"So what brought you to Dublin then—don't most New Zealanders head for London? There were always a couple of Kiwi solicitors or legal secretaries doing their big OE, as they called it, at the firm I worked for. They were very fond of the Friday liquid lunches, from what I remember—that and the Friday night drinks sessions."

"I'll have you know us Kiwis pride ourselves on our reputation of being extremely hard workers." Jessica said this tongue-in-cheek, remembering having joined in plenty of those Friday night drinks sessions herself over the years. "I suppose most Kiwis do head for London but then most head home when their visas run out, too. I've been in this part of the world since 2001, thanks to my Nana and Granddad hailing from Wigan and I did go to London initially. It wasn't for me, though. I flew over there on my own and the size of the city intimidated me. I just have one of those faces, I think." She shrugged.

"What do you mean, one of those faces?" Owen asked, topping up her glass.

"The kind of face that always attracts weirdoes. I must have soft touch written all over me because no matter where I was in London, they would seek me out and track me down. It was like I had a heat sensor they could home in on."

She saw Owen's expression. "No, truly it was. Listen, I once had a chap announce that I had really lovely hairs on my arm just before he began stroking them while I sat completely hemmed in by him on the Tube. The worst bit was nobody around me moved or came to my aid and that's when I—hey, it's not funny—it was pretty traumatic at the time, I will have you know."

Owen stopped grinning. "Sorry. I'm sure it was but it was a compliment of sorts."

Jess gave a little grin. "Yeah, well, one I could do without, thanks, and it was the kind of thing that could only happen to me. Anyway, after the hairy arm incident, I decided enough was enough and I headed over to Ireland to check out Dublin. I'd heard it was a boom town and it was my last-ditch attempt to see if I could make a go of things on my own before heading home with my tail between my legs and a mother waiting to tell me I told you so."

"It obviously all worked out then."

"It did, thanks to my two best friends and landing a pretty amazing job." She had him laughing again with her tale of how she came to meet Brianna and Nora before filling him in on her job at Marriotts that had eventually opened a door at the *Dublin Express* for her.

"You're an awfully long way from home. You must miss your family."

"Yes and no. It's one of those love-hate relationships. I miss them when I am here but when I go home to see them, I can't wait to get back to Dublin again because they drive me nuts. Especially my Mum." Jess rolled her eyes.

"Honestly, you've no idea. She's desperate to marry me off and refuses to believe it's a lost cause." Realising what she'd said, she cringed, apologising, "Sorry, that must have sounded awfully selfish, my moaning about my nearest and dearest after, well, after everything your family went through." The wine had definitely loosened Jess's tongue.

"No, it just sounds honest and pretty normal. After Amy died, there wasn't a lot of normal in our house but I remember what it was like before, when there was plenty of bickering and driving each other nuts going on under our roof, too."

From over on the bench, an egg timer suddenly pinged. Saved by the bell, Jess thought.

"It's seven thirty," Owen said, pushing his chair back. "That means it's time to feed Wilbur. It's dark out so I'll walk you over." His voice brooked no argument as he got the milk ready.

A chivalrous man—now that was a rare commodity in this day and age of equal rights, Jess thought, rather liking the masterful tone of voice but then he added, "Besides, I need to attach his drip bottle."

"Oh, right—well, I'm on dishes when we get back."

※

"SO ARE YOU WRITING the great novel in your spare time? Although I don't suppose a footloose and fancy-free young woman in Dublin has that much spare time." Owen was leaning against the wooden strut holding the middle of the barn up, waiting for Jess to finish feeding Wilbur. His attempt at nonchalance didn't really work and Jess looked up, unconsciously registering what a rugged scene he set.

"Oh, you'd be surprised how much spare time a footloose, fancy-free young woman has."

"Do I take that as a yes you are writing a book?"

"It's a very clichéd ambition. What writer doesn't aspire to writing a book?"

Wilbur made a soft snuffling noise and Jess felt her heart melt.

"You didn't answer my question."

"I know."

Their eyes met in a silent standoff before she sighed. "It's a sensitive subject and I don't like talking about it. The only people who know are Nora and Brianna. I want more than anything to write a book. It's seems like such a natural progression from what I have been doing all these years."

"So what's stopping you?"

"The ideas are all there but I can't seem to start it. Whenever I sit down to begin it, I go blank."

"Where do you begin when you write your column?"

"That's different. I get a tiny seed of any idea and then it just grows. The words come faster than I can type them." Jess shook her head. "If I am honest, I suppose what it really comes down to is that I am scared I won't be able to do it—you know, put together something of that scale."

Owen looked intently at her. "You'll do it when the time is right."

JESS WOKE WITH A START, casting her eyes frantically around the strange room. Where the hell was she and with a quick glance under the heavy covers...why was she in the nude? She spied a glimmer of sunlight peeping in through the crack in the curtains and as she remembered, her body relaxed again. Gosh, this was such a comfy bed, she thought, not wanting to get out of it but knowing she must. I'll just stay here a minute longer, she decided, stretching languorously and enjoying the feel of the warm linen under her toes as she reflected on what a surprisingly enjoyable time she had had the previous night.

They'd come back inside after settling Wilbur down for the night and done the dishes, chatting about inconsequential things as she washed and he dried. Neither had mentioned the dishwasher standing empty beside the sink. Once they'd finished clearing up, Owen had made them both a nightcap, which they'd taken through to the lounge to enjoy in front of the comfort of a blazing fire.

They'd sat in an easy silence, both lost in thought as they stared at the flickering flames. Owen's face was inscrutable but the frown that had marred his forehead during the day had softened. This was the sort of cosy companionship married people must experience on a nightly basis, Jess had realised and for the first time ever, she felt truly envious of the life Brianna shared with Pete. Imagine having someone to cook with every night, talk to every night and someone to have sex with every night—well, initially anyway. Jess liked to think she was a realist.

It was with these spinning thoughts that she became acutely aware of the intimacy of the situation she found herself in and suddenly she could no longer relax. Her face flushed at the direction in which her mind had taken her and terrified Owen would be able to read her expression, she drained her glass and announced she was bushed.

Owen had muttered something about catching the late news as she'd said goodnight and beat a hasty retreat to her room. Shutting her bedroom door firmly behind her, she'd sat until she grew chilled on the end of the bed, telling herself off for being so childish as to be unable to simply enjoy a man's presence without reading more into it.

Stripping off, she'd climbed under the covers, convinced she would be awake half the night due to the strangeness of finding herself in a pig farmer's cottage in a wild corner of Northern Ireland for the night. Her mind began ticking over what Owen had told her about Amy's short life and she knew she would have to stop mulling it over and over or she really would get no sleep. I'll think about Nick and what I should wear for the wine bar opening, she decided, surprised to find it was the first time she had thought about him all day. Her last conscious thoughts were that—heaven forbid!—her mother was probably right. Wool would not send the right signals out to Nick; she would raid Nora's wardrobe. Then, the next thing she knew, she was waking up. It must have been all that fresh air, she decided, having one more starfish stretch before reluctantly pushing the covers aside and getting up.

Having made herself as presentable as she could with her limited resources, Jess opened the door and wandered into the hall, where her nostrils were assaulted by the smell of toast. Owen was up and about then, she concluded, hoping that he wasn't cooking up a full Irish breakfast with lashings of bacon.

"Good morning," she said, entering the warmth of the kitchen.

"Morning. How did you sleep?" he asked, turning away from the pan of eggs he was in the process of scrambling.

"Really, *really* well, thanks. I haven't slept like that in ages—well, years actually."

"Aye, it's being in the country—you know, the absolute darkness you get without streetlights and the quietness. When my friends come over from London to stay, they say the same thing."

"You should bottle it and sell it; you'd make a fortune." He didn't raise a smile and Jess sensed she was back where she had started. That wall she had encountered the first time she had spoken to him on the phone and that he had put up between them for most of yesterday was firmly back in place. She felt let-down after having managed to knock it down last night only for it to have been rebuilt overnight. By the set of his shoulders as he hunched over the stove, she knew she could forget about the easy, relaxed banter they'd shared doing the dishes.

"The eggs are nearly done. Sit down—there's a pot of coffee on the table. I'll drop you to the station after breakfast."

"Oh, okay, thanks," she mumbled, doing as she was told. "Have I got time to pop down to see Wilbur before we have to go?"

"Aye."

Grumpy bugger with his friggin *Ayeing*, she thought, pouring herself a mug of the strong brew in the percolator in front of her. Owen joined her a few minutes later, placing a heaped plate of the yellowest-looking scrambled eggs she had ever seen in front of her. They were obviously laid by happy hens, she thought, noticing the fresh parsley he had sprinkled on top as a garnish—ever the gourmet and ever the grump.

Despite the awkward silence, Jess couldn't help but eat with relish—she was starving. It really must be all that fresh country air, she decided, scraping up the last little bit of egg before getting up to stack her plate in the dishwasher. "That was great, thanks. I'll head out to say goodbye to Wilbur, shall I?"

"Aye, alright, but don't be long."

She stomped across the dewy grass, oblivious of the beauty of the morning sun warming the surrounding fields in her annoyance at her host's moodiness.

Her foul temper evaporated a moment later, though, as she stroked Wilbur's warm, trembling body and her eyes grew hot and gritty as she said her goodbyes.

"Look after yourself, my little mate. I know that we have only just met but I'm really going to miss you, and I just know that you will grow up to be big and strong just like your brothers and sisters next door. Keep drinking that milk and you'll catch up to them in no time." Wilbur let out a little whimpering noise and, assured it wasn't just a one-sided conversation she was having, Jessica kissed her fingers and pressed them against him. "Don't you let any of the big pigs push you around…" She was about to start giving him a few more lessons in life as to what he could expect when he finally got out into the big wide world, when she heard a cough behind her.

She whirled around, embarrassed to find Owen standing there, and wondered just how much of her piggy pep talk he'd overheard but his face was, as usual, unreadable.

"We'd better get going if you're to get on that bus," he muttered, turning and walking away abruptly. She said one last goodbye to Wilbur.

The journey back to Ballymcguinness wasn't a long one but in the rattling silence of the Land Rover, it felt interminable. Jess stole a surreptitious sideways glance at Owen but his face was a mask of concentration as he tried to avoid the many potholes. She'd turned away, folding her arms firmly across her breasts and stared instead at the lush, patchwork fields. If that was the way he wanted to play it, she told herself, then that was fine; she would be Ms Professional too. After all, it wasn't as though she had come to the North to make a new friend. She had come as a journalist to hear a story, which she had done. Mission completed. It was time to go home now and write that story.

Owen screeched to a halt outside the school and the children on their morning break all stopped playing to stare over at them. Then, realising there was nothing more to see than a grumpy looking farmer and an equally grumpy looking woman, they returned to their games. The bus's timely arrival spared them from having to hang around awkwardly and Jess turned toward him as it pulled up beside them. "Well, er, thank you for everything."

"No problem."

God, it was like getting blood out of stone, she thought. "Right, well, I best be going then. I'll email you through a copy of the draft article when it's finished."

"Aye, that would be good."

"Okay, well...goodbye then." As she climbed aboard, she didn't see Owen turn on his heel and walk away; she was too busy breathing a sigh of relief. It wasn't Leery Len sitting in the driving seat but rather a woman who took her ticket with a cheery smile. Just as well, she thought; otherwise she wouldn't have been responsible for her own actions with the mood she was in.

As she sat down heavily in her seat, she glanced out the window and caught a glimpse of a girl with long dark hair standing on the pavement where she herself had stood a moment ago with Owen saying their awkward goodbye, but as she blinked, the girl vanished. She looked around for Owen's jeep; perhaps he was still there. Maybe he had seen her too? But all she could see was a cloud of exhaust fumes in the far distance. It had been nothing, nothing at all, she told herself. She was overwrought from all she had learnt about Amy yesterday; that was all. The bus juddered into life and Jess sat back in her seat, determined not to think about what she had just seen, and to her surprise, as the bus rolled through the little village and out onto the open road, she found herself feeling a little sad to be leaving Ballymcguinness behind.

Chapter Nine

"WHAT DO YOU THINK OF this one?" Nora was holding out a gorgeous LBD Jess had seen her wearing a couple of times. "You can't go wrong with a little black dress."

"You can if it is a woolly one, apparently, and little is definitely the operative word with that one. I don't think I'll fit it." Jess frowned, surveying the strip of silky black material dangling from Nora's fingertips.

"Go on, give it a try. You can always wear those support knickers your mam sent you over last Christmas but just make sure you whip them off and replace them with something more appropriate should things get fruity between you and Nick. Otherwise, he'll think you're off to do the Tour de France in a pair of nude-coloured cycling shorts!"

Jess laughed. Trust Nora to say it like it was. Lucky for her, she was heading into work after lunch so they had the morning to put together the perfect outfit. Standing in her bra and knickers in Nora's sumptuously feminine bedroom, she shivered. There had been a nasty frost this morning, a sure sign that winter was around the corner. She hoped Wilbur was faring okay with the sudden drop in temperatures. Taking the dress from Nora, she wriggled her way into it. "Zip me up, would you?"

"Okay, are you ready? Steady—on the count of three suck your tummy in—one, two, three, now!"

Jess breathed in as hard as she could and Nora wrestled the zipper into place and then took a step back. "Oh wow, it looks fab! The perfect dress for a cocktail bar opening. What do you think?"

Jess looked in the mirror. The dress was shorter on her than it was on Nora, finishing mid-thigh, but the no mini-skirts rule didn't come into effect until after she turned thirty-five so she could still get away with it, albeit by the skin of her teeth. From the scooped neckline to just under the bust, the dress was satin cream, which suited the red tones of her colouring and set off the gold flecks that decorated the green of her irises. The bottom half was a black silk sheath. There was no doubting that the dress was snug but it did hug her in all the right places. Buried in the depths of her wardrobe at home, she had a pair of black satin kitten heels, which would be just the ticket to complete the whole mini-skirted version of Audrey Hepburn *Breakfast at Tiffany's* look or, she corrected herself, Jessica Baré Cocktails at Esquires look. "You're right. It is perfect, just so long as I don't breathe out and don't sit down all night."

"Listen to your Aunty Nora. Wear those sucky-in knickers of yours and you'll be fine."

Jess changed out of the dress and back into her Wallis camel cords. They'd looked brand new when she whipped them off the hanger at the hospice thrift store, a bargain at two euros. Knotting the belt of the suede, fur-lined jacket she'd also been talked into buying that day, she flicked her hair out from under the collar. The old dear behind the counter had told her the jacket's caramel colour set the highlights off in her hair "a treat." She'd happily parted with another fiver—always a sucker for a compliment.

Dressed again, she wandered down the hall into the kitchen to join Nora for an overdue coffee and catch up. She didn't rate her chances of a piece of cake to go with that coffee—not if Nora was still Dukaning. Mind you, she mused with a rueful glance down at her own midriff, she couldn't really afford to be eating cake between now and tomorrow night anyway. Perhaps she'd try to snaffle one of those protein bar thingies Nora always had to hand instead.

"Okay, so what's the story, morning glory?" Nora asked, setting down a fragrant mug in front of Jess before reluctantly handing her a protein bar from the box on the breakfast bar. "They're not cheap these, you know."

"Thanks. Me and my magic suction knickers thank you for your support."

"Oh, well, I suppose it would cost me more in the long run if you split the dress," Nora said grudgingly as she ripped open the wrapper on her own bar before adding, "So come on, then, spill. What in the name of Jaysus were you doing in Ballyfrigginmcguinness on a pig farm? Brianna gave me some garbled story about how you'd gone up there to sniff out an idea for your column. I didn't get the whole rundown because she spotted Harry in the front garden piddling on the geraniums so she had to dash."

Jess laughed before saying, "I did head up to Ballymcguinness for a story." She began filling her in on how her recent purchase of *Snow White and the Seven Dwarfs* had led her to Amy's story. Nora sipped away in silence, her normally steely blue eyes filling with tears when she heard about the bomb and how it had cut Amy's life short all those years ago. Getting up, Jess got the box of tissues down from the fridge. Nora might come across as a tough nut but underneath it all, she was made of marshmallow like the rest of them. Handing her the box and waiting until she'd finished giving her nose a good blow, she began telling her all about Owen and his moods, the farm, and of course Wilbur. Nora's tears dried up and her eyes narrowed as she wagged a finger at her.

"Jessica Baré, I can see where you are heading with this and I am telling you, don't you dare go there!"

"What do you mean?" Jess looked at her friend, puzzled by her vehemence.

"I mean please do not do your usual trick of falling for the man with issues. Not this time, when you have someone waiting in the wings for you who is both successful and gorgeous but best of all very, very keen on you."

"Honestly, Nora, I don't know what you're talking about and by the way, you sounded just like my mother then. That's exactly the sort of thing she would say." Jess was indignant.

For her part, Nora was equally indignant. She didn't like being compared to anyone's mother. "I did not sound like your mother—well, okay, maybe I did, just a little bit, but to be fair, she has a point, as well as your best interests at heart and so do I."

Jess screwed her nose up; she was not liking the turn this conversation had taken.

"Don't look like that. You do self-sabotage; you know you do. It's like you have this weird kind of gravitational pull toward men with problems so far as your love life is concerned. You can't seem to help yourself. You think you will be the one to fix them." Nora shook her head. "Well, my friend, take it from me, you can't fix what happened to this Owen. It's truly awful and it's really sad but it happened and it's up to him to move on, which he obviously can't. Did he tell you why his marriage broke up?"

"No but then I didn't ask him because it was none of my business and not related in any which way to the story I am going to write. Which, may I remind you, is why I was there. It was work, not a romantic quest, thank you very much and for your information, I do not fancy him! I felt sorry for him, yes, but who wouldn't? And even you would have thought Wilbur was something special."

"Sorry, I beg to differ. I like roast pork and apple sauce far too much to be moved by an undersized piglet and if his being divorced has nothing to do with your story, how come it even came up?"

Jessica poked her tongue out at Nora. "You're a hardnosed woman, Nora Brennan. I am not even going to bother answering that and I *do* fancy Nick; of course I do—he's gorgeous. Man of my dreams material, which Owen is not."

"Alright, alright, truce—I believe you." Nora held her hands up in surrender.

"Good."

They ate their respective bars in silence. Actually, Jess thought, looking at the brown square before taking another bite, it wasn't too bad. Chewing on the chocolate raspberry-flavoured snack, she decided it was time to turn the tables.

"So Miss Know-It-All, what is it with you and the adventure sports?"

Nora grinned sheepishly. "All I can tell you about that is that I have met a man worth putting my life on the line for."

"Yes, maybe, but you're not being honest with him, are you? You are not the kind of girl who likes to jump out of planes for fun or hare down bike tracks made for goats."

"Honesty, shmonesty—it's overrated in relationships anyway." Nora nearly sent her coffee flying as she waved her hand to emphasise her point.

"But you hate anything that puts you the teensiest bit out of your comfort zone." Jess wasn't going to let it go.

"He's worth it." And with that, Nora closed the subject.

"WHOA, LOOK AT YOU. You're gorgeous!" Nick leaned in and kissed Jess on the cheek.

He smelt gorgeous, she noticed, inhaling deeply. It reminded her of the aftershave Owen had been wearing at dinner the other night. Under strict instructions from Nora, she'd had her hair blow-waved that afternoon and it fell softly around her shoulders in a halo of deep red waves. She'd made an effort with her makeup, too, spending ages making it look like she had no makeup on at all except for the deep plum lipstick she'd opted for to give her face drama—or at least that's what the magazine she'd copied the look from said it would do. As for the dress, well, it was worth feeling like a sausage stuffed into a skin that was far too tight for its meat filling if she got a reaction like that, she decided as he opened the car door.

She made sure she climbed in to the low to the ground sports car as ladylike as was possible in order to keep her secret support weapons discreetly under wraps. It was far too early in their budding relationship to give him a glimpse of those!

Nick manoeuvred the sports car with the expertise of a man who knew the streets of central Dublin well. He was in control and it was rather sexy, Jess thought, her eyes sliding to the right for a sly glance. His fingers, she noticed as they loosely gripped the steering wheel, were long, his nails well-manicured. Owen's fingers had been thick and calloused, a working man's hands. Stop it right now, Jessica! she told herself firmly as Nick suddenly swerved into a red-roped cordoned off area on Dame Street, where a young valet waited to take the car away and park it elsewhere.

She couldn't help but feel like a bit of a celebrity as Nick walked round and opened the door for her. He definitely knew how to make a girl feel she was special. Swinging her legs out, Jessica decided there would be no pics of her in the paper flashing her Nana knickers and so she was careful to keep her thighs firmly pressed together like the women in *OK! Magazine* always did before she stood up.

The bar they'd pulled up outside was rocking and in the chilly autumn dark, its brightly lit interior was like a beacon. She felt a jolt of pleasure as Nick put his arm around her waist and steered her inside.

Esquires was sleek and modernistic, exactly the kind of place Jess normally hated. Give her a cosy old pub with a roaring fire and a fiddler over that awful dunk, dunk techno music any day. However, after her second expertly shaken Cosmopolitan, she decided that maybe the dunk, dunk music wasn't so bad after all. Nick was being super attentive as he made sure her drink stayed replenished and guided her around the room, introducing her to the who's who of Dublin guest list.

"You know a lot of people," she leaned in and shouted in his ear.

"You have to grease the right palms in my line of business," he shouted back before guiding her over to an empty red leather settee pushed up against the floor-to-ceiling windows. Talk about a place to be seen, she thought, perching down on the edge of the settee. The dress did not allow for sinking back into sofas.

"We might be able to hear ourselves without bellowing here." Nick grinned at her. He had such great teeth, Jess noticed; they really were an orthodontist's dream. He was definitely a man who brushed and flossed twice daily. As he sat down next to her, he swallowed a mouthful of his Manhattan and she was glad he had chosen the smooth, masculine drink because it suited him. It might have been a tad off-putting if he'd ordered say, a *My Pink Lady* or a *Mimosa*. She looked at her own pink concoction. The problem with cocktails was that they went down so easily, she thought before draining it. With an empty glass, she listened, nodding every now and then in commiseration as Nick told her about the frustrating holdups his latest project—converting an old community hall into luxury apartments—was having.

"Some people just can't accept change or progress." He finished with a shake of his head and then, noticing her glass, he stood up and took it from her. "I just don't get the attachment to a cruddy old pile of bricks. Can I get you another?"

She probably shouldn't, Jess thought; she didn't want to get tipsy too early in the night or he'd think her a right lush but then again how often did a girl get access to unlimited free cocktails? "Yes, please," she chirruped.

As Nick disappeared into the crowd, she smoothed her dress before surveying the room, noticing the number of older paunchy gents. Standing next to them were gorgeous twenty-somethings, poured into their own versions of the LBD. They were tossing their long blonde hair over their shoulders and hanging off their escort's every word as they sipped their own prettily coloured concoctions. Money talked, alright. Why was it you hardly ever saw women with their middle-aged spread well and truly spreading, out and about with gorgeous twenty-something males unless they were out with their sons? So much for living in enlightened feminist times. Some things never changed, she thought ruefully, remembering her last transit in Bangkok airport where she'd been horrified at the sight of beautiful young Thai women heading off for new lives with men who were old enough to know better. Her thoughts were suddenly interrupted.

"Jessica, hi! You look deep in thought; what's on your mind?" It was Jo, a young reporter for the *Express*.

"Oh hey, Jo. I was just contemplating why it is money makes older men so much more attractive, whereas for women it just gives them a bigger budget to blow at the Botox clinic."

"You're far too cynical for such a gorgeous young woman, Jess."

"I'm not that young, Jo," she muttered, remembering the rogue squiggly grey hairs she had had to tweeze out upon arriving home from her blow-wave that afternoon. Not a good look, having what looked like three white pubic hairs sprouting from one's part line. It was then she noticed that Jo was not dressed in his customary old jeans, hoodie, and sneakers. He had dressed up for the occasion but the contrast of his flash duds against his too-long hair and bum fluff beard was odd. He looked like a boy playing dress-ups, she decided. Mind you, now that she was officially heading toward her mid-thirties, any man under twenty-five looked as if he should be in a cap and short pants. "I like the outfit," she lied.

Jo grimaced. "I feel like a prat. I had to borrow the pants and shoes off my flatmate but hey, I'd have come in a fecking toga if it meant scoring free drinks."

"Yes, I can see you drew the short straw, having to cover a cocktail bar opening."

"I know it's a tough job but somebody had to do it. So what are you doing here other than sitting about, contemplating deep and meaningful life questions and looking, might I say, very sophisticated?"

"Why, thank you sir." Jess grinned, guessing that to Jo, any woman over thirty would seem sophisticated. "Well, technically I am working, too, because I shall file my observations on our ageist society for comment on in my column sometime in the near future. Don't tell Niall you saw me drinking on the job." She winked and Jo laughed. "Actually, the fodder for my column is an added bonus. I was invited by Nick Jameson—he's over at the bar getting me another drink. He runs a property development business."

Jo frowned. "Nick Jameson? I've heard of him. Isn't he the guy behind Progressive Construction? They sail very close to the wind; you watch yourself there, Jessica. I am sure they were the guys behind that development a year or two back where that group of elderly people were ousted from their council flats. The guy swims with sharks. Not your type, I would have thought; what are you doing with him?"

She didn't get a chance to ask what he meant because at that moment Nick reappeared.

"Nick, this is Jo; Jo, this is Nick." She did her introductions but the two men didn't shake hands as Nick's were both full, which was probably a good thing judging by the surly look on Jo's face.

"Er, Jo's a reporter at the *Express*. He drew the short straw in the office and got to cover tonight's opening." Her giggle was a little too high-pitched.

"Tough job." Nick reiterated Jo's earlier sentiment but the younger man didn't raise a smile, instead nodding curtly as he said, "Right, well, I can't stand here gassing all night. It's time for me to mingle. Good to see you, Jess. Catch up soon, yeah?"

"That sounds good. See you, Jo—behave yourself."

Jo shot a swift glance at Nick before turning his attention back to her. "You behave *yourself* and make sure you don't get bitten, alright?"

"What did he mean about not getting bitten?" Nick frowned, watching Jo's back as he vanished into the small crowd gathered on the dance floor. He handed Jess her drink.

"Oh, it was just a silly joke, a work thing." Casting her eyes around the room for a distraction, she spied an orange spray-tanned wannabe from a reality TV show. "Oh look, isn't that, that girl Emma from *All Girls Together*? My God, that programme is the pits. Did you see the episode where she got into a catfight with one of the other contestants because she'd used her hair straighteners?"

BY THE TIME JESS HAD slurped down her sixth drink—having long since moved on from the cosmopolitans to a rather delicious banana daiquiri, which she had swiftly followed up with a pina colada—she had forgotten all about what Jo had told her. Nick really was good company, she thought, erupting into a fit of the giggles as he finished telling her a funny tale to do with an encounter he'd recently had with a woman determined to get to Ewan Reid through him.

"So Nora's got competition then?"

"If you count crazed stalker types as competition then yes, she does."

She laughed again and glanced round the room. It was after one a.m. and the crowd was slowly beginning to thin. If she were honest, the dunk, dunk music was beginning to make her head pound and she strongly suspected that if she were to mix another drink, she would be sick. Nick looked at her amused and raised an eyebrow. "Time to go?" It was loaded with promise.

Yes, Jess decided, getting unsteadily up from the settee; it was definitely time to go.

"I'll pick the car up in the morning," Nick said, draping a proprietorial arm across her shoulder as he steered her back through the bar. It was chilly outside and the queues for cabs were as usual of nightmare proportions, but as Nick leaned in and kissed her with a certain slow confidence, she knew that they'd find a way to warm up and pass the time while they waited.

JESS OPENED ONE EYE and then quickly shut it again. She was far too fragile to deal with the obnoxious sunlight streaming into this foreign bedroom in which she had wound up crashing the night. She rubbed her temples, groaning out loud and telling herself that at her age she really should know better. Her head felt as though an express train had mown into it sometime in the night. Actually, she corrected herself, make that morning because it had been gone one a.m. when they'd left Esquires. Running her tongue across her teeth, she shuddered; her mouth felt like something furry had taken up residence in it.

Curling up into the foetal position, she clutched her nauseous stomach. She must have been poisoned—yes, that was all there was to it. Some naughty kitchen hand in charge of plating up the hor d'oeuvres that had been passed around from time to time last night and to which she had helped herself to with relish had not washed his or her hands after going to the toilet. She was the victim of someone else's poor personal hygiene because the horrendous way she felt at this moment in time simply could not be due to the mismatch of alcoholic beverages that had passed her oh-so receptive lips last night. God, she'd kill for a lemonade icy pole!

At least she was still dressed, she thought, risking a glance under the duvet, though—oh mortification! The dress had ridden up to her middle over the course of the night, leaving her undergarments in full view should anybody have decided to sneak a peek. Nora would not be impressed, either, at her ridiculously expensive LBD having been used as a nighty. Oh well, Jess decided as she heard the shower in the en-suite stop running; she had bigger things to worry about than Nora. Besides, what she didn't know wouldn't hurt her. The door to the bedroom opened and she knew she was going to have to sit up and open her eyes. It was time to face the music or rather, Nick Jameson.

He had a towel wrapped around his waist and even in her current poorly state, Jess couldn't help but notice the definition of his stomach muscles and the tiny curling tendrils of hair running from his navel down to his...she looked up, deciding to concentrate on the droplets of water still clinging to his wet hair instead. He really was rather gorgeous, she thought, suddenly becoming aware of the dishevelled vision she must be. Oh my God, I probably look like a red-headed Gene frigging Simmons! She tried to nonchalantly calm her curls down by running her fingers through her hair.

"Good morning and how are you feeling?" Nick grinned at her before turning away to sift through his wardrobe. "I think that last daiquiri caught up on you last night."

Jess didn't think he'd buy her "poisoned due to poor personal hygiene" theory.

"Um, I've been brighter and I'm sorry I, uh..."

"Fell asleep on me?" He turned around, a coat hanger with a shirt and pair of dress pants in his hands. "Don't worry about it, although I can't say I wasn't disappointed." He winked at her, and Jess felt her stomach do a somersault and this time it wasn't down to the alcohol and cream swishing around in it.

"Would a coffee and a couple of painkillers help?"

"Oh yes, please—a strong coffee and some extra-strength morphine should do it," she croaked, trying not to look as he dropped the towel and got dressed.

"That bad, huh? I'll be back in a sec."

Nick left the room and Jess took a moment to look around. The décor of the room suited him. It was in keeping with what she remembered having seen of the rest of his apartment when they'd arrived back last night to carry on their snog fest in privacy. She flushed, flashing back to how they'd tumbled on to his bed and how things had been getting very hot and heavy, or to use Nora's turn of phrase, fruity—OMIGOD! Another thought occurred to her. What must he think of her and her knickers? He'd gotten up to go to the bathroom and she remembered thinking she should whip them off but everything went kind of black after that and she must have fallen asleep. "God, you're such a prize, Jessica Baré," she muttered, coming back to the present.

Nick's bedroom was modern, minimalist, and masculine all at the same time. But she didn't have time to be sitting here admiring the white ambience of his boudoir, she told herself, grabbing her purse. Rummaging inside, she produced her compact and snapping it open, gazed at the woeful reflection staring back at her with distaste. Oh yes, the look she'd thrown together this morning was very much KISS. Humming "I Was Made for Lovin' You", she began rubbing at the black smudges under her eyes, noticing that her dramatic lips had long since disappeared and were now dry and cracked, oh and crap—was that dried dribble snaking down the side of her chin?

Nick reappeared as promised a few minutes later. Jess didn't know why she was surprised he'd come back because it wasn't as though he could do a runner; she was in his apartment, after all. He handed her a couple of what she hoped would be miracle pills and a cup of coffee. Clasping the mug with both hands, she inhaled the rich aroma gratefully. He must have one of those fancy coffee machines, she decided, and taking a tentative sip, she was pleased it stayed down. She swallowed the tablets one after the other, willing them to take effect.

Nick looked amused as he sat down on the bed next to her. "Are you hungry? Because I do a mean bacon buttie."

Jess's tummy rolled violently as Wilbur floated before her eyes. "Um, no—the coffee is fine, thanks."

"Sure?"

"Sure."

"Look, I hate to have to do this but I've got a meeting I have to be at for ten. I can drop you home on my way if you like?"

Jess glanced at the bedside table clock. It was already nine. She didn't add, "So, no chance of a bit of the old morning delight then?" That would be sure to take her mind off the pain in her head. Mind you, in her current state she was not exactly looking or feeling like a femme fatale and she supposed she should be grateful not to have to venture outside to loiter on street corners, waiting for public transport.

"Yeah, that would be great, thanks, if it's not putting you out?"

"No, not at all."

Jess finished her coffee as Nick told her about the meeting he was going to.

"There's a couple of stay-at-home mums—you know, the type that call themselves home executives?" he sneered.

She didn't know of any mothers who called themselves that but she nodded anyway.

"They've got far too much time on their hands, blocking the sale of this decrepit bloody community centre that is a safety hazard anyway. I have to try to convince the Council that they're bored housewives with nothing better to do than hold up progress and it *is* progress. Who wouldn't rather add value to their property with luxury apartments in the neighbourhood instead of an eyesore of a public building?" His voice was steely and Jess remembered her conversation with Jo the night before.

Still, she thought he was a businessman and successful businessmen didn't set out to make friends with everybody nor could they afford to be sentimental. In his eyes, a building was bound to be just a building—bricks and mortar and no more. It was a good job Brianna wasn't privy to his views on women who chose to stay home to look after their children, though. She'd have set Harry on him.

A phone rang somewhere in the living room and Nick excused himself, giving her the opportunity to get out of bed, race to the bathroom to brush her teeth with her finger, and run a comb through her bedraggled locks.

Thankfully she'd found a pair of dark glasses to don for the ride home but when they pulled up outside Riverside Apartments, Nick took them off her. "You've got beautiful eyes; don't hide them," he murmured.

Jess blushed, beginning to make a joke about how bloodshot they were but he silenced her with a kiss.

"I'd like to see you again," he said, coming up for air.

"I'd like that too."

"I've got business down in Kerry over the weekend and then I'll be tied up for Monday and Tuesday dealing with this community centre crap but things should be settling down mid-week. How about giving me a chance to show off my culinary prowess on, say, Wednesday night?"

He wanted to cook her dinner despite her having black teeth on their first date, falling asleep just before a crucial moment on their second date, not to mention exposing her support knickers and waking up looking like Morticia Addams with red hair! "That would be lovely," Jess breathed, getting out of the car and watching as it sped off down the Quays, a sleek grey bullet weaving its way through the morning traffic.

She was walking on air as she made her way across the courtyard to her building, not even minding when a familiar voice said, "Oi, love, you're looking a bit rough on it this morning."

Chapter Ten

"OH MY GOD, BRIE, HE wants to cook me dinner! Even after the horrific impression I must have made. Can you believe it—I've met a man who actually cooks?" Jess shrieked down the phone. She had perked right up after having stood under her shower for fifteen minutes, allowing the pounding water to ease the pounding in her head. "I have never had a boyfriend who could cook, not ever." Of course she couldn't count the meal she'd enjoyed at Owen's because he wasn't her boyfriend. That was different, she assured herself. Besides, it wasn't as though he had had any choice in the matter. He was hardly going to let her starve and it wasn't as though there was a McDonald's just down the road.

"This Nick does sound pretty special from what you've told me. I can't wait to meet him."

"You'll love him," Jess gushed, though even as the words tripped from her tongue, she wasn't sure Brianna would be smitten, especially not if they got onto the subject of the desperate housewives holding up his purchase of their local community centre. It was all a bit too close to home and exactly the kind of cause Brianna liked getting behind.

"Hey, wouldn't it be great if you and Nora have both met your soul mates at long last! Ooh, you could have a double wedding and I could be bridesmaid or because I am married, do I have to be a matron of honour?"

"Brie, you're getting way ahead of yourself. I haven't even had sex with the man yet."

"No but you would have if you hadn't passed out."

"It sounds terrible when you say it like that."

The two women burbled on, happily discussing Nora and her death-defying activities all in the name of love, the latest Harry misdemeanour (he had laddered his mother's new tights to dress up as Superman, to which Jess had consoled Brianna by saying that it could have been worse—he could have been dressing up as Wonder Woman) until eventually the conversation veered its way around to Jess's spontaneous trip to the North.

"Believe it or not, I have never been across the border," Brianna said. "From what I've seen on the telly, it's like it's another country—you know, with the different currency, the British shops, and all those murals and flags everywhere."

"I didn't see too much of that side of things because you were bang-on about the bus. It more or less took the back roads all the way to Ballymcguinness. It was a complete nightmare."

Jess filled Brianna in on Leery Len to shrieks of laughter before moving on to Owen.

"Oh, that poor man and his family; it's just so sad." Brianna sniffed. "I don't suppose it's the type of thing you ever really get over, either. I wonder if that's why his marriage broke down; maybe he's never dealt with his grief properly because men don't talk about things like we do. They bottle it all up."

"No, to be honest, Brie, I think it was more likely his wife left him because he's a right moody bugger. One minute he's Mr Charming the next he's Mr Surly. If I had the space, I'd go for custody of Wilbur."

"Jess, you're terrible! Give the man a break; he's had a terrible time of it. You and I can't even begin to imagine what him and his family went...oh crap, is that the time? I have to run. I've got a meeting I have to get to. Sorry to rush off on you, babe. Ciao."

"No probs. I need to get on with some actual writing and not talking anyway."

As soon as Jess put the phone down, it rang again.

She answered it to hear Nora's harried voice. "It's me, sweets—tell all but try to tell all in five minutes because Ewan's taking me waterskiing and we're leaving in ten."

"Good God, Nora! It is frigging freezing outside today! And you hate getting wet." Jess was taken aback because her friend was definitely a lounge around poolside in her bikini girl who didn't even like to dip a toe in to test the water. Nope, the red swimsuit *Baywatch* run was definitely not for the Nora she knew and loved.

"It's not cold in the South of France and who knows? I might enjoy waterskiing." She did not sound convinced. "Anyway, I didn't phone you to talk about me. Come on, dish the goodies."

Jess gave a much-edited version of her antics the night before, knowing that Nora would be nowhere near as sympathetic as Brianna had been about the whole hideous undies, falling asleep debacle.

"Okay, so let me get this straight—you didn't have sex?"

"No, we were, uh, um, I actually I decided I wasn't ready so we just cuddled. He was a perfect gentleman."

"Jessica, Jessica, Jessica," Nora tutted down the line and Jess didn't need to see her to know she would be shaking her head. "Come on, it's me Nora you're talking to. You crashed out, didn't you? Mouth wide open, whole nine yards, full monty, dribbling crashed out." There was more tutting.

"Yeah." Jess sighed, knowing the game was up. "How did you guess?"

"Like I said, it's me you're talking to. Firstly, you never do well when you mix your drinks and secondly, since when have you ever not been ready when a gorgeous man happens along and you've had a skin full?"

Jess wasn't sure she liked this summarising of her behaviour, even if it was true.

"Oh my God, he didn't see your un—"

Jess was saved by the bell.

"Listen, Ewan's here so I've got to go but before I do, I have two words for you."

"What?"

"Lingerie and redemption. For God's sake, woman, go get yourself some decent underwear before your next date!"

Jess hung up the phone. She supposed Nora was right. Her Mum hadn't sent her any decent, saucy sets in ages. She seemed to have decided her daughter was a bit of a lost cause in that respect, especially if the slippers were anything to go by.

Moseying into the kitchen, she eyed her cupboards hopefully, deciding she needed something starchy and full of carbs before she could even think about doing any work. Opening the doors of the pantry, she surveyed the shelves hopefully. She'd done a Tesco's run last week, so she had plenty of food in. On closer inspection, though, it was all food that involved some sort of preparation on her part—be it adding milk to it or and this was definitely a no-goer—actually cooking. Frowning, she put the can of lentils back on the shelf and headed over to the fridge instead. Hmm...cheese, yogurt, some token carrots and broccoli—no, there was nothing else for it, she decided, slamming the fridge door shut. She'd have to hit McDonald's. Putting her laptop into its carry case and grabbing her purse, she headed out the door.

"EAT YER FECKING FRIES!"

Jess had gotten so lost in her work that she had forgotten where she was: the Mary Street McDonald's. Across from her sat a girl with stringy bleached hair, hardly old enough to be out of nappies herself. She was holding out a packet of French fries to a little boy perched in a high chair. He had a nose that was desperately in need of blowing and was far more interested in bashing the plastic toy that had come with his Happy Meal than eating his fries. The girl turned her pointy featured gaze toward Jess, who quickly looked away, not wanting her to give her the opportunity to ask, "What the feck are youse looking at?"

Sitting on top of her table were the bedraggled remains of a few stray pieces of lettuce, along with two empty Big Mac boxes. Jess sighed and looked at the two crumpled pieces of cardboard. It was another misdemeanour that she wouldn't be willingly sharing with Nora. Turning her attention back to her laptop, she decided to email what she had just typed off to Owen. She'd written it from the heart and she hoped he would realise that when he read through it. Typing a quick message inquiring as to Wilbur's health, she attached her article and hit Send. Closing down her laptop, she decided it was time to head home but maybe she'd just grab a large fries first.

AS JESS SPRAWLED SLOTH-like on the settee later that evening, she had two phone calls. The first was from Marian, who was telephoning on the pretext of giving her daughter a general update as to how everyone was at home. Once they'd established that everybody was fine and that Kelly and the Martian were going at it like rabbits (to which Jess had made gagging noises) in their efforts to conceive, she'd moved swiftly onto the business at hand. The real reason behind her phone call was to interrogate her eldest daughter as to how her date had gone.

"Did he pick you up in that sports car of his?"

"Yes, Mum."

"Did he hold the car door open for you like a proper gentleman?"

"Yes, Mum."

"Frank, he has good manners! He didn't drive like a maniac, I hope? Honestly, some of the teenagers your Dad and I see hooning around the neighbourhood now in their zoop-zoop cars are just accidents waiting to happen. Most of them can't even see over the steering wheel. It's ridiculous letting kids have cars like that, isn't it, Frank?"

"No, Mum, he stuck to the speed limit. It's pretty impossible not to; the traffic is nightmarish in central Dublin and besides, he isn't a teenager."

"What did you wear in the end?" She moved swiftly on.

"You'll be pleased to know I didn't wear my Anne Klein. I borrowed a lovely little black dress with a cream bodice from Nora. She gave it her stamp of approval and she is dating a movie star, Mum, so she knows her stuff."

"Thank God!—She didn't wear the wool outfit, Frank!—What about knickers? Did you take my advice with regard to your knickers?"

Jess heard her father's voice in the background, "*Marian!*"

"Sorry, Frank, but this girl of ours needs all the help she can get. Well, did you?"

"*Mum!*"

"Alright, alright, keep your knickers on."

Marian failed to realise her pun as she carried blithely on, "So what was the place he took you to like? It was a cocktail bar, wasn't it?"

"Yes. It was very posh minimalist with lots of polished chrome and expensive leather couches. A place to be seen and not at all my normal sort of hangout but the cocktails were free all night, which is definitely my kind of thing." Jess chortled silently, knowing this would irk her mother.

"Well, maybe it is high time it became your sort of hangout, my girl, and that you started to mix with a better quality of people."

Unbelievable, Jess thought, holding the phone away from her ear and poking her tongue out at the receiver but Marian was only just warming up.

"I hope you behaved yourself, Jessica Jane. You're too old to be making a holy show of yourself these days. I remember the time you staggered home after you'd been to a party at the girl Frankton's house."

"Sarah was her name, Mum, not 'the girl Frankton.'" Jess cringed; this was a story Marian had regurgitated more than once.

"She was a bad influence on you, that one, wasn't she, Frank? It was disgraceful behaviour on your part, my girl."

"Oh, for goodness' sake, Mum, that was years ago—I was seventeen! You have the memory of a flipping elephant. And for your information, as far as a first date goes, I was very well-behaved and Nick didn't mind the striptease I did on top of the bar later in the night at all."

"That's not funny. Sarcasm is the lowest form of humour."

"Well, what do you expect, talking to me like that? I am thirty-four-years old, not four."

"Once you become a mother, you are always a mother. I live in hope that one day you will understand that your baby is always your baby, no matter how big or how much of a smarty pants she might get."

"Yeah, I know you do, Mum." Jess was in danger of dislocating her eyeballs with the roll that followed that reply.

"So did you get on well together? At least tell me that."

"We did, actually. He is very..." Jess paused, chewing on her bottom lip. How would she describe Nick? An image of Galaxy bar smooth milk chocolate sprang to mind. "He's very charming and he's *really* good-looking."

"Did you have sex?"

"That is none of your business!"

"Marian, would you leave the poor girl alone!"

Good old Dad, Jess silently cheered, even though she knew it was a futile effort on his behalf. Marian would ignore him because she wasn't finished yet. Oh no, not by a country mile.

"Good. I was hoping you took my advice and that I can take that as a no because believe you me, it's really not a good idea on the first or even second date to give a man what he wants."

Jess cringed, knowing she was about to go off on a tangent; it was as inevitable as the ebb and flow of the tides.

"Now, I know you young people get up to all sorts these days but no matter how modern a man may be in his thinking, deep down they are all Neanderthals. If you can remember that, then you won't go too far wrong. Men are hunter-gatherers of old who don't like to think that their mate may have been collecting her nuts and berries too easily, if you get my drift?"

Good God. Jess shook her head. The worst thing was that this was actually her mother's convoluted way of saying keep your legs shut.

She grinned as she heard her Dad snort and say, *"Marian, I am just off to club a woolly mammoth to death for dinner and then I think I will drag you by your hair into the kitchen to cook it."*

"Ignore your father—he's another smarty pants. Where do you think you get it from? Deep down, men are old-fashioned when it comes to that sort of thing, so you'd do well to wait until at least your fourth or even fifth date before offering up the goods. Of course, you want to keep him interested, though, which is why I was so concerned over your choice of underwear. Think entrée, not the main and certainly not all three courses!"

Good grief. Home runs, entrees and mains—her mother's metaphors when it came to sex were appalling. It was a wonder she and Kelly had ever been conceived because Jess couldn't fathom how her mother had managed to communicate to her father that she was in the mood. *I have an itch that needs scratching* perhaps, or *there's some urgent plumbing to be done*? Either way, it was a good thing she didn't know the half of it, thought Jess, because there were some things in life that were just none of her damn business.

Not expecting a reply, Marian Baré ploughed on with her inquisition. "Did you make arrangements to see each other again?"

"Actually, we did. He's cooking me dinner next Wednesday night."

There was a loud clunk followed by a scrabbling noise and then silence. Finally and to Jess's immense relief, her father's voice came on the line.

"It's Dad here, sweetheart. Your Mum's come over all strange and had to go and lie down for a minute—what on earth did you say to her?"

Jess told him.

"Oh, well, that explains it. You'd better look out because the next thing we know, she'll be booking the church and arranging the flowers. You know what she's like." His tone grew sombre. "Listen, Jess, while I have you on the phone and your mother's a safe distance away, I wanted to tell you not to let her bully you where this Nick chap is concerned. She means well, and she wants you to be happy, but from what she's relayed to me, he doesn't sound your type at all. I know you've picked a few wrong-uns in the past, love, but this fella—a property developer with a sports car? Well, to be honest, Jess, he sounds rather oily."

Nick wasn't oily. Okay, yes, he was definitely smooth but not oily. "Dad, when have I ever let Mum pressure me? I like Nick, actually I like him a lot, but I have not managed to stay single well into my thirties by rushing into things, so don't worry, okay?"

"You're right and despite what Marian might think, you are old enough to make your own choices. Just make sure you make the right one. Now tell me, what have you been working on lately? Are you still busy cooking up a storm?"

Jess smiled. She could always count on her Dad to show interest in her work and she settled into her sofa, pulling the throw rug up under her chin as she began to fill him in on the Aherne family's sad story.

When she'd finished, Frank was quiet for a moment. "You're right, sweet; it is a story that needs to be told. Tell it well."

"Can I read you the draft I've written?" Her father, her biggest fan, was always keen to hear her work—raw state or polished—and though Jess preferred the impersonal nature of email by which to receive any criticisms, she knew she could count on her Dad to relay back only the positives. Getting the article up on her laptop's screen, she leaned forward and began to read. When she'd finished, Frank was silent for a moment, digesting what he had just heard before exhaling loudly.

"Powerful stuff, Jess. What a thing for a family to have to have suffered through. It's incomprehensible, you know, but the same thing will be happening to another family somewhere in the world right now as we speak. Look at what's been going on in Syria." He sighed. "It does make you stop and take stock when you hear a story like that, even if it is only for a short while. It puts all the trivial day-to-day stuff into perspective. We're one of the lucky ones, Jess—very lucky—and I know you and your Mum don't always see eye to eye, but she loves you. You know that, don't you?"

"Yeah, I know she does and I love her, too. She just drives me mad, that's all."

Frank laughed before asking, "This Owen fella sounds like a good man. Will you be seeing him again?"

Jess wasn't fooled by his attempt at nonchalance. It was a funny thing, she realised; had her mother asked her that question, it would have gotten her back up straight away. With her Dad, though, she could be honest. "Yes, he is a good man and he's been through a lot but he blows hot and cold all the time." Jess chewed her bottom lip agitatedly, remembering how whenever Owen had become conscious of feeling relaxed around her, his guard had gone back up. "Maybe it is some sort of defence mechanism. I'd definitely like to see Wilbur again, though. He was so cute and uncomplicated."

"I never thought I'd see the day when my daughter was smitten with a piglet and as for this Owen being a tad moody, well, perhaps he has good reason to be. From what you've just told me, life hasn't exactly dealt him a fair hand, now has it?"

"No, it definitely hasn't."

"I have a feeling your story isn't done yet either. You'll be seeing him and your wee runt Wilbur again soon."

Jess chose to misinterpret his words. "Yeah, you're probably right. If Owen is true to form, then he'll be difficult and probably want loads of editing done before I submit my final copy to Niall. Still, it would be good to have an excuse to see Wilbur again. I'd like to see him grow up into a big pig."

Her father laughed. "I thought women who didn't have children got cats or those white yappy dogs as substitutes, not pigs."

"Bichon Frises, Dad, and Wilbur is not my baby substitute."

Frank grew serious once more. "I know I don't say this to you very often, Jess. Nowhere near often enough but you do know that you're making us proud, don't you? What you've achieved with your writing, your own column—well, I want you to know that we are proud of you. That's not just coming from me either; Mum feels the same way."

Jess felt the hot sting of tears and blinked them away as quickly as they had come. She wished she could believe what he said where her mother was concerned but she didn't have time to dwell on it because speak of the devil, Marian—fully recovered—came back on the line.

Ten minutes later, Jess hung up the phone with relief. She felt drained by the grilling she'd just had over what she was planning to wear on her dinner date, where Nick lived, and the kind of property he developed. At least this time round, though, she had been able to reply satisfactorily. She'd only just finished flexing her fingers to do a spot of channel surfing when the phone shrilled again.

Oh no! Please, please don't let it be Mum again. She sighed and if she had been Catholic, she would have crossed herself but since she wasn't, she just wished she had splashed out the extra couple of euros for caller display. With a sigh, she leaned over and picked it up.

It was Owen.

Chapter Eleven

OWEN HAD TELEPHONED to tell her that he had received her emailed draft of "Amy's Story." Jess braced herself for a barrage of corrections but to her surprise he said he thought it read well. "It was hard to read my own words and see them laid out like so but you've written it well. It's not too flowery like." He finished by telling her he was happy for it to be submitted to her editor as it was.

Jess stopped slouching and pulled herself upright. This was high praise coming from someone like him who, she was quite sure, would not be shy in coming forward had he not liked what she had sent through to him. It was only right, too, given how close to his heart the article was that he should want it word perfect.

"I am glad you are pleased with it. It wasn't an easy thing for me to write." She wouldn't send him the bill for the two Big Macs. Comfort eating at its worst.

"Aye, I'm sure it wasn't."

"Do you think Amy would be pleased with it?" She held her breath because his answer mattered to her.

"Aye."

"Good."

An awkward silence stretched out between them which Jess finally broke. "How's Wilbur doing?"

"Not bad. He's hanging in there. He's a fighter, alright."

"Good. I've been worried about him."

"Well, you don't need to worry; he's in good hands. I know what I'm doing."

Jess could tell by his tone he was amused, though she didn't know why. He changed the subject on her before she had a chance to mull it over further.

"The reason I rang you was because I found an old family album I'd forgotten about and there were some pictures of our Amy in there that I thought might go with your piece."

"Oh, that would be great! I was going to phone you anyway and ask if we could use some pictures but I didn't know how you'd feel about it. Would you be able to scan them through to me?"

"Well, the thing is I'm down in Malahide tomorrow for a meeting. There's a new deli opening soon who are interested in stocking some of my produce and being a Saturday, I thought that you might be able to, uh... " His voice trailed off and Jess, getting the gist of what he was in an awkward roundabout way trying to say was, offered, "You'd like me to meet you in Malahide?"

"Yes. If you're free, that is. I thought we could have some lunch and you could take a look through the photos then."

Why did he have to make it sound like he was asking her to join him while he had his teeth pulled out? Remembering her father's words about him having good reason for being an awkward bugger, she decided she could afford to be gracious. "That would be lovely, Owen, thank you. If you hang on a minute, I'll let you know what time the Dart gets in."

Getting up, she retrieved the crumpled timetable from its home in the fruit bowl and told him she could be in Malahide for mid-day and so before they hung up, it was arranged that he would meet her off the train at the station.

JESS LAY IN BED THAT night thinking about him. She knew that beneath the taciturn exterior there lurked an insecure soul and when he let his guard down, she liked him. The man really was an enigma, she concluded with a yawn before dropping off to slumber the deep, uninterrupted sleep of the hungover.

THE NEXT DAY DAWNED with a brilliant blue sky peeking through the crack where her curtains didn't quite meet in the middle. Jess was pleased the weather suited the buoyancy of her mood and she tossed the duvet cover aside. Sitting up and stretching, she was profoundly relieved to find that physically she also felt like part of the human race once more. Getting up, she bounced down to the shower, peering into the mirror to see that the only remaining evidence of her cocktail overindulgence was a set of slightly puffy eyes.

They'd have gone down by lunch time, she thought before opening the shower door and stepping under the hot water stream. For some reason she washed her hair even though it didn't really need it and shaved her legs, although, she thought with a rueful glance down, they really did need it.

She dawdled over her hair, opting to wear it loose, and then fiddled around with her makeup before taking an age to decide what she should wear. Not that it really mattered, she thought; Owen wouldn't care if she showed up in a sack. He was a pig farmer, not a man about town.

She wasn't in a casual kind of a mood, though, she thought, tossing her jeans down on the bed and rifling through her wardrobe. A flash of green amidst the rainbow of colours caught her eye and she plucked out her classic 1930s sage green suit. She was getting a bit tired of the whole 80s look—there was only so far she could go with a double belt or leg warmers. Besides, she always got loads of compliments when she wore her sage suit. The colour set off the gold flecks in her hair.

Letting her towel drop, she began to get dressed. The jacket had a cinched waist that flattered her hourglass shape and the fitted pencil skirt finished at a respectable mid-calf length. Standing back to admire her efforts, she announced to her reflection, "Rita Hayworth, eat your heart out!"

All she needed to really look the part were a pair of elbow-length white gloves, a pillbox hat, and a little handbag. That might be going a little over the top, she decided, before grabbing her shoulder bag and heading out the door.

It was a bit hard mincing down the Quays as the skirt had definitely not been designed and sewn in an era when women power walked but nevertheless, lots of wiggling later, she managed to make it to Connolly Station in time to sidestep onto the northbound Dart.

To her surprise as Jess sat down in her seat and smoothed out her skirt, she realised she felt nervous. Her stomach was churning with the sense of anticipation she always got when she was going on a date. Which was ridiculous, she told herself, because this was by no means a date. If anything, it was a kind of business meeting and the only reason Owen had wanted to meet up with her was because he was probably worried about the quality of the old photos if he had scanned them through.

In an effort to distract herself, she decided to pass the time voyeuristically by staring down into the handkerchief-sized gardens attached to the back doors of the pebble dash houses they were now whizzing past. They afforded their residences no privacy in the slightest, she thought, noticing that some backyards were well tended while others were slovenly. Some had lines full of washing—talk about airing your dirty laundry. Imagine having your smalls on public display like that. Mind you, she wrinkled her nose as they passed a pair flapping on the breeze that could have set a ship a sailing, some of them weren't exactly small. Slowly, however, the residential vista gave way to a more eye-pleasing rural one and Jess settled back, enjoying the rest of the short journey.

As the train slowed before finally coming to a standstill at the pretty coastal town of Malahide's station, Jess spied a man pacing outside the newspaper kiosk. It was only as she stood draping her bag over her shoulder that she realised it was Owen. She hadn't recognised him, not because he looked different but because it was so strange seeing him out of context somewhere other than Glenariff or Ballymcguinness.

Jess's mind went into overdrive once more as, feeling as though she were in a scene from a wartime movie, she sidestepped down in what she hoped was an elegant manner from the train onto the platform in order to meet her beau just returned from the war. Except, she told herself sternly, he wasn't her beau and in the movies it would have been Owen getting off the train, not her. Even when she was having a fictional fantasy, the journalist in her liked to keep it fairly factual.

"Alright?" he asked in that gruff manner of his, and Jess crashed back to the present millennium. That was definitely not the way a returned soldier would greet his sweetheart and she was definitely not his sweetheart.

His eyes twinkled as he looked her up and down and she sensed he was laughing at her choice of outfit. She'd felt so good when she'd left home, too; now she felt vaguely ridiculous. There was something about Owen that made her own mood swing from good to sour smartly.

"So how was Wilbur when you left him this morning? I hope he'll be okay on his own," she asked tartly.

"Wilbur will probably outlive us all. He was fine. I should have him off the bottle soon."

"That's good news—he must be piling the weight on."

"Yes, he's getting quite porky."

Jess looked at him, startled—had he just made a joke? His deadpan expression gave nothing away.

As they got farther down the road, Jess began seriously regretting her outfit. She was beginning to feel like an un-dainty version of a Japanese woman in a kimono trying to keep up with Owen's long-legged stride. He glanced over at her and again she spied that hidden amusement lurking behind his eyes but at least he slowed down. Why the hell hadn't she gone with the acid washed jeans and leg warmers? Then she spied Malahide Castle and completely forgot about her choice of clothes.

"I went to a great Radiohead concert there. It was such an amazing venue," she said, pointing through the established greenery of the grounds to where eleventh-century stone ramparts peeked through the foliage.

"You wouldn't have struck me as a Radiohead fan."

"I'm not but the tickets were free."

He laughed. "Fair play to you. So what sort of music do you like then?"

"All sorts, really; it depends on my mood. If I am doing housework, then I like a bit of ABBA or if it's really heavy-duty stuff like window cleaning, then I always play my AC/DC CD. 'Thunderstruck' really gets my arms going." She made a circular motion with the palm of her hand to demonstrate. "If I am out with the girls, though, I like to relive my misspent youth and listen to anything from the nineties. Oh, and I love my New Zealand music collection, as well as anything by Coldplay. What about you?" She really hoped he wouldn't say Country and Western.

"I like all sorts too."

"That's a very evasive answer and one that won't do. Who is your all-time number-one favourite band?"

"That would have to be the Stones."

"The Rolling Stones?"

"You sound surprised."

"Hmm, it's just that now that you mention it, I kind of had you down as a Billy Ray Cyrus type of a guy."

Owen snorted and looked at her aghast. "Why on earth would you think I would be in to that shite? I don't wear a Stetson or cowboy boots, and I most certainly do not have a mullet."

"I don't know. Maybe because you are a country boy, I kind of assumed you'd be into the whole line dancing culture and don't knock Billy—'Achy Breaky Heart' was a classic."

He stared hard at her and she paused in her shuffling along to grin slyly. It was payback time for his silent mocking of her. Realising she was having him on, he laughed again and Jess decided she liked his laugh. It was warm and genuine and that harsh worldliness etched into his face lifted when he smiled. She wished he would laugh more because it suited him.

Malahide Marina came into sight with its surprisingly large number of gleaming white launches moored up to the jetties. Expensive apartments flanked either side of it. The smell of serious money wafted over toward them on the early afternoon breeze. Somehow Jess never visualised Ireland as a boaties paradise but then again when the rain finally stopped and the sun came out, its harbours were as beautiful as anywhere in the world so why shouldn't it be? Owen interrupted her thoughts.

"What do you fancy for lunch? And just so you know, I am not a quiche sort of a guy nor do I always have to have steak."

It was Jess's turn to laugh. "Fair enough. What about some good old pub-grub then?" She pointed halfway down the block to where a sign depicting a regal-looking cockerel was swinging gently back and forth out the front of a sprawling stone building.

"Aye, sounds good."

The weather, although sunny, wasn't overly warm and deciding it was too cool to sit out in the beer garden where they'd spied a few diehard smokers, they opted for a nook near the fireplace instead. The log burner was only just ticking over but it was enough to warm the room to a comfortable level. Jess shrugged out of her jacket and draping it over the back of her chair, looked around.

Yes, this would do, she decided; it was the kind of pub she liked, being cosy and traditional. A proper pub with none of that flashy chrome crap or couches made for perching in sight. Owen asked her what she'd like to drink and returned a moment later with a glass of wine in one hand, a pint of Guinness in the other, as well as a couple of menus he'd managed to tuck under his arm.

"Well, well, well, who'd have thought? A man who can multi-task."

"Aye, I am a man of many talents." He placed her drink down on the mat in front of her and handed her a menu.

It didn't take Jess long to decide what she was going to have: scampi in a basket. They were in a coastal town, after all, so it should be super fresh she thought, unconsciously licking her lips and oblivious of the startled look Owen gave her. He announced he was opting for the roast of the day, which Jess was relieved to see was beef and not pork. In her opinion, it would have been almost cannibalistic on his part were he to tuck into a helping of pork and crackling.

As he headed up to the bar to place their order, she spied the landlord, who was propping it up for the first time. He bore an uncanny resemblance to Rick Stein and she wondered whether they were related.

"Don't you think he looks like Rick Stein?" she said, inclining her head over toward the bar when Owen returned.

"Aye, he does a bit and he likes a drop of the old wine like Rick does too, by the look of him. I quite like his show."

"Yeah, me too, though I like the scenery as much as I enjoy the actual cooking."

"Ah, that's right—cooking's not your thing." He took a deep drink of his pint.

"That stuff's like a meal in itself; you won't eat your lunch," she admonished and saw that familiar gleam in his eyes as this time he took a deliberate slurp followed by lots of aahing.

"You sounded just like my Ma then," he stated, swiping his foam moustache with the back of his hand.

Jess frowned. "Well, it's true. I never quite acquired a taste for Guinness," she said. "For me, it is right up there with oysters, even though I only live a hop, skip, and a jump from the Guinness factory and Glendalough's Guinness Lake is one of my most favourite spots in all of Ireland." She was babbling, she realised, so forcing herself to shut up, she took a sip of her wine instead. It was just that if she didn't make small talk, she was worried he might lapse into that moody melancholy of his, and she didn't want that to happen, not when she was actually enjoying his company.

"So despite your aversion to a good old pint of the black stuff, you live near the Guinness factory? That's fairly central."

She nearly said, "Aye, it is" but stopped herself just in time. "I do, yes. It's a great spot to live down on the Quays. I can walk everywhere I need to go. Do you know Dublin?"

"Aye, a bit. I had a few nights on the tiles there that I woke up worse for wear from." He rifled through the breast pocket inside his jacket and produced a couple of photos, handing them to Jess. The first she saw was a classic school portrait of Amy. She really had been a pretty girl despite the missing two top front teeth she was proudly displaying with a broad grin. She looked so young; peering closer at her, Jess was sure she could detect that same glimmer she spotted in Owen's eyes sometimes when he found something amusing. Flipping it over, she saw someone, probably their mother, had written "Amy aged 6" on the back.

Six was the age she had been when she got her *Snow White and the Seven Dwarfs* book, Jess realised and turning it back over, she stared at the photograph, feeling the little girl whose name had been scribbled on the inside cover of her book come to life.

She would have been a popular child. Pretty girls always were, she thought, remembering Melanie Cox, who had set the trends at Hillsborough Primary where she had gone. If she wore her long blonde hair in pigtails, all the other girls arrived the next day at school with their hair in pigtails. She had pestered her mother for weeks about getting a pair of sneakers the same as Melanie's but her mother had been unable to grasp the enormity of having pink sneakers with blue trim and not plain old white ones.

Amy would have been a trendsetter, too; she could tell just by looking at her. Unlike Melanie Cox, though, Jess would have bet money on it that Amy would have been a fair and just queen of the playground as she delegated who got to take turns playing jump rope with her.

The other handful of pictures were far more relaxed and candid shots. One showed Amy kicking a soccer ball around in the garden with a young Owen. They both looked so carefree and Jess felt her eyes prickle at their naivety as to what lay around the corner. She'd never been to see a fortune teller and now she knew why. It was far better to be blissfully unaware of the cruel knocks that might be coming your way.

"Is that Tippy Toes?" she asked, glad of the diversion as she flicked to the last picture. Amy was holding a mangy-looking black and white cat. She had a look of total devotion on her face as she gazed at the cat who, looked like she would rather be someplace else.

"Aye, that's Tippy Toes—not exactly a thoroughbred, was she?"

"No." Jess laughed. "But I can tell she would have had personality. So is it okay if I take these?"

"Aye, but I would like them back sometime."

"Of course. I'll look after them, I promise." Their eyes met briefly and she felt her face flush, grateful that their food arrived at that moment. Jess inhaled the wonderful aroma of the sea coming from her basket and was pleased to note the generous pot of tartar sauce that came with it—there was nothing worse than a mean serving of sauce.

Owen's roast looked pretty good, too, and it came with a couple of her favourite Yorkshire puds. She wondered briefly if there might be any chance of swapsies but a quick glance at his hooded profile as he began sawing into his meat made her decide he probably wouldn't appreciate the suggestion.

"So when will your paper run the article?" he asked, loading his fork.

"I think Niall thought that it would be particularly poignant were it to run on the anniversary of…well, you know, but I'll tell you for sure once he confirms it and of course I'll send you the paper as soon as it's gone to print. Have you told your father about it?"

"Aye. He hasn't read through it yet. He'll pick it up when he's ready like. I think he'll be pleased enough that Amy will be remembered, though, and not just by us." He changed the subject then, making small talk about the other Ladybird books Jess had in her collection before asking, "So why the fascination with other peoples' cast-offs?"

It was not the most eloquently put question and it got Jess's back up. "Have you not heard the saying one man's junk is another man's treasure?"

Owen looked suitably chastened.

"Besides, to me they're not cast-offs; they are treasure. Anybody can walk into a shop and pick something brand new off the shelf if they have the money but where's the thrill in that? I get so excited when I stumble across a vintage designer label that I feel my heart beginning to pound and my palms get all sweaty." Oh dear, had she just made herself sound like a werewolf? "It's not just for the love of a good bargain either." She quickly carried on, "I like the fact that I won't see anybody else wearing what I am wearing and I don't know, maybe there is good reason for that." Jess shrugged and glanced down at her sage green ensemble.

"I think you look great."

"Really?"

"Aye." Owen looked embarrassed and busied himself with his roast taties.

"I found the most beautiful powder blue Wedgewood box the other day in an Oxfam shop that I am going to use as a jewellery box. It gives me such a buzz, imagining the stories that something like that could tell. I wouldn't be sitting here now with you, either, if it weren't for my fascination with things that have been pre-loved."

"No, I suppose not and I'm sorry. I didn't mean to sound flippant before—I was curious, that's all."

"Right then, put your money where your mouth is. I saw a thrift shop back on the High Street with my name on it. Come and check it out with me after lunch and you'll see what I've been talking about," Jess challenged.

"Alright then, I will." He held his hand out and they shook on it before resuming eating.

As he placed his knife and fork down on the plate, Owen leaned back in his chair with the contented look of a well-fed man. "Are you up for pudding?"

"I think I may just have a teensy bit of room left."

"It's good to see a girl who likes her food."

Unsure if that was a compliment, Jess reached over and took the sweets menu from him before deciding on the sticky date pudding.

Owen announced he was going to have banoffee pie.

Jess watched him walk up to the bar to order and gazing at his back bent over the bar, she wondered—not for the first time—why his marriage had broken up. The words were out of her mouth before he even got his bottom back down on his seat.

"Why did you and your wife split up?"

Owen looked at her in surprise. "What brought that on?'

"I told you I am a nosy rosie."

"Aye, you are that. I suppose it goes with the territory like." He didn't look annoyed, though, and Jess wondered whether he would answer her.

He toyed with his drinks mat for a moment and not looking up, replied, "I met Sarah in London through work; she was a lawyer too. She wasn't like the girls I'd grown up around and I liked the fact she didn't know about my family's past when we got together. It felt like a proper fresh start." He shrugged. "We lived together for a bit and then decided to get married. In hindsight, we were too young and by the time we moved into our thirties, we realised we had nothing left in common. We weren't the same people anymore; we both wanted different things." His eyes when he looked up were distant. "She loved living in the city whereas I think I always knew that I would go back to Ballymcguinness one day. It was a bonus that we split up before we got to the having kids part."

"How long were you married?"

"Eight years."

"Oh, that's quite a long time." It was a big chunk of his life, Jess realised, wondering whether he was as over his ex as he made out. She was surprised to find herself hoping he was.

Two bowls of calorific desserts were deposited in front of them and not wanting her pudding to get cold, Jess tucked in.

"God, that was delicious," she declared minutes later, leaning back in her chair and clasping her hands round her full belly. Realising she probably resembled a green Buddha, she quickly sat upright. Owen, too, looked well and truly satiated as, groaning, he got up to pay for their meal. Jess minced up behind him, getting her purse out, but he insisted on paying, telling her in that brusque manner of his that it had been his idea in the first place, therefore it should be his treat. His expression brooked no argument so she tucked her purse away again.

True to his word, Owen allowed Jess to lead him into the thrift shop she'd spotted earlier. It was a long, narrow shop cluttered with racks of mismatched clothes on the left-hand side of the wall. To the right were bookshelves filled higgledy-piggledy and bric-a-brac treasures lined the back wall. A changing room cubicle with a floral curtain on a rail screening it off was tucked away in the corner. Behind the counter sat an elderly woman clacking away with her knitting needles. Owen looked out of place as he lurked uncomfortably near the door while Jess began rummaging through the clothes.

"Here!" she called out triumphantly a moment later, holding a belted cream jacket aloft.

"That looks like something my Gran would have worn."

"For your information, this style happens to be all the go this autumn and if I were to pick up a jacket like this on the High Street, I'd pay around fifty euros easily but look, it's only three and a half euros."

"Maybe there is a reason for that," he replied, taking a step further inside the shop.

Jess ignored him, peering at the label inside the collar. "Plus it's made in England, not India, so it hasn't been knocked up on the cheap by some poor underpaid factory workers."

"And she's got a social conscience," Owen muttered, rolling his eyes.

Jess was determined not to be put off and putting the coat to one side, she carried on rifling through the clothes. She spotted a skirt she liked and then headed over to the shelf housing the books. There wasn't much there to get her excited—old Jilly Coopers and a couple of Sidney Sheldons but no children's books. She moved toward her last port of call in the shop, pausing to smile at the old woman knitting as she passed by the counter on her way to the bric-a-brac section.

As she spied the little green, leaf-shaped dish hidden amongst a mishmash of seventies pottery, Jess felt a familiar roaring start up in her ears; her heart began to race as her palms grew slippery.

Picking it up reverently, she turned it over and almost let rip with a jubilant, "Yes!" Its stamp declared it was, just as she had suspected, none other than Carlton Ware and…it had a price tag of a ridiculous one and a half euros.

"Owen," she hissed out of the corner of her mouth, inclining her head for him to come over. She did not want to attract the attention of any of her fellow shoppers or alert the knitting woman that she had spotted a true bargain.

Owen raised an eyebrow and came over to see what she was holding on to as though her life depended on it.

"What's that you have found then?"

"Shush, keep your voice down," she whispered, her eyes flickering around the room to make sure they weren't attracting any undue attention. "It's Carlton Ware. I can't believe it." She turned the dish over in her hands and showed him the stamp on the bottom. "It's collectable; isn't it gorgeous?"

Owen looked bemused. "It's a dish shaped like a leaf. So what use will that be to you?"

"I won't actually use it you-you-eejit!"

Jess moseyed up to the counter and handed the dish over nonchalantly. "I'll have this please."

"It's a pretty little dish, isn't it, dear?" The old biddy behind the counter put her knitting to one side and turned the dish over in her hands.

Jess sent up a silent prayer, asking for her not to spot the stamp. If it had been a hospice shop, she might have felt guilty enlisting God like this but since it was a community thrift shop, she was sure he'd be okay with it.

"That's one and a half euros ta, lovie."

She flashed Owen a triumphant *I told you so* look and handed over the money before telling the old dear not to worry about a bag. Then secreting it away in her own bag, she walked as fast as her skirt would let her out of the shop. To her surprise, when she turned around, Owen wasn't behind her. She waited a few moments until he appeared in the shop's doorway, toting a plastic bag. It was her turn to raise an eyebrow.

"It was a bargain," he said, opening the bag and showing her a thick Aran jersey to add to his Aran jumper collection. He had the good sense to look sheepish.

Chapter Twelve

"I THINK YOUR MAN THE pig farmer fancies you," Brianna said. "And I think you fancy him too."

"I do not and his name's Owen, not your man the pig farmer." Actually, Jess thought, she wasn't entirely sure how she felt. Her head had been all over the show since she'd had such an unexpectedly lovely afternoon with him yesterday. It had been an awkward goodbye, though, with neither of them knowing what to say. There had been no hint on his part that he would like to meet up again, either, with the only tenuous thread that suggested they might keep in touch being her promise to forward him the paper when it ran "Amy's Story."

She had made him promise to keep her up to speed with Wilbur's health, too, but whether he would or not—well, she could only hope. Hoisting herself with some difficulty back onto the train, she'd paused before sitting down to look back over her shoulder, mentally playing that childish game of "if he's still there it means he likes me" but his back was turned and he was already walking away. The train's doors had slid shut before it rumbled out of the station and that had been the end of that.

Now, Jess and Brianna were huddled inside their coats on a bench covered in seagull poop down at the beach in Bray while Harry disturbed crabs in their holes by poking a big stick down them.

"What about Nick?"

"Oh, no question, I definitely fancy him." Jess nodded emphatically.

A little too enthusiastically, in Brianna's opinion. "Do you? I wouldn't have thought he was your usual type, Jess, not from what you've told me."

"That is the point. Despite what everyone seems to think, my mother in particular, I am capable of fancying a man who is gorgeous, successful, and mentally stable. I don't always go for damaged goods."

"Hey, I'm on your side." Brianna reached over and gave her friend's hand a quick squeeze. "And I don't disagree with you. It's just that from what you have told me, your man Owen is good-looking and successful but he has one big thing you need that I am worried Nick might not have."

"Brianna, if you are talking about what I think you are talking about…"

"Get your mind out of the gutter, girl! No, I mean he is sensitive. You need a man who is sensitive and not some cut-throat businessman—that just isn't your style."

"Huh…you mean sensitive like Harry?"

Both girls turned their attention to Harry, who had moved on from stabbing crabs while they slept to beating a dead fish that had washed up onto the pebbles with his stick.

"Oh my God, Harry! Cut that out!" Brianna yelled, standing up and gesticulating for him to stop the carnage. Once he'd dropped the stick, she turned her attention back to Jess. "Whatever you do, don't ever have kids," she warned for the umpteenth time. "The stress is going to kill me. Honestly, one day I'm worried he will grow up to be a flasher, the next a cross-dresser, and then on days like this when the testosterone really kicks in, a serial killer."

Jess laughed and gave her friend her usual response to Harry's quirks. "He is a gorgeous, totally normal boy, and one day all those things you just spieled off will be funny anecdotes at his twenty-first."

"You think?"

"I know so. Listen, boys will be boys and like Harry, Nick's got a soft side, too. I think you need to meet him and see for yourself."

"Okay, I'm up for that. How about you both come to our place for dinner, if it all goes well with your date this Wednesday, that is? That way, Pete and I can check him out properly and I promise I will try to reserve judgement until then. I'll put the hard word on Harry to behave."

"Right! You have got yourself a deal. Dinner would be lovely and you'll get to see for yourself that Nick's lovely too. Now then," Jess said, tucking her flyaway hair behind her ears, "all we have done is talk about me. What's going on with you?"

"Oh, the usual busy, busy—you know how it is. I am heading out later this afternoon to make placards for a protest the play group is going to stage." She shook her head, causing her shoulder-length brown hair to bob up and down. "I really believe that corporate greed is the death of communities."

Jess didn't think it would go down too well were she to point out that if it weren't for big corporations, Pete wouldn't have a job so instead she gave her friend a pat on the back. "Good for you, Brie, standing up for what you believe in."

"Well, you just make sure you stand up for what you believe in and don't let yourself be bullied by Nora or your Mum where Nick is concerned, okay?"

It was the second time she'd been warned about letting herself get bullied in under two days: first by her father and now by Brianna. Was she really that much of a pushover? Jess pondered and speaking of pushovers. "So have you heard from Nora? The last time I spoke to her, she was off waterskiing in the South of France.'

"What! The South of France! Lucky madam, but she hates the sea."

"I know she does. She also hates mountain biking and skydiving but that hasn't stopped her. I swear, Brie, this Ewan is going to be the end of her. She'll have a bloody nervous breakdown if she keeps it up. I've tried talking to her but she won't listen."

Brianna shook her head. "She's mad. I'll have a word, so I will. I haven't spoken to her since last week, so I'm due to give her a call and tell her exactly what I think about her swanning around the South of France on a set of waterskis without telling me."

Jess shivered. The wind was losing its change of season chill and was feeling decidedly wintery today.

"Come on, you're turning blue it's getting so cold, and I think Harry's probably massacred enough sea-life for one day," Brie said, standing up and checking her backside for remnants of bird poo. "Let's head home for a cuppa."

JESS SUCCESSFULLY WHILED away the days until big date Wednesday by throwing herself into her work, taking time off only to heed Nora's advice and upgrade her underwear drawer. It was ironic, really, that the gorgeous pale green, French lace bra and briefs she had splurged on probably cost more than the entire contents of her wardrobe put together! She definitely drew the line at second-hand undies, though she'd mused as she carefully snipped the tags off and after the shock of her support knickers, Nick deserved every penny she had spent on her new lingerie. She must remember to tell her mother she had upgraded in that department, too, because it might shut her up for five minutes.

Actually, she thought, frowning, it was strange that she hadn't heard from her mother. She'd have put money on her ringing with a pre-date pep talk. She'd kept expecting the phone to ring, with half of her hoping it would be Owen with an update about Wilbur and the other half hoping Nick would ring just to see how she was. It had, however, remained stubbornly silent on all fronts. That was the thing with working from home, she'd thought, shooting the phone a nasty look; sometimes the silence got oppressive.

It wasn't until Tuesday morning, though, that she realised she'd been so busy tapping away at her laptop that she hadn't heard from Nora either. For all she knew, she could be laid up in a French hospital with a broken leg thanks to her ridiculous waterskiing expedition. What kind of a friend was she? Jess chastised herself, picking the phone up and while images of poor injured Nora swam before her eyes, she speed-dialled her friend at work.

Nora answered on the fifth ring. Instead of the usual harried "I am so busy" tone she reserved for work, her voice was despondent.

"Hey, you sound awful. What's up?"

"Nothing. I'm fine."

"No, you're not—spill."

"No, I'm not." Nora capitulated with a sniffling sound.

Jess knew better than to try to get to the bottom of whatever the problem was while Nora was at work. She was too much of a professional to offload between the hours of nine and five, so she decided to take affirmative action instead. "Right, that's it. Nora Brennan, I am calling a girly pow-wow. Be at my place, seven o'clock tonight."

"But I'm..."

"Nope. Whatever it is, cancel it. I'll ring Brianna. See you then."

Nora knew better than to try to argue. "Oh, alright—and Jess?"

"Yes?"

"Thanks."

"You don't have to thank me. That's what friends are for."

Jess hung up, frowning and wondering what on earth had her normally upbeat and in-control friend down in the doldrums. It was most unlike her to let a man affect her the way Ewan apparently was. "Don't let him have packed it in with her," she said aloud to the empty room before tapping out Brianna's number. Nora would be devastated if that were the case.

Brianna was home and the girls spent ten minutes speculating as to what could have happened between loves young dream before agreeing that Brianna was to be in charge of crisps and dips while Jess would get the crackers and whip up one of her famous cheese balls, a Kiwi party staple of old. They'd both buy wine. They had a feeling they were going to need plenty.

JESS STOPPED WORK LATE that afternoon in order to trot off down to Tesco's. She was a woman on a mission, tossing the necessary cheese ball ingredients of both cheddar and cream cheese, salad cream, chopped nuts and some token greenery—a bunch of chives—into her basket. Throwing in a box of crackers, she decided that if the circumstances were as dire as she suspected they might be, then they could be in need of serious reinforcements so she added a king-sized bar of chocolate to her groceries—just in case. When she got to the wine aisle, the only special she could find worth bothering with was an Australian sav, so muttering, "It will have to do," she plucked a couple of bottles off the shelf. Taking her stash up to the checkout, she received a sympathetic smile from the girl serving as her comfort food got stacked into a plastic bag. "I always find Milky Bar does the trick personally," she'd said, waving the bar of fruit and nut chocolate under the scanner.

As Jess had headed home to begin rolling her big cheesy ball, she thought to herself that chocolate was indeed the universal language of sisterhood.

BRIANNA HAD ORGANISED to pick Nora, who was obviously in no fit state to drive, up on her way over and the two women buzzed their arrival at one minute to seven. Jess poured three generous glasses of wine while she waited for their knock at the door. When it came, she opened it and was shocked by her first sighting of Nora. She looked dreadful and Jess couldn't stop the little gasp she emitted at the sight of her glamorous friend's bedraggled blonde locks. She had no makeup on, either—that was unheard of. What really got to her, though, was the fact that Nora was in a leisure suit and on her feet was something she never ever thought she would see her friend's dainty tootsies slide themselves into: Ugg boots.

Nora didn't do casual and Jess had had no idea she even owned a leisure suit, let alone Ugg boots. It was then that it hit home just how bad a way she really was in. Racing over, she wrapped her fragile friend in a bear hug. "Did you get a park okay?" Jess asked, looking over Nora's shoulder to Brianna, who was bringing up the rear, laden down with supplies.

"I'm in for the long haul," she replied, holding up her bottles of wine. "So I got Pete to drop us off. He'll pick us up on his way home from squash around elevenish—Harry's at my Mam's for the night."

The three women trooped through to the lounge where their glasses of wine were waiting.

Brianna sat down and kicked her boots off before tucking her legs up under herself and reaching for her glass while Nora collapsed down on to the settee and knocked her drink back in two gulps. Then, spying the cheese ball, she dived into it, scooping big chunks onto the artfully arranged crackers and shovelling them in her mouth as though they were on a conveyor belt. Brianna and Jess exchanged glances that asked *where had their friend the Dukan Diet Queen disappeared to*?

At last she stopped eating long enough to hold her glass out for a refill. "God, that's better. Your cheese balls really are the biz, Jess. I needed that."

Jess preened as she got up to get another bottle out of the fridge. "I've always maintained that there really are healing properties in a cheese ball. I think it must be the cheddar or maybe it's down to the cream cheese."

"Or maybe it's just down to all the horrific calories," Brianna said, snorting before she carried on with her crisp fest.

With their glasses topped up, Jess and Brianna tussled over the crisps and dip. The cheese ball was out of bounds—poor Nora needed it more than they did. Supping their drinks, they listened while Nora filled them in as to what had got her knickers in such a knot.

"Ewan wants us to...to do a b-b-b-" She sounded like a five-year-old sounding out her letters.

"Wants you to do what, Nora?" Brianna and Jess chimed patiently, both bewildered and each hoping she wasn't going to reveal some new sex act they hadn't heard of.

"He wants us to do a b-b-bungee jump together off the top of Liberty Hall."

Jess and Brianna looked at each other, shocked Nora was referring to Dublin's tallest building. "And I can't do it!" Nora wailed.

"Right, enough is enough!" Jess stated, getting up from her armchair perch to shove another loaded cracker in her friend's gob. It had an instant calming effect.

"You need to tell Ewan the truth. You can't keep pretending to be someone you are not and Nora, face it—you are not an adrenaline junkie."

"Why can't I keep pretending? I managed to pull off the mountain bike ride, skydiving and waterskiing, so surely that qualifies me? I just need to find a way to fight the fear." Nora's expression was petulant.

Brianna interjected, "Feck fight the fear! It qualifies you as an idiot, yes, because you were absolutely terrified doing all of those things and think about it. Where will it end? He'll have you white-water rafting down the Amazon, or swimming with great whites if you're not careful or, or..."

"Or leaping off tall buildings with a piece of elastic tied round your legs," Jess finished.

"I know, I know. My nerves are shot and look." She held out her trembling hands and both women looked in shock at Nora's chewed fingernails.

"Nora Brennan, listen to me. This is not you. You are not a nail-biter. You get your nails done once a week, for goodness' sake! I aspire to have nails like yours." Jess paused to gaze briefly at her own short clipped nails. Long nails were hopeless when you earned your money tapping out articles on a laptop. Her face took on a puzzled expression. "What I don't get, though, is how come you managed to skydive and all that other stuff but you can't do a bungee jump? What's so scary about that by comparison? Not that I'm encouraging you or anything." She popped a handful of dip-laden crisps in her mouth. "Yum. Brie, that feta and spinach dip is divine."

"Yeah, it is, isn't it? Marks had a special on, so I grabbed a couple."

"Excuse me, you're supposed to be helping me sort my life out, not talking about bloody supermarket specials."

"Sorry." Both women were contrite.

Mollified, Nora answered Jess's question. "I was naïve when I did the skydive. I had no idea what I was in for or how terrifying it would be. As for mountain biking," she shrugged, "anyone can ride a bike; I just pretended I was doing a spin class. Being flown to the South of France in a private plane helped take the edge off the waterskiing." Her blue eyes filled with fear. "But there is absolutely no fecking way I can throw myself off a building with nothing but a pair of pantyhose holding me up—not even if I popped a couple of Valium first!"

"Then tell Ewan the truth for your own sake, or you're going to give yourself a nervous breakdown."

"Okay, okay." Nora held up both hands in defeat. "You're right, I know and I will—I promise but he's in the States for the next two weeks filming."

"Well, as soon as he gets back, you come clean." Jess wagged a finger at her.

"What do I say, though? Ewan's said all along how great it is that he has finally met a girl who is into all the same stuff as him. If I tell him I'm not who he thinks I am, he is bound to give me the flick. He'll think I'm just as fickle as those fans of his who send through pictures of themselves in the nude all the time."

"Women do that?" Brianna asked, frowning.

"And men."

Jess raised an eyebrow. "Really?"

"Yep, really. Honestly, you two have no idea what celebrities have to put up with."

No, Jess thought to herself, she obviously didn't and the taste tester she had experienced of life in the limelight—finding an unflattering photo of herself plastered in the papers—had left her cold.

"You don't know that he'll think you're fickle," Brianna said, earnestly tucking her bobbed hair behind one ear. "Tell him that you've decided adventures sports just aren't for you after all but that you are happy to be his cheerleader. If he is as keen on you as you are on him, he will understand."

"I hope so because I have never felt this way before about anyone and girls, I am absolutely bloody terrified I'll lose him." Nora sniffed, her eyes filling.

Brianna pulled a tissue out from her sleeve and handed it to Nora. "It's clean, I promise. If he's a keeper, you won't lose him. Have a bit of faith in him," she advised wisely as both she and Jess got up and wrapped their arms round their friend. When they broke away, she blew her nose and managed a small grin before draining her glass with a slurp. "Anymore wine going?"

"So how did your protest go, Brie?" Jess asked as she filled Nora's glass and sat back down.

Brianna bought Nora up to speed with the play group she was so passionate should stay and her ties to it with Harry having gone to it twice weekly as a tot.

"You really are a sucker for a good cause." Nora shook her head. "Dublin's down-and-out would be lost without you."

"I would hardly call a group of mammies passionate about their community having a centre where their children can meet to play 'Dublin's down-and-out,' Nora." Brianna was indignant.

For Jess, however, as Brianna mentioned "a group of mothers" in the same sentence as "community centre," the penny had at last dropped. Gosh, she could be so thick, she thought, tipping her wine down her throat. Hang on, though, perhaps the group of mothers about which Nick had been so derisive were nothing to do with Brie and her band of merry mammies? Then again, what were the odds of more than one group of mums up in arms over the demolition of a building in a city the size of Dublin anyway?

"Er, Brie, what building is it that you're trying to save?"

"The Bray Community Centre. I thought I'd told you that?"

"Um, no, you didn't, actually."

"Ah, well, no matter." She shook her head, her face growing animated as she began to relay the latest. "The protest went really well. RTÉ even showed up with their cameras rolling. The infuriating thing is that the company behind the proposed project refused to meet with us. Bloody cowards, whoever they are. All they care about is money. I tell you, girls, they march in and destroy the lifeblood of small communities but I'm not going to let them destroy mine!"

Nora clapped her hands and drawled in an American accent, "You go, girl!"

Oh dear, thought Jess; now was not the time to mention the fact that she was ninety-nine percent certain the cowardly company Brianna was on about belonged to Nick. She already seemed to have made up her mind that he wasn't right for her and revealing that it was him behind her latest cause's proposed demolition would definitely not endear him to her. She decided she'd keep quiet about it for now and see how her date went tomorrow night. If they got on well and decided to see each other again as she hoped would be the case, then she'd have to come clean and tell Brianna. It would be up to her then as to whether she still wanted to have them both round for dinner.

For some reason, Owen's face floated before her but she batted him away, having a sneaky scoop of the cheese ball instead while Nora was fossicking in the fridge for further supplies.

They had broken out the chocolate and were cracking open the third bottle of vino when Brianna piped up with, "That Nick chap you set Jess up with is cooking her dinner tomorrow night."

Bugger, Jess thought; she'd wanted to steer clear of any conversation regarding Nick.

"Whaat! When did that happen?"

"He invited me over when he dropped me home last week."

"But you didn't tell me that when I rung you. I thought you'd never hear from him again after your Oscar-winning 'Drunk Woman' performance." Nora looked most put out.

"Well, you didn't exactly give me a chance to tell you, did you? You were too busy issuing orders about my needing to upgrade my knickers and before you ask, for your information, I have done so."

When Pete arrived to pick his wife and Nora up shortly after eleven after a hard night bashing a little black ball around a court, he looked perturbed when Jess answered the door. He didn't like to ask why she had a pair of lacy green knickers on her head nor why Nora was taking aim at his wife with the matching bra.

JESS WOKE THE NEXT morning with the nagging headache that signified she probably shouldn't have had that last glass of wine last night. Oh well, she thought, squinting and sitting up; it had been fun, and she and Brianna had successfully completed their mission, which was to get their friend laughing again. Besides, she decided, shrugging into her dressing gown and padding through to the kitchen, the headache was nothing that poached eggs on toast and a good strong cup of coffee wouldn't fix.

She spent her morning finishing her column for the week. Her inspiration this week had come from last night's girly get-together. It had been brewing since her encounter with the snooty shop assistant from the haute couture shops she had ventured into with Brianna and been cemented by the lass on the checkout at Tesco's the day before. She'd decided to write about the unspoken and universal language that existed between women and how some women were part of the sisterhood and some definitely weren't.

Having emailed her final draft off to Niall, she was debating whether beans on toast was a good idea for lunch or whether she might be better going for something like a chicken wrap from the Spar shop down the road when the phone rang. It was Nick.

The conversation was short and sweet as he was on his way to a meeting. Jess crossed her fingers and hoped it wasn't over in Bray. He told her he would swing by around seven thirty to pick her up. She'd hung up thinking he had sounded very masterful and she'd felt her stomach knot in excitement at the thought of the night to come.

For once she didn't have to spend hours agonising over what to wear because Nora had taken it upon herself the night before to choose what outfit she should wear. "You need to dress to impress for a man like Nick because Ewan told me he usually dates model types," she'd declared knowledgably as she hauled a cream sixties swing dress out of Jess's wardrobe. "This, girlfriend, is the perfect dress for in-home dining." Handing it to Jess, she disappeared back into the wardrobe again, reappearing a few moments later looking like the cat that got the cream as she held up a pair of matching heels. "Wear your hair down," she ordered bossily before picking up Jess's new bra and pinging it across the room at her.

Nick was fifteen minutes late and Jess had just finished re-checking her makeup in her powder compact for the third time since she'd plonked her bottom down on the cold vinyl in Riverside's foyer. She jiggled her crossed legs in an effort to stop thinking about the fact she needed the loo and to prevent the bare backs of her thighs from sticking to the seat. Brianna always said she had a Woolworths bladder but this was down to nerves, Jess thought, peering out into the dark for any sign of slowing headlights. She was loath to wait outside on the street for him and not just because of the nip in the air but because the last time she had loitered out there waiting for a ride, a passing Japanese tourist had said, "Kon niche wa—how much?"

Taking a deep breath in order to calm the butterflies, Jess glanced down at her dress. At least she knew she looked good. She sent Nora a mental ten out of ten for choice of outfit because as she had tottered past in her cream heels, Puff the Magic Dragon had just about fallen out the window between drags. She'd also bumped into Gemma from across the hall for the first time in ages. Dressed as per usual in head-to-toe skin-tight black and clutching a water bottle, she was of course coming back from a workout.

"Jess—wow! You look fantastic. Have you got a hot date?" She'd winked but then she'd ruined it by going on at her about joining her down at the gym again.

No chance, thought Jess, wondering whether Gemma was on some sort of commission. Perhaps she got free membership if she managed to recruit new members. Jess's musing as to Gemma's motivations were interrupted by a toot. Nick was outside. As she pulled open the heavy doors, the sounds of Justin Timberlake emanated forth. She ran over to the car and as she climbed into the seat next to him, her heart skipped a beat. He looked gorgeous in a crisp white shirt and jeans, his hair still wet from a shower. He turned the music down and as he leaned toward her, she caught a whiff of that same delicious aftershave before she lost herself in the kiss that followed.

It wasn't until a group of lads walking up the Quays began calling out, "Whoa! Go on, get in there, mate!" that they broke apart. Nick grinned cheekily at her before revving the engine and expertly weaving the car out into the evening traffic.

Chapter Thirteen

"I'M SORRY. THIS HAS never happened to me before." Nick lifted the bed covers and gazed dolefully at the culprit.

It's never happened to me before either, she thought. Jess felt as deflated as Nick's partner in crime. It happened—she knew that, of course—but why did it have to happen to her tonight? "It's okay," she lied.

"It's not you, Jessica; it's me."

My God, all these clichés, Jess thought. "It happens. Don't worry about it—truly, Nick, it's fine."

"Not to me it doesn't. It's the stress of this bloody community centre business."

"It's not going well then?" Jess squeaked, feeling like Judas knowing what she now knew.

"No, it's not. This bunch of hormonal homemakers is holding everything up with their whingeing to the Council. They have no idea about the real world or how much money is riding on this thing."

Jess felt her face heat up and was glad that the room was dimly lit. He would not be impressed if he knew that one of the hormonal homemakers to which he referred was her best friend and actually, she thought, she didn't particularly care for the vehemence in his tone.

They lay side by side in his Californian King-sized bed under crisp white sheets, their heads resting on the twin pillows. At that moment in time, Jess wished she still smoked; it would have given her something to occupy herself with instead of lying next to him in an awkward silence.

The evening had started off so well too, she thought, closing her eyes and wishing herself away. When they'd arrived back at Nick's, he'd unlocked the front door and she had been assailed by a delicious smell that she'd pinpointed after several discreet sniffs as rosemary and roasting lamb. Yum—lamb was her favourite and her mouth had watered as she decided that Nick was definitely a smooth operator. Sitting on his designer white couch, she watched him set the scene by lighting candles and putting a CD on his stereo.

He disappeared into the kitchen and reappeared with two balloon-like wine glasses, a rich red liquid swimming well under halfway in each of them. Accepting the glass, she took a tentative sip. It was delicious and she made a mental vow not to knock it back—she didn't need to go down the blackened teeth road again.

"Do you like it?"

"I do. It's very, um, full-bodied." She hoped that didn't sound like a hair advertisement.

"A bold, meaty red is how it was described to me. I bought it from a boutique vineyard in Mendoza, Argentina. The Argentines are voracious meat eaters and the owner assured me that it is the perfect accompaniment to roasted meat. I hope you like lamb?" he'd asked, sitting down next to her. His thigh brushed hers.

"I come from a country where the sheep outnumber the people, so yes, I like lamb." She'd smiled. In the background, his state-of-the-art stereo began crooning something low and throaty. Norah Jones perhaps? Jess wondered, trying to distract herself from the warm pressure of his leg next to hers.

"Did I tell you how lovely you look tonight?" Nick murmured, taking her glass out of her hand and placing it on the glass-topped table in front of them. "That's a beautiful dress."

Jess sent a telepathic thank-you to Nora and felt a shiver of anticipation as he moved toward her. She felt as if she were starring in a seduction scene from a movie and she definitely hoped it would venture into the realms of the pornographic before the night ended.

He was such a good kisser; closing her eyes and leaning into him, she allowed herself to relax and enjoy the sensation of his body next to hers. His hands began to roam freely and she quivered involuntarily as he reached her breasts, stroking them gently through the sheer fabric of her dress. He'd pulled away then, leaving her feeling slightly bereft as he got up to tend to the meat.

"There's nothing worse than dry lamb," he'd said, tossing her a mischievous look over his shoulder, and Jess got the distinct impression he was well aware of the state he was leaving her in.

By the time he served their meal, she had composed herself again and smoothing her hair down, Jess got up to join him at the opposite end of a large glass-topped table. All this glass—it was definitely not a child friendly home, Jess noted, imagining the field day Harry would have putting his fingerprints everywhere. But then why should it be?

Nick had excelled himself: the lamb was cooked to perfection, the roast potatoes were crunchy on the outside and deliciously moist and fluffy on the inside, and the side serving of spring vegetables, even though it was autumn, were al dente. Jess wasn't surprised by the excellence of the meal; she knew enough about Nick now to know he was the type of man who wouldn't attempt to do anything unless he could do it well.

"You obviously enjoy cooking because this is superb," she said, her knife sliding into a perfectly pink piece of lamb. Her mind flashed back to another conversation with a surly farmer from the North who had followed this theme and she shook the images it conjured away.

"I do when I get the time but I have a limited repertoire."

"Well, it's broader than mine."

"That surprises me." He raised an eyebrow. "I really enjoyed reading about your culinary adventures, trying all the different cuisines on offer around Dublin. It was very amusing. You are a talented writer, Jessica."

Jess flushed, unused to praise and unsure how to accept the compliment gracefully. She decided to brush it aside. "I managed to combine my two great loves with that series, eating and writing. It was lots of fun but I am afraid I am the kind of girl who needs to be shown how to do something ten times before I master it. It all went in one ear and then flew out the other."

Nick laughed. "Which country's cuisine was your favourite?"

"I would have to say I enjoyed the Creole course the most. Probably because it was so different to anything I have tried before but on a weekly takeaway basis, I am definitely an Indian fan. What about you?"

"I love Thai. There's a great restaurant just down the road from here that I usually eat at once a week. They do wonderful fish cakes. Perhaps I could take you there and convert you sometime?"

Jess felt her cheeks stain again. "That would be lovely." For him she would definitely forfeit her Malabari Prawn in favour of fish cakes.

Nick served a wine, which he told her would offset the sweetness of the dessert he'd prepared. His knowledge of wines was impressive, Jess thought, raising her glass to her lips. All she knew about the crushed grape was that if it was crisp and cold, then she usually liked it. As for dessert, well, it was a foregone conclusion that it wouldn't be the Tesco's Bavarian chocolate pie that usually made an appearance at any dinner parties she held.

It was a ramekin of crème brulee that was placed in front of her and even she knew that this was a temperamental dessert. Nick's, however, was set just right and when he produced a miniature blowtorch to caramelise the sugar, Jess had almost swooned. Just wait until her mother heard about tonight, she'd thought, dipping her spoon into the deliciously delicate custard—Marian would go into orbit. It had been such a long time since she'd been treated like a princess, Jess realised, and she had to admit to loving every minute of it.

Nick had been insistent she leave the dishes when she had stood up in readiness to clear the table, suggesting they go through to the living area and enjoy a post-dinner drink instead. Her head swam at the sight of all the different spirits on display, clustered together on a silver tray atop a unit that also housed his vast CD collection. She wondered what types of music other than the jazz CD currently playing he liked as she decided upon a Baileys on the rocks. Sitting curled into the corner of the couch with her heels discarded on the floor beside her, she took a sip of the icy liquid, deciding that it was indeed just as the advertising proclaimed, like liquid silk. Nick had opted for a whisky. It was a man's drink, she thought, trying to stop her mind from wandering below the belt as she forced herself to pay attention to his adventures in Dubai earlier that year.

"You make it sound like a city built of gold." She laughed, looking at him over the rim of her glass. He had replied that it might as well have been for the vast amounts of money that circulated around the city built on sand.

Their eyes had locked then and she had seen the unspoken promise of what was to come as his had darkened. With a suggestive half-smile playing at the corners of his mouth, Jess had allowed him to take her by the hand and lead her through to his bedroom where, he'd assured her, they would be far more comfortable.

Feeling a delicious shudder of anticipation, she had stood almost immobilised by the bed as his hands roamed the contours of her body while his tongue had probed the inner sanctum of her mouth with a sensuous slowness that was beginning to drive her crazy. Allowing him to unzip her dress, she raised her arms obligingly as he lifted it over her head before pushing her back on the bed. Her eyes half closed as their arms and legs tangled together.

Nick unhooked her bra with the precision of the well-practised, and the sensation of skin against skin was almost more than she could bear but she was glad he'd left her panties on for the time being. For what they had cost her, she wanted him to get at least one good gawk at those babies before they hit the deck. To give credit where it's due, he did look impressed as he paused mid-manoeuver before pulling them down and allowing her to shimmy free of them. He stood then and began undressing slowly to reveal a taut and defined body. He definitely worked out, Jess thought appreciatively as she shifted into a skinny position, hoping he wouldn't notice that she definitely didn't.

He moved alongside her and Jess felt a tension building inside her as his hands stroked gently between her legs. Her hand eagerly searched out his equipment—this was always the crucial moment, she thought as she homed in: would she be disappointed or pleasantly surprised? As her fingers sought, found, and closed around the package deal, she decided she wouldn't be disappointed. Nick groaned and pulled away from her rhythmic stroke, leaning over to open the bedside cabinet drawers in search of a condom.

Thunderbirds, we are go, she thought, closing her eyes only to open them a moment later when nothing happened. Glancing down, she watched in horror as like a balloon deflating without the audible hiss, it was all over rover.

And so here they were, lying side by side like two naked strangers, drowning in a huge expanse of snowy linen. His bed was ridiculously oversized, Jess thought, risking a sideways glance. She felt a surge of pity at the sight of Nick's normally confident features looking so uncertain. What had happened wasn't his fault and as she had told herself earlier, these things did happen. Logic told her it had nothing to do with her but of course her ego wasn't so sure. It was hard not to take it personally, she mused; still, she needed to be the bigger person and harden up. Oh God, she had it on the brain! Rolling onto her side, she raised herself up on to her hip and decided to be brave because she was not going to lie here in this uncomfortable silence any longer. "Nick, it's really not a problem. These things happen and like you said, you have an awful lot of stress in your life at the moment, so if you would rather I left then I understand. Do you want me to go?" Her eyes were round green orbs as she looked at him, unsure as to how she would react if he told her he wanted her to go.

Nick shook his head emphatically, looking like a little boy who had lost the running race and forfeited first prize. "No, of course I don't want you to go. I wanted tonight to be just right and it's kind of humiliating, that's all." He managed a wry smile. "I am only thirty-nine-years old so I didn't think I qualified for Viagra just yet but apparently I was wrong."

"I'm sure it was just a one-off," Jess soothed.

"I hope so." His expression was woeful. "I can't promise I will be good company." Reaching over, he stroked her arm. "But I'd like you to stay and please believe me when I tell you that it is nothing to do with you. You are a beautiful woman, Jess, and what just happened is most definitely down to me, not you."

Suddenly Jess didn't care if they lived in harmonious celibacy for the rest of their days; it had been a long time since a man had showered her with such compliments. She wasn't going anywhere.

"I've always been driven when it comes to business and I don't know how or when to switch off."

"I can imagine how high pressured your line of work is," she soothed, stroking his cheek. Actually, she wouldn't have a clue but it sounded good.

"You're great, you know that, don't you?" he said, planting a gentle kiss on the tip of her nose.

He stretched his arm out along the pillow in invitation and Jess moved under it, laying her head on his shoulder. Her body moulded into his and she relaxed, enjoying the sensation of being held—though not quite as much as she had been enjoying other sensations earlier. Still, she would take what she could get, she decided as her eyes grew heavy and began to close. The wine, the dinner, the Baileys, and her sexual misadventures had taken their toll and with a little sigh, Jess drifted into oblivion.

She knew it was early when she woke because she could hear the dawn song. She couldn't remember the last time she had heard the birds in all their morning glory. The pigeons that congregated on the rail of her mock veranda of a morning weren't exactly what you would call songbirds. Reaching across the bed for Nick, she began patting around and realising the space next to her was empty, her eyes popped open. Where was he? She listened out for sounds of life—a toilet flushing, a kettle boiling—but there was nothing bar the birds. Deciding to investigate, Jess got up and pulled last night's dress back over her head before padding through the silent apartment to the kitchen. Sniffing for clues like Inspector Cloueseau, she deduced from the lingering aroma of coffee and toast that Nick had been up and then her eyes fixed on a note propped up against the kettle.

In the kind of precise handwriting she would have expected him to have, he informed her that he had to be on the road early as he had a meeting in Cork. He'd be back late afternoon, so he would phone her then. In the meantime, she was welcome to stay and make herself at home for the day.

Jess sighed. So there'd be no lingering breakfast followed by a spot of morning delight then. Glancing round the empty apartment with its minimalistic styling, she suddenly felt very lonely. Not even waiting to make a much-needed cup of coffee, she picked up the phone and called a cab. She wanted to go home.

OPENING THE DOOR TO her apartment, she stepped inside with relief that she hadn't been subject to cat calls from Puff the Magic Dragon as she'd crossed the courtyard because she was not in the mood. He must be doing some work for a change, she decided, kicking the door shut behind her—that or he'd decided to pack in the smoking. Wandering into the lounge, Jess's eyes swept the room with a stranger's eye. How would Nick perceive the organised chaos that she liked to think of as home? Would he see her eclectic collection of treasures as just that or would he think of them as junk?

On the wall beside the antique oak sideboard Brianna and Nora had clubbed together to buy her for her thirtieth birthday, insisting she needed it to display her bits and bobs, was a set of six blue and white Tunisian tiles.

When they were arranged together, they formed a picture of an urn. She had haggled for an age with a leathery-skinned man in forty degree heat whilst scooters swerved around her in a souk in the town of Monastir to buy them. The aroma of foreign spices had still been in her nostrils as she had marched back triumphantly to her hotel with her carefully wrapped parcel. When she looked at those tiles, she could still see the twinkle in that cunning old man's brown eyes and in her head, she could still hear the early morning call to prayer that signified she was indeed somewhere very foreign.

Then there was the dainty Royal Doulton china cup and saucer set she had bought on a girl's weekend down in Galway many moons ago. With a smile she recalled how she, Brianna, and Nora had had the kind of fun that only the young and single can have that weekend. She'd been wandering the town's cobbled streets on the Saturday morning, nursing a sore head in search of greasy sustenance, when she'd found herself being drawn inside the dark and dusty antiques shop. As she had opened the door and a bell had rung somewhere near the back, she had half expected a pixie to materialise behind the counter. The little old woman who appeared a moment later had indeed been the proud owner of a set of pointy ears. Jess had been reminded of the little shop where the Wishing Chair in Enid Blyton's stories had been discovered and though she hadn't found a wishing chair of her own, she had found the cup and saucer set.

She couldn't help but think of Owen as her eyes settled on her latest acquisition—the Carlton Ware leaf dish. While he would give her a hard time about all the tat she had collected over the years, she knew that he would enjoy listening to the tales that went with them. She frowned, unsure if Nick would ever see the merit in anything second-hand.

Having made a good strong brew and followed it up with a hot shower, Jess dressed for comfort, not company, in her trusty elephant suit. She decided to shake the melancholic feeling that had settled over her for no particular reason that she could pinpoint, by firstly scoffing down what remained of the bar of chocolate from their girly night in. Then, she would phone Brianna and ask for her take on Nick's little problem. Nothing was sacred between friends, she thought, breaking off the last square before picking up the phone.

Brianna was, as Jess had known instinctively, most sympathetic to her plight; it was why she had chosen to ring her and not Nora, who would have grilled her for hours on her bedroom technique.

"I know where you are coming from. It's happened to Pete a couple of times—God, he'd kill me if he knew I was telling you—men are funny like that, aren't they? It's always been when he is under pressure at work, so don't read anything into it, Jess. I know it's really hard not to take it personally, though, because until Captain Pete is back at the helm, I can't help but wonder if he has gone off me or something."

Captain Pete? Jess didn't want to pursue that one. "That's exactly how I felt, even though I knew it was stupid."

"Well, it was stupid because he is obviously smitten but what has your man so wound up anyway?"

Oh crap, now she'd done it. Did she tell her Nick was the driving force behind the proposed demolition of her community centre or just leave it? Jess chewed on a fingernail, deciding to take the easier option and leave it, muttering something instead about the finance he was trying to get together for the project he was working on not being straightforward.

"So are you going to see him again?"

"I hope so. He said he would phone me later today."

"Well, that's good, isn't it?"

"He hasn't phoned me yet."

"It's only ten in the morning, that's why. Now what about organising this dinner at our place so I can meet him and be bowled over by his wonderfulness too?"

Jess cringed; she couldn't keep Nick hidden away from Brie—she was one of her best friends, after all. No, if she wanted to keep on seeing him then she'd just have to bite the bullet and hope to hell that neither of them put two and two together.

"I'll mention it to Nick this afternoon—when suits you and Pete?"

"What about Saturday night? It's short notice but then our social life is sorely lacking these days."

"So is mine because Saturday night is good for me too but I'll let you know for definite once I've spoken to him. Oh and Brie, don't mention our little chat to Nora, will you? You know what she's like; she'll go straight out and buy me a copy of the *Kama Sutra* or something."

Brianna laughed. "You're right, she would. Don't worry. I won't say a word."

"Thanks." Jess decided to change the subject. "Now then, how's my favourite wee man?"

"Harry?"

"Who else?"

"Well, he might be your favourite young man but he is not mine. The little toad decided it would be a good idea to ask a lady at our local Tesco yesterday afternoon why she was so fat but he didn't just leave it at that—oh no, not my Harry. Nope, he went on to ask her was she not making healthy choices in her shopping? The poor woman had a box of frozen cream puff eclairs in her hand at the time. Apparently Harry's class has been learning all about making good choices when it comes to food. I was mortified."

Jess was still laughing when the phone rang again two minutes later.

It was Nora wanting to know how her dinner date had gone. Jess glossed over the main event, thanking her friend for picking out her dress and telling her what she wanted to hear—that it had been fantastic. It was only a little white lie after all, she justified, because the foreplay had been amazing and she was fairly sure the rest of it would have been too, if Nick hadn't got a puncture. Besides, she didn't want to get into it again; what she really needed was some advice.

"Nora, you know how Brie's involved in trying to save the Bray Community Centre that houses the play group she used to take Harry along to?"

"Yes, she mentioned it the other night. She's pretty passionate about it."

"I know—that's the problem."

"What's the problem—I'm not with you?"

"Nick's behind the proposed demolition of it."

There was silence for a moment and then Nora exhaled loudly before uttering Jess's earlier sentiment. "Crap."

"My thoughts exactly. And now Brie's insistent that I bring him round for dinner to meet her and Pete. She wasn't keen on the little bit I had told her about him anyway but when she finds out it is his company wanting to knock the centre down, she'll go mad. What do I do?"

"You'll have to tell her because she is bound to find out sooner or later anyway. Besides, it is Brie's problem, not yours. There is nothing not to like about Nick. He is successful, handsome, and charming—do I need to go on? Business is just that—business. It is not personal."

It was true Nick was all those things, Jess thought, but Nora wasn't finished yet.

"Brianna will just have to drop the bleeding hearts routine and get over it."

It sounded harsh but Jess supposed she was right. "I guess so but the thing is I can see her side of things, too. It is sad how companies like Nick's come along and knock the stuffing out of small communities by tearing down buildings that have been their hub for years. And all because money talks. It just doesn't seem right."

"Now you listen to me, Jess," Nora said in that tone of hers that left no room for discussion. "Nick Jameson is the best thing that has come your way in a long time. Don't go spoiling it for yourself by jumping on Brie's soapbox. You know what she is like. By this time next month, she will have forgotten all about this community centre of hers and she will be signing up to save the fecking pigeon or some such thing."

"Yeah, I know what you mean and in Nick's defence, I have to say that I have never been wined and dined quite so thoroughly." She sighed. "It was lovely but what if Brie doesn't forget all about it this time?"

Nora had an urgent call come through and had to go, leaving Jess feeling perturbed because in the space of half an hour, she had more or less lied by omission to her two best friends about the man she was seeing. It was something she had never done before and it left a sour taste in her mouth. She didn't get a chance to dwell on it, though, because no sooner had she hung up the phone than it rang again. Good God, she muttered, what is this place—a frigging Bombay call centre?

"Hello?" she snapped.

"Jess." A wary voice greeted her. "How are you? It's Owen."

At the sound of his Northern twang, her mood brightened. "Owen, hi! I'm fine, how are you?" She didn't give him a chance to answer, asking instead, "How's Wilbur getting on?"

"Actually, that's why I am calling. Wilbur's sick."

Chapter Fourteen

OWEN HAD ASSURED HER down the phone that it was just a cold Wilbur had come down with but Jess knew that in an animal for which the odds had already been stacked against like Wilbur, a cold could be a serious thing.

"I'm sure he'll pull through but I thought you'd want to know. I promised I'd keep you up to speed like."

"I'm on my way," she'd shrieked, hanging up on him before he could talk her round. Logic was telling her Wilbur was a pig and she was being ridiculous but logic had nothing to do with the swarm of emotions that had engulfed her upon hearing Owen's voice and the news that Wilbur was ill. She phoned Brianna for the second time that morning. It rang and rang and Jess tapped her foot impatiently, muttering, "Come on, Brie, pick up." Until, at last she answered.

"Hello." Brianna panted as though she had just finished the New York Marathon.

"Can I borrow your car?"

"Is that you, Jess?"

"Yes, sorry."

"Bloody hell, I was on the loo—you know what my piles are like."

Jess did indeed know all about Brianna's post-childbirth five-years-of-hell piles but had no wish to get into a discussion about them at this moment in time.

"And the phone rang for so bleeding long I thought something must have happened at school with Harry so I had to get off. I only spoke to you five minutes ago. What's the emergency?"

"Sorry, Brie, but it *is* an emergency. I just had a call to say that Wilbur's sick, so I need to get up to Ballymcguinness again as soon as I can."

"Who's this Wilbur? I thought your man's name was Owen and who told you that you have to get up there right away?"

"Brie!" Jess was impatient; she didn't want a confab about it all—she just wanted to get up there. "Wilbur's the piglet I told you all about. You know, the little runt like in *Charlotte's Web* that I got to feed."

"Oh right, I'm with you now, sort of."

"Well, he's sick and I have to get up there. Christ, if anything happens to him and I am not there!"

"Okay, Jess—are you listening to me?" Brianna snapped, not expecting an answer and if she were there, she would have given Jess a slap to bring her round; however, the silence down the other end of the phone satisfied her that she had her friend's attention. "Take a deep breath—in through the nose and out through the mouth."

The sharp tone was an anomaly for Brianna and it shocked Jess into doing what she was told.

"Good girl; now take another one. That's it and again, one more for me. Right now, are you calm?"

"Yes." No, she bloody wasn't calm, Jess thought, snorting through her nostrils and exhaling noisily out of her mouth as she wondered why Brianna was using the routine she usually saved for Harry when he got a graze on his knee or stubbed his toe on her.

"Jess, sweetie, I want you to put things into perspective. Wilbur is a pig, okay?"

"I thought you, of all people, understood, Brie. He's not just a pig to me."

"If you say he's your baby, I will have you committed. Anyway, you don't have to be Einstein to work out that it's not this Wilbur you're breaking your neck to go up and see. It's a pretty convenient excuse if you ask me. Did Owen ask you to come?"

"No, not exactly and I don't know what you mean about it being a convenient excuse—it is Wilbur I am going up to see." Jess studied her thumbnail before beginning to chew on it agitatedly. She might have been playing dumb but she had a fair old idea what her friend was implying and maybe there was more than a grain of truth in it, but she was still hurt. Wilbur was so small and vulnerable and he needed her to be on his side. Okay, so her feelings for Wilbur might be seen by some as irrational—but not by Brianna, surely? She could always count on Brie to take her side. So what if she was unconsciously misplacing her maternal instincts? She couldn't help how she felt.

Sensing she might have gone too far, Brianna suddenly backtracked and announced that yes, alright, Jess could borrow her car so long as she had it back to her that evening because she had a meeting to go to. Jess had wasted no time and so, grabbing her purse and shoving her feet into a pair of trainers, she'd slammed the front door behind her and headed for Bray.

It took her well over half an hour to get to Tara Station and as she stared out the window while the familiar scenery she normally adored whizzed by, she didn't see any of it. She was too busy mulling over why it was that when you really needed to get somewhere in a hurry, things always seemed to conspire to hold you up. Like the group of American tourists she had gotten stuck behind on the Quays. She'd had to bite her lip to stop herself from yelling at them to "move their fat arses!" By the time they did and she made it to the station, the train she wanted to be on had just been pulling out and she'd had to wait an age for the next one. Now, it was with a sigh of relief that she felt the train slow as they pulled into Bray Station.

Jess spied Brianna's familiar blue Golf Estate in the car park and was pleased her friend had driven down to meet her, as it meant she wouldn't have a ten-minute jog up to her house.

"Brie!" She waved and as she made her way over to the car, Brianna climbed out to greet her.

"Hi, you made it then."

"I nearly assaulted a group of Americans on my way but yes, I made it at last without causing them grievous bodily injury. I hope you didn't have to wait too long?"

"I brought my book so it wasn't a problem." Brianna grinned, handing over the keys, and then looked shamefaced. "I'm sorry about what I said earlier. I had no right to pass judgement like that. It's that time of the month and you know what I get like. Pete always says I'm like Jekyll and Hyde when I'm due on. He reckons he can see the evil change in my eyes."

"I know where you're coming from. God help anyone who tries to get between me and a bar of chocolate round that time. Besides, if it was you haring off into the wilds of County Down to see some piglet, I think I would have something to say too."

The two women giggled and then hugged quickly before Jess slid behind the wheel of Brianna's car. "Do you want me to drop you home?"

"No, you get going. A walk will do me good. Exercise is supposed to ease PMS, isn't it? Mind how you go and I'll see you tonight."

Jess slammed the door shut and gave her friend a wave before sliding the gear stick into drive and putting the pedal to the metal.

She only slowed once during her journey, having been flashed a warning by an oncoming vehicle that there were gardai up ahead. She took her foot off the accelerator and by the time she spied their vehicle half hidden on the side of the road by shrubs, she was driving at a sedate pace. A sideways glance as she drove past revealed they were far more interested in the contents of their sarnies than her. Good, she thought, revving up again; the last thing she needed was the holdup of being issued a speeding ticket. She doubted the gardai would grasp the gravity of her circumstances if she were to tell them she were speeding because she had to get to Ballymcguinness lickety-split to see a sick pig.

The rest of the journey was a blur of tarmac until she at last slowed to drive down the main street of Ballymcguinness. It was like *Groundhog Day*, she thought, casting her eyes left and right, soaking up the familiar sight of Katie Adams chuffing on a ciggy outside the hairdressers and Billy Peterson arranging his fruit and vege outside the grocers. Old Ned was sitting on the wall and he raised his stick as she drove past in greeting. There was something strangely comforting about the familiarity of it all, Jess thought, driving past the school. It was deserted; class must be in, she decided, as she wound her way out onto the country lanes that would take her to Glenariff.

Owen must have heard the car's tyres crunching on the gravel, she thought, wrenching the hand brake up and climbing out of the car. Either that or he had been peering out the living room window in anticipation of her arrival. She hoped it was the latter, comforted by the sight of his rangy frame clad in a familiar Aran jumper and cords tucked into his wellies as he strode toward her. Jess's eyes narrowed as something darted out behind him. It was Jemima. Arching her slender white neck, she fixed her beady black eyes on Jess and hissed.

Right, Jess thought, slamming the car door shut, in no mood for the snotty goose's shenanigans; two could play at that game. She met Jemima's imperious gaze with her own flinty one and sent a mental message that if she didn't watch it, she'd fix it so she saw her on her dinner plate this Christmas with lashings of stuffing and gravy. There was a momentary standoff and you could have heard a pin drop but it was Jemima who dropped her gaze first and, seemingly haven gotten the message, waddled off round the back of the cottage. "Just call me the goose whisperer," Jess muttered under her breath, turning her attention back to a bemused Owen.

"What was that all about?"

"Oh, nothing. Jemima and I just came to a private understanding, that's all." Jess smiled sweetly at him, waiting for him to tell her that he was glad she'd come. His face, however, had darkened.

"You didn't need to come all this way," he growled and then gesturing at the car, he asked, "Whose is that?"

"My friend Brianna's and yes actually, I did need to come." It wasn't the greeting she had been looking forward to as she risked life and limb driving up here and her own mood dipped. What had happened to, *"Jessica, thank God you came!"* Followed by a tight bear hug from which he would only break away to steer her over to the barn where they would talk in grave and hushed tones beside Wilbur's sickbed. Huh! she thought, taking in his furrowed brow; it didn't look like that was about to happen. Trying to impress the drama of the situation on him, she told him, "Wilbur's sick—there was no way I couldn't not come. I have to see him. Where is he?"

It was a stupid question, she admonished herself, beginning to head over in the direction of the barn. Where did she think he would be—tucked up in Owen's bed with a hot-water bottle, a thermometer hanging out of his mouth?

From behind her, Jess heard Owen mutter something and she swung round, not quite catching what it was he had said. By the look on his face, however, she was fairly certain she wasn't meant to have either. Okay then, she told herself, if that was the way he wanted to behave, he could sod off. Picking up her pace, she promptly stood in something brown and squishy. She didn't turn around to see whether he had noticed; instead, she hastily scraped her trainer back and forth on the grass before marching onwards. Asshole, she said to herself, as though it was his fault she had trod in whatever it was she had just smeared all over the grass. If he wanted to be an ass, well, that was his problem. Besides, it wasn't him she had driven all this way to see. Nope, she decided, pushing open the barn door; as far as she was concerned, Owen bloody Aherne could just stick his bad mood where the sun don't shine.

When she stepped inside, she was greeted with a cacophony of squealing from an overexcited mummy pig and her piglets housed inside the first stall. "Hello girls, calm down. It's only me, Jessica. I've come to see young Wilbur again." They paid no attention and carried on with their ruckus. Making her way down the barn, she saw the light under which sat Wilbur's little box and, raising her eyes heavenward, she asked that he, "Please, please be alright." Kneeling down next to the box, she was oblivious of the hardness or the cold of the concrete floor as she reached in and gently stroked the piglet's little tummy. Beneath her hand, she could feel his body trembling with the effort it took to raise his head to see who it was that was rubbing his tummy. "It's me, Wilbur—Jess. I've come back to see you."

He dropped his head back down apathetically and Jess watched his laboured breathing for a moment before sensing Owen's presence behind her. "What's wrong with him?" she asked, her own voice tremulous.

"Like I told you over the phone, I am fairly certain it's just a cold. There was no need for you to come all this way."

"Well, I'm here now, aren't I? So stop going on," Jess snapped. "And what do you mean when you say that you're *fairly* certain it's only a cold? Have you not had the vet out? What if it's the flu?" A thought crossed Jess's mind then and her hand shot off Wilbur's quivering stomach as though she had been scalded. What if he had swine flu? All her maternal instincts were momentarily forgotten because—and this caused her to break out in a sweat—what if she now had it! She cast her eyes around the barn, half expecting the men in white space suits to appear, announcing they were now in a no-go zone and that the barn had been cordoned off until the risk of infecting the outside world had cleared.

Owen must have read her mind. "It's not the flu. I am not going to be responsible for a pandemic across all of Ireland, so you can relax."

"Well, how can you be certain if you haven't had the vet out?" she asked, her mouth setting in a stubborn line.

"I do have some experience in looking after pigs, you know."

Jess knew she had reached a crossroads. She could continue to pursue the subject by stating that yes, he was a pig farmer but that did not make him a vet or she could have a bit of faith in him and concentrate on why she had come. She decided to let it go and turned her attention back to her reason for coming in the first place.

"Come on, Wilbur; rally round, mate. Do it for me, please."

"If it makes you feel better, I've given him the equivalent of paracetamol to take his temperature down and he's been having plenty of fluids." Owen shrugged. "Aside from keeping him warm, that's all I can do."

"What about chicken soup?"

"What?"

"Chicken soup—that's what you're supposed to feed people with fevers, isn't it?"

"You do know that Wilbur's a pig, don't you?"

"Yes, of course I do. I only thought..." Actually, she didn't know what she had thought. It was the shock of seeing Wilbur so poorly, that was all. She felt tears beginning to sting her eyes and was annoyed with herself. The last thing she wanted to do was show weakness in front of Owen. He wasn't a tea-and-sympathy sort of a guy.

True to form, though, he decided to prove her wrong and his permafrown softened. "Why don't we go up to the house? I'll make you a cuppa. You probably need one after the drive up here."

Jess swiped angrily at her eyes. Why did he always have to turn around and be nice just when she'd decided once and for all that he was a total arse? Standing up, she picked the bits of hay stuck to her elephant pants off. He was right; she was parched but not quite ready to defrost. "I don't want to put you to any trouble," she stated with a formal sniff.

"Aye, it's no bother. A spot of company would be good," Owen replied, walking out of the barn without a backward glance.

Jess stood there for a moment longer, thinking back to the last meal they'd shared. He could have fooled her. And did he mean he liked *her* company or just company in general? "The man's a complete mystery to me, Wilbur," she muttered, bending down to give him one last scratch behind his ear. "I'll come back down to see you in a little while; rest up now, little one."

The Aga was on as Jess stepped inside the kitchen and the warmth made her feel instantly at home. Owen was bustling around at the kitchen bench, a study of domesticity as he asked, "White and one? That's how you take your tea, isn't it?"

"Yes please," Jess replied and not waiting to be asked, she pulled out a chair and sat down at the table. Her nose twitched as she realised it wasn't just the warmth from the Aga that gave the kitchen such a homely feel; it was the smell of fresh baking permeating the room. When Owen turned round a moment later, he had a plate of buttered scones in one hand and her cup of tea in the other.

"You didn't make those, did you?" Jess asked, her mouth dropping open.

"Aye," he replied, placing the tea down in front of her and the scones in the middle of the table before pulling a seat out opposite her and sitting down.

"How on earth did you learn how to bake scones? They are supposed to be a Kiwi staple right up there with pikelets and I can't even bake them." Mind you, thought Jess, helping herself to one, that wasn't saying much.

"Me Ma. Amy wasn't interested in cooking and the like, only licking the bowl, but I used to follow Ma round the kitchen like a shadow. She was forever telling me to get out from under her feet."

Jess soaked in this information, trying to imagine a much younger version of the man before her trailing around after his mother as she whipped up wholesome treats for her family. She couldn't so she bit into her scone instead. The butter dribbled down her chin; it was delicious. There was nothing so comforting as a cup of hot sugary tea and a scone, she thought, wiping her chin with the back of her hand.

"Not quite chicken soup but I think it will do the trick," Owen said with a smirk.

"They're fantastic," Jess mumbled between bites. "My Mum's a great baker, too. She makes these biscuits called Yo-Yos that are my absolute favourite. They're horrifically fattening, though, and a complete cholesterol nightmare but so, so yummy. I didn't inherit her baking gene, I'm afraid." She shrugged. "I'm a lost cause. I couldn't even get my fudge to set in third form home ec."

"It's not hard; it's basic science. I'll show you sometime." Owen's normally tan colouring turned ruddy and before Jess could respond, he changed the subject. "Any word for definite on when the article will run?"

"Niall, that's my editor, said it will be going in the weekend paper this Saturday, October the twentieth. I was going to ring you and let you know that it was definitely going ahead but you beat me to it."

"Thirty years to the day."

"Yes, thirty years to the day. I think I mentioned that Niall felt running it on the anniversary of Amy's death made her story all the more poignant." Jess cringed, seeing his face, and instinctively reached across the table to rest her hand on his arm. "Sorry, poignant sounds so trite, I know, but it does seem right somehow to run it then, don't you think?"

"Aye."

Her hand resting on his arm suddenly seemed a trite gesture in itself and removing it, she busied herself picking at the remains of her scone. "I've arranged for a copy of the *Express* to be couriered to you on the Saturday morning."

She desperately wanted to ask how *he* really felt about having it all raked up but his expression didn't invite the question, so they sat in silence for a few moments, each lost in thought. For Jess's part, she was surprised to realise that on this visit, she hadn't felt the ghost of Amy between them until now. In fact, she hadn't thought of her at all and she hoped that didn't make her disrespectful in any way; it was just that her purpose for coming had nothing to do with Amy.

It was true that life did go on but it startled her to realise that perhaps for Owen his sister's shadow was always there. When he looked up from his teacup, he had obviously decided to change the subject. "So what have you been doing with yourself since I saw you in Malahide?"

It was a poor attempt at small talk, Jess thought, gazing at the bottom of her own cup. "Oh not much—working, catching up with my girlfriends." She was reluctant to mention Nick, deciding it was none of his business anyway. "What about you?"

"Looking after the pigs."

Well, if ever there was a conversation stopper, that was it. Jess shifted uncomfortably in her seat before helping herself to one last scone. As she hoed it down, "Barracuda" erupted from the depths of her handbag. Owen's eyes widened as she fished it out and put a stop to the blaring tune:

"What the feck do you think you are doing at the pig farmer's again?" a voice shrilled down the line at her.

It was Nora.

Adopting a sweetness and light tone, Jess replied, "Yes, I got here without any problems. Thanks again for letting me use the car. I'll have it back to you by six tonight at the latest. Bye and thanks again." She thought she heard Nora shriek her name as she hung up but she couldn't be sure.

"That's an interesting choice of ringtone."

"What? Oh yeah. That was my friend Nora's idea of a little joke. It's beginning to wear thin. I can't bake and I am pretty much a technophobe, so now you know all my secrets."

Owen looked blank but Jess couldn't be bothered explaining. She suddenly felt drained by the day's events and with a sinking sensation, she knew she'd only be able to avoid Nora for so long before she got short shrift from her. As for Owen—well, his moods were like the shifting tides and she had had enough. "Look, like I said, I have to have the car back for six so I might just go out and say my goodbyes to Wilbur now before I head away, if that's okay?"

"Aye, fine by me," Owen said, not looking at her as he got up and began clearing the table.

Jess knelt quietly next to Wilbur, who despite the amazing ruckus coming from the pen near the entrance, was sound asleep, making little snuffling noises here and there. Her heart melted. "I really hope you make it, little buddy, but I think this time it's going to be goodbye for good. I can't see myself coming back here anytime soon so you are just going to have to be strong on your own." Blinking back the tears that threatened, she got up and turned to walk out of the barn. Owen was blocking the entrance way with a peculiar expression on his face.

"Why did you come here today?" he asked, not moving aside.

"You know why I came."

He was studying her so intently she had to look away.

"I came to see Wilbur."

"Was it just Wilbur you came to see?" His voice was gruff, belying what really lay behind his words.

It was then that Jess knew if she were to look up, Owen would kiss her.

Chapter Fifteen

THE INTENSITY OF FEELING that swept through Jess as Owen's lips connected with hers took her by surprise and she was glad that his arms had looped their way around her back, supporting her and stopping her from falling. The sounds around them faded out and the only thing she was conscious of was the sensation of his tongue as it gently explored her mouth. Her arms wound their way over his shoulders, snaking up to the back of his neck, where her fingers tangled themselves in his hair. She pressed her body closer to his, feeling his hardness growing.

The sound of a cough followed by a cheerful male voice saw her eyes snap open.

"Ahem. I hope I'm not interrupting anything."

At the sight of a kindly looking man with unruly grey hair and a stomach straining to be freed from his shirt, they broke away from each other like two cats who had just had a bucket of cold water tossed over them.

"Um, Jessica Baré, this is Michael Riordan, our local vet."

Jess noticed the requisite *All Creatures Great and Small* brown leather case; of course he was. Michael Riordan held out his hand and Jess took it, receiving a firm handshake.

"I decided to take your advice after all and give him a call just to be on the safe side."

The look that flashed between Michael and Owen didn't go unnoticed by Jess. She was fairly certain she was being humoured.

Michael's prognosis was just as Owen had said: a common cold. He looked at Jess with a twinkle in his eye as he told her that considering Wilbur's size, he was doing remarkably well. "Aye, he'll grow into a fine young boar, mark my words," he stated as they followed him out to his jeep and Jess could have sworn she saw him wink at Owen.

She was distracted from pursuing this train of thought by the sudden chill that coursed through her. The sun had dropped low in the sky. It must be getting on for four, which meant she was going to have to head away if she was to keep her promise and get the car back to Brianna in time.

She was tapping her foot impatiently, not knowing what would happen between her and Owen now the moment had passed while he and Michael conferred over by his jeep. Both men suddenly paused mid-conversation, startled by the burst of song emanating from her handbag once more.

"Sorry, it's my stupid phone," Jess said, retrieving it and in her haste to shut it up, she quickly answered, wishing she hadn't as she heard Nick's voice.

"Jess, hi. I am sorry I had to head away so early this morning. I'm on my way back from Cork now and I thought if you were still at my place, I'd stop off and grab us some Thai from the place I was telling you about."

Oh shit, Jess thought, taking a few steps away; of all the times for him to phone. "Um, I'm not at your place, actually. I'm in Ballymcguinness," she squeaked.

"Where the hell is Ballymcguinness?"

"It's in the North, County Down to be exact. I, uh, I am following up on a story I have been working on." She tried to ignore Owen, who was staring over at her with a perplexed frown. Luckily, Michael Riordan hadn't finished bending his ear and she was relieved when he focused his attention back on the affable vet.

She lowered her voice. "Nick, my friend Brianna has invited us around to their place for dinner on Saturday night. It's short notice, I know, so if..."

"What was that? Jess, can you speak up? I can hardly hear you—Jaysus, you really must be in the back of beyond with reception like that," Nick interrupted.

Jess repeated herself, raising her voice only marginally before adding, "If you can't make it, I understand." She was half hoping he would say he was busy, allowing her to delay the inevitable confrontation between him and Brianna but he didn't. Besides, after what had just happened outside the barn, she no longer knew how she felt about him.

"There's nothing I can't cancel on Saturday. I'd love to come but is there any chance of seeing you tonight? I've meetings in Dublin tomorrow then I'm staying overnight in Cork tomorrow night because I've got some serious schmoozing with potential investors around the golf course first thing on

Saturday morning. I was kind of hoping we could finish tonight what we didn't really get to start." He gave an apologetic laugh.

Jess cringed. She couldn't believe it had been less than twenty-four hours since she'd been in his bed and that less than half an hour ago, she'd been snogging someone else! What was that saying, feast or famine? And what did that make her? No, she wouldn't go there, she decided, shaking her head; she had to focus on the fact he was going to come to Brie's for dinner. That meant she would have to come clean with both of them. It wouldn't be fair to put either of them on the spot like that. Jess rubbed at her temple. Her head had begun to throb and the one thing she did know for sure was that she couldn't face seeing Nick tonight. She needed to sort out how she felt.

"I won't be back until late and then I have to type up an assignment I've been working on; it's due first thing tomorrow." The lie tripped easily off her tongue and she noticed that she was once more the focus of Owen's shrewd gaze. The vet had climbed into his jeep and with a wave and a clunking of gears was heading off down the drive.

"What's all that noise?" Nick asked.

"It must be my phone. You're right, the reception is bad. Look, I'll have to go." She didn't give him a chance to say goodbye, hanging her phone up and tossing it in her bag as if she had been handling a hot potato, only to fish it back out to switch it off. She didn't want to talk to anyone else.

Looking at Owen, she felt suddenly self-conscious at the thought of what would happen now. It was kind of like the nervous anticipation she'd felt as a teenager on a date at the movies, waiting for that arm to slide along the back of the seat to rest on her shoulder. She also felt rather silly at his having dragged the local vet out just to appease her.

"Important call, was it?" He raised an eyebrow and his stance with his hands in his pockets was one of feigned indifference.

"No, it was nobody." She knew he knew she was lying and the awkwardness in the air between them grew palpable. Jess decided to change tack. "You didn't need to do that, you know—call out the vet. It probably cost you a fortune just to be told what you already knew. I would have trusted your judgement." She inclined her head in the direction of the retreating jeep as it turned on to the main road.

"Aye, well, Michael's an old family friend. He doesn't charge through the nose and the problem is I don't trust myself."

What the hell was that supposed to mean? Jess wondered, looking at the ground and scuffing at the loose shingle with her sneakered toes. She was suddenly aware of what she was wearing—hardly the femme fatale, dressed in her elephant suit and trainers, but then she hadn't expected to be accosted at the barn door either. Or had she? Was Brianna right about her real motivation for coming here today? And what about Nick? She suddenly felt overwhelmed. She didn't know what the heck she was doing or what she was playing at. All she did know was that she had to put some space between her and Owen.

The need to clear her head and get some perspective on what had transpired that afternoon and how it had made her feel was overwhelming. She couldn't face pussyfooting around Owen and his cryptic mixed messages. "I, um, I have to get going." Fishing her keys out of her pocket, she jangled them purposefully.

"Aye, I suppose you do."

So he wasn't going to make this easy for her then, she thought, not knowing why she was surprised. When in the short space of time that she had known him had he made anything easy?

"Right, well, let me know how Wilbur gets on, won't you? I'll send you a copy of the paper as soon as it's gone to print." She was playing the professional, deliberately re-building the wall between them before he could do the same to her.

He nodded and Jess turned away, cutting a slow path over to the Golf, half hoping to feel his hand on her shoulder stopping her—making up her mind for her. But as she slid into the driver's seat, she saw that he was still standing in exactly the same spot he had been a moment earlier, with his hands still shoved in his pockets.

Well, stuff you! she thought, wrenching the key and, as the car roared into life, she felt as though she had imagined the whole scene in the barn entrance. Pushing her foot down hard on the accelerator and haring off down the drive and out of Owen's complicated and messy life in a hailstorm of loose shingle, she wondered whether perhaps she had. Jess didn't see the girl with the black hair rest her hand gently on Owen's shoulder before he turned and walked heavily back inside the house.

THE DRIVE BACK TO DUBLIN was non-eventful and Jess pulled into Brianna's driveway at five fifty-five, pleased to have kept her word in getting the car back on time. Despite heading out to a meeting that evening, Brianna invited her in for a glass of wine, eager to hear how her day had gone.

"Do you want to stay for dinner? Sure, I don't have to leave for over an hour yet and we're not having anything fancy—just Spag-Bog but there's plenty to go round. I always make enough to feed an army."

Jess wasn't hungry and she wasn't really in the mood to talk about what had happened, not even with Brianna. Besides, truth be told, she was the teensiest bit peeved that she'd blabbed to Nora about her whereabouts for the day. "No thanks, Brie. I'll have this and get going."

Brianna had poured them both a glass of red from the bottle of pinot noir she'd had opened on the bench. She liked a drop while she cooked and they were sitting at the dinner table, the smell of onion and garlic heavy on the air. The relaxing scene was shattered by a bloodcurdling scream permeating the house. It had come from upstairs and Jess's eyes swung toward the stairs in alarm.

Brianna rolled her eyes. "Oh, pay no attention. It's Harry's bath time; poor old Pete will be drowned, so he will."

Jess managed a small smile but tonight not even Harry's shenanigans could lift her mood and she quickly downed the rest of her glass. She didn't want to intrude on the Price family's weeknight routine. What she really wanted to do was head home, change into her pyjamas, and open up a bottle of red of her own. She pictured herself curled up on the couch with a large glass with which to sip away on while she watched a mind-numbing TV show she would eventually nod off in front of.

Brianna interrupted her thoughts. "So come on, then, don't be holding out on me—how did you get on today? How was your pig?"

For a moment, Jess wasn't sure which pig Brianna was referring to—Owen or Wilbur?

"Is he going to live?"

Ah, Wilbur then. "Yes, I think he probably will."

"Why so down then? Did something happen with your man?"

"He's not my man and I'm not down. I'm just tired and I had best be leaving you to it," she answered, standing up and pushing her chair in just as another scream shrilled. Both women looked toward the stairs this time. "That sounded serious—you better go and give them a hand up there."

"Harry's developed this fear of the water since he snuck down the stairs and saw *Jaws* on the telly a few weeks ago. It's all Pete's fault; you know how he loves his old horrors, so he can bloody well deal with it."

Jess knew for all her fighting talk, Brianna would be up those stairs, sorting the two men in her life out the moment she'd gone.

"I'll phone you tomorrow. We'll talk then, okay?"

"Alright then; that sounds good." Brianna looked hard at her friend. "Are you sure nothing happened today, Jess? Because you look awfully pale."

"No, I'm fine, truly—just worn out from the driving. I'm not used to it and thanks again for the use of the car."

Brianna followed her to the front door, pulling it open before giving her friend a quick hug goodbye. "Do you want me to get Pete to run you down to the station? He'd be glad of an excuse to escape."

"No, it's only down the road. I'll be fine." Jess was looking forward to stretching her legs after having sat in a car for the last couple of hours. As she headed down the path, Brianna called out after her, "Oh, I nearly forgot to ask. Did Nick get hold of you? And are we on for Saturday night?"

Jess stopped; she'd forgotten all about Saturday night. Crapity, crap, crap, it was all getting too much. Brianna and her campaign, Nick and his development, Owen bloody Aherne and poor wee Wilbur, Nora on the rampage—when did her life get so complicated? She knew she should go back inside and fill Brianna in properly on what development it was that Nick was working on but she simply couldn't face any more drama in her day. "Yes, Nick's free. We'll be there. You go back inside; you're letting all the heat out," she called back, hoping against hope that the topic of Bray Community Centre wouldn't rear its head on Saturday night.

"Great. Is sevenish alright?"

"Sevenish is fine."

Brianna disappeared back inside and shut the door.

LATER THAT NIGHT, JESS fulfilled her fantasy by curling up on the couch in her cosy flannelette pyjamas, a glass of red in her hand as she tried to lose herself in the god-awful reality TV show she'd tuned in to. It was no good, though; it couldn't hold her attention. She didn't feel like doing a Bridget Jones and wallowing in the mess she was making of things, either. No, she frowned, she was more in an angry woman Melissa Etheridge sort of a mood. Sod Owen and his mixed bloody messages. She got up and began rifling through her CDs, looking forward to joining Melissa in belting out "Like the Way I Do."

The phone rang just as she pulled it out of the rack and Jess sighed, looking at it with dread as she debated whether or not to answer it. It was probably Nora and, deciding she might as well get the lecture over and done with, she reached over and picked it up.

"Jessica, darling, it's Mum phoning to see how your dinner date went."

God! The perfect end to the perfect day. Jess wrinkled her nose before having a big slug on her wine. "Hi, Mum. It was fine, thanks." As the wine slid down her throat, she knew that *fine* just wouldn't cut the mustard, not with her mother.

"Fine? What does that mean? And are you drinking?"

Jess took a deep breath and her voice came out in one big long sigh. "A glass of wine, yes. It doesn't make me an alcoholic, Mum, and what I meant was that I had a nice time. Nick cooked a lovely meal and he was a real gentleman. We will be seeing each other again on Saturday because Brianna's invited us over for dinner."

"She's drinking alone, Frank, and give me patience—it's like getting blood out of a stone trying to hold a conversation with your daughter. Listen to me, my girl, I didn't put us on a family and friends calling plan to have you fob me off. I want the details. What did he cook you? What wine did he serve? Did you have, ahem..."—her mother tittered girlishly—"*dessert?*"

Jess cringed at the pathetic double entendre. "Mum! That is none of your business." Besides which, she wasn't really sure her mother would understand if she said sort of.

"Alright, alright—no need to be coy. At least tell me what you ate."

"He cooked roast lamb and it was delicious, dessert was crème brulee, and he served a red with the lamb and a white that offset the sweetness of the brulee. He knows all about wine and stuff," she added dully.

"Well, for someone who has been wined and dined and treated like a lady, you don't sound very enthusiastic. What's the matter?"

Before she could stop herself, it was out of her mouth. "I've just had a big day, that's all. I drove up to Ballymcguinness again because Wilbur the little runt I befriended got sick." As soon as she'd finished her sentence, she knew she'd made a big mistake in confiding what she'd been up to. There was a deathly silence down the other end of the line and then an ear-splitting shriek sounded. Jess held the phone away from her ear, completely unprepared for what she heard next.

"You're doing it again, Jessica Jane Baré. You're damn well doing it again. Frank, I told you this would happen!"

"Calm down, Mum! I have no idea what you are on about."

"You're falling for the pig farmer with the past instead of the property developer who could offer you a future—that, my girl, is what I am on about."

"No, I'm not." Jess flushed. "Wilbur was sick so I went to see him, that's all, and the article I wrote about Owen's sister Amy being killed in a bombing during the Troubles is running this weekend. I was glad of the chance to tell him in person because the story coincides with it being the thirtieth anniversary since it happened. It's called being sensitive to your source, Mother, and that's it—end of story. There is no reason for me to see him ever again and anyway, I just told you I am seeing Nick on Saturday for dinner."

"That as may be but I know how you work, Jessica. Your heart's not in it anymore. I can hear it in your voice. This pig farmer fella tells you his sob story and you melt. If Nick were to announce he was going in for a double leg amputation on Monday or, or oh I don't know, that his cat was terminally ill, then you'd be all over him but unfortunately he has no problems, no issues to work through. He is normal. N-O-R-M-A-L, Jessica." Marian spelt it out and then carried on, "Well, I am not having it! This time, I am not going to stand by and let you sabotage things for yourself. You are too long in the tooth to mess about like this."

"Gee, thanks, Mum."

"Don't be sarcastic with me, young lady." There was the sound of heavy breathing down the phone and then the muffled sound of her parents conferring in the background. Jess realised her mother must have put her hand over the receiver. This was not boding well, she thought and in the next moment was proved right.

"It was going to happen sooner and now I am glad I decided to make it sooner."

"What?"

"I have retired, Jessica. It was time for me to hang up my socks. As of last Friday, I became a free woman."

Jess refrained from adding *shouldn't that be knickers she'd hung up* but she didn't think her mother would find it funny at the moment; besides, she was getting an uneasy feeling in the pit of her stomach that she really wasn't going to feel like joking around shortly.

"I felt it in my water. I knew that you were going to need me more than Smith & Caugheys does. So, I've talked to Dad and your sister and we've all decided it's for the best. I am coming to Ireland."

"What?"

"I'm coming to Ireland."

"No, Mum, you can't!" Jess wailed in horror.

"Oh yes, I can, my girl. Your sister's taught me how to surf the Net and I've been gurgling all sorts of bargain return flights that I can book online. Your father's insistent I go budget now that I've retired."

God spare me the computer jargon, Jess pleaded, making a mental note to ring Kelly and give her a mouthful once she managed to talk their mother out of coming over.

"In fact, I have my eye on a deal that could have me at your place by the middle of next week."

Good grief, she really was serious. Jess flailed around, desperately groping for reasons she couldn't possibly come. "What about Dad? He might have said it was okay for you to come here but he would, wouldn't he? You know how useless he is at looking after himself. He'd never cope without you." Yes, that was a good one; Jess's tensed shoulders relaxed as she finished playing her winning *Dad can't even boil an egg* hand.

"Women always rally round a man left to fend for himself and if they don't, the neighbours will look after him. There's your sister, too; she can help out and I will leave him plenty of frozen dinners. He won't even know I'm gone."

"Well, well..." Jess blustered, "Well, what about Kelly and Brian? They'll never manage the kids without you to help out."

"Your sister and her husband will just have to miss their date night for once. Might do them good to give that side of things a rest or I am going to wind up with more grandchildren than I know what to do with," Marian muttered.

The fear was building in Jess's stomach like a volcano about to erupt. She couldn't think of anything else that might make her mother change her mind. It was last-resort time. "Put Dad on for me!"

"Don't bellow like that, Jessica; it's unladylike and a please wouldn't go astray—Frank! Your daughter wants a word."

"Hello, sweetheart." His tone was wary.

"Dad, you can't let her come here, you just can't. You know it wouldn't work. Say something to stop her."

Frank sighed. "Jess, love, you know as well as I do that when your mother sets her mind to something, there is no stopping her, and I am telling you there is no stopping her. She is coming to Dublin and to be fair, it's not just about sorting out whatever it is you're playing at with these two fellows. She wants to see where you live. You've been gone a long time, you know."

"Yeah, I know, Dad." She didn't add that there was a reason for that.

"To be honest with you, she needs a holiday. What with working full-time and helping Kelly out these last few years, well, she deserves a decent break. Your sister runs her ragged with those kids. It won't do Kelly any harm to have to stand on her own two feet for a bit, either; it might make her appreciate just what Marian does for her. And it will do you and her good to spend some quality time together on your home turf."

Crikey, that was the longest speech she had heard her father make since Kel's wedding. "Well, I don't think it's a good idea. In fact, I think it's a terrible idea. Besides, she's just told me she's retired so I don't know what you're going on about her needing a rest for. If it's a holiday she's after, well, Fiji is a lot bloody closer." God, what a nightmare. Jess got up, cradling the phone in the crook of her neck and shoulder as she topped up her glass. "If she comes here, she'll do nothing but criticise me the whole time. You know what she's like."

"Love, your mother just wants to see where her eldest child has been living for the past decade. You are making a mountain out of a molehill."

"No, she doesn't. What she wants is for me to marry money and breed. She's never approved of any of the choices I've made—not with work or with men. Why do you think I love living here so much? There's nobody going on at me all the time—that's why." She sounded like a petulant child even to her own ears but she couldn't help it.

"Listen to yourself! Grow up, Jessica!"

Chastened, Jess felt like she was twelve years old again, caught pinching the milk money for sweets, as he carried on. "Do you know Marian's friends all roll their eyes behind her back when she starts in on the 'our Jessica's got her own column in a Dublin newspaper, you know' because they've heard it so many times. She just wants you to meet someone who you can make a commitment with. What mother doesn't want to see their child settled? And look at it this way: this might be your golden opportunity to prove to her that you are capable of making the right decision all by yourself." The spark of anger dissipated and he deftly changed the subject. "Anyway, enough of all that. When does the story you wrote about the young girl who died in that bombing run? I'd like to read it."

"It goes to print this Saturday—thirty years to the day that Amy was killed."

On the other side of the world in his brick house in Hillsborough, Frank Baré sat shaking his head. "Do you know, I remember Philip Sherry telling us about the bombings and troubles over there in Northern Ireland on the six o'clock news. It's hard to believe it was thirty years ago and that you are all grown up and living over in that part of the world now."

"I live in the Republic of Ireland, though, Dad; the Troubles never really touched the South."

"I find that hard to believe. It's all one land mass, isn't it?" He didn't give her a chance to answer. "Will you be going up to see your chap in Ballypintofguinness, the one who has your mother's knickers in such a knot, when it runs? It won't be easy for him seeing it all laid out in print like that, I shouldn't imagine."

"Bally*mc*guiness and I've told you before he is not my chap. No, I won't be going up to see him because he hasn't asked me to, so make sure you tell Mum that. Owen's a very private person and he wouldn't appreciate me just showing up." She studied the hangnail on her thumb. "His father's in a retirement home nearby so I think he will probably spend the day with him."

"Ah, he's a loyal son. I like that."

"And a right moody bugger to boot."

"Pardon?"

"Nothing."

"You will be sending us a copy of the article, though, won't you?" he asked again.

Once a month, Jess faithfully sent copies of her weekly column cut out of the paper to her parents. "If Mum's such a whiz kid on the computer these days, you two could always read it online."

"Your mother's relationship with the Internet is very new and I have a feeling it won't last. Besides, she likes to have a hard copy of your column so that she can pass it round her friends."

That was news to Jess, and she felt herself softening a little where her mother was concerned. "Really? Well, okay then, I'll post it off as soon as it's run."

"From what you read to me last time we spoke, it sounded like you were trying to get a moral point across to your readers, not just relaying to them what happened. Am I right?"

Jess thought for a moment. Her dad's perception amazed her because until he'd mentioned it, she hadn't realised that was exactly what she had tried to do. "I hadn't thought about it like that but I suppose that was what made it so special to write. It sounds a bit pretentious but I don't usually get the opportunity to be thought-provoking and I hope I have managed it. Maybe it will make people contemplate the ongoing effects war has on innocent families because what happened to Amy should never happen again in Ireland. I want her to become real to the reader and not just a casualty in an old fight." Brianna's face sprang to mind. "My friend summed it up when she said hearing what Owen had to say made her want to go and hug her son. Families are just too precious to be destroyed by one senseless act." As she finished her impassioned speech, she realised Frank Baré was indeed a clever man. He had just set her up.

"Exactly, Jessica. Think about what you just said when your mother arrives."

She knew he was right and she loved her mother—of course she did—but she was just so damn annoying at times. "Point taken."

"Good. Anyway, Mum wants another word with you so I'll say cheerio, sweetheart."

As she listened to her mother burble on excitedly about her impending trip and how she couldn't wait to visit Trinity College and Dublin Castle and all the other sights, the realisation that there was nothing she could say or do that would change things sank in. She was coming to Dublin whether Jess liked it or not.

Chapter Sixteen

ON SATURDAY MORNING, the twentieth of October, 2013—thirty years to the day that sixteen-year-old Amy Aherne from Glenariff Farm in Ballymcguinness was killed—her story ran in the *Dublin Express*. It was spread over two pages in the colour weekend supplement and it made for an arresting read:

Amy's Story
By Jessica Baré

This story starts with a children's book published in 1969, a fairy tale bought by a mother in Northern Ireland on behalf of her youngest child to give to his sister for Christmas 1976. It's no fairy story, though, nor is it just the sad relaying of brutal facts that ended in Lisburn in 1983. It might have finished there, though, if not for her family and had that little book not found its way to me. I don't mean to sound proprietary because neither the book nor the story I am going to tell you belongs to me. This is Amy's story and in order to tell it to you, I have to begin where it all began.

My full name is Jessica Jane Baré or Second-hand Jane, as my friends have started to call me. Why? Well, it's because I love the pre-loved—just like that old cliché, someone else's junk is my treasure. My real passion, though, is for old children's books—it's something about the smell of them, I think. It conjures up the innocence of a bygone era of children called Dick and Ann and tea at five o'clock, trapped forever within their much-thumbed pages. I covet the Ladybird Series 606D books in particular—the classic fairy tales every child grows up with: Rapunzel, Cinderella, The Elves and the Shoemaker, and most pertinent of all Snow White and the Seven Dwarfs. It wasn't the bold black typeface, however, that had me poring over the books as a child and hoarding them as an adult but Eric Winters' fabulously detailed illustrations. They brought those stories to life and were the source of a childhood fascination with witches, fairies, princes, and princesses. The delicate colours of the foxgloves planted by the thatched cottage's flag stone path, the grand white Bavarian styled castles in which as a little girl I had no doubt I would one day grow up to live in, were a world away from the suburban pocket of New Zealand I inhabited. When a young imagination is fuelled, though, the impossible becomes possible. Good versed evil within those pages and always won. If only we could hold onto that analogy forever.

I often wonder, when I open my books to find another boy or girl's mark inside, whether that faceless child felt the magic, too. Who were they, these little people who had scribbled their names inside books long since forgotten by adulthood?

Snow White and the Seven Dwarfs arrived with neither pomp nor ceremony but rather by mail thanks to an online auction I was determined to win. Inside the tatty cover, in precise, big print was the dedication:

To Amy with love from Owen Christmas 1973

Beneath this, scrawled in orange pencil pressed deep into the cardboard, she had forever made her mark:

Amy Aherne
Glenariff Farm
Ballymcguinness
6 years old

As I looked at the scribbled inscription, I began to wonder. Who was she, this six-year-old girl from the seventies? Was she a dreamer like me, who was now learning the hard way that princes don't just pop up every day and that there are an awful lot of frogs out there? Or perhaps she was a realist who didn't believe in a man supplying her with a ready-made happy ever after? Might we have been friends if we had met? Where was she now? What had she grown up to do with her life?

I felt a compulsion that was almost a physical tug. It was one that I have never felt before—this overwhelming need to know. I would find her and tell the story that lay within the name inscribed in the storybook. What I found, though, was not at all what I expected. Amy didn't leave school early and take the first job she was offered so she could buy records, clothes, and makeup like her girlfriends. She didn't wind up pushing a pram before her time either. Nor did she pack her bags and head off to the city to share a grotty flat with other intellectuals while she studied hard and solved the problems of the world. She didn't put a foot on the bottom rung of the corporate ladder to begin her ascent, all the while trying to fit a life in around the demands of her chosen career. The full moon never shone down on her while she partied the night away in a bikini and sarong on a Thai beach with her drunken compatriots. As for meeting Mr Right, well, he never got the chance to show up, so she never knew what it would have been like to set up home with him and look after their babushka doll babies together.

The choices we take for granted as ours to make, the mistakes we know will push us off course along the way that only make the getting back on track all the sweeter, all of that was taken away from Amy in the futile tit for tatting of a war that could never really be won.

I began my search for who this little girl was and who she had become with the high-tech precision of a bungling journalist who resorted to the white pages and a foot-in-mouth phone call to Owen Aherne. The four-year-old boy who had long ago given his sister the book I held in my possession was now a man in his forties, who still lived at the family farm in Ballymcguinness. After the shock of a blundering journalist with the wrong accent barging into his past, we figured out the book's journey away from Amy to an eBid purchase in 2013 began with the need for extra spends and a sale at a church fete. That sorted, he laid the facts bare:

Amy was two years older than me and she was turning into a bit of a tearaway. The day it happened, she'd told our Ma that she was going to her friend Evie's house and Evie told her Ma she was coming to ours. Instead, the girls caught the bus up to Lisburn.

Amy had her eye on a lad who worked up that way, so Evie told us later. She'd met him at a dance and was determined to see him again, even though according to Evie he didn't want to know her. We never found anything else out about him apart from the fact he was a Catholic boy who'd had the gall to show his face at a dance in Banbridge. The local lads took umbrage at this boy talking to one of "their" girls and he'd received a kicking for his trouble. I think that for Amy, it smacked of Romeo and Juliet—an impossible love in her eyes, which made her chase after him and read all the things sixteen-year-old girls read in to situations where there is nothing but a busted nose and broken ribs to read at all.

Things were bad back in '83. So she knew that there was no way in hell she'd have been allowed to go anywhere near Belfast or the like if she'd asked. Ballymcguinness is a dot of a place, though, claustrophobic for young people. The girls had itchy feet and the element of risk in going somewhere they knew full well they had no business in going was exciting to them. It would give them a bit of kudos with their pals—something to show off to them about. They were six foot tall and bulletproof. Besides, we were all so bloody naïve, tucked away from the worst of it all. The fighting always seemed to be happening somewhere else, not in our backyard.

Evie told us later that she'd left her bag in the coffee shop they'd been hanging out in for most of the day. Amy had been eyeing up this lad she fancied as her Romeo, who worked across the road from the café at a garage. They'd sat smoking cigarettes, trying to look sophisticated, drinking manky, bottomless coffee until it was time to get the bus home. Evie ran back down the road to fetch her bag while Amy waited at the bus stop outside O'Hara's Butchers. There'd be murder to pay at home if they missed the last bus and got caught out.

It was a Loyalist bombing that went wrong. A meeting was due to be held in the back of the butcher's. Christopher O'Hara, an IRA hard man in his day, and his cronies were supposed to be gathered there except they weren't and seven innocent people, including my sister, were killed instead. We were told she died instantly and that she wouldn't have suffered, which was a blessing for her but of no comfort to me Ma, who spent the rest of her life suffering. It's a hard thing to accept that you've no body left to bury, just the pieces left behind. Me Da was an armchair Unionist back then who liked to spout off with his pals down at his local, Murtagh's Pub, on a Saturday afternoon but after what happened to Amy, he never stepped foot in there again—he lost his spark.

Owen's since returned to the North to take over the running of the family's farm after having lived abroad for many years. He has found a sense of peace in returning to a simpler life he once knew well. His mother passed away eight years ago as a woman who never recovered from her loss and his father has retired to a home in Dundrum, a man who never recovered from his losses. What happened to the Ahernes' daughter was not their fault but parents will always second-guess their every action that culminated in an event that was ultimately out of their control.

The cottage where the family lived has been renovated and modernised but you can still feel Amy's presence there. She's not just in the photos that dot the fireplace mantel—a visual reminder of a girl who was loved—there is a sense of her everywhere.

So who had she been, this young woman hovering on the brink of adulthood and a world that was hers for the taking?

Well, like the story goes, once upon a time, there was a child who was fair of face. She lived in a pretty cottage with her mother, father, and younger brother. She had lots of friends and she liked to play dress-ups and hold tea parties for her dolls. Here was a little girl who loved to read, to dream and to dance—she was to her family and friends a delight who made them smile each and every day. As she grew and the hormones exploded, she dipped her toe in and began to test the waters of independence: a normal teenager who loved her cat and her best friend, ogled pop star's posters, played her records too loud and dreamt the big dreams of the adolescent while her mammy told her to get in the bathroom and wash that muck off her face! Everything was new and fresh and exciting and all the more so for not being allowed to do it.

The Amy I found was a beautiful little girl who was full of life and laughter; she would become a young woman on the cusp of a life that could have been exceptional or could have been ordinary—it was ripe for the picking but either way, it should have been hers for the taking.

She left behind a cat that pined, friends who would never forget her, and a family who were broken—blown into pieces like she was. I've since taken her book home where it belongs and I've told her story and in doing so, I know that Owen and his father hope that Amy's legacy is one that will make you—whoever you are—think about what really matters.

The sixteen-year-old girl she grew to be was motivated by fashion, not by politics, and the depth of the secular hatred whispered about by some and shouted about by others bewildered her.

"We're all human beings so why can't we all just get along?" she once asked her Da to which he replied, "It's not that straightforward, Amy, love."

"Why not? It doesn't seem that complicated to me." And with a shrug of her shoulders, she walked away.

Sometimes it's the most simplistic ideologies that make the most sense.

JESS'S BOSS NIALL, who normally took the hardnosed route when it came to bestowing praise on his journalists, in case they took it to heart and asked for a pay rise, telephoned her late that morning to congratulate her on a job well done. He informed her that the paper was going to be inundated with reader's responses to her story because Letters to the Editor were already flowing into his inbox thick and fast.

"It might make some of those buggers up there so keen to stir it all up again think," he'd growled down the phone in his customary gruff voice.

Nora had been next to ring. "Oh, it's so sad, sweetie; no wonder you've been spending time with the pig farmer. I get it now but you know the past is the past and you've got to look to your future." She had sniffed and then in typical Nora style, she'd changed tack and announced that she could just imagine Ewan playing Owen should the rights to a movie ever be sold. She'd gone on to suggest Megan Fox for the role of Amy but then changed her mind, saying she was too old for the part and it probably wasn't a great idea throwing Megan and Ewan together, even if Megan was married.

"Er, Nora," Jess had cut in, "Owen doesn't look anything like Ewan, and I don't think he would want his family's tragedy being Hollywoodized, not even if Daniel Day-Lewis himself offered to play him but hey thanks for the thought—gotta go." She'd disconnected the call with a shake of her head. She dearly loved her friend but honestly sometimes.

Brianna had kept to her traditional role in their friendship by being the sensitive one. "Oh Jess, what a waste of a life; it's just so sad."

"You sound surprised," Jess replied, puzzled. It wasn't as though Brianna wasn't familiar with what had happened to Amy.

"It's completely different having it laid out in black and white and those photos of Amy—well, they bring her to life and you can see her potential, how beautiful she was. It really brings it home what a tragedy it was." Brianna sniffed loudly. "Do you know I felt ashamed reading it because I still can't believe that kind of brutality happened in the country I live in, even though I have always *known* that it happened. Does that make sense?"

"Yes, I know what you mean. It does seem surreal now and the Troubles have been so romanticised, especially by Hollywood, but it was as bloody as any war." She shook her head, remembering the conversation she had just had with Nora. "Life goes on, though. Look at Croatia—the tourists have been going back there for years even though the countryside's still littered with unexploded landmines."

"You're right." Brianna's voice quivered. "Do you know, Jess, I don't think I'd be able to carry on if anything was to happen to Harry?"

"Owen's mother didn't either, not properly."

"Have you spoken to him yet? The poor man! If it's brought out all these emotions in me then I can't imagine how he must be feeling having his family's story laid bare like that for all to see."

Jess squirmed. She knew she owed him a phone call but she couldn't bring herself to ring him, not just yet. The uncertainty of the reception she would get was holding her back and she had spent the morning hoping instead that he would phone her. "Um, no, I thought it might be better to let him ring me, you know, when he feels like talking—if he feels like talking, that is."

He was the person whose voice she had been on tenterhooks to hear each time she'd picked up the phone that morning.

"Why?"

"You don't know Owen." Jess gave a sardonic little laugh. "Neither do I, for that matter, because he is the most self-contained man I have ever met. That's why I thought it would be better to leave him alone today to deal with this in his own way. He'll be in touch if he wants to be."

"Don't give me that. It sounds like an excuse if ever I heard one. Did you stop to think that maybe he finds it hard to reach out after everything he has been through? I think you owe him a phone call at the very least to see how he is doing." Brianna was a tough love advocate.

"I know you're right. It's just..." Brianna, of course, was not privy to the whole story.

"Just what?"

"Nothing, it's nothing. I'm just being pathetic." Jess felt awful for being unable to face the possibility of rejection but it was something she was going to have to grin and bear. She did owe it to him because it was her who had started all this and set the article in motion, so the very least she could do was to let him know she was thinking of him. "I'll ring him now."

"Promise?"

"Promise."

Dialling his phone number before she could talk herself out of it, Jess held her breath as it rang and rang before finally clicking over to the answering machine. At the sound of Owen's voice explaining he wasn't home, her eyes began to prickle. She sniffed and cleared her throat and then as the beep sounded she left her message:

"Owen, hi, it's Jess. I, uh, I just phoned to see how you were doing. I hope your copy of the *Express* arrived okay and that you are pleased with the way it all came together. Um, Niall phoned to tell me the response from readers has been phenomenal. I'll forward you the copies of all the Letters to the Editor. Anyway, I, uh, I hope you're okay with it and that Wilbur's doing okay and that your Dad is okay. Okay, um, bye." God, what was with the non-stop okays? She hung up, hoping she hadn't sounded too much of a babbling idiot because she hated answerphones at the best of times and this was not the best of times.

On the floor spread out in front of her was the *Express*. "Amy's Story" in its bold black typeface gazed back up at her. Her eyes flitted over the familiar text before settling on the photo of Amy holding her disgruntled cat tightly. She had been so vividly beautiful, so alive. As the tears plopped down her cheeks, staining the newsprint, she hoped that seeing their sister/daughter remembered in a story like this had somehow helped Owen and his father today and that they felt she had done good by her.

SATURDAY EVENING ROLLED around, leaving Jess with the much more imminent worry of her mother gate-crashing her life in the near future and dinner that evening with Nick at Brianna's.

Marian had emailed her flight details through that afternoon and if she were honest with herself, Jess had been glad of the distraction. Her mother was flying some godforsaken airline Jess had never even heard of and arriving Tuesday night. When she meant business, she did not muck about. Speaking of whom, Brie and Nora had been over the moon when she'd rung them back to tell them her news.

"We've heard so much about her over the years, I can't wait to meet her," Brie had gushed.

"You say that now," Jess had muttered darkly.

"What do you mean?"

"You'll see for yourself soon enough."

"Ah, I am sure she's lovely. Now then, did you ring your man?"

"I did but there was no answer so I left a message."

"He hasn't rung you back?"

"No, he's probably with his father for the day."

"Oh gosh, you don't think he'd do anything stupid?"

"Brie, don't even go there. Of course I don't." God, she could be dramatic. Jess frowned, not wanting to admit to herself how much she would like to hear Owen's voice.

"No, of course he wouldn't; he's lived with it all these years, so he has." Brianna did not sound convinced.

"So what are you cooking us for dinner tonight?" Jess asked, brightly deciding to distract her friend before she suggested they begin phoning hospital emergency departments.

"It's a surprise."

"Right, well, I shall look forward to being surprised," Jess lied, thinking it may well be Brianna who was surprised. "See you at seven."

"See you then."

Nora, upon hearing of Marian's impending arrival, had been happy to hear she had an ally on her way over. "If anybody can stop you chucking Mr Right away, it will be your mother because you've certainly not been paying any attention to me." Nora seemed oblivious of Jess's protestations that she wasn't chucking Nick anywhere—she would be seeing him that evening for goodness' sake! She was beginning to feel like Ross in that *Friends* episode where he kept telling everyone that he and Rachel were "on a break." God help her when Nora and her mother did get together; she shuddered. It would be bad enough for her having to cope with the pair of them but she wouldn't put it past them both to frogmarch poor Nick down to the registry office!

In the meantime, though, she had to get through this evening first so she pushed all thoughts of Owen and her mother aside with a swipe of the new lippy she'd bought from Boots that morning. Smacking her lips together, she leaned in closer to the mirror and inspected them. She wasn't sure about the shade but the sales assistant had assured her that red was this season's colour and that its brick undertones would do wonders for her pale complexion and auburn hair. Oh whatever, Jess thought, stepping back from the mirror disinterestedly. Sales assistants were full of shite; everybody knew that. Pushing her hair back over her shoulders to inspect her outfit, she turned this way and that. She'd dressed in a pair of high-waist, wide-legged black pants she'd owned forever and a day, teaming them with a pretty cinnamon 1950s top that had a silk bow under her boobs. It was very flattering in the way it fell and the colour did wonders for her eyes; at least, that was what Nora had told her.

"You'll do," she announced to the reflection staring back at her from the mirror and, satisfied she was as ready as she would ever be, she picked up her purse. With one last glance at the silent telephone, she paused for a moment. Should she try phoning Owen again? No, if he wanted to talk to her, he would be in touch, she told herself sternly before heading out the door.

A strange sight greeted her as she strode through the flood-lit quad. Gemma, dressed in her usual sporty attire, was standing astride a man, her trainer clad foot planted firmly on his stomach as he pulled himself up into what looked like a sit-up.

"Come on, are you man or mouse? Put some effort into it, for God's sake! I want a hundred more," she shouted, looking like some sort of dominatrix queen except instead of a whip, she was brandishing a water bottle. Spying Jess, she waved her over. "Off out again, Jess?" She grinned before raising an eyebrow. "It must be serious."

"It might be," Jess replied enigmatically. "Never mind me, though. What an earth are you doing?" There was something very familiar about the man Gemma was doing God knows what to, she thought, studying his flushed face and pained expression.

"This is Jimmy from apartment forty-four up there." Gemma pointed in the direction of Puff the Magic Dragon's lair. It was him! Jess realised as he paused to give her a half-hearted wink and rasping out an, "Oright, love?"

"Did I say you could stop? No, I did not! Get back into it, man!" Gemma yelled and with a look of half terror, half admiration, he did as he was told. "He's been hanging out his apartment window whistling at me whenever I walk through the courtyard for weeks now and he finally asked me out but I said I'd only go out with him if he stopped smoking. Exercise helps keep his mind off the fags."

"Oh, right." Jess felt vaguely betrayed at the news she wasn't the only one on the receiving end of his whistles but then again, she thought, looking at the sweaty red face with a shudder, rather Gemma than her. "Good for you, Gem. Got to run. Bye."

Nick was running late again. Considering she was by nature a punctual person, this grated and Jess tapped her foot impatiently in the foyer, feeling a stab of irritation pierce the grey cloud that had been hovering over her all day. She hated to keep Brianna waiting too, knowing that she would have gone to loads of trouble. The evening was not off to a good start and she hadn't even left her apartment building yet!

By the time Nick pulled up at seven twenty, she had bitten two fingernails down to the quick. As she raced outside, she was assailed by both the cold night air and the bass line of Justin Timberlake once more. Ducking down and clambering inside the idling car, she couldn't help but wonder what was wrong with a bit of good old Dire Straits or even Floyd—they just seemed that little bit more masculine for someone of Nick's era—but to her relief, he turned the stereo down before leaning over to kiss her on the cheek.

"You are looking particularly stunning tonight," he murmured, stroking her hair, his voice thick. With that compliment, Jess felt her irritation disperse as he indicated right and merged out into the flow of evening traffic.

Deftly swerving to avoid a bus busy pulling out, Nick cursed the driver under his breath before regaining his equilibrium. "I read your piece in the paper today. It was pretty powerful stuff—not your usual style." His eyebrow was raised in query as he glanced over at her.

"No, not my usual style at all. How did your trip down South go?" Jess changed the subject, not wanting to discuss Amy or Owen with him. It felt wrong and she was glad that for the rest of the drive to Bray he was content to fill her in on Cork and his prowess—or lack of it—on the golf course. She'd have found his commentary amusing if she didn't have such a sense of impending doom where the evening ahead was concerned.

"Hey, are you alright? You seem a bit preoccupied." Nick's expression as his face was momentarily illuminated by a street light was concerned.

This was her chance to come clean and tell him who Brianna was before they met face to face in about five minutes' time. She had no choice. It wasn't fair to either of them not to say something and so, licking her bottom lip,

Jess took a deep breath, opening her mouth to explain just as Nick braked violently. Her head snapped forward as the car skidded to an abrupt halt. Slamming his palm down on the horn, Jess saw in the car's headlights a fluffy white cat pause to glare at them before sticking its tail in the air and meandering off the road.

"Bloody cat! It came out of nowhere. Sorry about that—are you okay?"

Jess rubbed her neck. "Yes, I'm fine; a bit of a fright, that's all. At least you didn't hit it."

And just like that, the moment for confessing all had gone.

"Okay, you turn right here and see that white picket fence up there on the left? That's where we are going."

Nick pulled over, flush with the kerb, before getting out of the car and coming round to open her door for her. Treat her like a princess he may but Jess felt as though she were on her way to the gallows as she literally led him up the garden path.

"DO YOU KNOW YOU LOOK really familiar? I'm sure we have met somewhere before," Briana said, glancing back over her shoulder as she led Nick and Jess through to the warmth of their dining room. Pete stood by the sideboard, wrestling with a bottle of red and, as Brianna turned to smile at them both, Jess felt her insides contract. Any moment now there would be fireworks.

"Do I? I don't think we've met before," Nick replied to her question, smoothly holding out the bottle of wine he had bought with him. "It's a 1986 cabernet. I'm Nick, Nick Jameson. It's lovely to meet you."

"Are you sure we haven't met?" Brianna frowned as she took the bottle from him.

"Positive. I never forget a face, especially not a pretty one." He shot Jess a peculiar look as Brianna did the introductions.

"Nick, this is my husband Pete—Pete, Nick." Pete gave up on the bottle and leaving the cork screw sticking out of the top of it, he held his hand out in greeting. "I hope your wine's screw top, mate." He shook hands with the taller man in front of him.

Jess risked a sideways glance at Brianna, whose mouth had dropped open. Uh-oh, she thought, as her friend clamped her mouth shut and shot her a nasty look.

"Could you come and give me a hand in the kitchen for a sec, Jess?" Her smile was sweet but her tone was saccharine and Jess was not fooled.

"Um, yeah, of course." She dragged her heels behind her friend.

"Where's Harry tonight?" Maybe a change of subject would stave off the bollocking she was about to receive.

"At his Nana's and don't try to fob me off. It's bloody well him, isn't it?" Brianna hissed once they were out of earshot.

Jess didn't say anything, studying the floor tiles beneath her feet instead.

"For God's sake, Jess, why didn't you tell me you were dating the man who wants to tear down our community centre!"

"Shush, Brie, keep your voice down! I didn't tell you because I knew you'd go mad, that's why. Please don't say anything."

"I won't make a scene—my mammy raised me better than that. But you should have told me instead of putting me on the spot like this. I am not happy with you." Brianna prodded her in the chest and Jess had the grace to look shamefaced. "I knew there was something up with you where he was concerned but I just put it down to his being a bit too good to be true and you being wary. I mean *it's a 1986 cabernet and I never forget a pretty face*. Really, Jess?"

It had been a bit cringe-worthy. "I'm sorry, Brie; I really am. Could you please try to keep an open mind about him tonight, though, for me? I know that if you just give him a chance, you'll see past all that other stuff and you'll like him. The community centre—well, it's just business to him; it's not personal."

"Don't push your luck because it feels pretty bloody personal to me right now," Brianna muttered, piling little pieces of brown toast with oysters atop them on to a platter.

Jess decided to take her friend's advice and not push her luck. Brianna not giving out to him was the best she could hope for under the circumstances and as her friend carried the nibbles through to the dining room, she arranged her own face into a cheery smile and marched out to join Nick and

Pete. Somehow they would all get through the evening. It could have been worse—at least Nick had been none the wiser as to whom Brianna was.

IT HAD BEEN A MOST peculiar dinner party, Jess concluded as she hugged Pete and Brianna goodnight. The food had been delicious—Brianna had done them proud on that front—but she had also artfully steered the conversation away from Nick's line of work and talked about Harry for most of the night. Granted, he was a fascinating subject at the best of times but being a childless couple, the topic of children wasn't one Nick and Jess could contribute much to. In fact, Jess had thought if Brianna kept it up, Nick would be heading for the snip on his way home. She was sure he had been in danger of nodding off at one point. For his part, he had sneaked in the odd golfing titbit whenever Brianna paused in her monologue to draw breath, which wasn't often.

She had managed to stick a few jibes in, too, about the importance of having somewhere in the community to meet up with others when you were at home with a small child twenty-four/seven. Pete, bless him, puzzled by the strange undercurrent at the table, had gabbled on about his latest project at work. Jess had tuned out as she always did when Pete got started on that subject but at least it was a topic Nick could relate to. She'd been on tenterhooks all night and had hardly said a word through dinner but to put a positive spin on the evening, at least they had gotten through it with no showdown of clashing opinions. It might have been awkward but at least it had been civil and the food, judging by everybody else's clean plates, had been great.

Waving their hosts goodbye from where they stood backlit in the front door, Jess decided she'd phone Brianna and thank her in the morning for keeping quiet. It wouldn't have been easy for her, she thought, sliding into the passenger seat. The temptation for her to slip Nick a dodgy oyster or spit in his chicken parmigiana must have been huge. She crossed her fingers and hoped Nick didn't come down with any food poisoning symptoms in the next twenty-four hours as he got behind the wheel and slammed the door shut.

Jess glanced over at him and was startled by the thunderous expression on his face. Before she could ask what the matter was, he had gunned the engine into life and taken off down the street at a rate of knots that would have impressed a Concorde pilot. Oh dear, she cringed, hoping Brianna and Pete had already gone inside. Nick's hasty exit would not endear him further to her friend because last year she had spearheaded the "Slow Down in our Community" campaign.

"Nick?" Jess asked, clutching at the sides of her seat. "Is everything ok?"

She saw his bottom jaw muscles clench and he slammed his hand against the steering wheel. "No, it's bloody well not! I don't know what you were playing at, Jessica, but that holier-than-thou friend of yours is the main rabble-rouser holding up my Bray project. She's costing me a shitload of money."

Jess squirmed. "I know. I'm sorry but she's not holier-than-thou; she's just very committed to her cause. You must see her side of things?"

He turned to glare at her, his knuckles white against the steering wheel. "So you knew then? And no, I don't see her side of things at all. Bloody do-gooder."

Jess studied her own hands, which were now clenched in her lap. "I twigged awhile back but I didn't know how to tell you or her." She looked over at him. "I really am sorry but come on, Nick, be fair. I feel awful for not saying anything but what you do with your work—well, it's nothing to do with me—us. And Brie is a grown woman who backs her own causes. I didn't want to get caught up in the middle."

"So you said nothing while I confided the problems I was having with my project." He shot her look of pure disgust and shook his head. "I recognised her as soon as she opened the door and let me tell you, it took supreme willpower on my part not to turn and walk away but I decided to give you the benefit of the doubt. I figured maybe you didn't know what your little pal gets up to in her spare time so I kept quiet and played nice for your sake. It's a shame you didn't show me the same courtesy."

Neither said a word for a moment until Nick made her jump. "Jesus, Jessica!" Spittle flew from his mouth. "Have you any bloody idea how much money I have tied up in this?"

Jess squeaked. "A lot?"

"A tonne and I stand to lose the lot thanks to that stupid cow and her cronies." His voice was a snarl. "I can't stomach women like that; they have no life outside the home so they create their own little dramas."

"Hey!" Jess didn't like his tone at all; it was pure venom. This was a side of Nick he obviously kept well-hidden underneath his smooth veneer. "She's not a cow—she's one of my best friends and for what it's worth, I think she has a point. That community centre is a good thing—it brings people together. The only people who will benefit from a shiny new apartment complex are the developers."

It was a barbed comment and Jess was certain that were it physically possible, Nick would be emitting steam out of his ears. She decided it was best, considering he was behind the wheel, to keep her mouth shut for the duration of the ride home. So, they sat in tense silence until he pulled up outside Riverside Apartments. She was about to say a curt goodnight when he was upon her. Pulling her to him by her hair which he had wrapped his hand in, he began kissing her so roughly it made her mouth and teeth hurt. He shoved his free hand up her top and groped at her breasts. Jess could feel the violence lurking just beneath the surface and it took her a moment to react.

"What do you think you're doing? Get off me!" She shoved him off her and managed to open the car door, all but falling out onto the pavement. Scrabbling to her feet, she slammed the door shut and then, with one last sneer in her direction, he was gone, leaving nothing but smelly exhaust fumes in his wake.

Jess hurried inside and headed for her apartment. As she closed the front door behind her, she leaned against it for a moment, feeling sick at what had just happened. How could she have misjudged him so badly? She breathed deeply for a few minutes and then burst into tears as the shock hit her—the way he had turned on her like that had really frightened her.

As her heart rate slowed to its normal beats per minute, she made herself a milky cup of sweet tea, shoving down a couple of chocolate biscuits that had somehow survived the week in her pantry. The sugar hit made her feel better and taking the mug through to the living room, she sat down on the settee, nursing it between both hands. Nick's reaction had shocked her; she could see now why he was so successful at what he did because using bully-boy tactics was obviously second nature to him. Needing to tell someone what had just happened in order to make it a reality in her own mind, she picked up the phone and punched out Nora's number.

She answered after the sixth ring. "Hello?"

"Hi, it's me."

"Hey, Jess! I was just saying goodbye to Ewan. God, I can't wait until he gets back—only five days to go. I tell you, Skyping just doesn't have the same allure as phone sex. You feel kind of silly peering into a computer screen, making lusty noises. What are you doing home, anyway? I thought you'd be spending the night at Nick's."

Jess let out a little sob. Life sucked.

"What's up?" Nora asked, alarmed.

It all came flooding out and when she'd finished, Nora announced she would personally hunt Nick Jameson down and cut his gonads off. Jess wouldn't put it past her and she spent the next five minutes trying to dissuade her friend from becoming the next Lorena Bobbitt.

"He didn't get the chance to do anything *that* bad; it was just the way he did it. He was so angry with me, Nora; it was horrible. It was like being mad at me turned him on or something. Ugh." She shuddered at the memory.

"God, I'm so sorry, Jess. I had no idea he was a sicko. I feel awful pushing you at him the way I have been—it's just that he seemed so nice. I only wanted you to be happy."

It was a sentiment she had heard a lot lately. "I know you did and I thought he was nice, too," Jess replied despondently. "Appearances can be deceptive but you know, Nora, if I am honest, I think I knew something wasn't right with him. He reminded me way too much of a Galaxy chocolate bar."

"Smooth, you mean?"

"Yeah and if you have too much of it, you feel sick." She burst into tears. "What's wrong with me? Why do things like this always happen to me? If the men I meet aren't losers then they are nut cases. It's not fair."

"Hang tight, sweetie. I am on my way over."

True to her word, Nora arrived half an hour later with a bottle of wine tucked under her arm. By the time she tucked Jess into bed sometime in the wee hours of Sunday morning, neither girl was feeling any pain. Nor did they have any voices left, having screeched so loudly to Melissa Etheridge that the neighbour had banged on the wall.

The next day being Sunday, Nora telephoned Brianna to fill her in on what had happened. Then after a spot of name dropping, she managed to get them a lunchtime seating at Peploes, the popular wine bar on St Stephens on the Green.

"A long lazy liquid lunch is just what you need," she insisted, marching Jess off to her room, ignoring her protests about not being hungry as she told her to get dressed. "Rug up, though; it looks pretty fresh outside."

Stepping onto the pavement outside Riverside Apartments, the two women were hit by an arctic blast and Jess was glad she had taken Nora's advice and dressed warmly. Tucking her hands into the sleeves of her coat, she picked up Nora's brisk pace, the cold air clearing her head as they marched down the Quays.

They arrived at the oh-so classy eatery opposite the Green bang-on midday. Brianna, eager for the unexpected time out from family life, was already there waiting with a glass in hand at the bar. As the threesome were greeted and led over to their sumptuously laid table, Jess decided Nora had been right. This was just what she needed and after glancing at the menu, she decided she was starving after all. She would have to splurge on a starter and a main, oh and quite possibly dessert, too! It all sounded just too delicious.

Over wine and an entrée of Brie aux Filo, Jess apologised to Brianna.

"I'm sorry for putting you on the spot the way I did last night. I wasn't a very good friend, putting myself first like that."

"Ah, don't be silly. You have every right to date who you want. I was out of order sounding off at you the way I did. I just wasn't expecting to know Nick when you arrived last night, that's all, and you weren't to know what an arse he was. Though..." she added with a wink, "I did try to tell you he sounded a bit too good to be true."

"Like a Galaxy bar," Jess and Nora chorused.

"Good parallel. You need a man who is a bit rough round the edges, Jess, but he's got to have a heart of gold like yours, too."

Jess was assailed by an image of Owen as Brianna, obliviously smearing her toasted brioche with pate, asked, "Hey, have you told your mammy it's all off?"

"There's no point because it's too late to stop her coming now; her flights are all booked. Anyway, a wasted trip will serve her right for being so gung-ho about marrying me off."

"She'll be devastated."

"She'll get over it," Jess muttered.

"When does she arrive?" Nora asked.

"This sodding Tuesday, can you believe it? I tell you, girls, we'll drive each other mad spending all that 'quality' time together. A few days I can do but two weeks under the same roof?" She shook her head.

"We'll help keep her busy," Brianna assured her and Nora nodded her agreement.

"Yeah, it will fly by, you'll see."

"Thanks." Jess wasn't convinced.

"You know, I feel pretty stupid, too." Nora changed the subject. "I thought Nick was perfect for Jess. It goes to show what an appalling judge of character I am. I hope I haven't made the same error of judgement in Ewan."

"Ewan is not Nick! Besides, you said they hardly know each other these days," Jess stated firmly and glad to take the spotlight off herself for a moment, she asked, "Have you told him how you really feel about adventure sport yet?"

"I was going to wait until he got home next week but I blurted it out last night when we were Skyping in between—"

"Spare us the gory details—we're eating, thank you very much. So what did he say?"

Nora looked coyly at them. "You were both right; he was great about it. He said I should have told him instead of putting myself through the paces like that but that any girl prepared to do what I had done to impress him was worth having around. I am going to be his cheerleader from now on and watch from the sidelines, which suits me just fine."

"Oh Nora, that's great! Do you know, I still can't quite believe you are dating a movie star."

"Me neither," Brianna reiterated.

Nora smiled and then dropped her gaze, studying her glass for a moment. "I don't think of him like that. I did at first but once you've seen someone sit on the loo first thing in the morning, it kind of brings it home that it's just a job. Albeit a very well-paid and glamorous one but at the end of the day, it's just a job and he is only human."

"Albeit just a fecking gorgeous one and I want to propose a toast." Brianna slurred slightly; she wasn't used to wine in the middle of the day. "To the best friends a girl could have."

"To the best friends a girl could have." The girls raised their glasses and clinked.

"It's my turn now!" Nora insisted, holding her glass up again. "To rough and ready men with a heart of gold for Jess and to the lovely Pete and to Ewan."

"To the man for me, wherever he may be, and to the lovely Pete and Ewan," Jess echoed as they did another round of clinking. Then Brianna and Nora looked at her expectantly. "Your turn."

"Okay—um, here goes. To slimy, bad tempered freaks with erectile dysfunction not getting their own way—long live the Bray Community Centre!"

"Yay! That's the attitude, Jess—get mad, not sad." Nora leaned over and patted her hand before raising her glass along with Brianna. "Long live the Bray Community Centre! Now then, can we get down to some serious drinking?"

The three women laughed and charged their glasses.

"You know, Jess, I am a firm believer in getting right back on your horse and riding it or in your case the pig, so what about it? How does the land lie with your pig farmer chap?"

"Stop calling him my pig farmer, Nora; his name's Owen."

Over the second bottle of wine, Jess's tongue well and truly loosened as she filled her friends in on what had happened in the barn during her mercy dash to Ballymcguinness.

"I knew there was more to it!" Brianna shrieked, causing heads to turn.

"You sly old thing, you making out you were only concerned with the piglet's health. How is porky by the way?" Nora said.

"It's Wilbur, as you well know, and I don't know how he is because I haven't heard from Owen since then."

Then both girls asked, "So what are you going to do about it?"

Jess shrugged as her dish of Dublin Bay prawn risotto was placed in front of her. "Nothing. What can I do? He made it pretty clear it was a spur of the moment mistake and he never phoned me when Amy's story ran. If he wanted to talk to me that would have been his cue to call, surely?"

"I thought I told you that you should ring him."

"I did but he wasn't there, remember? So I left a message. He's never phoned me back." Jess shrugged but the girls weren't buying her affected indifference.

"Well, I think you should try again." Nora pointed a fork full of potato smothered in rosemary at her.

"Yes, me too."

"No bloody way. I do have some pride, you know."

"Barracuda" broke out, much to the shock of their fellow diners and, blushing, Jess rescued her phone from her bag. "You can bloody well change this back to a normal ringtone, Nora Brennan." She glanced at the caller display and paled. "It's him. Oh my God, it's him."

"Who? Nick? Right, give me the phone." Nora looked at her friend's orb-like eyes and held her hand out, looking like she was ready to do murder.

"No, not Nick—Owen."

"Well, fecking well answer it then!"

Chapter Seventeen

FROM HER VANTAGE POINT on the bridge, Jess could see that Owen had gotten there first. With downcast eyes, his hands were thrust deep in the pockets of his jeans to protect against the biting wind as he scuffed the pavement with the toe of his boot. At the sight of him standing outside her apartment building, her legs literally felt weak and she gripped the railings to steady herself.

She'd panicked at first when she answered the phone, feeling sure he was going to tell her that Wilbur was no longer with them. Or, that he and his Dad had hated seeing "Amy's Story" in print and the whole thing had been a huge mistake. Asking him to hang on for a sec, she'd gotten up from the table, unable to concentrate because Nora and Brianna were climbing all over each other in their desperate attempt to eavesdrop. Frowning at them both, she'd mouthed "behave" before walking the expanse of the restaurant to brave the elements outside. Having been assured Wilbur was on the mend, she wrapped her spare arm around herself, wishing she'd put her coat on as she braced herself to hear what he had to say.

"I wanted to thank you for what you wrote and me Da asked me to let you know that he thought you made a grand job of it."

Jess exhaled. "I'm so glad. I was worried it might have been too much for him."

"No, he's a tough old bugger, my Da."

A chip off the old block then, Jess thought, waiting for him to get to the crux of his call.

"He's had to be, you know, and it was a good thing reading about Amy in the paper like that because it meant we talked about her and Ma—the good times as well as the bad. Instead of both burying our head in the sand and pretending it was a day like any other. Anyway, the thing is, I'm in Dublin for the day and I wondered whether you might be free to meet up somewhere. It's short notice, I know…"

The casual indifference behind his words irked her. She wasn't in the mood to jump to, not after the way things had been left the last time they had seen each other. It just seemed hard—too much of an effort required that she just didn't have the energy for. Maybe if he had called her yesterday before everything that had happened with Nick, she might have been more receptive but today she wasn't in a happy space where men were concerned at all.

"I'm out for lunch with the girls at the moment, sorry."

"Ah."

They both drifted into silence and Jess, shivering, watched a young couple padded out in matching puffa jackets wandering toward the Green on the other side of the road. Between them was a toddler who could have passed for a Teletubby waddling along, holding both their hands as they entered the park. The woman was carrying a loaf of bread with her spare hand and Jess felt a pang. She wished her life were so simple that Sunday afternoons could be spent strolling St Stephens Green with people she loved, feeding the ducks. Not standing outside a restaurant freezing while she dealt with an unpredictable Northern Irish man with a troubled past.

Owen cleared his throat but Jess stubbornly maintained her silence and her stance; she was not going to make this easy for him. He didn't have the monopoly on moodiness and it was him who had rung her, after all, so let him sweat it out.

"What about meeting up when you've finished your lunch like?"

So he was prepared to wait for her? That boded well but hang on a sec, Jess cautioned herself; don't get ahead of yourself. For all she knew, he could just want to collect the photos of Amy he had loaned her. "Why, is it urgent?"

"Aye, it is in a way. I owe you a proper apology like for the way I behaved the other day and I'd like to do it in person."

Well, she hadn't expected that. Was he sorry for kissing her or was he sorry for the way he had acted as though it should never have happened afterwards? There was only one way to find out and if he was going to be magnanimous then so would she. "Okay, I've finished eating, anyway. I could meet you at mine in an hour for a coffee—that way, I could give you your photos back too. Does that suit?"

"Aye, an hour would be grand."

Jess gave him directions and then hung up before heading back inside to the warmth of Peploes where Brianna and Nora were chomping at the bit to find out what had transpired.

"Why did you not suggest meeting him here so we could get a good look at him?" Nora asked, her bottom lip sticking out.

"Because, Nora, you two would scare the living daylights out of him."

"I think she wanted ease of access to the bedroom." Brianna leered over the rim of her wine glass.

"Oh my God, you don't think that when I said meet me at my place for coffee, Owen would have heard meet me at my place for sex! Do you?"

"Calm down, Jess. If you said coffee, then he'll be expecting coffee, not you in sexy lingerie and for the love of Mary, go and get that piece of parsley out from between your teeth before you head off!"

HE STILL HADN'T SPOTTED her on the bridge and Jess savoured the moment it gave her to compose herself. He was dressed in his civvies—as she had come to think of his non-farming attire: jeans and, squinting into the weak afternoon sunlight, a blue jumper that wasn't an Aran knit.

She didn't know what today was going to bring; that was the thing with Owen—she never knew. All she could hope for, she decided as she steeled herself to carry on across the bridge, was honesty on his part. Her hands clenched into fists at her side. And if he started to pull any of his moody bullshit, well, she'd... She didn't get past that thought because looking up, Owen's gaze locked on hers. He waved out and began striding down the Quays to meet her.

Trying surreptitiously to smooth her hair, Jess hoped she didn't look too dishevelled. The wind had all but blown her down Grafton Street and along the Quays.

"Hello."

"Hi."

They danced around, each self-consciously, on the cracked old pavement for a moment. What was the protocol when it came to greeting someone you had snogged passionately the last time you had seen them? In the end,

Owen decided a kiss on the cheek was appropriate and when his lips brushed against her skin, Jess felt as though she had been scalded. Taking a step back, she waved in the direction of Riverside. "You found it okay then?"

"Aye, your instructions weren't hard to follow. There is only one River Liffey and one Guinness factory in Dublin, after all."

Jess's shoulders relaxed as she spied that familiar twinkle in his eyes and they began walking toward the apartment building's entrance. "What about parking—did you get one alright?"

"Aye, I got one round the back, no problem, thanks. You could have warned me about the mad pigeons, though." He indicated a white and brown stain on his shoulder. The pigeons that congregated daily around the side streets behind the Quays were a mangy-looking lot, always scrounging a crumb. They had a vindictive streak, too, if you didn't produce the goods, hence the poop.

Jess wrinkled her nose, hoping he wouldn't notice the tremor in her hand as she pushed open the main doors. "They are a bit of a nuisance. I'll get a cloth to sponge it off when we get up to mine."

Owen followed her through the foyer out into the quad and the first thing they saw was Jimmy flat on his back. Gemma was standing over him with one foot firmly planted on his stomach again.

"Come on, you great big lump—sit up! You've another twenty-five before you're finished." Her ponytail swished back and forth as she shook her head. "If I don't talk tough, he doesn't even try. How's it going, Jess?" Then, spotting Owen, her face lit up. "Well, hello there. You must be Jess's mystery man?"

Jessica could have kicked her and would have but the other girl was quite obviously stronger than her. "Gemma, this is my *friend* Owen; Owen, Gemma. Gemma is acting as Jimmy here's personal trainer while he tries to quit smoking."

"Howrya." Jimmy wheezed pulling himself up.

"Twenty-four to go—get on with it, lard ass!"

Gemma grinned at them both, looking like butter wouldn't melt. "I'm really enjoying this and there's good money to be made in personal training so I might go solo—you know, quit the gym."

"Good for you, Gem. Catch you later." Jess was eager to be away before she tried to recruit her.

"She'd do a roaring trade if she wore a leather mask and cracked a whip," Owen muttered and Jess laughed as she pushed the lift button.

"She is a bit scary, isn't she?"

"Fecking terrifying!" They grinned at each other and as the lift door slid open, the ice between them thawed.

Flicking her gaze round the living room a moment later, Jess was glad she'd tidied up a bit before she'd headed out with Nora that morning. There was no underwear drying on the clothes rack or dirty dishes piled up on the bench. Yes, all in all, the place was looking respectable. Owen had glanced around the room with curiosity etched on his face before being drawn to the windows with their view of the smoking stacks of the Guinness factory. Flicking on the kettle, Jess busied herself by fossicking under the sink for an old cloth he could use to clean himself up with. She didn't see him crouch down to flick through her collection of old books.

"Janice Bohan."

She looked up startled, rag in hand. "Pardon me?"

He held out a battered copy of *Rapunzel*. "This book once belonged to a lass by the name of Janice Bohan. Seeing all these here brings home the randomness of you deciding to find out about our Amy."

"I suppose it does when you look at it like that." Jess frowned at the suitcase stuffed full of all the other names she could have chosen to trace. At the fleeting memory of a dark-haired girl she thought she'd seen watching her and Owen, she wondered, "You know *Snow White and the Seven Dwarfs* was the last book I needed for my collection, so maybe it was just meant to be."

"Aye, maybe it was." Putting the book back, he wandered over to inspect her shelves full of treasures before turning around to face her. "It's just what I pictured. All this—it's you."

"Is that a good thing or a bad thing?" Jess handed him the cloth and waited for an answer while he rubbed at his shoulder. She looked around the room, trying to see the apartment through his eyes.

Placing the rag down on the bench, he finally answered. "Oh, it's definitely a good thing."

He pulled her toward him then and lowered his mouth to hers. For someone as gruff as Owen, his lips were incredibly soft and his caresses were so gentle, too gentle. Jess pushed her body up against his, trying to convey the urgency she felt for them to be closer. Pulling away, she took him by the hand and led him through to the bedroom.

Afterwards, she lay exhausted with her head on his shoulders. Her hand rested lightly on his chest, feeling the sweat their lovemaking had left behind cooling beneath her palm. She had read somewhere once that happiness was in those perfect moments captured briefly, fleetingly throughout life. This was happiness, she decided, as Owen stroked her hair rhythmically. As the anaemic rays of autumnal sunlight faded from the room, he did what she wished he had done from the start. He began to talk and this time, he let the complicated layers that manifested themselves in that hard shell he'd let grow around him peel away.

"I know I have behaved like a schizophrenic shite but I wasn't sure I could open myself up to feeling anything romantic for anyone again."

Jess lay listening as he confided his fears of being unable to put the past to rest and of wearing his sister's untimely death like an oversized suit for the rest of his days.

"What made you come today then? What is it that has changed?" she asked, leaning up on her elbow and tracing a line down his cheek. He needed to shave but she liked the roughness of the prickles beneath her fingertips.

"I missed you, and I knew I would have to step up to the mark or I would lose my chance with you for good. That's mostly why I came but I also realised that at some point since I met you, I *have* moved on. Maybe it was all the talking about what happened and seeing it type-written so I could read it objectively for the first time. You know, take a step back and put it in the past or maybe it was simply time that did it? It's supposed to be a great healer, isn't it?"

Jess nodded. She didn't have firsthand experience with the grieving process but as a writer, she was familiar with that and all the other wise old adages.

"Whatever it was, I feel now that she's at peace up there." He raised his eyes to the ceiling and Jess's green eyes followed suit, unsure what she expected to see other than the smattering of fly poo that adorned it. "I feel like I have done right by her, and I know that she wouldn't have wanted me making a pig's ear of the rest of my life because of what happened to her." He smiled at his little joke meant to lighten the weight behind his words and Jess punched him playfully on the arm.

"That's the second truly terrible pig joke I've heard you drop now."

"Aye, sorry; it goes with the territory and I couldn't resist." He cuddled her closer to him, breathing in the scent of her hair for a moment. "You know, reaching that thirty-year marker and re-reading our family's little bit of history yesterday—well, it was like a chapter in my life that has coloured things for far too long finally closed. Talking to me Da yesterday, I realised it's different for him. He's given up and accepted that he will always live with it. Amy was his girl and he won't get over Ma's passing, either, but I have to move on. Neither Ma or Amy would have wanted me to bury myself in the past." He paused to wipe a tear that had escaped from the corner of Jess's eye away.

"Don't cry. It's a good thing you've done, coming into my life the way you did. I'll always remember them both, of course I will, but for the good stuff from now on. Not the one bad thing that came to pass and shaped everything else that came after it. That would be nothing but an insult to the people they were. I can see that now." He sighed and if he had been wearing them, it would have come from the bottom of his boots before exhaling slowly. "You know, I hope that reading how Amy was killed might just make someone—whoever—think before they go down a road they've no business going down."

Jess took his metaphoric meaning to be that if one person took on board that no good came from fighting a fight no one could really win, then it had been worth sharing his family's pain. It was her sentiment, too.

She lay there listening to him breathing, thinking over what he had just told her. He had said everything that she thought she needed to hear him say but there was still something bothering her. "What about Sarah?" She referred to his ex-wife. "Is she still part of that oversized suit you've been wearing all these years?"

Owen turned to look at her in surprise. "Did you think that?"

"I don't know; you haven't exactly been an open book."

"Neither have you."

"What do you mean?"

"You were seeing someone, weren't you?"

So he had registered her call from Nick the day she'd done her mercy dash to see Wilbur. "Is that why you turned cold on me after we'd kissed at the barn?"

He looked a little shamefaced at that. "Aye, I suppose. I was jealous and like I said, I didn't want to put myself in a position where I might be exposed but then I decided you were worth getting burnt by."

"I am not going to hurt you, Owen, not ever." She kissed the tip of his nose. "Believe me, he wasn't worth getting jealous over and it was over before anything really got started. It's been you all along." She'd fill him in one day on what had happened with Nick but not now.

"I'm glad." He kissed her and then pulled away to look at her, his expression serious. "The way I have been was never anything to do with Sarah. When that was finished, it was over and I walked away from her and our marriage, that life, without a backward glance and so did she." Owen shook his head. "We were just a bad fit, Sarah and I. I think we both knew we had made a mistake the moment we said 'I do' but it was too late then. The problem all along has been that from the moment I picked you up at the station and watched you being harangued by Mad Bridie, I knew you were going to be a very good fit."

Jess had never known the kind of certainty where it is instinctive that you have met the right person before either. It was overwhelming but as she lay in the darkened room enjoying the contentedness it had brought with it, a thought sprang to mind unbidden. Bugger! She had forgotten about the oversized suit problem of her own that was heading her way—her mother. It was only two days until she set foot on Irish soil.

∽

ON TUESDAY EVENING at seven, the tin can that was part of the fleet belonging to the budget Cheap-Cheap Airline her mother had been forced to fly, thanks to what she termed her husband's tightfisted tyranny, touched down. Its wheels, as they skidded down the damp Dublin tarmac, sent a spray of water up in the air and the airline's bright yellow canary logo was just visible in the gloom of the evening. Marian Baré was officially in the country.

As Jess hopped from foot to foot in the Arrivals hall waiting for her to clear Irish Customs, she let her mind drift back over the last couple of days.

Owen had stayed that night and they'd only dragged themselves out of bed to order pizza. When it arrived, they'd taken the box straight back to bed with them. Propped up on pillows, feeding each other slices, they'd marvelled over the fact, like new lovers do, that pepperoni supreme was both their favourite. What other things would they find out they had in common over the course of time? The sense of a new beginning was tangible and it had been heavenly. The being with Owen, not the pizza obviously, Jess reiterated to herself. Although now, as her tummy grumbled at having been given no dinner, the pizza took on a divine status too.

Wrapping her arms around her stomach in an effort to shut it up, she remembered with a frisson of excitement how they'd made love again. "We need to work off all those cheesy calories." She'd laughed, nuzzling into his neck. Despite the need to burn off the carbs, it had been slower this time. The urgency of before was in the past and they took the time to explore each other's body.

Afterwards, as they'd talked into the small hours, Jess had taken a deep breath and come clean about her mother's impending visit. "I love her but honestly if she'd had her way, I would have had an arranged marriage years ago to a lawyer or a doctor even an accountant so long as he was a chartered one."

Owen listened to her with an amused expression as his fingertips played an imaginary tune on her shoulder.

For her part, Jess realised how she must sound. "I'm sorry, Owen. I shouldn't moan to you of all people about her but I'm dreading Tuesday, I really am."

Owen would have none of it, though. "Ah, she can't be as bad as all that? Not if she made you." He smoothed her hair away before kissing her on her forehead. "When will I meet her?"

"You don't want to meet her; she's a right old snob." Jess shook her head. The prospect of her mother and Owen in the same room together filled her with alarm. The feelings she had for him were far too new and precious to let her mother stomp all over them with a few thoughtless remarks.

"Aye, I do; she's your Mammy, and I want to prove my intentions toward her eldest daughter are honourable. I can turn the charm on when I need to, you know."

Jess raised an eyebrow. "You—charming? Not an analogy I'd have used."

"I said when I need to." His face was illuminated by the hall light shining into the room as he grinned down at her. "You're not planning on hiding her away from me, are you?"

The thought had crossed her mind, yes, but she could see the question behind his eyes.

"It's nothing to do with you. It's Mum—the way she is—but you're not going to take my word for it, are you?" How could she explain to him that the whole reason her mother was hot-footing it over to Dublin was to try to steer her away from him and in the direction of the dodgy developer with distemper? Okay, so she hadn't told her what had happened with Nick yet but even if she did, it would make no difference. She was coming to Dublin and there was no way she would ever warm to the idea of her daughter hooking up with a pig farmer with, as she saw it, a "past."

"No, I'm not, so how about you bring her up to the farm on Saturday? She can meet Wilbur. If I don't win her over then, he will if she's anything like her daughter."

The idea filled Jess with horror and as Owen carried on, the horror deepened.

"You could stay the night or just come for the day? It's up to you." He winked at her then. "Of course, if you stay the night then I'll get to have my wicked way with you again."

Jess looked at Owen, aghast. She didn't know which idea was worse: that of her mother staying on a pig farm or actually having sex while her mother was in the same house? Either scenario was a complete nightmare but she couldn't see a way out of it without hurting Owen's feelings. That was something she wasn't prepared to do for anyone and especially not for her mother. Besides, the thought of not seeing him for a whole fortnight while she played hostess with the mostest was unthinkable. Nope, there was nothing for it; she'd just have to buy her mother a set of wellies and tell her to soldier on.

The plan began to form. She'd ask Brianna nicely if she could borrow her car again—that way they could just go up for the day. Mum might just be able to behave herself for six hours but throw in a night as well? Jess shuddered; she knew that would just be asking for trouble. Who knew, though? If the opportunity presented itself, she might get to whisk Owen away for some alone time in the barn. Wilbur's sweet little face flitted to mind—he'd just have to shut his eyes and cover his ears.

They'd drifted off to sleep not long after that conversation and the next morning Jess had spooned into his warm and solid body, revelling in the fact that he was there and not part of a dream from which she would wake. The discarded pizza box on the floor further cemented the reality of the previous evening, as did the odour it was emitting. Owen was still out for the count, so she'd taken advantage by sitting up and watching him while he slept. God, he was beautiful; her eyes drifted over his broad strong features, his wide mouth. She giggled as he let out a little snore, waking him up, and he'd opened his eyes. As his gaze focused, he smiled lazily before grabbing her.

"What's so funny?"

"You—you were snoring."

"I don't snore."

"Oh yes you do."

He'd silenced the argument with a kiss and then their day had started off with a bang, literally. After showering and a quick breakfast, Owen announced reluctantly that he had to get back to Glenariff for the animals. Jess didn't want him to go but she didn't want him leaving Wilbur unattended either. It was probably a good thing, she mused, watching him tie his boots. She really did have to get this week's column written because she was going to be busy with her mother from Tuesday night onwards.

Wrapping her in a big hug and kissing the top of her head, Owen promised to ring her that evening. Neither of them knew what the next step for them would be. It was something they were going to have to wing as Ballymcguinness was not just around the corner. Nor was there any chance of Owen upping sticks and moving to Dublin, but she was getting ahead of herself as usual, Jess had told herself. She had to get through this Saturday with her mother first.

Her apartment had felt bereft without Owen's big presence filling it and she'd drifted around aimlessly, trying to settle down to do some work but ultimately when Brianna phoned, she was grateful for the distraction.

She was abuzz with the news that Bray Council, over the course of the weekend, had come around to her way of thinking. They'd pulled out of the deal Nick had been trying to negotiate. His company was not going to be allowed to proceed with any development on the site. The sale was null and void, and Brianna was over the moon. "It's karma for how he treated you the other night," she'd stated gleefully. "See, Jess, I might not know shite about shite but I do know right from wrong!"

"Have you been watching *Erin Brockovich* again?" It was Brianna's all-time favourite film.

"Yeah, that movie always makes me feel so empowered and that is exactly how I feel at the moment—like I took on the big boys and I won."

"That's exactly what you did do and I for one am very proud of you for holding firm to what you believe. Well done, Brie."

"Thanks." Her jubilance disappeared. "Hey, Jess, there's no hard feelings, I hope, where Nick is concerned, is there? You did mean what you said yesterday, didn't you?"

"I meant every word and I am glad he is not getting his own way. You were right about communities needing a place where people can go to get together. That's not something Nick can relate to; his world is ruled by the almighty dollar, not people."

"Euro actually."

"Euro, pound, punt—whatever! Anyway, enough about him. Owen stayed last night."

Brianna shrieked down the phone. "Oh my God, you didn't waste any time. I thought it was coffee he was coming over for, not sex? Details, please!"

Nora had rung on her lunch break and between stuffing down a sandwich—the Dukan diet was a distant memory—she, too, demanded the details. "I have to live vicariously through your sex life until Ewan gets back on Monday, so come on, spill!"

She listened to her friend gush and in her guilt for pushing Jess toward Nick, she resolved to be open-minded where Owen was concerned. He might be a pig farmer from Northern Ireland with a family tragedy lurking in his past but on this occasion she was prepared to trust Jess's judgement and give him the benefit of the doubt. "You know, from what you have just told me, I think that this is one man who you might just have helped heal."

"He said he feels like he can put the past where it belongs now—in the past. I just hope Mum's prepared to be as magnanimous as you because he has invited us to the farm on Saturday."

"Wow! He does mean business. Your mam will be impressed by that; I mean, he's obviously serious."

"Yeah, seriously mad inviting her up. He has no idea what he's in for."

"Give your mam a bit of credit. I am sure that once she meets him, she will see exactly what you see in him."

"You reckon? I think all she will see is a pig farmer with a thick accent."

Nora tried to cover her laugh and it came out as a snort. "Sorry, it's just that it is not the most salubrious of job titles." Her tone grew sage. "Like I just said, Jess, I reckon it's time you cut your mammy a bit of slack."

"You are forgetting I know her—you don't."

"Fair play to you, I suppose."

They'd changed the subject then, with Nora informing her that Ewan had been really pissed about Nick's behaviour and wouldn't be hanging out with him again anytime soon. "He reckoned Nick just liked being seen out with him because it was good for his public profile—a spot of free publicity, so to speak. In Ewan's line of business, you learn fast who your real friends are."

"Yes, I suppose you do."

Owen kept his word, ringing just after nine that evening. Her mother had been banished from her brain as she had lost herself in his sing-song accent while he gave her Wilbur's health report before filling her in on his day.

Jess blinked, coming back to the present as the doors in front of her finally slid open to disperse the first load of weary travellers. They trickled forth in a steady flow and she scanned their crumpled faces one after the other in anticipation of the familiar one she was expecting. As they came and went with no sign of her mother, she experienced a twinge of anxiety. Where was she? If she hadn't seen the Cheap-Cheap plane land with her own two eyes, she might have fretted that its engines had given up the ghost somewhere over the Atlantic. But it *had* landed, which could only mean her mother had been delayed by Customs.

Oh no! Surely Mum wouldn't have attempted to smuggle in her homemade Yo-Yo biscuits, knowing they were her favourites? She wouldn't put it past her to try. Jess chewed on her thumbnail, unsure of what to do next.

As she began envisaging the wrestling match between her mother and a surly customs officer over a tin of biscuits, the doors opened once more and released a frazzled and none-too-happy-looking passenger—Marian Baré.

"Mum!" Jess stepped forward to greet her, taking in her dishevelled appearance as she did so with shock. Her normally coiffed auburn curls were limp and hung in straggles around her face. Her makeup was non-existent, aside from the black smudges under her eyes, giving her face a zombie-like quality, and her clothes, which would have been immaculate when she left Auckland two days ago, were now stained and crushed. Something was missing, too, she thought as Marian sagged into her arms. Taking a step back from the embrace and holding her at arm's length to steady her, Jess realised what was wrong. She had no bags with her.

Chapter Eighteen

"WHERE'S YOUR LUGGAGE, Mum?"

"My suitcase is in Taiwan. That means I have no clothes, no makeup, and no hair rollers!"

The latter, Jessica knew, for her mother was a true tragedy indeed to have to bear.

"Calm down, Mum; we'll sort it out. They do have shops in Dublin, so if your case isn't here by tomorrow, I'll pop out and get you a few necessities. In the meantime, you can borrow anything you need from me. I don't understand, though; what the hell is your luggage doing in Taiwan?"

"They forgot to load it on the bloody plane, didn't they, but I have given the airline your address and been assured it will be couriered there by tomorrow afternoon at the latest. I blame your father, Jessica. If it wasn't for his insisting I fly budget now that I am officially retired and we are a one-income family… It's all part of his new belt-tightening regime. I have a good mind to phone him when we get back to your place to tell him that unless he books me a return flight with Air New Zealand, I am not coming home. I refuse to put myself through that…that journey from hell again!"

Jess's eyes widened. If it came to that, she'd bloody well foot the bill for the new booking.

"It's true, you know, that saying that you get what you pay for. In the last forty-eight hours, I have been to Taiwan, Bangladesh, and touched down in most of the states belonging to the former USSR. I have had a small child throw up in my lap, and I have sat next to a woman for the last ten hours of my journey with Tourette's syndrome and a fear of flying—can you imagine?"

Jess burst out laughing at the picture her mother had just painted.

Marian looked aghast. "It's not funny, Jessica. We didn't even get any inflight perks. Not so much as a cup of coffee." She stared hard at her daughter and then her own mouth twitched and she, too, had to laugh.

"Come on, Mum—put it behind you. You're here now, so let's get you home for a cup of tea and a hot shower. You look like you could do with one." She started laughing again and then, linking her arm through her mother's, she led her outside of the terminal building to the waiting taxi rank. Perhaps the next fortnight mightn't be so bad after all.

"Welcome to Ireland, Mum."

True to her word, the first thing Marian had done upon stepping inside Jess's apartment was insist on phoning Frank. Once she'd made her call, she had found herself being herded off to the shower and now freshly scrubbed and smelling sweet, she lay prone on the couch, waiting for Jessica to finish making her a cuppa.

"I appreciate the loan, darling, but these pyjama bottoms are too tight."

"You'll be fine, Mum; just don't bend over." Jess handed her a steaming mug. "It's hot, so be careful. Do you feel better after giving Dad what-for and having had a hot shower?"

"Hmm, yes, thanks. Both were very cathartic." She blew on her tea and then took a tentative sip before resting her head back on the settee. "I must say, you have this place looking lovely. It's a proper home. Well done, sweetheart."

Jess stood a little taller; she was pleased. She hadn't been sure what her mother would make of apartment living but then she went and spoilt it.

"Yes, I can definitely see the benefits of living in a complex like this when you're single. Much more secure but of course it would be no good for a family."

Right, Jess thought; it was time to burst her mother's bubble. "Actually, Mum there's something I need to tell you."

"Oh my God, you're not pregnant, are you?"

"Oh, for goodness' sake!"

"Sorry, dear, it's just a conclusion most mothers jump to when their daughters utter those words."

"Well, I am not pregnant. What it is...is that well, what's happened is..."

"Spit it out, Jessica."

"I won't be seeing Nick anymore." The relief coursed through her. There, she'd told her; it was out in the open now.

"Oh." Marian sipped at her tea, not glancing up to meet Jess's eye.

"Is that all you're going to say?" Surely it couldn't be that easy, Jess thought dumbfounded.

"No, darling, it most definitely is not all I am going to say but I just need a moment."

Later that night, as she lay in bed with her mother sleeping the deep sleep of the jet-lagged next door, Jess processed her reaction to the news that Nick was no more. To be fair, once she had finished crying into her cuppa, she had calmed down sufficiently to listen to Jess's explanation as to what had gone wrong in the short space of time since their last phone call.

Marian had switched pretty smartly from sorrow at the loss of a potentially suitable son-in-law to anger as Jess relayed the way in which he had treated her. She, too, had been keen to join Nora in a Lorena Bobbitt styled hit but Jess had assured her there was no need. He was history, she informed her. "I've moved on, Mum." That was when she told her about Owen, injecting a tally-ho kind of joviality into her tone. "You'll get to meet him on Saturday. We are going up to the farm for the day."

"Jessica, Jessica, Jessica." Marian had shaken her head sadly. "What happened to this Owen's sister was tragic but it's his tragedy, sweetheart; don't go making it yours, too. I can see how you could have got swept up by it all but we have been down this road so many times, my girl. When will you ever learn? You can't fix people; they have to want to heal themselves."

Her remarks sent up a flare of irritation. "You've only been here an hour, Mum, please don't start going on about the whole wounded bird thing. I had an idea to write a story around a name in a second-hand book and that story happened to be a sad one but it is his sister's story, not Owen's. I don't need to fix him because he isn't broken, so please don't prejudge him on something that happened in his life that he had no control over. That wouldn't be fair."

She watched as the struggle played out on her mother's face. There was so much she obviously wanted to say but was fighting against spurting it all out and getting into an argument so early in the piece. She was too weary for that and so miming that her lips were sealed, she declared, "Alright, I won't say a word more about him."

Yeah, right. Jess fixed her with a steely glare. "And you will keep an open mind on Saturday and you will be nice? Promise me."

"Alright, alright. Yes, I promise I'll behave."

There wasn't much more to say after that and feeling her hackles slowly settle down, Jess went off to rustle them both up a light supper of scrambled egg and toast.

She waited until Marian had gone to bed to ring Owen, filling him in about the lost luggage and her mother's journey from hell. He'd sympathised and told her about his day, informing her Wilbur was steadily gaining weight before they'd said a drawn-out good night to each other. She hadn't even hung the phone up and she was missing him, she realised, wrapping her arms around her legs and resting her head on her knees.

Rolling over in bed, eyes wide open and staring into the darkness, she conjured up the feeling of him lying next to her. Oh yes, where Owen was concerned she had it bad.

The next morning after breakfast, Jess managed to dig out an old pair of curling tongs that would suffice until Marian could get hold of her heated rollers and handing over her makeup bag, she gave her free rein with it.

After much discussion about what she would wear for the day, "I am not wearing any of your oddball thrift shop ensembles," she had stated, giving her daughter's authentic Boho skirt and boots the once-over before settling on the elephant suit. She didn't really have much choice because it was the only new thing Jess owned and it was also the only outfit that would fit her.

Actually, Jess thought, tossing her mother a soft pink scarf to brighten the outfit, it suited her.

"It doesn't look too bad and at least I will be comfortable." She'd sniffed, giving her hair one last primp, looking much more like Jess's mother and not the vagrant she had picked up from the airport yesterday. Then, they headed off for a day's sight-seeing.

The morning passed in a blur of hopping on and off the open-topped double decker that did the rounds of the city. Thankfully the weather behaved itself and although it was cold, at least it wasn't wet. They were too busy soaking up the city's history to talk about anything more serious than the sights they were seeing and Jess was enjoying seeing Dublin through a newcomer's eyes again.

It gave her a sense of pride as they wandered through the grounds of Trinity College to go and view the exquisite Book of Kells housed there. For her part, Marian was completely blown away by Christchurch Cathedral, marvelling at the fact it had been in existence since the tenth century. She'd had her photo taken next to the statue of Molly Malone on Grafton Street, laughing as Jess sung the first verse of the song that had become Dublin's unofficial anthem:

In Dublin's fair city
Where the girls are so pretty
I first set my eyes on sweet Molly Malone
As she wheel'd her wheelbarrow
Through streets broad and narrow
Crying cockles and mussels alive, alive o!

Jess had arranged to meet up with Nora for lunch in Temple Bar and being a nice day, the area was heaving. They picked their way along the cobbled street to Café Vivaldi, where she spied her friend. Nora was already sitting under one of the big umbrellas, having bagged a seat in the small outdoor area in front of the eatery. Good, thought Jess as Nora waved out; it was a place to sit and "be seen"—Mum will be in heaven. There was nothing like a spot of people-watching on a nice day in Dublin.

Nora's dark glasses were firmly in place and a latte was in front of her as she relaxed in the unexpected bonus of winter sunshine. Pushing her glasses up onto her head, she scraped her chair back and stood up with a wide and welcoming smile. Marian, an apparition in elephantine grey, enveloped her in a warm hug, nearly knocking her off her Valentinos.

"I've heard so much about you over the years; I feel like I already know you, my dear, and it is lovely to finally put such a pretty face to the name," she enthused.

"Sure, it's great to finally meet you, too, Mrs Baré." Nora didn't know it but she had just scored herself ten out of ten for pronouncing Baré in the correct manner first pop.

"Call me Marian, dear." The two women sat down and Jess, grinning at Nora, pulled a chair out and joined them.

"Isn't the atmosphere just lovely? There's such a buzz about the place." Marian sighed contentedly as she gazed around at the teeming foot traffic.

"Yes, Dublin always comes alive when the sun comes out and this is a lovely spot to sit and just watch the world go." Nora smiled, pleased her suggested meeting spot was being so well received.

"And the coffee's great, too—Mum, what do you fancy?"

"A large latte and a sandwich would be lovely—you choose. It's so nice to sit down, Nora; I tell you, we've been on the go all morning."

Nora had already ordered so Jess left Marian filling her friend in on their morning's activities and headed inside to order.

When she reappeared with their table number in hand, the two women had moved on to the subject of Ewan. Marian was asking for the lowdown and Nora was only too happy to fill her in.

Their various sandwiches and paninis arrived and the conversation flowed.

"I love your outfit, Marian; it looks casual but smart at the same time—the perfect choice for sight-seeing." Nora was staring at the older woman's pant suit; there was something about it that looked really familiar but she couldn't quite put her finger on it.

Jess sniggered. Nora fancied herself as such a fashionista, she'd be horrified when she realised it was her trusty old elephant suit.

"Thank you, dear; it's actually Jessica's. My case got left behind in Taiwan so I had nothing with me but the clothes I was standing in."

Nora's face was a picture when she twigged and as her mother chatted on, Jess felt herself relaxing in the warmth afforded by the sun. She didn't know what she had been so uptight about her Mum coming over for. All that wasted energy worrying when it was all going to be fine. Today, in the unseasonal bright weather, all those little idiosyncrasies of hers that normally grated seemed muted. Or at least they had...

"So what do you make of this Owen Jessica is so keen on then, Nora?"

Jess's shoulders stiffened. "Mum, you promised you weren't going to say anything more until you've met him for yourself."

"I was only asking Nora's opinion of him." Her mother protested innocence. "What's wrong with that if you've got nothing to hide?"

Nora squirmed. "Actually, Marian, I can't say too much about Owen because I haven't met him yet either but from what Jess has told me, he sounds lovely. I am not passing further judgement until she does introduce us, moreover—not after the botch-up I made introducing Nick."

Marian's eyes narrowed. "Yes, he was a bit of a wolf in sheep's clothing but you weren't to know, dear. I get to meet Owen on Saturday. Jess is driving us up to this farm of his. I can't say I'm looking forward to that."

"Mum!"

"I meant going to a piggery for the day, not meeting this new friend of yours. I don't know, Nora; she's always been the same—so defensive." Marian smiled conspiratorially at Nora as though Jess weren't seated right next to her before getting to her feet and announcing she had an urgent call of nature to attend to.

"God, she never changes! Nobody else can wind me up as fast as she can. She's such a bloody snob." Jess huffed as her mother disappeared inside the café, resisting the urge to poke her tongue out at her retreating back.

Nora grinned and patted her friend's hand. "She's your Mam—that's what they do to their children. You just take her too seriously, that's all; she doesn't mean anything by it and at the end of the day, it's your best interests she has at heart. I really like her. I can see a lot of you in her, actually."

"Nora Brennan, take that back—you cannot!"

"I can too. You have the same eyes and hair—hers is just shorter, that's all."

It wasn't the first time Jess had heard the comparison made. "Yeah, well, that's where the similarities end and the only reason you're so taken with her is because she wanted to hear all about your favourite subject—Ewan—so as she can go home and tell all her Mahjong friends that she met the girl who is dating Mr Movie Star."

Marian re-joined the conversation and when there was no further mention of Owen, Jess felt her mood lighten again. Nora's hour-long break flew by and after they'd said their goodbyes to her, Jess tried to persuade her mother to go on the Dublin Viking Tour—she'd never admit it to anyone but she'd always wanted to go on the bright yellow amphibious vehicle that toured the city. The tour culminated in a "splash down" at the Grand Canal Docks but Marian wasn't keen and wouldn't be persuaded. She didn't want to get her carefully curled hair wet.

Instead, they wandered through the Grand Post Office. Jess pointed out the bullet marks from the 1916 Easter Rising, engraved for all time in the building's pillars. As her fingers ran over the indentations, she couldn't help but think that this was where it all started. Those men who had taken part in the Rising with such a justifiable, downtrodden passion could never have known the spinoff that would happen sixty-odd years later to a girl from Ballymcguinness. Shaking the morbid thoughts away, she linked her arm through her mother's and led her back out to the street. They moseyed along O'Connell Street so that Marian could call into one of the many souvenir shops dotted around the city to stock up on all things leprechaun. Laden down with bags, Jess suggested one more port of call—it was on their way home anyway and besides, they'd earned a drink: the Brazen Head, Ireland's oldest pub.

Sitting with her pint of perfectly poured Guinness in front of her—when in Rome, Marian had giggled as she placed her order and if Jess hadn't known better, she would have thought her mother was flirting with the handsome young bartender—she was in raptures as she soaked up the atmospheric interior of the little pub.

"This is just how I envisaged an Irish pub and look! They even have fiddlers playing on the weekend!" She pointed to a poster on the wall with such enthusiasm that Jess felt a surge of warmth toward her. How was it she could love her Mum so much one minute and then in the next want to thump her?

Marian was very giggly and the careful façade with which she normally carried herself had definitely slipped as they made their way home two drinks later, unaccustomed as she was to tippling in the afternoon. Jess had been horrified when she'd caught her blowing a kiss at a geriatric lorry driver who was leering out the window at them while they crossed the road. She'd taken her mother to task as well as by the elbow, steering her straight home after that incident.

To Jess's dismay, Gemma and Jimmy were in full "discipline" workout mode as they entered the quad and Marian had laughed fit to burst at the sight of them before asking who did they think they were: "Jane Fonda and Richard Simmons?" Then, crossing her legs, she'd hobbled off in the direction of Jess's wing as fast as her little legs could carry her, muttering about wetting herself if she didn't get to the loo quick smart. Jess scurried after her, tossing an apology over her shoulder to Gemma and Jimmy, who called after her demanding to know who the hell Jane Fonda and Richard Simmons were.

Marian made it to the bathroom in the nick of time and Jess had only just popped the kettle on to make her mother a strong cup of coffee when the intercom sounded, heralding the fact that her lost luggage was no longer lost.

"Well, thank goodness for that! I feel I can relax and get properly into the holiday mode now," Marian said a few minutes later as she heaved her bulging case up onto her bed.

"You could have fooled me, Mum. You looked like you were doing a pretty good job of getting in the holiday mode this afternoon."

"Yes, well, that Guinness did rather go to my head but what goes on tour, stays on tour, eh Jessica?"

Jess cringed. It was not an appropriate saying for one's mother to come out with.

Oblivious of her daughter's discomfort, Marian began rummaging through her case. "Here you go." She held a Smith & Caughey's bag aloft triumphantly. "I had one last splurge before I lost my discount. They are all YSL so they shouldn't ride up your bottom."

Jess peeked inside the bag at the array of midnight blue, emerald green, and ruby red lace and silk—knickers, knickers and more knickers. Now this was the mother she knew and loved and it was definitely a step up from the slippers. Maybe she didn't think she was such a lost cause after all. "Thanks, Mum, they're gorgeous."

Marian wasn't finished yet, though. Tossing trousers and a couple of jumpers to the wayside, she produced a tin from the depths of the case. "These are for you, too, sweetheart."

Opening it up and peering inside, Jess's face split into a big grin because it was full of the butter-filled custard biscuits she loved. "Yay! Yo-Yos—my favourite!" She hugged her mum, feeling a surge of love for her as she told her to leave the rest of her unpacking until later. "Come on, let's go and have a couple of these with our coffee."

The unaccustomed alcohol, jet lag, and the busy day took its toll on Marian and by seven that evening, she was tucked up in bed. Jess cocked an ear and grinned from her vantage point on the couch, hearing her snoring. She'd just flicked the television on when the phone rang. It was Owen and she found herself unable to stop the silly smile spreading across her face at the sound of his voice.

They chatted about all the inconsequential happenings in their day. Owen laughed when she told him about her mother's un-motherly behaviour with the truck driver and how she nearly wet herself laughing at the sight of Gemma and Jimmy. "I'm looking forward to meeting her; she sounds a case."

Jess changed the subject then, asking after Wilbur.

"Aye, he's doing grand. He'll be ready to join his siblings any day now. I miss you," he'd finished, his voice growing husky.

Jess was glad there was nobody there to see the goofy look on her face as she said, "I miss you too." She'd have liked to have said that she couldn't wait for Saturday but truth be told, she was dreading it.

MOTHER AND DAUGHTER spent Thursday amicably riding the Dart in either direction with no mention of Owen. Instead, Marian kept up a running commentary, filling Jessica in on how her father had decided to retire at the end of the year and how her sister was so excited about the idea of a new baby when it happened but that she had no idea how she'd manage with five. "The children will have to help out more. You know, when I was Mia's age I used to..."

Jess let the conversation flow over her, enjoying hearing all the trivia that was part and parcel of family life. She did miss being part of it all firsthand sometimes, instead of always hearing the family's news after the event. They had morning tea in Malahide and as Jess sat in the quaint little café with her mother sipping a cup of tea, a plate of scones with jam and cream between them, she couldn't help but recall her last visit to Malahide. How things had changed, she thought, checking her phone to find a saucy text message from Owen. She blushed as she read it, too embarrassed to send one back with her mother sitting right there.

Marian, partial to a bit of namedropping at the best of times, thoroughly enjoyed hearing who lived where as they rode the train down to Greystones later that afternoon. "Wait until I tell them all at Mahjong that I saw Enya's castle and I swear that was Rick Stein outside that lovely little pub in Malahide."

Jess smiled to herself. It had been a nice day and it wasn't over yet; they still had time for a wander along the beach and a quick drink at the pub before they'd need to get the train to Bray. Brianna had invited them for an early dinner as Pete was working late.

"SO MARIAN, WHAT DO you think of our fair city then?" Brianna asked, passing her the bowl of scalloped potatoes. "Harry, eat with your mouth closed, please. Remember your manners."

"Oh, I love it! All the history and culture is just wonderful. We are such a new country in New Zealand by comparison. Jessica has been showing me a fabulous time and it's marvellous to meet her lovely friends and to see where she lives at long last."

Jess was impressed at her mother's use of so many different adjectives and looking across the table at her, saw how animated her face was. She crossed her fingers under the table and hoped that same enthusiasm would carry through to Saturday when she met Owen.

"From now on when she telephones us, I'll be able to picture exactly who, what, or where it is she is talking about." Marian paused as she concentrated on spooning the potatoes onto her plate, her face donning a petulant expression. "Not that she phones us much—it is usually the other way round."

"Oh, Marian, I am sure that's not true."

It was actually, Jess thought, feeling a frisson of shame. She'd have to start making more of an effort but just as she'd promised to faithfully phone home once a week, her mother opened that big mouth of hers again.

"Of course, Brianna, I'm only here for a fortnight and I'd have liked to have gone down to Cork this weekend to kiss the Blarney Stone but Jessica's informed me we're going up North to a pig farm to meet this man friend of hers instead."

Jess bristled. "Oh well, at least I'll be saving you from a bout of herpes by not kissing the Blarney." The much-kissed piece of rock at Blarney Castle was a tourist favourite with the legend stating that doing so would bestow whoever kissed the stone with the gift of the gab, something her mother didn't need to worry about, Jess thought, fixing her with a black look.

"What's herpes, Mam?" Harry's eyes were big, his mouth open in a vision of masticated peas.

"Sorry," Jess mouthed at her friend.

Brianna decided avoidance was the best reply. "Oh well, you're not missing much, Marian; you can't get near the place for tourists normally. Now going up North, well, you will get to see the real Ireland and the scenery up that way is just stunning. From what Jessica's told me, too, Owen's farm is like something out of a storybook. Sure you'll have a lovely time, so you will."

Good old Brianna, Jess thought, flashing her friend a grateful smile as she passed the carrots over.

"Harry and I grew the carrots together, didn't we, poppet?"

Harry nodded.

"I'm finding involving him in the garden is a great way to get him to eat his vegies."

"Oh, I agree. Kelly—that's Jessica's sister—says the same thing and she has a wonderful vegetable garden on the go."

"Yeah, that Dad tends for her," Jess muttered.

Marian ignored the comment. "Have you met him then, this pig farmer friend of Jessica's, Brianna?"

Jess's knife hovered over her plate; she wished her mother wouldn't use that tone of voice each time she referred to Owen's profession.

"No, not as yet but I am sure I will get to do so in the near future. I am looking forward to it. He sounds divine."

"Do you think so?" Marian raised a haughty eyebrow and Jess's leg twitched violently under the table with the urge to kick her.

Oblivious of her daughter's leg spasm, she cut into her chicken breast to reveal the ham and cheese stuffing inside; then not giving Brianna a chance to answer, she popped it in her mouth, chewed and declared it to be delicious. "Is there any chance of passing some cooking tips on to my daughter? I always say a woman needs to be a maid in the living room, a cook in the kitchen, and a whore in the bedroom." She tittered in that irritating "all girls together" giggle of hers, except they weren't—all girls together.

"Mum! That's Jerry Hall's quote, not yours, and remember who else is at the table." Her eyes flicked toward Harry, who was looking perplexed once more by the strange adult conversation going on over the top of his head.

"Mam, what's a whore?"

After dessert and with Harry out of earshot, a lively chat between Marian and Brianna had ensued about all the horrible things little boys get up to. Marian had come up trumps with her tale of how her grandsons Ethan and Elliott's favourite pastime was crossing swords in the shower in order to pee all over one another but Brianna had been the hands-down winner with the Harry and the poo on the compost pile story. The three women had stared in silence at the empty bowl of home-grown carrots and then Jess had announced that if they were going to catch the eight p.m. train, then they had best be making a move.

As they made to leave, Brianna pulled Jessica to one side, whispering out the corner of her mouth, "I like your Mam, Jess, I really do. Once you get beneath that front she tries to put on, she's a sweetie but I tell you what, if Harry decides to tell his class all about whores and herpes for news tomorrow, I will hold her personally responsible."

JESS HAD ARRANGED TO take her mother into the Guardian's Office for the grand tour on Friday and when it rolled round, it was much to her relief that this was one outing they managed to get through with no further faux pas on Marian's part.

Chapter Nineteen

AS BRIANNA HAD RECEIVED no complaints from Harry's teacher about the use of inappropriate language when she went to pick him up from school on Friday, she agreed to keep her promise regarding her car. The freak snowstorm that would render the roads impassable that Jess had been praying hard for did not eventuate and when she drew her curtains on Saturday morning, she saw the day had dawned cold but clear. There wasn't so much as frost on the ground.

The route North was more familiar to Jess this time round, with no hidden surprises in the form of gardai eating their lunch roadside. She noticed her mother, who had maintained a running commentary since they left Bray and to which she had tuned out by the time they passed through Drogheda, grew quiet. They were driving alongside the outskirts of Newry with its rows of duplicate houses, Irish flags flapping brazenly on the breeze.

They were making good time, Jess thought, glancing at the dashboard before turning her attention back to the road in front of her. At least the weather being good meant that her mother was seeing the Irish countryside at its best. She tapped her foot gently on the brake to slow as they arrived at Dundrum and couldn't resist pulling over for a spot of morning tea. It was such a pretty village and Marian seemed quite smitten by it as she peered out the window at the ruins of the castle.

However, as they drove down the hill a short while later and Ballymcguinness popped into view, her feeling of impending doom deepened. Owen's little village was more functional than aesthetic and she didn't want to give her mother any more negative ammunition with which to fire.

In an effort to endear her to the delights of small Irish village life, she pointed out Katie Adams puffing away on her perpetual ciggy as she stood outside the pub and Billy Peterson, who was arranging pears this time outside his grocers—they must be in season, Jess said cheerfully as she spotted Old

Ned still sitting on the wall. He raised his stick to them in salute and Marian tittered in the passenger seat.

"Goodness, this place reminds me of that old nursery rhyme, you know the one? *The butcher, the baker, the candle stick maker*. It's certainly not somewhere I could ever picture you living, Jessica. You take after me in so much as you are a city girl. What on earth would you find to write about living here?" Her mouth dropped open and Jess followed her gaze to the left, where she spied Mad Bridie in her dressing gown and slippers, trying to get on a bicycle.

"There you go, Mum, see—there's plenty to write about in the country when you look a little closer. There's always a lot more going on than meets the eye in a small community." Jess had no idea whether this was true or not but she wasn't going to sit by in silence and let her get away with making unfavourable remarks to do with a way of life she was clueless about. "And for your information, I happen to like the country. You can't beat all that clean, fresh air."

"All that methane, you mean." Marian shot a disparaging look at the cows happily chomping at the lush grass in the fields they were now driving past. "And since when did you like the country?"

Jess thought for a moment and then the answer came to her clear as a bell. "Ever since I met Wilbur." It was true, she realised; that little piggy had brought her and Owen together and had inadvertently put a lot of things into perspective for her about what was important in life and what wasn't.

Marian frowned and shook her head in that way of hers that spoke volumes and as they wound their way around the hedgerow lanes, Jess sent up a silent prayer for today to go well. She might well be approaching her midthirties but that didn't mean she didn't still need her Mum's approval.

Brianna's Golf Estate bounced up the driveway, hitting every puddle along the way, and Jess made a mental note to pop it through the car wash before she returned it. Glenariff came into view and did her proud by looking every inch the storybook farm cottage with its lime-washed walls nestling against a backdrop of green.

"Oh, Jess, it's lovely. I feel like we've just driven in to the pages of a Beatrix Potter book." Marian dropped her defences as she clapped her hands delightedly. "Oh and look, there's even ducks!"

As if on cue, Jemima and her cronies had picked that moment to come waddling around the side of the cottage for a dip in the pond.

"Actually, Mum, they are not ducks—they are geese and watch the mean-looking one in the middle. She's their ringleader. I call her Jemima, and I wouldn't trust her so far as I could throw her and believe me, I'd like to."

Marian laughed. "Jemima Puddle Duck? You loved that book when you were a little girl. Come to think of it, you loved anything by Beatrix Potter but then you moved on to fairies and Enid Blyton. Do you remember all that hoo-ha over Noddy and Big Ears?"

Jess wasn't listening; she was busy leaning over into the back seat. "Here you go, Mum. You might want to take your heels off and put these on. They'll save your shoes." Jess handed her a pair of blue plastic wellies. Cheap and cheerful but they'd do for the day.

"I will not wear gumboots!" Marian looked at them aghast before climbing out of the car. She stood and smoothed her trouser suit down before squelching straight into a pothole-filled puddle.

Oh dear—Jess would have giggled if she wasn't wound so tight—they were not off to a good start. With lemony lips, Marian took the proffered boots and sat back down to change into them just as Owen appeared in the doorway. Waving over, he pushed his sock-clad feet into his own set of boots and strode forth to greet them.

As he approached, Jess's tummy did that strange flip-floppy thing it always did when she saw him. He looked so ruggedly handsome; she'd never known a man who could carry off cords and a woolly jumper the way he did. She watched amazed as his face broke into a welcoming grin before he took her startled mother by both hands and kissed her on the cheek.

"Welcome to Glenariff Farm. It's lovely to meet you, Mrs Baré." He took a step back, still holding her hands in his as he studied her face. "Jessica, you told me it was your mother who was coming, not your sister."

It might have been a line as old as the nearby hills of the Mourne Mountains but it worked and the lemon lips disappeared, to be replaced by a flirtatious smile along with a bat of the eyelashes.

"It's lovely to meet you too, Owen, and thank you for inviting us up for the day."

"Come on, don't be standing about in the cold." Owen took Marian by the elbow and gently steered her around the potholes and into the waiting house.

Jess lingered behind for a moment, not quite believing what she had just witnessed. Surely that charming chap who had just wooed her mother couldn't be the taciturn farmer she was fairly sure she had fallen head over heels with? As Marian disappeared into the warmth of the cottage, Owen looked back over his shoulder at her and winked before mouthing, "Told you so."

It was easy for Jess to tell her mother was impressed by the cottage as Owen ushered her around by the way in which she held her back straight as she peered at the various furnishings, recognising them for the quality pieces they were. She lingered over the photos on the mantelpiece before picking one up and asking, "Is this your sister, Owen?"

With her nerves jangling as to what his reaction would be, Jess went and stood beside him in silent support but he simply nodded, bemused as Marian continued to stare intently at it.

"What a beautiful, beautiful girl," she said finally. "Jessica's told me so much about her, you know, and of course I've heard all about the wonderful article she put together for her newspaper." Marian put the photo back before looking up at him with watery eyes. Then resting her hand on his arm, she murmured, "Such a tragedy, young man; my heart goes out to you and your family."

"Aye, well thank you, Marian—it's alright if I call you that, isn't it?"

She nodded. "Yes, please do."

She was such a phony! Jess stared at her mother in disbelief—not once since she had arrived in Ireland had she asked about Amy nor had she shown any interest in the piece she had written. All she had been concerned about was the fact that Owen must be some kind of depressive because of it all and made non-stop snide remarks about his career choice.

Marian's nose twitched and her smile was warm as the unshed tears quickly evaporated. "Now tell me, Owen, what is that wonderful smell?"

"I hope you're both hungry because I have made a pie that could feed the five hundred, so I have." His eyes twinkled, enjoying his role of the benevolent farmer.

Jess felt so edgy she didn't think she'd be able to eat a thing. She trooped behind him and her mother into the kitchen, feeling like she was going to the gallows. The trusty Aga was putting out the heat and true to his word, a steaming casserole dish topped with a dense golden pastry sat in the middle of the table alongside a bowl of salad and a cob loaf. Her mother looked as if she was in love as Owen pulled a chair out for her and asked her what her preference was. "White or red?"

Hoping it would help take the edge off, Jess opted for a glass of red, which she downed in next to no time while Owen dished up the pie. It was as she'd known it would be, delicious, and she managed a few bites while listening to the conversational banter bounce back and forth between Owen and Marian. Her hand froze, a piece of bread mid-way to her mouth, as without warning Marian moved from the innocuous swapping of pie recipes to the business at hand. Helping herself to a second serving of salad, she began drilling Owen about the farm.

Jess put the bread down, knowing it would taste like sawdust to her now and sitting back in her chair, she clasped her hands tightly in her lap, her nails digging into her palms as Owen explained to Marian how long the farm had been in his family and what being able to keep it going by free-farming the pigs meant to him. It was money that talked where Marian was concerned and his familial, free-range sentiments would score no brownie points with her, so Jess decided to knock the conversation right off course. "Hey, Mum, did I tell you that Owen was a very successful commercial law solicitor in London for years?" She didn't need to add *not just a pig farmer* because it lay thick on the air and on the tip of her tongue.

Marian shot her daughter a peculiar look but Jess didn't notice nor did she register Owen's furrowed brows.

"No, you didn't tell me that. It wasn't for you then, Owen?"

Jess wasn't going to give him the chance to open his mouth again just yet and waving her hand airily, she said, "Oh, he needed a career break, that's all. London's London—it will always be there." Pushing her chair back, she stood up to clear her plate. With a glance at her mother's stunned face, she was satisfied she had successfully sold Owen's earning capabilities to her. He was, she had implied with her clever phrasing, a "professional" who chose to masquerade as a farmer for the time being. Plate in hand, she gestured toward the garden and suggested they head outside to see Wilbur.

"Aye, that's a good idea, Jess. Marian, do you want to come with us or would you like to stay here in the warm?"

Jess crossed a finger behind her back but there was no contest where Marian was concerned—another cup of coffee in a cosy kitchen or traipsing across muddy fields in order to see some pigs?

Jess virtually skipped along behind Owen as he led the way to the barn. It felt like months, not just a few days, since they had last been alone together and she couldn't wait for some one on one time with him and to see Wilbur, of course. If he didn't slow down, though, she'd need a rest, not a snog fest, by the time they got to the barn. Crikey, he was setting one heck of a pace as he cut across the mushy paddock. She smiled to herself, thinking he was obviously as keen as she was to be away from the eagle-eyed Marian.

As he heaved open the barn door, she finally managed to catch up to him. In her eagerness to see Wilbur, though, she pushed past him and made her way down the barn, passing the sow and her piglet housed in the stall next to where Wilbur's box was. Where were all the other piglets? she wondered briefly but then seeing the heat lamp had been turned off and that the box was empty, her eyes flailed round the barn bewilderedly. As her gaze settled back on the fat sow lying on her side, hungry piglet suckling greedily at her, an understanding suddenly dawned. That piglet was Wilbur. She looked over to where Owen was still standing in the doorway for confirmation and he nodded.

Jess wandered closer to the stall but not too close because she didn't want to disturb the little family and she stood silently watching the wondrous scene. He had made it—Wilbur was out of the danger zone; just look at him being nursed by his mother! Before long, he'd be up to size and joining his siblings foraging outside in the paddock. It was a beautiful sight, watching him bond with his Mummy like that and she wanted to share it with Owen but he still hadn't moved. She looked across at him, intending to beckon him over but the look on his face stopped her and with a sense of trepidation, she left the happy scene to find out what was wrong.

"Are you okay? I know Mum can be hard work with her airs and graces but you just have to take her with a pinch of salt. Don't let her get to you."

"It's not your mother who has the problem, Jess—it's you."

"What do you mean?" Jess looked up at him, puzzled, and reaching out, she touched his arm for reassurance but he brushed her away, his irritation palpable. Taking a step back, she looked up at him, her face demanding to know what the problem was because she was damned if she knew.

"What was all that malarkey in there about me being a lawyer? I am a pig farmer, Jess. It's what I do and it's what I love. I won't apologise to anyone for my life because it's a good one and it's an honest one."

Jess opened her mouth to protest but he shook his head and held up his hand to keep her at arm's length. "No, let me finish what I have to say. If you can't accept me for who I am, how do you expect your mother to? Jaysus, Jess, the reason I left London in the first place was to get away from people who were so caught up in worrying about what others thought. It's not for me, that kind of life, and I didn't think it was for you either but I have read you all wrong."

"But I'm not like..."

He didn't stick around to hear her explanation, flashing a look of disgust at her before striding down the paddock away from the cottage and away from her. By the set of his shoulders, Jess knew there was no point in going after him. Besides, what would she say? What he had said was true. She had been trying to make him out to be someone he no longer was and if he were still that person, she probably wouldn't want to be with him anyway. So why had she done it? To keep her bloody mother happy, that was why. She wanted him to be someone she would approve of for once. As his figure grew smaller, she felt sick with the realisation that he had trusted in her and despite everything she had said about not hurting him, she had done exactly that.

Jess used the time it took her to squelch back across the field to the cottage to get mad. As she stomped back into the kitchen, oblivious of the trail of muddy footprints she was leaving behind her, Marian demanded, "What's happened, Jessica? You've got a face on you that looks like a smacked bum and where's Owen gotten to?" She looked over Jess's shoulder to the empty garden behind her.

"Come on, Mum. Get your bag—we're going." Jess snatched up her own handbag and headed back out the door.

"But where's Owen?" her mother asked again as she scurried out after her daughter in her pop socks, pausing at the front entrance to climb back into her wellies.

"He's out looking after his pigs, which is what he does for a living and if you weren't so damned well hoity-toity about people and their professions, then he wouldn't be so damned well pissed off at me!" Jess stormed across the driveway toward the car, determined not to cry and not waiting to hear her reply, just as Owen hadn't waited around to hear hers. She was oblivious of the fact that Jemima was stealthily bringing up her rear, and she'd clambered inside the car, slamming the door shut before the goose got the chance to lunge and peck. So Jemima arched her long neck in Marian's direction instead and made a beeline for the older woman. She was standing transfixed by the advancing goose, semi-defenceless in the no-man's-land between cottage and car.

Much splashing in puddles, bad language, and hissing on both their parts ensued along with bag waving as Marian tried to shoo the bird away until, finally bedraggled but not beaten, she slid into the sanctuary of the passenger seat.

Eying her filthy pants with distaste, she tried to brush the worst of the mud off, muttering, "Thanks for your help." When no reply was forthcoming, she looked across at her daughter. Registering her mutinous expression, Marian wondered whether perhaps she might be better off taking her chances with Jemima again.

She didn't get a chance to further consider her options, though, because Jess, not even waiting for her mother to do her seat belt up, had put her foot down on the accelerator and was haring off down the drive and out of Owen's life once and for all.

"Jessica!" Marian gasped. "What on earth has got into you? Slow down, for goodness' sake."

Remembering it was not her car she was driving and that she had no axe to grind with Brianna, Jess grudgingly slowed. In the seat next to her, her mother's sigh of relief was audible.

"That's better. I don't fancy being sent home in a budget body bag. I'd probably wind up in Taiwan too."

Jess refused to smile, feeling her mother's eyes upon her.

"What were you ranting on about me being—what was it you said before? Hoity-toity?—yes, that was it."

Jess didn't say anything, concentrating instead on the bends in the road ahead of her.

"I hardly think that's a fair comment because I'll have you know, Jessica Jane, that I have been on my best behaviour today. I did not turn my nose up at anything and I kept my word and gave Owen the benefit of the doubt just like I said I would and guess what? Surprise-surprise! I liked him. He is a lovely young man, so if anything you should be sitting there saying I told you so instead of getting yourself into such a stew. So come on then, my girl, tell me what was it that got you in such a state all of a sudden?"

"You, Mum! It was you who got me in such a state! You wound me up like you always do, because no matter what I do and no matter what choices I make, you always manage to make me feel like I don't measure up! Not in my job and certainly not in my love life. Well, I am sorry I am such a big, fat disappointment to you." Jess banged her hands down on the steering wheel.

"Calm down, Jessica. I have no idea where all this is coming from." Marian looked at her daughter in alarm, wondering whether she was having some sort of breakdown.

"Nothing I do is ever right where you are concerned and no one I meet is ever good enough, so I spouted off all that crap about Owen being a successful lawyer to make you like him. How could you not like him if you knew he was a lawyer? Only a professional will do for your daughter, after all. Except now he says I am not the person he thought I was and I don't think he wants to see me ever again." Jess broke into big gulping sobs.

"Right, enough is enough, Jessica Jane Baré! You cannot drive in this state—you will kill us both." Marian gestured at the tractor that was meandering toward them and taking up most of the lane. "You, my girl, are going to pull over and let Farmer Ted there on his tractor pass and then we are going to sort this ridiculous notion you seem to have about what makes me tick once and for all."

So it was that next to a field full of cows on a cold early winter's afternoon in the depths of County Down, Northern Ireland, Jess and her mother had a long overdue chat.

Marian toyed nervously with her rings, fighting back tears. "I have never meant to make you feel like you didn't measure up. Good grief, Jessica, I am so proud of what you have achieved! I mean, just look at you." She turned in her seat, gesturing to where Jess sat hunched over in hers, her face hidden behind a curtain of hair. Leaning over, she smoothed her daughter's hair back from her face and tucked it behind her ear. "That's better. I can see your beautiful face now and you are beautiful, Jessica." Her voice softened. "Do you know that when I look at you, I can't believe the baby your father and I raised is all grown up now? Where did she go, that little girl of ours, our firstborn who always had her nose buried in a book?" She sighed. "The time goes by so fast, Jess, and it only seems to speed up even more once you have children. We've made mistakes along the way. I know we have but we did our best and do you know that when I look at the life you've carved out for yourself, I'm fit to burst? There you are, with a wonderful career doing something you love, living in a fabulous city with fabulous friends and here's me," her right hand patted her chest, "finally getting to be a part of it all, even if it is only for a few weeks. If I have been disapproving of your choices in the past, it's because you never brought anyone home who was anywhere near your equal." She reached over and stroked Jess's cheek. "Remember when you were little and you brought that sparrow inside that the cat had got at?"

Jess nodded.

"You were so determined to make it better. You even made it a little bed in an old shoe box and set up a nursing station in your wardrobe but the poor thing never stood a chance, even with all that TLC. You were beside yourself when it died."

The memory still made Jess feel sad. She couldn't fix it—make it better—and it had been a lesson in life that had taken her a very long time to learn.

"It broke my heart seeing you like that and I couldn't stand to sit back and say nothing while I watched you get upset time and time again with the choices in men you were making. I just wanted you to be happy, not weighed down by someone else's problems."

Jess wasn't ready to be appeased just yet, so she sat head bowed, making little snivelling noises until her Mum did what she really wanted her to do. Unbuckling her belt, Marian leaned over and pulled her daughter into her arms, cradling her close. Snugged against her like she was, Jess felt like a child again. She wished she was because life had been a lot less complicated back then.

"I know what I can be like." Marian continued, "Lord knows your father tells me off often enough but I can't help myself. It just bubbles up inside me, this need for people to think I am something special, and things just pop out of my mouth before I can stop them. I suppose putting on a posh front is my way of trying to hide behind what I really am."

Jess pulled away from the embrace and rubbing her eyes, she looked at her mother, wondering what she was going to say next. "What do you mean?"

"A woman who did nothing much with her life, that's what I mean, Jess. I was married at nineteen, remember, and I don't regret that or the fact you girls came along so soon afterwards for one minute so don't get me wrong on that count. It's just that I never finished my hair-dressing apprenticeship and after awhile, staying at home and being a wife and a mother was all I knew how to do. That was fine at the time because that was what most women of my generation knew. We were the queens of the Edmonds cookbook. But then the times changed and suddenly women were getting careers and becoming independent. What we did—being homemakers—didn't seem so important in society's eyes anymore. Do you know Kelly tells me she can actually see people's eyes glaze over when she tells them that she's at home with the children?"

It was true, Jess thought; she'd heard Brianna bemoan the same thing on numerous occasions and the derisive way in which Nick had described stay-at-home mothers had been appalling.

"Then when my time did come, and you girls were at an age where I could think about what I wanted to do with the rest of my life, what did I go and do? I got a job selling knickers, that's what."

"There's nothing wrong with knickers, Mum—we all need them."

Marian raised a small smile. "Glad to see you still have your sense of humour and I know there is nothing wrong with it. I enjoyed my time working and the other girls were great fun but selling underwear was never going to set the world on fire, was it? And there was you, growing up with all this talent and making a life for yourself, independent of me. I was scared you saw me as a bit of a let-down and I never knew what to say to you, this high-flying, gorgeous girl of mine. I suppose that's why I pushed so hard for you to meet someone and settle down because then you'd be living the sort of life that I could relate to. I'm so sorry, Jessica." She broke off with a sob.

Jess rubbed her mother's back. "Oh Mum, you should never have felt like that. I am who I am because of you and Dad and all the opportunities you gave me. You were the people who gave me the confidence in myself to put myself out there and give things a go because I knew that if I failed, I could always come home and that you would always be there to pick up the pieces. Having that kind of stability behind you makes life a whole lot less scary." She paused to fish out the packet of tissues she could see peeking out of the pocket of her mother's handbag and handed her one. "You know, I think being a mum is the most important career choice any woman can make and I hope that if I ever become one, that I can do half the job you did with me and Kels." She leaned in and kissed her mother's cheek, noticing the lines that were there now where the skin had once been smooth. Lines that would one day etch themselves onto her face, too. Where had the years gone? "You were always there for us, Mum—all the running us around to this group or that. Dropping us off and picking us up from our friend's houses, all those hundreds of packed lunches and afternoon teas that were always waiting for us after school. You put us first the whole way through. There is no sacrifice greater than being a mum. Just look at everything you still do now for Kelly and the kids. She'd be lost without you and although I might not always show it, I need my Mum, too."

"You do?" Marian's eyes were the mirror image of Jess's as they looked properly at each other. Nora was right, Jess thought; the similarities had always been there—she'd chosen not to see them for the longest time.

"Of course I do. Who else do I know who can bake Yo-Yos like you?"

Marian laughed, swiping at her tears with the tissue and then, taking the rest of the packet off Jess, she pulled out another and gave her nose a good blow. "Aren't we a pair of silly gooses?"

"Don't mention geese!" Jess snorted. "Oh Mum, you should have seen yourself stomping around that puddle, wielding your handbag at Jemima."

Marian began laughing, too, and the tension that had filled the car such a short while ago dissipated.

"I love you," Jess said once she'd got her giggles under control.

"I love you, too."

Marian pulled the sunshade down and wiped away the streaks of mascara her tears had left behind before turning her hand to Jess and swiping away the black smudges under her eyes. It reminded her of when she was a child and her mother would spit on a hanky before wiping her face with it when they were out. Just like she had done when she was a child, too, she wiggled to escape but to no avail. Satisfied she'd cleaned up the worst of the damage, Marian reached into her bag, producing a lipstick. "You need some colour; you'd scare the birds if I stood you out in that paddock, so come on, put this on. At least we've the same colouring."

Jess stared at her. Her heart was breaking, she felt physically ill, and her Mum wanted her to put lipstick on as if that tiny tube of colour would cure all ills? "I don't need lipstick on in order to drive the car back to Dublin and the way I feel at the moment, I really don't give a stuff what I look like. Let's just get back on the road so I can get the car back to Brie's."

Marian smile beatifically. "Well, you might want to give her a quick call and say we'll be a bit late getting back. She'll understand because we are not going back to Dublin, sweetheart, not until we've been back to the farm and you have sorted things out with Owen."

Jess shook her head. "No way. Nice try, Mum; you didn't see Owen's face, though. I have blown it with him. He doesn't want to see me again."

"Now listen to me, young lady—just because we have had a heart-to-heart doesn't mean I am going to stop sticking my oar in. I'm your mother and that's what mothers do. It is our birthright. Now, put the lipstick on, then start the car up and do a U-turn."

Jess frowned at the narrow country lane; even if she did as she was told, she didn't have a hope in hell of performing a U-turn—a six-point turn at best. She could put the lippy on, though. As she angled the rearview mirror and applied a layer of russet red to her mouth, her mother said, "Honestly, sweetheart, do you think I am about to let the best man who has ever come your way slip through your fingers so easily?"

And as Jess put the lid back on the lipstick, Marian shook her head in that way of hers that spoke volumes.

Unprepared to go Round Two with Jemima, Marian opted to wait in the car. "Don't you dare come back out until you've kissed and made up," she bossed, casting a wary eye across the drive. "And watch out for that bloody goose."

The front door of the cottage was locked, so Jess wandered around to the side of the house. Peering through the French doors, she spied Owen looking like he meant business as he chopped something at the kitchen bench. There was a glass of half-drunk red wine next to him and even from her vantage point outside she could smell the unmistakable aroma of browning onions. Typical male, she thought; food was the last thing on her mind. She watched him for a moment, trying to summon the courage to tap on the door until, feeling like a Peeping Tom, she at last knocked.

Owen swung round, nearly tipping whatever the contents of the pot he had in his hand all over himself. She heard him swear and then grabbing a tea-towel, he wiped at the stain spreading down his pants, gesturing at her to come in with his free hand.

"Jaysus, Jess! You scared the crap out of me! I nearly wore all the bloody stock!"

"Sorry, I didn't mean to startle you." She shifted from foot to foot, unsure of the reception she was expecting. "What are you making?"

"A beef and mushroom in red wine casserole."

"Oh, that sounds nice—very, er, hearty."

He stopped wiping and looked at her. "It is but that's not why you came back, is it? To see what I am cooking for dinner?"

"Um, no, I came back to apologise, if you'll let me." Jess took his silence for acquiescence and so she told him of all that had transpired between her and her mother after they had left that afternoon. "You were right in what you said. It was me with the problem. I was trying to impress my Mum, who didn't want me to impress her at all. Even though she *was* impressed because she thinks you are lovely, by the way. And as it turned out, that's all she has wanted for me all along—to be happy. Does that make sense?"

"Aye, in a roundabout way, it does."

"The thing is, Owen, I don't think I can be happy without you. You are everything I have ever wanted and it took me so long to find you that I am absolutely terrified of losing you." Jess felt her face flush with the sentiment and her hands grow clammy at the fear that he would reject her apology as being too little too late.

"Where is Marian, by the way?"

Jess frowned; she had just laid her heart on the line for him and he wanted to know where her mother was. "She's waiting in the car and she said I am not allowed to come back out until we have kissed and made up."

"Well, then, we better not keep her waiting."

Owen took her in his arms and in that fleeting second before Jess closed her eyes, guiding her mouth to meet his, she saw the shadow of a young dark-haired girl smiling at her before, with a wave that Jess instinctively knew was goodbye, she faded away.

Then they kissed and made up.

Epilogue

Two Years Later

JESS AND OWEN BOTH said 'Aye' do in a civil ceremony held in the grounds of Glenariff Farm in high summer. All the guests said it was a beautiful service that went off well and that nobody had really noticed the celebrant's mispronunciation of Jess's surname thanks to Marian stepping up so smartly to put her right—"It's Beret, dahling, not Bare."

Jess shouted her entire family over for the wedding with the proceeds of the best-selling novel she wrote during her year's sabbatical in Ballymcguinness. The bride did not wear white as she didn't feel it was appropriate given the basketball-sized belly she was sporting. She did, however, wear a vintage 1930s gown she let out around the middle, having picked it up for a song at the Enable Ireland charity shop on George Street in Dublin.

Nora, Brianna, and Kelly weren't happy about having to wear secondhand bridesmaid dresses but once threatened by the bride-to-be with pink 80s puffballs if they weren't compliant, they stopped their complaining and on the day looked gorgeous in their respective flapper dresses. The mother of the bride, meanwhile, was radiant in an outfit reminiscent of Mrs Middleton's at William and Kate's do.

The only real hitch in the day was when Harry, Ethan, or Elliott (they each pointed the finger at the other) left the gate to the paddock open and several pigs—including Wilbur—tried to gate-crash the proceedings.

Needless to say, roast pork was not served at the wedding breakfast and Jemima was not invited.

The End

From the Author

HELLO, MY NAME'S MICHELLE Vernal, and I hope you enjoyed reading Second Hand Jane and that at the very least it made you smile! If so then leaving a review would be so appreciated. I'm Mum to Josh and Daniel and am married to the super supportive Paul. We live in the garden city of Christchurch, New Zealand with our three-legged, black cat called Blue. BC (before children) Paul and I lived and worked in Ireland, the experiences we had there have flavoured my books although my new novel The Promise is set on The Isle of Wight. The Promise is a book written with heart. I was adopted in 1971 in Winstanley, Great Britain. My parents emigrated to New Zealand shortly after. It was only after having my children that I sought out my birth mother. She hails from Southampton, a ferry ride to the Isle of Wight, and we've forged a great long-distance relationship. It also turns out I am distantly related to Molly Downer, the last witch on the Isle of Wight – how could I not write a story set on the island once I found that out? Read on to find out more...

Sign up for my VIP Newsletter here (I promise not to bombard you!): www.michellevernalbooks.com

The Promise

Readers' Favourite – Five Stars

Two women from different generations brought together by another's wrongdoing.

When British backpacker, Isabel Stark happens across a car accident on a lonely stretch of road in the South Island of New Zealand her life changes forever. The sole passenger, Ginny Havelock asks her to make a promise before she passes away—to find Constance and to say she's sorry.

Isabel's a lost soul who's been drifting through life unsure of where she fits, and the promise she made in New Zealand haunts her upon her return to the United Kingdom. Her only clue as to finding Constance lies within a conversation held at Ginny's funeral. It takes her to the Isle of Wight.

In the 1940's sixteen-year-old Constance's life on her island is sheltered until the death of her brother; Ted brings the reality of war crashing down around her. He leaves behind his pregnant young widow Ginny. When Constance meets a handsome Canadian airforce man, she's eager to escape her grief and be swept up by first love. It's a love which has ramifications she could never envisage.

When Isabel and Constance's paths finally cross will Ginny's last words be enough for Constance to make peace with her past? And in fulfilling her promise will Isabel find a place she can call home?

'A wonderfully heartwarming, touching and romantic story.'
Tammy Robinson author of Differently Normal

'The Promise is engaging, delightful and hugely entertaining.'
Readers' Favourite

AVAILABLE ON AMAZON

Printed in Great Britain
by Amazon